About

Janice Preston write historical romance. A standalone reads, she lo stories set in the same Regency world, and many of her books include book-hopping characters. When Janice isn't writing she enjoys reading, swimming, pottering in the garden when the sun is shining, and travelling when she can. She fuels her imagination with endless cups of coffee, is far too keen on unhealthy food, and is an expert procrastinator.

Regency Rogues

Regency Rogues:

Talk of the Ton

JANICE PRESTON

MILLS & BOON

First Published in Great Britain 2020
By Mills & Boon, an imprint of HarperCollins*Publishers*
1 London Bridge Street, London, SE1 9GF

REGENCY ROGUES: TALK OF THE TON © 2020 Harlequin Books S.A.

From Wallflower to Countess © 2015 Janice Preston
Scandal and Miss Markham © 2017 Janice Preston

ISBN: 978-0-263-27954-2

MIX
Paper from
responsible sources
FSC www.fsc.org **FSC™ C007454**

This book is produced from independently certified FSC™ paper to ensure responsible forest management.

For more information visit: www.harpercollins.co.uk/green

Printed and bound in Spain
by CPI, Barcelona

FROM WALLFLOWER
TO COUNTESS

To my friend, Morton Gray.

We've shared an exciting, unpredictable journey since we first met on the steps of Birmingham Library. Thank you for your generosity, your support and your wonderful imagination!

Prologue

August 1810

The single state had much to recommend it, Lady Felicity Weston mused as she crossed the landing of Cheriton Abbey on her way downstairs for dinner. She was beholden to no man: no man to criticize her appearance; no man to dictate her activities; and, most important of all, no man to threaten the barriers she had erected around her heart.

Her life was content.

As she reached the head of the imposing staircase, Felicity froze. A man, dressed in shirt and breeches, was bounding up the stairs two at a time. His shirtsleeves were rolled up, exposing tanned, muscular forearms. He wore no neckcloth, his open shirt collar exposing the strong column of his neck. With his thick brown hair wet and dishevelled he looked virile and slightly dangerous. Felicity's mouth dried. Just two steps down from where she stood, he glanced up and slammed to a halt.

Felicity's stomach flipped as she recognized the Earl of Stanton.

One of the most eligible bachelors of the *ton*, Stanton was a catch coveted by zealous mamas and ambitious daughters alike. And admired even by disregarded, unprepossessing spinsters who had watched his star from afar and had once—for one brief, uncharacteristic flight of fancy—wondered what it might be like to catch the attention of such a man.

Of all the men in the *ton*, it was Stanton who had drawn her eye, time and again, during her come-out five years before. But he had never noticed her.

Never asked her to dance.

Never escorted her to supper.

And that had suited her—even then—perfectly. She had seen little of him in the intervening years but she might have guessed Stanton would be amongst the guests at Cousin Leo's house party. They were close friends.

His chest expanded as he hauled in a breath, his chocolate-brown eyes regarding her with apology but no hint of recognition.

'I beg your pardon.' His voice was a rich baritone. 'I'm aware I am a little late, but I did not think anyone would be coming downstairs for dinner quite yet.'

He swept long fingers through his hair then climbed the remaining stairs to Felicity's level. Up close, he smelled of rain and horses and leather…and very *male*. Felicity stepped back involuntarily. His lips twitched.

'I apologize for my unkempt appearance. I was drenched coming up from the stables and I left my coat downstairs, where it might drip with impunity.' He sketched a bow. 'Stanton, Miss…?'

A craven impulse to proffer a false name was swiftly quashed. Much good that would do her if they were to spend the weekend at the same gathering. Besides, Felicity was in no mind to turn into a simpering miss over an attractive gentleman in his shirtsleeves. Her gaze lowered without volition, drinking in the breadth of his shoulders and the strength of those arms. She raised her eyes to his, and caught his expression of wry amusement.

She straightened, lifting her chin. *Arrogant wretch*. She would do well to remember arrogance was a trait that often went hand in hand with wealth, status and a handsome face.

'Felicity Weston, my lord.'

She was unsurprised by his perplexed frown. She attended society events rarely now and knew she had faded from memory. She had become accustomed to such a reaction upon introduction and it no longer embarrassed or hurt her, it simply was. People inevitably struggled to place her within the Weston family, not quite believing she was so closely related to her handsome parents and siblings.

Her sense of the ridiculous bubbled to the surface, prompting her to bestow a kindly smile upon his lordship.

'It is a thankless task, I fear, to try and second-guess my position within the Weston clan. Allow me to enlighten you: I am the sister of Ambrose, Earl of Baverstock.'

'*Sister?*'

'I am afraid so. Quite shocking, is it not?'

'Not at all,' came the swift rejoinder. 'My apologies for my shocking lapse in memory.'

'Oh, I do not take offence, I can assure you. Yours is a reaction I am quite accustomed to. Indeed, I believe I should almost miss it if I failed to provoke such a response. For otherwise, you see, I might be *quite* overlooked.'

Stanton held Felicity's gaze in silence, then his eyes narrowed. 'You are—'

'Unbecomingly frank?' Felicity tilted her head and raised her brows.

'Frank, yes. Unbecoming?' He stepped closer, his gaze locked on to hers. His voice deepened. 'Hmmm. Unusual, perhaps.'

Felicity battled her instinct to retreat, ignoring the flutter deep in her belly, knowing this kind of intimate verbal sparring was a game to men like Lord Stanton.

'I shall accept that as a compliment, my lord. After all, one would not wish to be considered in the common way.'

His eyes crinkled as he laughed. 'No, indeed, Lady Felicity. No doubt I shall see you later, when I am more appropriately attired. My apologies once again for my appearance.'

'Unnecessary, I assure you, although…it did cross my mind to wonder…'

He raised one dark brow.

'...is it the new *mode* for gentlemen to dispense with neckcloths? I am quite out of touch, I fear. And also—' she added quickly as his mouth opened, '—is the rolled-up sleeve now quite the thing? Or might they both, perhaps, be an affectation restricted to sporting gentlemen, much like the Belcher neckerchief?'

Stanton's lips firmed. For a split second, Felicity feared she might have prodded his lordship too far. After all, many men did not take kindly to being teased, but then she recognized the glint in his—quite beautiful, now she came to think about it—velvety-brown eyes. A muscle in his jaw bunched, then he threw his head back and laughed. Felicity's gaze snapped to the dark curls exposed by the open neck of his shirt. An involuntary shiver trembled through her.

'I shall add incorrigible to unusual, Lady Felicity. If you wish to know why I am more *déshabillé* than the mere removal of my coat might indicate, why not ask?'

'Sir!' Felicity raised the back of one hand to her forehead in mock horror. 'How could you suggest such a thing? It would be *most* improper for a lady to quiz a gentleman she barely knows about his activities.'

'Indeed it would. However, as you have made so bold as to raise the subject, I shall enlighten you. I was assisting my groom in the stables with a poultice.'

Felicity sobered. 'One of your horses is lame? I am sorry to hear it. I hope he will soon recover.'

Stanton smiled. 'Thank you. It is merely a precaution. I am sure there is no cause for alarm.' He bowed. 'My apologies once again, Lady Felicity.'

'That is quite all right, Lord Stanton, you were not to know I would have the audacity to appear before the allotted time for dinner. You may rest assured your lapse in standards will not become public knowledge.'

Felicity bent a gracious smile upon his lordship and then

sailed down the stairs, her head high. One thing she had learned during her brief sorties into polite society was to do the unexpected and, always, to walk away first. That way, she was never the one left standing, open-mouthed.

Chapter One

Late August 1811—Bath

'Mama, I should like you to arrange a marriage for me.'

Felicity held her breath as she leant back against the solid strength of her mother's sitting-room door. Lady Katherine Farlowe reclined upon a rose-coloured sofa, clad in a pale pink chiffon robe trimmed with swansdown. Her already huge blue eyes widened as she stared at her only surviving daughter.

'Oh, my *darling* girl. I am so happy for you.' Lady Katherine arose elegantly and wafted across the room to Felicity. 'Who is the lucky man?'

Felicity braced herself as her mother enveloped her in a scented embrace. 'I don't know.' Her voice was muffled against her mother's breast; the swansdown tickled her nose. 'That is why I am asking you to arrange it.'

Lady Katherine released Felicity and stepped back, a frown creasing her soft white skin. 'But…I do not understand. Why? What about love? Do you not want to be happy in your marriage?'

Felicity bit back her cynical riposte. Her mother was an incurable romantic. Felicity knew better. Love, particularly unrequited love, was agony. She had seen it with her sister. She had lived it with her mother—a woman who was adept at closing her eyes and her mind against all unpleasantness. No, she was determined to never feel anything for her husband other than friendship. She would not, like the other women in her family, fall victim to the heartache of unrequited love.

Besides, at four-and-twenty, and after having been on the marriage mart for nigh on six years, the chances of Felicity making a love match were close to zero. She could not recall any man showing her particular attention, despite being the daughter of an earl and possessing a respectable dowry. She had lived her life overshadowed by the beauty of her mother and of her older sister, Emma, before she died.

'I would like my own household,' she said, in reply to her mother's incredulous questions, 'and, eventually, children.'

She felt the heat building in her cheeks as she said the words. She had never admitted that dream out loud before, not even to Beanie, her old nursemaid, but at least her desire for children made this previously unthinkable decision more tolerable. She would wed—if her mother could find her someone suitable. Marriage had become the best of a poor set of options available to her.

'Come and sit by me, Felicity.'

Mama was clearly overjoyed, despite the further proof of her daughter's lack of feminine attributes. She had long despaired over Felicity's sad lack of looks, of her inability to make the best of what she had and of her consistent refusal to pander to the mores of society and the expectations of a young woman by seeking a husband. As time had passed, and as Felicity had aged, Lady Katherine had expected less and less of her. And that had suited Felicity perfectly.

Until this past year.

Felicity banished all thought of her new stepfather, Mr Quentin Farlowe: the sole reason for this drastic step. She could never admit that to her mother—the slightest criticism of the latest love of Lady Katherine's life would be met with tears and reproaches and, ultimately, stubborn denial.

Lady Katherine took Felicity's hand, turning it over in her own lily-white hands.

'Tsk. I declare, Felicity, if only you would use Bloom of

Ninon on your skin, as I have begged you to do, time without number, you would have hands to be proud of. Like mine,' she added, with satisfaction, as she extended her arm and splayed her plump, bejewelled fingers. 'You will want your husband to be proud you wear his ring, will you not?'

Will I? 'Well, Mama? Will you arrange a marriage for me?'

Lady Katherine sighed. 'How I can have given birth to an unromantic soul like you, my darling, I have no idea. Even your dear Papa, God rest his soul, was more romantic, and that is not saying a great deal.'

Felicity pondered this observation of her late father's character. She had watched her parents' marriage: her mother, hopelessly besotted; her father, benignly indulgent of his wife—as long as she did not interfere with his pleasures. Her mother had been deeply hurt by her father's careless neglect and by his *affaires*. And now, as for her mother's new husband... Felicity clamped down her stewing resentment. It seemed it was the way of aristocratic gentlemen—to pursue their own pleasures, including other women, without regard for the pain it caused.

'Now, who is there?' Lady Katherine tapped one finger against her perfect Cupid's bow. 'There's young Avon. You've always been close, and he is heir to the duke.'

'No! I beg your pardon, Mama, but I should prefer an older man. Not only is Dominic younger than me, he is like a brother. I could never marry him, even if he were ready to settle down, which he is not. No, I do not want young, or handsome, or popular. I want *ordinary*.'

I cannot marry a man I might fall in love with. I will not risk that.

She could not delude herself that her husband would love her. If neither Mama nor Emma, with all their beauty, could engender such feelings in the men they had loved, what chance did Felicity have?

Felicity watched as her mother visibly swallowed her

disappointment. 'Well, it all sounds most unsatisfactory. However, I am sure you know your own mind, Felicity. You always have been an odd girl. Not like my poor, dear Emma…' The all-too-ready tears brimmed over, spilling down Lady Katherine's smooth cheeks. She heaved a sigh, raising a hand to her chest as it swelled. 'Very well, Felicity. I shall consult with the duke. He will surely know of someone. I shall write to him immediately.'

The Duke of Cheriton—Cousin Leo—was Felicity's joint guardian, together with her mother, until such time as she married or reached the age of thirty, whichever came sooner.

Felicity must hope he would find some pleasant, unremarkable gentleman with whom she might be content.

Chapter Two

'Stan. Good to see you.'

Leo Beauchamp, Duke of Cheriton, clasped the hand of Richard Durant, Earl of Stanton, in a firm grip as they met in the elegant hall at Fernley Park in the County of Hampshire, Richard's family seat.

'Your Grace,' Richard said, grinning, fully aware Leo hated his friends to stand on ceremony. 'Have you come up from Cheriton today?'

'No. Bath, as a matter of fact.'

Richard raised his brows. 'Bath? I had not thought you were in your dotage quite yet, old chap.'

Leo cuffed Richard playfully on the ear. 'Enough of your cheek, pup,' he said, although he was only seven years older. 'I was not there to partake of the waters.'

'Care to enlighten me as to why you went there?'

'I was summoned by my cousin Baverstock's widow on family business.'

Richard knit his brow. 'Baverstock? Oh, yes…quite the beauty, his widow, if I remember rightly.'

'Yes, she was…is… She remarried in April. Farlowe.'

Richard whistled. 'Went to welcome him into the family, did you?'

Leo snorted. 'Hardly. I tried to warn her off, but she was as determined to have him as he was to secure her. Her income alone will be enough to allow him to live like a nabob.'

'Fortunate fellow, falling on his feet like that. I could

wish Charles such luck. Mayhap a wealthy widow would remove him from my back.'

Charles Durant, a distant cousin, was Richard's heir, and regularly applied to Richard to settle his debts. Richard thrust aside his momentary qualm at the thought of Charles ever inheriting the title and the estates. He was fit and healthy and had every intention of living a long time.

A footman opened the salon door as they approached and they dropped the subject as they joined Richard's other guests—gathered for the first evening of a shooting party. It was an all-male event, as Richard's mother was away from home, visiting an old friend.

The messenger arrived as dusk fell on the second day of the shoot. The weather had remained fine, the birds were plentiful, and beaters and shooters alike were happily exhausted after a successful day. The news of the death of Lord Craven—an old school friend of Richard's—in a fall whilst out hunting shook them all but, for Richard, it was particularly painful, resurrecting the dark, agonising time when his older brother, Adam, had been killed in a shooting accident sixteen years before. Richard had been away at school at the time and, poignantly, it had been Craven who had comforted him when he heard the news.

He had returned home to find his parents changed beyond recognition: his father almost mad with grief, scarcely eating or sleeping, and his mother bitter and withdrawn. His parents had barely communicated with each other or with him. Richard had inherited the earldom at the tender age of seventeen, after his father had followed Adam into the grave and, since then, it seemed to Richard that his mother's only interest in him was as a means to secure the succession of the title.

Many an argument had raged over his refusal to contemplate marriage to protect the title and estates, but he had held fast. He was one of the most accomplished sportsmen in the *ton*. He led a full and active life and was universally admired and feted for his prowess on a horse, his precision with the ribbons, his expertise with an *épée*, his shooting skills, and even his invincibility in the ring. He was in no hurry to don leg shackles. The only obstacle to his contentment was his mother's persistent harassment about the risks he took, and her refusal to retire to the dower house until there was a new mistress to run Fernley Park.

But now…Craven's death made Richard question his stand. If he did nothing, might his mother's great fear of Charles laying waste to the estates be realized?

The atmosphere after dinner that evening was sombre. Most of his guests settled down to play cards after dinner, but Richard declined to join them, in no mood to play the convivial host. He wandered into the library, where he found Leo, alone, pushing chess pieces around a board in a desultory manner.

'Care for a game?'

Richard shrugged, and pulled up a chair. Preoccupied and uneasy, he found it nigh on impossible to concentrate on the game, his thoughts dominated by his mother's diatribes about sporting activities and premature death.

He moved his bishop and cursed under his breath as Leo swooped with his knight to seize the piece. He looked up to meet Leo's quizzical gaze.

'Things on your mind, Stan?'

'Craven; hard to believe, isn't it?'

'Sad business. It must bring back unpleasant memories for you.'

'It does.'

Leo had been a close friend of Adam's and a frequent visitor to Fernley Park during his youth. He had supported Richard through those lonely years after his father's death, having experienced for himself the pressures of inheriting such power and wealth at an early age. They had been friends ever since.

Richard reached for a bishop, hesitated, then withdrew his hand. Moving it would expose his queen.

'How old was he? Thirtyish?'

'Two-and-thirty: the same age as me. We were at Eton together.' Richard fell silent, still contemplating his next move. He reached for a pawn. 'It's brought home my responsibilities, though. There's no shying away from it: I've decided it's time to settle the future.'

Now the words were out in the open, Richard, paradoxically, felt better. The tension that had plagued him throughout the evening began to dissipate.

Besides, marrying will have the added bonus of removing Mother to the Lodge.

The thought of Fernley Park without his mother made even marriage seem appealing. Her presence constantly reminded him of his failure as a son and he was conscious he avoided coming home, leaving more and more of the business to Elliott, his bailiff. Remorse filled him at his antipathy towards his own mother: all he could feel for her was filial duty and responsibility. Since Adam's death, she had withdrawn any hint of affection for him. And then his father had... He swallowed hard. If only he had tried harder. Been a better son.

Could I have stopped him? Would he still be here?

His father's death had rocked what remained of their family and shifted their world on its axis. Scandal had been avoided but neither he nor his mother had been the same since.

'Much as I like Charles,' he added, placing his pawn on a square at random, 'I cannot risk him running the estate to ruin.'

'Indeed. He is a somewhat profligate young man.' Leo moved his queen, capturing the pawn Richard had just moved. 'I hear the duns are sniffing at his heels again.'

'So soon? I only bailed him out last year. I thought his debts were all cleared.'

'I have no doubt they were. I believe I cautioned you at the time not to throw good money after bad.'

'You did, and I should have heeded your advice. You've never steered me wrong yet.'

Leo smiled. 'I like to think I still have some uses,' he murmured, moving a rook. 'So, you are thinking of marriage. Might I enquire as to the identity of the lucky lady?'

Richard huffed a mirthless laugh. 'I have no idea. There is no one who springs immediately to mind. As long as she's well born, is of an amiable and compliant nature, and is not minded to interfere with my life, I am sure I can find someone to suit.' He picked up his bishop, hesitated, then took one of Leo's pawns.

'Aha,' Leo said, with satisfaction, as he swooped on Richard's queen. 'Mine, I believe.'

Richard sighed. His mind was definitely not on the game. They had barely begun but, studying the pieces left on the board, he could see he was in trouble.

'A marriage of convenience?' Leo said. 'Are you certain that is what you want? A compliant wife?'

'Why ever not? I have no interest in a love match and, if I crave excitement, I can find plenty outside my domestic arrangements. No. A nice, compliant lady, content to run a comfortable household and to look after my children—that will suit me very well.'

'In that case,' Leo said, 'I might know just the girl for you.

'Checkmate.'

Chapter Three

Mid-September 1811

Felicity sat before the mirror in her bedchamber at Cheriton Abbey as the maid loaned to her by Cousin Cecily—the duke's younger, unmarried sister, who had raised his children after the death of his wife—dressed her hair. It was hard to garner any enthusiasm over Anna's efforts, although Felicity did silently admit—with a twinge of guilt at her disloyalty—that the result was an improvement on poor Beanie's usual effort.

Miss Bean, nursemaid to all three Weston children, had acted as Felicity's maid since her sixteenth birthday, but her advancing age and failing eyesight had made travelling to Cousin Leo's estate impossible. It was time, Felicity had finally accepted, for her beloved Beanie—more of a mother to her than her own mother had ever been—to retire.

The house party had been organized for the duke's seventeen-year-old daughter, Olivia, in preparation for her *début* the following spring. A party of fourteen, plus the family, Cecily had told Felicity when they arrived from Bath an hour ago. Felicity was stomach-churningly aware, however, that she was also to meet her prospective husband.

'There, milady, you're ready,' Anna said. 'I must go now and help Lady Cecily—the family usually gather in the drawing room at six o'clock.'

'Thank you for your help, Anna. Have all the guests arrived?'

'I believe so, ma'am.'

Felicity's palms turned clammy and her stomach seemed to rise up. How she wished she could simply turn up at church one day to find a stranger awaiting her at the altar. Surely that would be preferable to this wretched charade? She forced her thoughts away from the ordeal to come, recalling that Dominic, Lord Avon—Cousin Leo's eldest son and Felicity's childhood playmate—would arrive tomorrow. Buried in Bath, as she had been for the past six months, she was eager for news from Westfield, the orphan asylum in London both she and Dominic supported whenever they could.

A thought struck her. What if her husband disapproved of her charitable activities? Might he ban her from involvement with Westfield, as her stepfather had tried? He would have that right—the right to command and control her. A chill raced over her skin, raising gooseflesh on her arms.

It is nerves. You will feel better once you have met him.

Fretting over something to come was the worst part: it was the lack of action—the sense of being tossed and turned by events without any control, like a piece of driftwood caught in a current—that allowed such fears to tease her. She could stay alone with her thoughts no longer. Dragging in a breath, Felicity left the sanctuary of her bedchamber and headed for the stairs.

At the head of the magnificent staircase, she looked down and pictured *that* scene a year before. Stanton. A pleasurable feeling coiled in her belly at the mental image of his lordship in his shirt sleeves and breeches. Would he be here this weekend? It was likely, she realized, with a shiver of anticipation she swiftly banished. Despite their encounter on the stairs, Stanton had barely noticed her again as he had flirted with and charmed the other guests during the remainder of that weekend, living up to his rakish reputation.

Whoever her prospective husband might be he would

be bound to show to disadvantage against the earl. Most men did.

And is that not precisely what you want? Did you not stipulate a quiet, ordinary gentleman for your husband?

She swallowed the nerves playing havoc with her insides as she descended the stairs and entered the drawing room to await the other guests and her future.

Leo ushered Richard to one end of his magnificent library, where a small leather-upholstered sofa and two matching armchairs were placed invitingly around a stone-carved fireplace in which logs crackled merrily.

'Well? Are you going to tell me who she is?'

All through dinner Richard had been trying to guess the identity of his prospective bride. Why on earth had he not demanded to know before travelling all the way to Devon? All he knew was that she had asked her mother to arrange a match for her.

Leo's silver-grey eyes gleamed. 'Patience, dear boy.'

Richard glared at Leo, who met his look with raised eyebrows and a bland smile. *He's enjoying this, the wretch.* They had been friends for fifteen years—Richard knew that look. Biting back his irritation, he sat on the sofa whilst Leo poured them both a brandy before settling into one of the armchairs. Richard tipped his glass, savouring the warmth of the fiery spirit, waiting.

'My ward, Lady Felicity Weston.'

As he digested Leo's words, Richard conjured up a mental image of Lady Felicity. They had not been neighbours at dinner and so had not conversed, but she had appeared monosyllabic and subdued throughout. Perhaps it was nerves, knowing she was to meet her future husband? He dredged up the memory of their encounter last year, but this girl had shown none of the spark and wit she had exhibited then.

Her mother, in contrast, was the life and soul of the

gathering, but too loud and foolish for his taste. The other daughter—she had died young, he recalled—had inherited her mother's beauty, but not so Lady Felicity. No wonder she had jested about being overlooked, for it was no more than the truth. Certainly, next to her flamboyant parent, she slipped into anonymity.

A further image arose, from his perusal of the occupants of the drawing room before the meal. Lady Felicity—head to one side, eyes bright, hands animated—had been chatting with Leo's sister, Cecily, who had clearly found it hard to contain her giggles. Then Felicity had looked up. Their eyes met, and immediately all her liveliness had leached away. He had barely noticed at the time.

He chose his words with care. Leo, he knew, was fond of her.

'She is a little insipid, is she not?'

An image of his mistress of the past year materialized in his mind's eye. Harriet—now *there* was a woman: curvaceous, experienced, uncomplicated, fun. He frowned into the amber liquid swirling in his goblet. What had been his stipulations for his future wife? *Well born, of an amiable and compliant nature, and not minded to interfere with my life.* He had said nothing about appearance and, indeed, why should her looks matter? She was not ugly. She was…plain.

'She doesn't show to advantage next to her mother,' Leo said, 'but she's a good girl, she has a kind heart, she wants a family, and she's the daughter of an earl. And Lady Katherine's father was a marquis, so her breeding on both sides is impeccable. Or have you changed your mind, and now desire a love match?'

Richard glared at Leo, who met his eyes with a grin. He leaned forward and gripped Richard's knee.

'Are you sure you want this, Stan? Neither Felicity nor her parents know your identity, and need never know if you do not wish to proceed.'

Was he sure he wanted this?

No. He had not thought to wed for several years to come.

But Craven's death weighed on his mind, as did the premature deaths of his father and his brother. He was loath to agree with his mother but, if anything *should* happen to him... It was not about what he wanted any longer.

It was his responsibility.

His duty.

His decision.

'My mind is made up. I must secure the future of the title and estates.'

Leo leaned back. 'So, given that you are still minded to wed, how do you wish to proceed? Is it to be Lady Felicity?'

He had a choice. He could either choose to settle the matter now or he must seek another bride. The thought of suffering the matchmaking efforts of determined mothers and importunate fathers during the coming months in London was enough to bring him out in hives. Which left...

'She is very young.'

'She is almost five and twenty; older than she appears.'

Richard felt his brows lift. He had thought her younger. At least she had a spark of personality, although her dress sense was appalling—that pale-pink gown she was wearing tonight had done her no favours, and her figure, probably the reason he had thought her so young, was almost boyish. But, on balance, would he prefer someone like her mother—beautiful, but empty-headed and fluttery? No, that would drive him demented in a trice. At least Felicity had demonstrated a sense of humour and a down-to-earth manner he could countenance.

As long as she did not entertain girlish notions of his falling in love with his own wife, he thought Lady Felicity Weston would suit nicely.

'Very well, Lady Felicity it is. At least I can deal with you, and not Farlowe, over the settlements and so forth.'

Leo grinned and gripped Richard's hand. 'Welcome to the family, Stan. I will go and extract Felicity and Katherine from the throng, hopefully without causing too much speculation.'

It was not long before he returned with Felicity and her mother. Richard stretched his lips into a smile as he stood up, pushing a hand through his hair, smoothing the unruly curls back.

He hoped he concealed his true feelings with more success than Lady Felicity. Her expression as she came through the door, and their eyes met, was one of sheer horror.

What was so very special about Lady Felicity Weston to suggest the Earl of Stanton was not a good enough match for her?

Chapter Four

Richard had no further opportunity to study his bride-to-be. Lady Katherine sailed past her daughter and captured his hands, standing so close her floral scent made his nostrils twitch. She gazed up at him through fluttering eyelashes. Already knocked off balance by Felicity's reaction to him, Richard's muscles quivered with the effort not to snatch his hands from her mother's soft, moist grasp. From the corner of his eye he caught the resigned look that passed between Leo and Felicity. Mayhap he was not the only person who found Lady Katherine a touch overwhelming.

'My dear, dear Stanton. Such joy…oh!' She giggled breathlessly. 'How droll am I? Joy is my dear girl's middle name: Felicity Joy. Does that not suit her a treat, Stanton? I am certain she will bring you as much joy as she has brought to me and her dearest papa—God rest his soul—and now to my beloved Farlowe.'

Richard extricated his hands. 'Indeed.' He shot a baleful look at Leo, who shrugged and grinned before manoeuvring Lady Katherine to the sofa facing the fire. He then proceeded to engage her in conversation, leaving Richard to get to know his intended.

Which proved to be as difficult as drawing blood from the proverbial stone. Felicity, her face quite colourless, had taken her place beside her mother, her attention firmly on the flames as Richard sank into the nearest chair. Her expression was hard to read but her rigid posture and tight fists told their own story. Something—something about him, he must conclude—was not to her liking. Contrarily, her seeming reluctance fanned his determination to proceed with the marriage.

'Well, Lady Felicity, who could have guessed when we met on the stairs last year that we would be here now, discussing our forthcoming marriage?'

'Indeed, my lord.' Still she avoided eye contact, staring into the fire.

Richard, momentarily nonplussed, continued to study her. Nondescript was the most fitting adjective he could conjure up. She was a touch taller than average, with a slight build. Another woman of her stature might be described as willowy, but, somehow, Felicity was not quite tall enough, and not quite slender enough, to earn that accolade. Her features were regular, her complexion dull. Her oval face was a shade too long and her chin a touch too determined, for delicacy. Her nose was straight, but a little too strong to be considered dainty, and her mouth was… Richard paused in his appraisal. The compression of her lips did little to disguise their rosy fullness. They, at least, could be declared alluring.

Her brown hair was pinned up in the Grecian style, with curls—already wilting—framing her face. Her eyes were a striking amber and, at this moment in time, they stared dully ahead as Felicity sat straight-backed, her hands white-knuckled in her lap.

What was she thinking? According to Leo, Felicity had asked her mother to find her a husband, but her reaction to Richard almost suggested she would be entering the union against her will. Richard hoped not. Now he had made his decision he was impatient to proceed. He vowed to win her over.

'It's a pleasant evening, Lady Felicity. Would you care to stroll on the terrace?'

She looked directly at him for the first time since she entered the room. Try as he might, he could not read her expression. Before she could answer him, though, Lady Katherine intervened.

'Of course she would, Stanton. Go along, Felicity. I am sure you do not need chaperoning if you are with your intended. I declare I have never been so happy in my life—except, of course, when my dear Farlowe proposed. Who would have thought that I would be mama-in-law to the Earl of Stanton. I shall be the envy of everyone. I cannot wait to see their—'

'Mama, please.' Felicity cut across her mother's monologue as she stood up.

Richard rose to his feet with a guilty start. He had been on the brink of becoming mesmerized by Lady Katherine's inane chatter.

Felicity, cheeks splashed with colour, shot a glance at him before lowering her gaze. 'Thank you. I should enjoy a breath of fresh air.'

She took his arm and they left the library via one of the French doors. It was dark outside on the terrace, but lamps at intervals along the balustrade cast weak pools of light to soften the shadows.

Richard placed his hand over Felicity's, where it lay on his arm. It was chilled, despite the mildness of the evening.

'You are chilled, Lady Felicity. Shall I fetch your shawl?'

'I am warm enough, thank you, my lord.'

'Richard. Please. We need not stand on ceremony with one another; unless, of course, you have doubts about our marriage?'

Her eyes flicked to his face, then returned to their contemplation of the flagstones at their feet. Richard stopped beneath one of the lamps and took her hands in his.

'Forgive my blunt speaking, but you do not appear happy. Am I ousting a preferred suitor?'

'No, there is no other, although I had not thought… I did not realize… Oh, heavens, I cannot find the words.'

Felicity tugged her hands free and turned to stare into

the darkness of the surrounding gardens. Her arms were wrapped around her waist and she looked somehow very vulnerable, standing there alone. It crossed Richard's mind that she was self-contained: she gave the impression she was used to relying on her own resources. He shook his head in self-deprecation. Harriet *would* be impressed. She was forever castigating him about his lack of insight and yet, here he was, analysing his bride-to-be as though he had known her for years. He thrust away all thought of his mistress. It felt, somehow, disloyal to think of her whilst in the company of his future wife.

He put his hands on Felicity's shoulders, the bones fragile beneath his fingers. 'Try. I won't bite, you know. I should prefer to start off with honesty between us, if we are to live together with any degree of comfort.'

Her shoulders tensed as she inhaled. Then she turned, and regarded him, her eyes as rueful as her smile.

'This is ridiculous. You are right. If we are to wed, we need to understand one another. And, I admit I have doubts. Not about you. Well, that is…' She paused, her brows drawn together in a frown. 'No, that is untrue. It *is* about you, but it is about me, also. You and me. Together. You see, I hadn't thought…I never presumed to be presented with such a… such a…*catch*, if you do not object to my calling you that?'

Richard bit back a smile. He had been called a catch many times, he was aware, but never to his face before. And never by an earnest-faced female who appeared to believe herself unworthy of a 'catch' such as he.

'You may call me what you will,' he said, 'as long as you promise not to use such insultingly offensive terms that I shall be forced to take umbrage.'

She laughed, revealing a glimpse of white teeth. 'Umbrage? I always thought that to be a state applied to elderly dowagers. Do you sporting gentlemen consider it a fittingly masculine trait, my lord?'

This was better. The spirited girl he remembered from

last year had surfaced, her face alive with laughter, her eyes bright.

'Perhaps umbrage does not quite convey the precise meaning I hoped to convey,' he conceded. 'Which word, in your opinion, should I have used, if I am to portray a suitably manly image to my future wife?'

Disquiet skimmed her expression, then vanished. Had he imagined it? Was it the bald reminder that she would be his wife that had disturbed her? Her countenance was now neutral, but her eyes remained watchful and she made no attempt to answer him.

'Would you have preferred me to use "offence" perhaps, or "exception"?' He leaned closer to her, and said, 'I do not, you notice, suggest "outrage" for that, I fear, would not meet with your approval any more than "umbrage". It is too synonymous with spinsters, would you not—?'

Felicity stiffened. 'Do not make fun of me, sir. I may be a spinster and, therefore, in your eyes, a poor, undesired thing, but I have feelings and I have pride.'

'Felicity, I promise I intended no slight. The thought never crossed my mind that you might think I was making fun of you. I was…I was… Oh, confound it! Come here.'

He had run out of words. He clasped her shoulders and drew her close. A finger beneath her chin tilted her face to his. He searched her eyes. They were shuttered. She was rigid in his arms. Was she scared? Had she never known a man's kiss? The thought, strangely, pleased him: knowing his wife had never experienced another man's touch. But he must take care not to frighten her. He lowered his head, slowly, and put his lips to hers.

He almost recoiled in shock. He had expected ice. What he felt was fire.

Chapter Five

Felicity's heart clamoured in her chest as Richard's lips claimed hers. One arm swept around her back, the other hand cupped her head. His lips were warm, surprisingly soft and tasted of brandy. They slid, slowly, tantalizingly, over hers and she felt her own lips soften and respond. A tingling thrill shot through her, all the way to her toes. Her fingers tightened on his sleeve as her belly squeezed in a strange but not unpleasant way. That kiss ended too soon for Felicity and as the reality sunk in—that this man would indeed be her husband, would be entitled to kiss her and caress her and much more—her heart faltered.

How could she resist falling in love with such a man? She was under no illusion that he might ever love her. Unrequited love had caused far more beautiful women than she to suffer. She saw an image of her future—lonely and desperate—stretching before her.

Richard smiled down at her. She searched his face. It confirmed her fears. Even in this dim light, she could read the amusement that lurked in the depths of those velvety eyes. And why would he not be amused? A naive spinster and the experienced man about town: would that not set the precedent for their marriage? Could she protect her heart? Through the lit windows of the library she could see her mother and the duke, deep in conversation. She must tell them as soon as possible that she could not marry Lord Stanton. She peeked at him again. He looked bored. That settled it, then.

'Perhaps we should go back inside. Mama will be wondering where we are.'

His lips twitched as he glanced through the window. Felicity felt a lick of heat, deep inside, remembering their warm, silken caress.

'I suspect your mama has forgotten our existence for the moment.'

Nothing would prevail upon Felicity to admit he was right. 'Nevertheless, I think we have been out here long enough.'

Richard sketched a bow. 'As you wish, my lady.'

Felicity studied him surreptitiously as she took his arm. Starkly handsome, his close-fitting black tailcoat and trousers emphasized his masculinity. Not only was Stanton one of society's most eligible bachelors, but Felicity was aware he was also widely acclaimed for his sporting prowess. The hard muscle of his arm under her hand attested to his strength.

He seemed not unkind.

He had a sense of humour.

He was nigh on the perfect man.

Just not for her.

Felicity wrapped her shawl closer around her and knocked on her mother's bedchamber door. She glanced along the corridor, praying no one would see her. The sick dread churning the pit of her stomach would not go away. She must speak with Mama and tell her of her decision, or she would never be able to sleep that night. The sooner she halted Lady Katherine's inevitable runaway enthusiasm for this match, the better.

She heard a faint voice from within, and entered. Lady Katherine was in the massive four-poster, reclining in a sultry pose against the stacked pillows. When she saw her daughter, she sat up, pouting.

'Felicity. I thought you were my darling Farlowe. What is it? Will it take long?'

Thank goodness her stepfather was still downstairs with the other men. It would be hard enough to persuade Mama to understand without Farlowe there to stir the pot.

Felicity perched on the edge of Mama's bed.

'Mama, I cannot marry Lord Stanton.'

'What?'

Felicity flinched, her mother's piercing shriek loud in her ears.

'I am sorry…'

'*Sorry?* You are the most ungrateful little… Why? You asked me to arrange a marriage, and I have set up an alliance with *the* most eligible bachelor of our acquaintance, and you have the *boldness* to suggest he is not good enough for you? Oh! Where are my salts? You *infuriating, stubborn* girl…'

Lady Katherine's face was pink with fury. Felicity found her mother's smelling salts and watched her wave them beneath her nose.

'Mama, I am sorry to distress you, but if you will listen to me—'

'Listen to you? I listened when you asked me to arrange your marriage. Finally, I thought…*finally*, Felicity is behaving as a modest young woman ought. But I was mistaken. You still imagine you are too good! Too good for the likes of Stanton, of all people.'

'I do not believe I am too good for him,' Felicity said, heart sinking. Once Lady Katherine had worked herself into such a state, she was unlikely to heed anything other than her own point of view. How Felicity wished Beanie was here to confide in.

'Well, I should think not. Now, if it was poor, dear Emma who had caught the eye of such a man…mayhap *she* could believe herself too good for him.'

Felicity thrust down the pain of once again being unfavourably compared to her sister.

'May we discuss this in the morning, Mama?' *When you are calmer.* 'I am sorry to upset you, but I would try to make you understand why I must refuse Stanton.'

Lady Katherine straightened in the bed, sparks shooting from her blue eyes. 'I do believe you are serious, you ungrateful chit. You always were stubborn, and unbecomingly *forward* with your opinions. Well, we shall see what Farlowe has to say about *this*.'

'My stepfather can have no opinion on my betrothal,' Felicity retorted. *If only you had never married him, I wouldn't be obliged to marry* anyone. 'The decision is mine. You cannot *force* me to accept Stanton.'

'But *why*, Felicity, darling?' Her mother changed tack, wheedling. 'I don't understand. Most girls would *swoon* at the thought of catching such a man.'

'The problem is that he is *too* good a catch, Mama.'

'Too good? How can a man be too *good* a catch?'

Felicity struggled to find the words. How could she possibly explain without insulting her mother and dragging Emma's name into the argument? Her mother would—and not for the first time—accuse her of jealousy.

'I wish for a quiet, retiring gentleman, Mama. Lord Stanton is popular. He is always the centre of attention. Please try to understand.'

I am afraid I will fall in love with him.

The words she could not say near choked her. A man like Stanton, in an arranged marriage, would develop the same carelessness her father had demonstrated towards her mother; the same indifference Farlowe was now beginning to demonstrate, a mere six months into their marriage. Such indifference in a marriage of convenience would be tolerable. But that *same* indifference, if she were to fall in love with her husband... A handsome face with warm brown eyes materialized in her mind's eye and her lips tingled in memory of his kiss. She could never resist him. She knew it as surely as she knew her own name.

Stanton was one of the most attractive men she had ever seen, with his dark brown, wavy hair, his deep, soulful eyes, and his fine figure. Since their encounter last year, she had added those strong, muscular arms and the glimpse of dark chest hair to the tally of his attractions. And now she had experienced his kiss—how could she ever withstand such an onslaught? She might be inexperienced, but she suspected that kiss had triggered only the merest hint of the passion buried deep within her. No, she dare not expose her heart to such a man. That way, for sure, would result in heart-break and despair.

'Well, I do *not* understand, you provoking girl. Oh, where is Farlowe when I need him? I need his support. No one understands my trials.'

'Please, Mama, may we speak again in the morning, before the betrothal is announced?'

'The duke and Lord Stanton have agreed to announce the betrothal after dinner, tomorrow evening. But do not think the delay will favour your case, my girl, for my mind is quite made up. Just think, I shall be the envy of all, when our news becomes known.'

'Mama, I cannot marry a man merely in order that you can boast to your acquaintances.'

'Oh! You would make me sound the most uncaring parent in the world, Felicity. Have I not always put your welfare and happiness at the very top of my priorities?' Lady Katherine sank back against the pillows and waved her salts beneath her nose again, her eyes closed. Then they snapped open and she sat up, nailing Felicity with a triumphant stare. 'The duke has approved the match. He believes you and Stanton will suit very well. Do you dare to question *his* authority?'

If her mother was to start invoking the duke's authority, Felicity knew she must concede her argument for now and try again tomorrow.

'Goodnight, Mama. I hope you sleep well. I shall come to see you in the morning. Please try to understand—I want to be content in my marriage but I cannot believe Stanton will prove a *comfortable* husband.'

She bent and kissed her mother.

'Do not think I shall yield on this, Felicity. There are times when you must realize that your elders have more worldly experience than you and know what is best.'

Chapter Six

A bright morning saw Felicity up and about early, her determination not to wed Lord Stanton stronger than ever. He had prowled through her restless dreams, stirring strange and unwelcome yearnings deep within her. She had woken from those dreams, her heart racing, her skin hot and damp. And that was merely the result of a single kiss.

As she made her way downstairs it was apparent there was no one else up, other than servants, but that suited Felicity: the only person she wished to speak to was her mother, unlikely to be awake at this hour. Felicity crossed the library and let herself out on to the terrace, where she had strolled with Lord Stanton the previous evening.

She paused at the spot where they had kissed. Her pulse quickened at the memory even as the ever-present fear wormed through her belly. Unrequited love. She could not, would not risk it. It was unrequited love that had so wrecked Emma's life that she had climbed to the roof of Baverstock Court and…

Felicity turned abruptly from the spot and headed for the flight of stone steps that led down into the garden, laid out in a formal style dissected by stone-flagged paths. There were gardeners already at work, weeding and collecting leaves, so she did not linger but followed the central pathway to an arched gap cut into a tall beech hedge. Through the gap was another pathway, and she turned left, knowing the stables were to the right. They, like the garden, would be a beehive of activity at this time of the morning.

A short distance along the path she reached the small rustic gate she remembered from her childhood. It led to a grass path that wound through a copse of ornamental trees before opening on to a vista of Cousin Leo's lake. Water always soothed her. When she eventually wed she would have, if not a lake, then at the very least a pond, preferably near to the house, so she could see it every day; a large pond, with water lilies, and fish, and a bench to sit on. Daydreaming pleasantly, Felicity continued towards the lake.

'Good morning, Felicity Joy.' The deep voice startled her from her reverie.

'Oh!' Her heart leapt into her throat as she looked around.

Lounging at one side of the path, broad shoulders propped against the trunk of a copper beech, was Lord Stanton.

Felicity felt her face heat. *Why must I blush now?* She could never blush prettily, like her mother or Emma. Then she gritted her teeth. Why should she care how she blushed? She could never impress Stanton with her appearance, and she was not about to try. Besides, had she not already decided he was not for her?

'Good morning, my lord. You are up early. I had not expected to see anyone out and about quite yet.'

'I am sorry if I startled you. I had a restless night. It is not every day a man meets his future wife for the first time.'

Felicity eyed him with suspicion. Was he poking fun at her? 'It is not too late to change your mind.'

His dark brows snapped together. 'And what, precisely, do you mean by that, Felicity Joy?'

He pushed away from the tree and prowled towards Felicity, his attention never leaving her face. She resisted the urge to retreat.

'You sound as though you might welcome a change of heart.'

'Why were you leaning against that tree?' Felicity asked. 'Are you waiting for someone?'

'You.' Stanton was close now, gazing down at her.

She held his gaze, her heart pumping a little too fast to be explained away by her walk. He was so handsome. Too handsome.

'What do you mean?' Her voice sounded breathless. It reminded her of her mother, which fuelled her irritation. She had no wish to flutter every time a man paid her any attention. She cleared her throat. 'You could not possibly have known I would be walking here.'

He grinned. 'I was returning from a stroll by the lake. I saw you coming from a distance, so I thought I might wait for you. And see when—indeed, *if*—you would notice my presence. It seems I am not the only one who is preoccupied. You, too, appear to have much on your mind, and not all of it pleasant, judging by your expression.'

'And if I maintain that is my normal expression?'

Stanton crooked his arm. It would surely be churlish not to take it. They continued towards the lake.

'Then I should say that your life is, perhaps, not very content. I should like to see a smile on your face always, Felicity Joy.'

He halted, tugging her around to face him. He lifted her chin with one finger, and Felicity was instantly transported back to the night before. She tensed. Was he going to kiss her again? His sensual lips curved, and she tore her gaze from them with an effort. His head dipped. If she was not marrying him, she should pull away, and yet…without volition, she swayed closer, relishing the heat radiating from his body. Her entire body softened as she breathed in his scent: a heady mixture of soap, fresh air and maleness.

He studied her, his expression serious.

Goodness, what must I look like? She really had not expected to meet anyone this early. She had splashed cold water on her face, pulled on the closest gown to hand and dragged a comb through her hair before roughly plaiting it, too preoccupied with her dilemma to worry about her appearance. How she wished it was possible to return to her childhood, when she had visited Cheriton Abbey and spent many carefree days exploring the grounds without a care as to how she looked.

The gentle sweep of Stanton's thumb beneath her eye broke into her thoughts.

'It appears I was not the only one who slept ill last night. What is it that troubles you? I can tell you are not overjoyed at the prospect of marrying me, but I confess I am at a loss to understand it. It seems to me we should make a success-ful partnership. We both, as I understand it, want children. Will you not confide in me about your doubts? I have no wish for a wife who feels she has been pressured into a union she actively dislikes.'

Her heart stuttered. 'It is not that I would dislike being married to you.' Far from it, if she was truthful. She re-called her words to her mother the night before. There was enough truth to sound believable. 'I have seen you enough times in London, sir. You are popular. You are always at the centre of attention. I specifically asked Mama to find a quiet, retiring gentleman for my husband.'

Stanton's brows drew together. 'Do you mean you wish to retire to the country entirely?'

'No. I enjoy country life, but I also enjoy spending time in London as I have interests there. I take little pleasure in society balls and parties, however.'

'Then I see no reason why our union should not prove mutually beneficial, Felicity. I would never insist we live in each other's pockets, particularly once an heir is born. Many marriages are conducted in such a fashion, with dis-cretion. I would be happy for our marriage to be the same.'

But I would not. Not with you.

She was so afraid she would grow to love him, par-ticularly now, when he had shown such gentle—and unexpected—understanding. And his words—his expec-tations of their marriage merely reinforced her fears. She was to be used as a vessel to produce an heir. And, without doubt, a spare. Like a brood mare. None of which she really objected to. Indeed, it was what she wanted: a quiet husband to live on the periphery of her life. But Stanton was not, and never could be, he.

'What do you say, Felicity Joy? May I pay my addresses to you? I should like to propose in the customary manner —and to hear your reply—and not just drift into an understanding.'

Chapter Seven

Felicity bit her lip. She would regret her decision either way, but better to suffer disappointment now, and be done with it, than to live in lonely suffering and heartache for the rest of her days. She did, however, need to talk to her mother again first.

'I am sorry to be indecisive, but might I give you my answer later? I should like time to think about what you have said.'

Stanton stepped back and bowed. 'Of course you may. I would not for the world wish to rush you. It is a momentous decision.'

'Thank you. If you do not object, I shall return to the Abbey now. And I will give you my answer later this morning, if that will suit you?'

'Of course.'

Felicity walked back along the path through the trees. She rounded the bend, and her heart sank. Her stepfather, Quentin Farlowe, had just stepped through the gate into the copse. It was too late to turn back, for he saw her almost immediately.

'There you are, miss,' he called.

Felicity cursed under her breath. He strode towards her, frowning, his thin lips barely visible.

As he reached her she lifted her chin. 'I am on my way to see Mama. There was no need to search for me.'

'I disagree. You have worked your mother into the devil of a state. What can you possibly object to in Stanton?'

'I will discuss it with Mama and my guardian.'

Farlowe's fingers bit into her arm. 'We will settle this now. I will not have your mother upset.'

No, of course you won't. No doubt it disturbed your sleep. How Felicity longed to throw those words at her stepfather, but she refused to stoop so low. 'I have no wish to upset Mama either. I am sure we will reach some accord.'

He dragged her close, glaring down at her through narrowed eyes. Felicity coughed as a wave of Farlowe's pungent hair oil pervaded her nostrils. The sickly smell contrasted sharply with Stanton's fresh, spicy scent.

'You've been a thorn in my side ever since I married your mother, looking down your nose at me. Why do you not want Stanton?' He bent his head close to hers, his breath hot against her skin as he whispered in her ear. 'Is he too much the man for you, miss? Are you scared of your wedding night? Mayhap I can be of assistance? Provide a little tutoring so you will not—'

'Let me go!' Felicity struggled against his viselike grip on her arm. 'When Mama hears what you—'

Farlowe laughed. 'But she won't find out, will she? You forget—I know you, *Lady* Felicity. You won't say a word to your mama because you hate to upset anyone—'

'Farlowe!' Stanton's voice cut through the air like a whip.

Farlowe looked round, but did not release Felicity as Richard strode towards them, fury pounding his veins.

'Merely a familial misunderstanding, Stanton; nothing for you to concern yourself with.'

The rogue didn't even have the grace to look ashamed. Richard wondered what he had whispered to Felicity. Judging by her expression, he had not been sharing a friendly word of advice.

'Oh, but I am concerned, Farlowe. Anything that distresses Felicity distresses me. Take your hands from her.'

'We have not finished—'

'Yes, we have.' Felicity twisted her arm free. 'I told you, sir, that I will discuss the matter with my mother and the duke. They are my guardians, not you.'

Richard levelled a long look at Farlowe, who blanched. Good. The savage anger in his breast must be reflected in his expression. He would have dearly loved to draw the scoundrel's cork, but would not do so in front of Felicity. Next time they met, though, Mr Quentin Farlowe would have a few questions to answer.

Glancing at Felicity, Richard was struck once more by her forlorn expression. Much as he would like to place all the blame for her dejection at Farlowe's door, he could not deny she had been troubled even before the incident with her stepfather. Was Leo mistaken? Was a marriage of convenience not Felicity's choice, but at the instigation of her parents?

'Would you be so good as to escort me to my mother, Lord Stanton?'

'My pleasure, Lady Felicity.'

When she took his arm, Richard noticed she leant on it a little more heavily than before as they headed back to the Abbey.

'Are you quite well, Felicity? Farlowe…he looked a little rough back there.'

Felicity's fingers tightened on his sleeve. 'He is not a particularly nice man,' she said. 'It is one of the reasons I asked Mama to find me a husband.'

So it *was* her choice. Her doubts, then, were definitely about him.

'Your mama is happy with him, though? He is not… cruel in any way?'

The faintest of sighs murmured past his ears and he had to tilt his head to catch her words. 'No, not overtly cruel. But there is cruelty and there is cruelty.'

Richard pondered that statement. After half a minute, when he was no wiser, he said, 'I fear that statement is a little obscure for this early in the morning. What do you mean?'

Felicity's head snapped round, her eyes stricken. 'Oh,' she gasped, 'I am sorry, I had quite forgot…that is…what I mean is that Mama has high expectations of my stepfather. I do not think he has the character to meet those expectations. Does that make sense?'

'I suppose it does. Your mother, if you will forgive me for saying so, is a lady who would require her husband to dance attendance on her. I surmise, from your explanation, that Farlowe does not view his role in quite the same way?'

'No, indeed. His role—in his opinion—is to live as high as possible, doing precisely what he wishes, with Mama's money. Oh! I do beg your pardon. That was most unbecoming in me… I'm afraid my stepfather brings out the very worst in me, despite my best intentions to let his shortcomings fly over my head without comment. Somehow—' she smiled, ruefully '—my basest nature seems to rear its head whenever he is involved. I think we shall never live comfortably together.'

'Which is why, as you say, you seek a husband. And, yet, you seem reluctant to accept my suit. I am beginning to feel quite deflated, Lady Felicity.'

'Oh, no.' She stopped walking and turned to Richard, her eyes big with concern. 'Please, no, I do not want you to think…to believe… Oh.' Her protestations ceased and her eyes narrowed. 'This is quite ridiculous as well you know, my lord. We both know very well that no other woman would view your suit with the slightest hesitation. The reasons for my indecision are…well, they are… Oh, I cannot say more than I have already. You said you would wait for my answer until later this morning, and I must ask you to honour that.

'Thank you for your escort. I shall be quite safe from here.'

Richard stood at the bottom of the main staircase, watching as Felicity climbed the sweep to the next floor.

'Good morning, Stan. Enjoying the morning air with your betrothed?'

Richard did not turn to look at Leo. 'I am not sure "enjoying" is quite the right word, Leo. And neither, if I read the lady correctly, is "betrothed". I must confess to a certain bemusement. Lady Felicity—if I have understood our, at times, quite muddled conversation correctly—is about to turn me down flat.'

Chapter Eight

'Now hear this, young lady, and hear it well.'

Lady Katherine stalked up and down her bedchamber, gesticulating. Until this very minute, Felicity had not dreamed she might fail in her attempt to avoid marriage to Lord Stanton. She sank onto a chair by the window, her legs unaccountably shaky, as her mother continued to pace.

'You asked me to find you a husband.'

'Yes, that is true, but—'

'No buts. I have found you an eminently eligible man, one who must be far beyond anyone you could have hoped for.'

'Yes, but—'

Her mother quelled her with one look. A feeling of unreality washed over Felicity. This determination in her normally persuadable mother was new, and she knew who to thank for it. *Why, oh, why did Mama marry that man?*

'I have spoken with the duke this morning—yes, already, at this unearthly hour—and he has confirmed his belief that you and Stanton will suit. He knows you both. He will hardly match one of his closest friends with someone unsuitable.'

'I do not believe Stanton and I will be compatible, Mama.'

'I have discussed this with Farlowe…'

Felicity sprang to her feet. 'I might have known *he* was—'

Her mother continued as though Felicity had not spoken. '…and we are agreed. You have a choice.'

'A choice?' Felicity stared at her mother, hope stirring. 'Who?'

'Not who. What. Our conversation last night left me vastly unsettled, Felicity, and I was still awake when my dear Farlowe retired. I told him of your stubbornness, and he suggested—'

'Did I hear my name mentioned?'

'Farlowe. My darling. Such a valiant but wasted effort on your part, searching for this wretched girl. But no matter, for she is here now, and I am about to reveal her options.'

Felicity caught Farlowe's smirk. Cold sweat prickled over her back. He wanted her out of their lives as much as she did. What was her mother's alternative? A nunnery?

Oh, please. We are not living in the pages of a Gothic novel. 'Very well, Mama. What is my alternative?'

'You said you wanted a family and we have found you a perfectly eligible suitor. You either accept Stanton or you will never wed. You will end your days living with us as my companion and, after I have gone, you must depend on the charity of your dear brother. You will forever be the poor relation.'

Felicity's knees threatened to buckle. She grabbed the back of a chair.

'You cannot prevent me finding a husband of my own,' she said.

'And you have proven yourself oh-so successful in that endeavour to date, have you not, Felicity?' Farlowe said. 'And do not think you will be permitted to squander good money on those urchins and thieves you are so fond of. You will have no need of such a generous allowance as your mother's companion.'

She could not win. In order to find herself a husband, she would have to allow herself to be courted. She must risk her heart whichever way she chose. The alternative: remaining with her mother and Farlowe—to have to endure his leers and his constant crude remarks about virgins—was sim-

ply intolerable. And she would not even have the release of
involvement with Westfield.

She must capitulate. Her choice was, in reality, no choice.
But she would move mountains in order to protect her heart.
On one thing she was adamant: she must *never* fall in love
with Lord Stanton.

Richard turned from his contemplation of the portrait
hung over the mantel and watched Felicity approach.

'Lady Felicity. I am honoured you have consented to
hear my address.'

He scanned her features. She looked no more enthusiastic than she had earlier. Her eyes refused to meet his as
she curtsied.

'The honour is all mine, my lord.'

Richard gave himself leave to doubt that. The hopeless
resignation in her voice matched her whole demeanour. He
felt a scowl crease his brow and hastily smoothed it away.
Not that she'd noticed; her eyes were fixed on a point somewhere beyond his right ear.

*Why not end this farce now? There are plenty of girls
available who would swoon at the idea of marrying you.
Why tie yourself to a woman who doesn't want you? Haven't
you experienced enough rejection from your own mother?*

Was it the challenge? Part of his determination to marry
Felicity was precisely *because* of her indifference. The other
part... In his mind's eye, he saw Felicity struggling against
Farlowe's grip. Could he really abandon her to life with
that rogue?

She was well born, compliant and desirous of a family. Leo was convinced they would suit one another and
Dominic—Leo's twenty-year-old son and heir, who had
arrived home earlier that afternoon—had even sung Felicity's praises, assuring Richard there was more to her than
might be apparent on the surface.

He thrust aside his doubts. There would be time enough

once they were wed to discover what she feared. She would not be here if she was completely averse to him personally. Would she?

He took Felicity's hands: fragile, the bones delicate in his grasp, the skin chilled. He felt a tremor wash through her, and squeezed reassuringly. Whatever her doubts, she was not shy, she had proved an entertaining conversationalist, and the way she had returned his kiss suggested she would be neither afraid nor reluctant to explore the physical side of marriage. That kiss! His loins stirred as his gaze dropped to her mouth without volition. He studied her full, shapely lips. She was not as insipid as he had first thought—Leo was right, she merely did not show to advantage beside her mother. She had a neat figure and her smile was infectious, lighting her whole face.

He was sure this marriage was the right decision for him, and that he and Felicity would rub along well together. His life was full and satisfying. He boasted a wide circle of like-minded friends with whom he shared an interest in a variety of sports. And, once he was wed, his mother would remove to the Lodge and he would happily spend more of his time at Fernley attending to the estate.

What he was less certain of was if it was the right decision for Felicity, standing quietly, her hands limp in his. Richard focused on her.

'Lady Felicity, would you do me the very great honour of accepting my hand in marriage?'

Her features appeared carved out of rock. Not even an eyelash flickered.

'Yes. Thank you.'

Her voice was as colourless as her complexion. His jaw clenched. He moved closer. She stepped back. He tightened his grip and tugged until her body was pressed full length against his. Another tremor ran through her as he wrapped one arm around her waist. But she did not look away. She held his gaze as he lowered his lips to hers.

Her lips were sweet and soft and relaxed as he kissed her and they opened readily enough. She allowed him to explore her mouth but she made no attempt to kiss him in return. She merely permitted the kiss. Dissatisfied, Richard was about to tear his lips from hers when he registered her tension. It was as though he held a statue in his embrace. Despite his earlier thoughts, he wondered if she was, after all, wary of the intimate side of marriage.

'Relax,' he whispered against her lips. 'This is meant to be enjoyable.'

He feathered butterfly-light kisses over her cheeks, her brows, along her jaw then nudged her head to one side to nibble at her earlobe. Suddenly, she exhaled with a *whoosh*, and the long rigid muscles down her back softened under his hands. Her body relaxed against his and she lifted her hands to his chest and pushed.

'I am sorry. This is hard for me. I wonder…might we wait until after we are married? Someone might come in.'

'We are newly betrothed, Felicity. We should be allowed a celebratory kiss, do you not think?'

Again, her expression eluded him as she wiped her hands down her skirts. Nerves? He would give much to understand what was going through her mind right now.

'Very well,' he said. 'We will wait until after the wedding. Speaking of which, I am minded to wed as soon as possible, if that is agreeable to you?'

He quashed the thought he was being unfair. He couldn't escape the feeling that, if given time, Felicity would renege on her acceptance, and he was suddenly determined not to afford her the opportunity.

'If you return to Bath tomorrow, I shall call in the Bishop's Office at Wells on my way through and procure a Common Licence. We will not then have to wait for the banns to be read, and we could marry by the end of the week.' His sense of fair play intervened, forcing him to add, with reluctance, 'Or do you need more time to prepare?'

Felicity straightened. 'No. That will not be necessary.' Finally, there was a hint of conviction in her tone. 'I shall go and inform Mama of our plans. Thank you for understanding,'

Understanding? Richard wasn't sure he understood anything about his bride-to-be.

Chapter Nine

'My lords, ladies and gentlemen.'

The hubbub of conversation faded as the assembled guests turned their attention to the plinth set up at one end of the huge ballroom to accommodate the musicians. That evening had seen the surrounding families invited to Cheriton Abbey for a ball. Felicity had dressed, with a little more attention to her appearance than usual, in her favourite evening gown of primrose silk, knowing all eyes would be on her at some point during the evening.

The duke stood impassively on the plinth, awaiting the undivided attention of his guests whilst Stanton cupped Felicity's elbow and guided her to the front and side of the throng. Despite her fears, Felicity could not suppress a *frisson* of excitement at the thought of marrying such a man. He was in his element, here in the ballroom. It was unfortunate she was not.

Her mouth dried as Cousin Leo began to speak and heads turned in her direction. Her lips clung to her teeth, foiling her attempt to smile.

'You might at least attempt to look happy.'

Stanton's breath scorched her ear. Felicity inhaled, his spicy male scent pervading every cell of her body. She pushed her thick tongue between her lips and her teeth in an attempt to moisten them. She was vaguely aware of a murmured exchange between Stanton and Cousin Cecily, who stood nearby. A glass was thrust into her hand.

'Here. Take a sip. It will help.' A large hand settled—

comfortingly—at the small of her back, its heat penetrating the delicate silk of her dress, warming her even as a shiver of awareness snaked down her spine.

She registered only an occasional word of Cousin Leo's speech as she sipped the punch. She glanced sideways at Stanton and smiled her thanks just as Cousin Leo said, 'I am sure you will all join me in wishing them every happiness in their life together.'

A low hum swept the room and then people were surrounding them, smiling, congratulating, shaking Stanton by the hand but also eyeing Felicity: speculating, slightly incredulous. She stood tall, steadying her nerves, aware this was but a tiny taste of the attention she would experience in London. She had a choice to make; a choice that might inform the future of this union with Stanton.

She could either shrivel or she could bloom.

She inhaled, braced her shoulders and curved her lips as she responded to their many well-wishers, grateful for the comforting presence of Stanton by her side, deflecting much of the attention away from her, protecting her, until people were distracted by the musicians tuning their instruments.

'Well, Fliss. It's official now. You are to be a married lady.' Felicity spun round in delighted response to the familiar voice in her ear.

'Dominic! I did not see you there.' She lowered her voice. 'It still feels unreal. I never wanted to marry…oh! I dare say I should not have said that.' She glanced round apprehensively.

Stanton, engaged in conversation with Cecily, appeared not to have heard.

Dominic, Lord Avon, laughed. He was a younger version of his father: tall, elegant and suave with the same black hair and silver-grey eyes. 'Well, I think it will be the making of you.' He raised his voice. 'Congratulations, Stan. Mind you take care of my favourite cousin.'

'Oh, I will,' Stanton said as they shook hands.

'Have you come down from London, Dom?' Felicity asked. 'It is such an age since I was there. Tell me, how do they go on at Westfield?'

'What, and where, is Westfield?' Stanton enquired.

Felicity's mother and stepfather joined the group at that moment and, hearing Stanton's question, Lady Katherine immediately claimed his attention.

'Oh, it is merely some nonsense of Felicity's, Stanton. Nothing for you to concern yourself with for I am persuaded Felicity will have vastly more important matters to occupy her once she is married.'

Before Felicity could respond, Stanton said, 'You may indeed be confident of Felicity's future preferences, my lady—and I bow to your superior knowledge of your daughter —but I do find in myself a desire to know what Felicity has to say on the subject.'

His voice held the perfect hint of apology, and Felicity could not be quite sure if he had just delivered a most elegant setdown to her mother. As she pondered, he glanced at her and she caught the devilish glint in his eye. She pursed her lips, trying to suppress the laugh that bubbled in her chest.

'My dear, would you care to enlighten me?' Stanton's voice and expression were suitably grave as he tilted his head and raised a brow. 'I asked you about Westfield, if you recall.'

'It is a haven for thieves and pickpockets,' Farlowe interjected. 'That is what it is. A waste of good money. It shouldn't be allowed, that's what I say.'

Her stepfather had never struck Felicity as a perceptive man, and now he sank to new depths in her estimation. How could the man be so blithely oblivious to Stanton's scowl?

'It is my allowance, sir, and I spend it how I please,' she said.

'Felicity! Do not put dear Farlowe down in that unbecoming manner. Why, whatever will Stanton think—'

'Stanton,' interrupted a silky-smooth voice, 'thinks his

future wife has her own opinion and should be allowed to voice it without interruption.'

'Oh, good man, Stan. Well said,' Dominic said, laughing.

'Dominic—' Cecily grabbed her nephew's arm '—the dancing is about to start. Would you be so good as to stand up with your elderly aunt for the first?'

'Oh, transparent, dear aunt. Come then, let us leave the newly betrothed and their relatives to play at happy families.'

Cecily led Dominic away and Felicity breathed easier, knowing he was more than capable of adding further fuel to an already fraught situation.

'Westfield—' she turned to Stanton '—is an asylum in Islington for orphans and destitute children. I've supported it for five years, and Dominic became involved about a year ago.'

'And will you tell Stanton where you find these *orphans* and *destitutes*?' Farlowe's voice rose in anger. 'The criminals you willingly consort with?

'I tried to talk some sense into her, Stanton, I promise you, but the provoking girl would not listen to me. Mayhap you will have more success in curbing her wayward tendencies.'

'Wayward tendencies?' Dark brown eyes turned to Felicity, appraising her. Heat washed over her skin. He bent his head, his lips close to her ear. 'I am intrigued, Felicity Joy. Positively intrigued.'

Felicity suppressed her tremor as the small hairs on the back of her neck stood on end, swallowing past the sudden constriction in her throat.

'They are children.' She struggled to keep her attention on Farlowe, 'They cannot help the things they must do to survive.'

'Pshaw!'

'Well, what would you do, Mr Farlowe, if you were starving?' Felicity's customary caution vanished. 'Might you not be tempted to steal a loaf of bread? Or pick a coin from someone's pocket?'

Farlowe bristled. 'Might I remind you, miss—'

'Come, my darling.' Lady Katherine, after one look at Stanton, tugged at Farlowe's arm. 'Let us dance.' She pouted and cajoled and finally succeeded in dragging her husband to join a reel forming in the centre of the room.

Felicity's heart sank. Why on earth had she risen to Farlowe's provocation? She glanced up at Stanton. Would he be appalled by her lapse in manners? He was staring after his future parents-in-law, his expression a study in perplexity. He switched his attention to her and raised one dark brow.

'Thieves and pickpockets, Felicity Joy?' One corner of his mouth quirked up. 'Might I enquire what other dens of iniquity you frequent?'

Chapter Ten

He was neither appalled nor, it seemed, dismayed that Felicity had argued with Farlowe. It appeared he was diverted.

Felicity swallowed her giggle. 'Do not tease me, Stanton, I beg of you.'

She could cope with Stanton in this playful mood. But when his voice deepened, and his eyes fixed on her in that particular way...intense...the heat of promise swirling in their depths...another shiver caressed her skin as her insides looped in a most peculiar way. She willed her voice not to tremble.

'Did you ever hear such nonsense? What infuriates my dear step-papa, of course, are the donations I make to the school. He even, would you believe, suggested I should pay him rent for living under his roof instead of contributing to the living costs of the children.'

'His roof?'

'Indeed. As soon as he and Mama wed he made it very clear to me upon whom my future depended. Which is why—'

'Which is why you are willing to marry me?' Stanton looked around the ballroom, then grabbed Felicity's hand. 'Come. Let us go somewhere quieter. I am curious to discover something of those wayward tendencies your mama warned me about.'

Felicity's insides swooped again but the thought of being alone with Stanton made her hang back. She wasn't ready. She needed to harden her heart against him, prepare herself for the intimacies to come. He stopped and looked round. Studied her face, then smiled, his eyes crinkling as he shook his head.

'Felicity Joy, whatever am I to do with you? Come. Shall we dance?' He sketched a bow and, at her nod, led her to join a nearby set.

The energetic country dance afforded them scant opportunity or, indeed, breath to talk further and it was not until supper that they continued their conversation. The other guests—in a rare show of consideration—allowed the newly betrothed couple to eat their food in relative privacy.

'We have much to discuss.' Stanton deposited a plate piled high with food in front of Felicity.

'I find I am not very hungry, sir,' Felicity said, her stomach clenching at the sight and smell of the food. 'What do you wish to discuss?'

'The wedding itself is in hand. Leo and I met with your mother and Farlowe earlier and it has been agreed the wedding will take place on Thursday morning, as long as the rector is available to perform the ceremony. Will that give you enough time to prepare? Your mother was anxious about your dress.'

'I have a suitable dress I can wear, my lord.'

'Good. Farlowe has undertaken to speak to the rector as soon as you arrive home tomorrow and, as I already told you, I shall call on the Bishop of Bath and Wells to procure the licence on my way to Bath. As long as the rector has some spare time before noon on Thursday there is no reason why we cannot be married on that day. If not, we shall have to wait until we can be fitted in.'

It all sounds so businesslike and unromantic.

Of course it is, you fool. It is an arranged marriage. Sentiment and romance do not come into it.

She buried any hint of regret deep inside. She did not want love. It was her decision. Love hurt. Love destroyed.

She watched as Stanton played with his wine glass, his long fingers stroking the stem. Was he not quite as composed as she imagined? He must be like granite if he did not feel some emotion. Marriage, even a marriage of convenience, was not to be entered into lightly.

And yet, here they were, two virtual strangers, planning their wedding. She gazed around the room. The chatter of the other guests intruded, dispersing the haze of unreality that had enveloped her.

'Will you tell me more about Westfield? How did you become involved in such a place?'

She tensed. Would he disapprove? His question reminded her of the power this man would wield over her. He was, surely, more open-minded and charitable than Farlowe? She gripped her hands in her lap.

'It was established by my childhood friend, Jane Whittaker, and her husband, Peter, who is a schoolmaster. Jane inherited a large house and some money from her great-aunt, and they set up a school to help the children of the poor better themselves.'

'It is a school, then.'

'That was the original intention, but Mr Whittaker's brother is a magistrate and he told them how many orphans were brought up before him, so they decided to provide a home for orphans too. The children are taught their letters and numbers and, as they get older, we find them placements with tradespeople and in households, where they are trained to become useful members of society.'

'Which trades?'

There was no denying the genuine interest in his voice.

'Any and every trade you may imagine. Shoemakers, coopers, butchers, tailors, milliners—we try to match the child to some trade they have an interest in or aptitude for. That, I must confess, is where both Dominic and I can help, as well as collecting donations, of course. We can be most persuasive. We seldom meet with a flat refusal to take a child.'

'I was astonished to hear of Avon's involvement.'

'He was very young when his mother died and that experience nurtured in him a kinship, of sorts, with children who are orphaned. However painful his loss, how much worse would it be to lose both parents and to have no family or wealth or position to fall back on? When he heard about Westfield, he was eager to help.'

Felicity paused, studying Stanton's expression. She might as well tackle the subject now. It would ease at least one of her worries.

As if he could read her mind, Stanton said, 'I should like to visit this place with you, after we are married, Felicity. And, in case you were worrying I might be of the same opinion as Farlowe, allow me to set your mind at rest. I shall not raise any objections to your involvement with Westfield, as long as you do not put yourself in any danger.'

Felicity's tension eased. 'Thank you.'

Chapter Eleven

On her wedding day Felicity rose early, unable to sleep despite the exhaustion of travelling up from Cheriton the day before. She sat by the window, mind and stomach churning with equal intensity.

The ceremony did not worry her. But the afterwards… the afterwards was the rest of her life. That did not merely worry her, it terrified her.

A tap at the door broke into her reverie and Beanie's familiar, smiling face, deep cracks fanning out from the corners of her faded brown eyes, appeared.

'You are awake,' she said, shuffling into the room, followed by the kitchen maid carrying a tray. 'I said you would be. There you are, Nell, put the tray down and off you go. Did you manage to get any sleep, my lamb?'

Felicity's throat tightened at the familiar endearment. How would she manage without Beanie? She had raised Felicity, been more of a mother to her than her own had ever been. And the other servants were like members of her family.

'Are you sure you won't come with me…us, Beanie?'

'Bless you, dear. If only I was ten years younger. But I am too old now to get used to a new home and fresh faces and strange ways of going on. I am content here in Sydney Place. I shall miss you but at least it will oblige you to take on a trained lady's maid at last.'

'Oh, Beanie, as if I care for that. You know I would much

prefer you. Do not forget, I shall be in an unfamiliar place full of strangers, too.'

'Ah, but you will be the mistress. And you will have your new husband by your side. And you are young. No, my lamb, I will not change my mind, but I shall enjoy seeing you when you visit. Come now, drink your chocolate and try to eat some bread and butter.'

Felicity picked up the cup of chocolate and wrapped her hands around it. 'This will be enough. I cannot face—'

'Or I've brought up a slice of Cook's apple cake, if that might tempt your appetite?' Beanie picked up the plate and followed Felicity to her chair by the hearth. 'I know you, Lady Felicity. At the first hurdle, your appetite flies away with the fairies. You must eat something. You do not want your stomach gurgling in the church because you haven't eaten, do you?'

Felicity burst into laughter. 'Oh, Beanie, I am going to miss you. Gurgling stomach, indeed.' But she did as she was bid and, after sipping the warm chocolate, she nibbled on the cake and the hollow swooping inside eased to a flutter. Not perfect, but better.

After Felicity bathed and dried her hair by the fire, Beanie helped her to dress. Her gown was of fine white muslin and she would wear a lace-trimmed cap on her head. Her delicate silk shawl, white shot with primrose, and a pair of dainty primrose slippers, would complete the ensemble.

'You look lovely, my dove.'

Later, after Beanie had dressed her hair, Felicity stood before her mirror scarcely able to believe what was happening. She...Felicity...always the plain, overlooked member of the family...was about to wed society's most eligible and desirable bachelor. She pinched at her cheeks to bring some colour to her face. That was better. She tried a smile. Better still. As long as she did not forget to smile, she could at least look attractive for her wedding, and for Stanton.

'Darling.'

Felicity started. She hadn't heard her mother come in, so lost in her thoughts had she been.

'Let me look at you.'

At Lady Katherine's prompting, Felicity twirled a circle.

'You look very well, my dear. Oh, to think of it. Lady Stanton. I never dared to believe you would make such a match, Felicity. Now, if had been Emma…' Her voiced faded into silence and she sighed before continuing in a determinedly bright tone: 'Still, it is your future we must look forward to now, dearest. Except…' She moved closer and began to fiddle with Felicity's hair. 'Oh, dear, I knew I should have sent Wilkins to you but, as dear Farlowe said, who then would have helped with *my toilette*? It is important I should look at my best, as mother of the bride. We do not want Stanton to think he is marrying into a family of peasants, do we?'

Felicity stepped back, out of the reach of her mother's fidgety fingers. 'Please, Mama, do not fret about my hair.'

'Oh, you have ever been a tiresome girl, Felicity. Tiresome and stubborn. Now, the carriage will be outside in twenty minutes—darling Farlowe bespoke it last night after he saw the rector. What a truly attentive and selfless stepfather he has been to you, has he not?' She paused, regarding Felicity with raised brow.

'Indeed, Mama.'

Words cost nothing, particularly as she would no longer reside under the same roof as Farlowe. That was reason enough for the step she was about to take. She was rewarded with a glorious smile.

'Mama, there is something…before we go. Tonight…' Felicity hesitated, feeling her cheeks glow. She had never spoken on such intimate subjects with her mother before. 'Tonight…what will it be like? What should I do?'

'Do?' Lady Katherine's cheeks grew pink. 'Why, Felicity, I cannot believe you wish to discuss such matters with

me. It is for your husband to instruct you. Do as he says and, remember, it is your duty to please your husband at all times in such matters. That is all you need to know.'

Richard sat in the front pew of the Abbey Church next to Leo. The rector was searching through the Bible on the lectern, the sound of shuffling pages loud in the near-empty church.

Richard reviewed the messages he would send the minute their nuptials were complete. The *Bath Chronicle* and *The Times* would publish formal announcements and he had written letters ready to be taken by courier to his mother at Fernley Park and to the London address of his heir, his distant cousin, Charles Durant.

He had also penned a more personal letter to his mistress of the past six months, Harriet, Lady Brierley. Harriet's image formed in his mind's eye—soft, voluptuous, enticing—and a pang of regret speared him at the knowledge he would never again... He cursed silently, then cast a guilty look at the rector. Thinking about his mistress on the morning of his wedding was bad enough but blasphemous thoughts in church...? He offered a silent apology to God and vowed to exercise tighter control over his thoughts.

His letter to Harriet, besides informing her of his marriage, had ended their *affaire*. The impulse to walk away surprised him—had he not deliberately sought a marriage of convenience in order not to change his life? Harriet was discreet and their *affaire* was not common knowledge but still he had felt honour-bound to end it out of respect for Felicity. He consoled himself with the thought he could always take another mistress in the future, once his heir was born.

'You are quiet.' Leo's voice dragged him from his thoughts.

'Merely ensuring I have not forgotten anything,' Richard replied. 'Announcements and so forth.'

'You are still minded to leave for Fernley Park immediately after the ceremony?'

'I am. I apologize for the lack of a wedding breakfast, but the thought of accepting Farlowe's hospitality...' Richard shuddered.

'Indeed. And it would be a poor start if you knocked your new father-in-law senseless before the ink is dry on the register, would it not? Do you intend to travel all the way home today?'

'I do. I want our first night as a married couple to be under my...our...roof. I have no wish to spend our wedding night in some inn by the wayside.'

'You will both be exhausted by the time you arrive, after travelling all day yesterday as well.'

The bells began to strike the hour and the door at the back of the church creaked open to admit Lady Katherine. She wafted down the aisle, alternately smiling and tearful, flourishing a delicate, lace-edged scrap of a handkerchief with which she dabbed at her eyes. As she settled in the pew opposite his, Richard bent his head, concentrating on his hands, clenched into fists between his knees. The fuss and the flutter eventually subsided and he looked up in time to see the rector signal to someone at the back of the church.

This is it.

His insides quaked in an unfamiliar way and he experienced a sudden urge to flee which he quashed ruthlessly. He was doing the right thing for all the right reasons.

'Nervous?' Leo's whisper was accompanied by a steady hand on his shoulder.

'No.'

He stood up and turned to watch his bride glide down the aisle on her stepfather's arm. His breathing—which only now did he realize had quickened—steadied and slowed. As Felicity neared, her attention fixed firmly on the rector, Richard recognized that his brief attack of nerves must be as nothing compared with hers. He willed her to look at him and was rewarded when, only a few feet away, she did.

Her eyes were shadowed, and her lips compressed. Doubt emanated from her and Richard's own doubts re-emerged. If the match was so distasteful, why was she here?

And yet…and yet…he recalled their conversations; their kiss. She was not indifferent to him. She wanted—she had said as much—to wed, and to get away from her stepfather. He would make sure she did not regret their union. She was to be his wife.

His. To have and to hold. He would protect her, and care for her.

He would fulfil his part of the bargain.

He reached for her hand, to reassure her. She flashed a grateful smile, transforming her face, and his own nerves settled. Her fingers twitched within his grasp, then curled around the edge of his palm. As one, they turned to face the rector.

Chapter Twelve

A small crowd gathered around the three carriages as they lined up outside the Abbey. Richard and Felicity emerged to a muted cheer, followed by a swell of speculation as Felicity's name was passed from onlooker to onlooker. The crowd pressed closer, and Richard heard Leo's name mentioned, followed by his own as the speculation got louder.

Leo, Lady Katherine and Mr Farlowe were close behind them, followed by the few friends and servants who had been in the church to witness their wedding.

'How handsome you looked, walking down the aisle, Farlowe.' Lady Katherine's voice rang out. 'And you, dearest Felicity, you looked very nice, as you came into the church. It is a shame you were seen to such disadvantage next to your stepfather, do you not agree, Stanton?'

'My love, I beg of you,' Farlowe interjected hastily. Richard had caught the man's eye and glared at him with such intent that Farlowe had paled. 'This is Felicity's day—'

'Oh, Felicity is used to me running on, aren't you, darling? She isn't a girl to take offence.'

'I take offence,' Richard said quietly. *Blast the woman. Why must she continually undermine Felicity? She clearly believes the only characteristic of any virtue is beauty.* 'If you will excuse us, my wife and I have a long journey ahead of us.' He held out his hand, smiling at Felicity. 'Come, my dear.'

Felicity shot Richard such a furious look, he stared. Did

she not want him—her husband—to speak out and protect her? A glance at Leo only elicited a resigned shrug.

'She is my mother. She loves me in her own way,' Felicity hissed before turning to her mother, who rushed to embrace her.

'Oh, Felicity, I did not mean anything by it, you know I did not. You know how I rattle on sometimes. I shall miss you so much, my darling.' Lady Katherine's eyes brimmed with tears as she flung her arms around her daughter.

'And I shall miss you too, Mama.' Felicity's voice was thick with emotion.

Not for the first time Richard realized that his upbringing, and his current relationship with his mother, had ill prepared him to understand the subtleties of other people's families. He only had to think of Leo's large, boisterous brood to comprehend what he had missed in his childhood. Mayhap Richard could learn something of family from his new bride, and top of that list appeared to be forgiveness. Richard vowed that, as his wife, Felicity would get all the support and kindness she deserved. Then his own children would grow up secure and happy in a contented household such as every child surely deserved.

Felicity said her goodbyes to the rest of the congregation, speaking to each one in turn. The last, an elderly, stooped lady, got a hug and a kiss.

'Stanton?' Felicity beckoned him.

Richard felt his brows contract. Stanton? She should call him Richard. Everyone else called him Stanton.

An uncertain expression crossed Felicity's face and Richard smiled, to show her he was not annoyed. How little they knew of each other—negotiating their relationship at the moment was akin to walking over swampy ground, not knowing where the soft, treacherous patches might lie. He must be more mindful, pick his way more carefully, until he knew her better.

'Yes, my dear?'

'May I present Miss Bean? She was our governess and, since we all grew up, she has shouldered the thankless task of being my maid.'

'Oh, nonsense, Lady Felicity; I mean, Lady Stanton,' the old lady quavered. 'You are the least demanding person I know.' Her eyes were red and swollen; as she stared up at him, Richard recognized the milky cast that spoke of failing sight.

He clasped her outstretched hand. 'I am pleased to meet you,' he said, and was rewarded by a grateful smile from Felicity.

'You see, Beanie? He is quite normal, and I shall be quite safe with him.'

A tear tracked down Beanie's cheek as she clasped Felicity's face between her gnarled hands and kissed her on the cheek.

'Goodbye, my dove.'

On the brink of mounting the steps into the carriage, Felicity turned to her mother. 'Mama, promise me you will take care of Beanie.'

'Why, Felicity, of course I shall. Hurry along, now. Whatever will Stanton think of you, keeping him waiting over your maid's welfare?'

Richard thought, but did not say, that he was rather proud of his new wife for caring for the elderly woman. He handed Felicity into the carriage, and climbed in behind her, after shaking Leo's hand. They waved, and soon left the City of Bath behind.

After a few lacklustre attempts at conversation, Felicity said, 'I do apologize, Stanton, but...'

'Richard,' he said.

A rueful smile crossed her face. 'Ever since my come-out I have known of you as Stanton. I fear it will take me some time to get used to calling you Richard, but I assure you I do not intend any slight if I forget once in a while.'

'In that case, I shall promise not to feel slighted. What were you about to say?'

We are as two strangers, the politeness in the way we converse, the way we glance at each other and look away as if fearful of catching the other's eye.

'I was about to say I am so weary I fear I shall be quite unable to keep up my end of any conversation. Would you think me dreadfully rag-mannered if I try to sleep?'

'Not at all. We shall stop for refreshments at the Old George at Salisbury. I shall wake you then.'

He was, if anything, relieved. He settled in the corner of the carriage, then beckoned. Her eyes rounded.

'You will be perfectly safe, Lady Stanton. I am not about to ravish you in a moving carriage, no matter how well sprung.'

Felicity's lips twitched. 'Such a relief.'

'Come, sit here, next to me. You can rest your head on my shoulder. It will be more comfortable.'

A slight hesitation, then she shifted along until their thighs touched. Richard put his arm around her shoulders, manoeuvring her until she was leaning against him. Several minutes passed.

'You can relax, Felicity Joy. I shall do nothing other than hold you, you have my word.'

A few more minutes and then a quiet huff of breath, followed by the softening of the wooden figure next to him indicated that she had, at last, relaxed.

After several weary hours and only one brief stop after Salisbury, other than to change the horses, the carriage drew to a halt. Richard stirred, biting back a groan as pins and needles coursed through his arm. He peered through the window. Fernley Park. Stiff muscles forgotten, he disentangled his arm from Felicity and eased her upright.

'Welcome to your new home, Lady Stanton.'

'What? I mean, I beg your pardon?' Her voice was muffled and, from what he could see of her face in the dim light cast by the oil lamps either side of the steps leading up to the front door, she looked bleary-eyed.

'We are home,' he repeated. 'Fernley Park.'

'Home?' She straightened and her hands flew to her head, patting at her hair. 'Where is my bonnet?' Felicity's bonnet, and a warm cloak, had been placed in the carriage before their wedding, ready for their journey.

Biting back a grin at her agitation, Richard grabbed the bonnet from the opposite seat.

'Allow me,' he said, and she sat obediently whilst he pinned the hat on to her head and tucked stray hairs neatly away.

The carriage door opened. Beyond the coachman, Richard could see Trick silhouetted in the front entrance. He climbed out of the carriage, stretched, then turned to hand down his wife.

His wife. How strange that sounded.

'Trick, this is your new mistress, Lady Stanton. My dear, this is Trick, the butler.'

'Good evening, Trick,' Felicity said with a smile.

'Good evening, milord, milady. I trust you had a pleasant journey.

Richard laughed. '"Pleasant" is not quite the word I should choose, but it was uneventful.'

'Which is all one can hope for,' Felicity commented as she entered the hall and gazed around.

'Indeed.' Richard eyed his bride. It was their wedding night. She looked exhausted and he felt no less fatigued. 'Is my mother in the salon?'

'Yes, milord.' Trick crossed the foyer and entered the salon. Richard led Felicity in his wake. 'His lordship and Lady Stanton have arrived, milady.'

His mother, impeccably dressed as always, stood to greet them, poker straight, unsmiling. Richard silently mocked himself for daring to hope his marriage might have softened her; might have, somehow, bridged the chasm that had yawned between them ever since his father's death. She had never been a relaxed and loving parent—a result of her strict upbringing—but neither had she been this aloof.

How had they become virtual strangers?

'Stanton. You are home.'

His mother scrutinized Felicity from head to toe and Richard knew, with a sinking certainty, she would find much to disapprove of in his actual marriage, despite her constant nagging at him to wed.

As Felicity's fingers tightened on his, the familiar, complicated muddle of emotions he always experienced in his mother's presence continued to churn deep in his gut.

Chapter Thirteen

Felicity battled her fatigue, sensing this first meeting with her mother-in-law could be crucial to their future relationship. Lady Stanton, tall and slim, her steel-grey hair scraped back from her face, stood erect and unsmiling, her eyes raking Felicity. Determined not to be intimidated, Felicity squared her shoulders and lifted her chin.

'Mother, I should like to present to you my wife, Felicity. Felicity, this is my mother, Lady Stanton.'

Felicity curtsied and smiled. 'I am pleased to meet you, my lady.'

'You may address me as Mother.' No words of welcome. No congratulations. No smile. 'You had better sit down.'

Mother! Something close to hysteria bubbled and swirled inside and Felicity clamped her teeth shut lest it escape. Richard squeezed her hand, and she steadied. Was her mother-in-law really so indifferent to her son's marriage? Cousin Leo had suggested Lady Stanton would be delighted her son had finally wed, but the reality appeared somewhat different.

'We have come to pay our respects, Mother. Felicity is exhausted and will retire immediately. There will be time tomorrow for better acquaintance.'

Felicity stared at Richard's clipped, formal tone. Why were they so awkward and formal with each other?

'Come along, my dear.'

Felicity resisted Richard's attempt to turn her around. Despite her tiredness, she had every intention of establishing her own relationship with her mother-in-law: she would not become a mere extension of her husband, with no opinions of her own.

She held the dowager's steely gaze. 'Goodnight, Mother,' she said. 'I apologize, but Richard is right. I am very tired and I am, I fear, incapable of conversing in anything approaching an intelligible manner tonight. Please forgive me.'

She then allowed Richard to escort her to the door.

'One moment.'

They paused. The dowager glided towards them. 'Stanton. There is a matter I wish to discuss, before you retire.'

'Of course, Mother. Allow me to ensure Felicity is cared for first.'

A kind-eyed, middle-aged woman awaited them in the hall.

'Mrs Jakeway, please take Lady Stanton to the Countess's suite. My dear, Mrs Jakeway is the housekeeper here.'

Mrs Jakeway bobbed a curtsy. 'Welcome to Stanton, my lady.'

Felicity smiled, murmuring her thanks.

'Your luggage arrived an hour since, milady, so it is all unpacked ready for you. Would you like a bite to eat in your room? Shall I ask Cook to send something up?'

Mrs Jakeway glanced at Richard as she spoke, and he said, 'I am sure her ladyship can manage a little something. Please do so.'

While Mrs Jakeway sent a message to the kitchen, Richard drew Felicity aside. She suddenly realized, with a resounding thump of her heart, that it was her wedding night and that this man could now visit her in her bed whenever he pleased. Her suddenly sensitive skin glowed, and her mouth was sucked dry as fear and anticipation swirled in a heady mix.

'Felicity?' Richard bent his knees, bringing his face level with hers. 'I will see you soon.' He held her gaze until she nodded her understanding. He smiled, lifted her hand and pressed warm lips against her skin.

As Felicity followed Mrs Jakeway up the long, curving sweep of the stairs, she glanced behind her. The dowager had joined Richard in the hall and they stood face to face, postures identically strained. They made no attempt to lower their voices.

'Where is her maid?'

'Indisposed.'

'Shocking! Jaunting around the countryside without a maid in attendance. Do you expect one of the household staff to fill the gap?'

'For a day or two only, Mother. I shall send to Winchester tomorrow to appoint a lady's maid. I am sure the house can spare one of the maids for so short a time.'

Felicity paused on the landing. It was wrong to eavesdrop, but they were being so indiscreet she had no compunction in listening to more.

'Lady Felicity Weston. Baverstock's daughter. And how old is she? Not in the first flush of youth, by the look of her.'

Her mother-in-law's voice dropped, but Felicity still caught some of her comments.

'...expected you to do better...dab of a girl...well bred, I suppose...'

'That is enough! You will kindly not criticize my wife, either to me or to anyone else.'

They disappeared inside the salon. Felicity joined Mrs Jakeway, waiting along the landing.

The Countess's bedchamber was spacious, decorated in restful shades of cream and blue, with tall, south-facing windows. The fireplace had a carved oak surround and the room was furnished with elegant rosewood furniture. The bed itself was massive, as wide as it was long, with posts at each corner, and a tester overhead, but no hangings to draw around for privacy and warmth as there would have been in earlier times. The bed dated, Mrs Jakeway informed Felicity, from the sixteenth century, and countless generations of Countesses of Stanton had slept there.

Two doors led from the bedchamber and Mrs Jakeway led her first to an adjoining sitting room with a chaise longue by one of the three windows and a sofa before the fire. There was a delicate escritoire, for correspondence, and a small round table with two chairs was set before the centre window.

'When the old master was alive, Lady Stanton spent much of her time up here,' Mrs Jakeway said.

'I do hope Lady Stanton was not obliged to vacate these rooms on my account?'

'Oh, no, milady. Don't you be fretting about that. Her ladyship moved out after the old master passed away, and insisted his lordship moved into his father's apartments immediately. He was barely seventeen, poor lad. It was...' The housekeeper clamped her lips shut. 'Come, I will show you the bathroom.'

She led the way across the bedchamber and through the other door into a small antechamber, dominated by a large bathtub, half-full of water. Steam gently curled into the air, scenting it with violets and a fire flamed in the grate, a wooden airer hung with towels nearby.

Felicity eyed the warm water longingly. 'Is that for me?'

'His lordship's orders,' Mrs Jakeway said. 'He sent word from Bath as to what time to expect you. The bed is aired and ready, however, if you prefer not to bathe tonight?'

'Oh, no, Mrs Jakeway, it is *just* what I need. Thank you for going to all this trouble. Could you send a maid to assist me, please? I'm afraid my own maid was unable to travel.'

'No need for that, milady. I shall help you tonight.'

Felicity was soon undressed and sank with muscle-soothing gratitude into the bath. She leaned her head back against the rim and closed her eyes, sighing with pleasure.

'My hair was washed this morning, Mrs Jakeway, so I can manage now, thank you.'

'Very well, milady.'

Felicity heard the door open and close again. Her mind drifted, veering away whenever her thoughts ranged near Richard and the coming night. She did not want to think. She simply wanted to be. She slipped a little lower into the water, every inch of her from the neck down bathed in scented heat. She felt underwater for the linen washcloth and spread it, sopping wet, across her face. If only she could remain here and if only the water would stay this warm. She breathed slowly and deliberately, the washcloth moving in time with her breaths. It was already cooling. Reluctantly, she reached for it and pulled it from her face.

A tap at the door behind her brought her crashing back to the here and now.

'Who is it?' *Please let it be Mrs Jakeway or one of the maids.*

'Would you like your back scrubbed, Felicity Joy?'

Her heart scrambled into her throat. Her arms thrashed, attempting to cover her nakedness, even though she knew he could see nothing.

Yet.

He had only to step a little further into the room. Her stomach churned as her flustered brain sought an escape, but there was no cover within reach.

Nothing.

Chapter Fourteen

'Felicity!'

The sharp command penetrated Felicity's panic and she stilled.

'If I had wanted to spy on you in your bath, I could have done so,' Richard said. 'However, I did, as you will recall, knock at the door.'

He sounded amused, but was that also a hint of exasperation in his tone? Felicity peeked over her shoulder. He was in the open doorway, shoulders propped against the jamb, arms folded across his chest. He smiled at her, shaking his head.

'I am not your enemy, Felicity. I did not intend to scare you. I met Mrs Jakeway on her way to fetch your supper and I came to see if you required any help.'

His voice and his words were patient and soothing, much as one might speak to a horse set into a panic. Had she overreacted? From Richard's point of view, no doubt she had done exactly that. They were man and wife. And yet... and yet...

'Thank you.' Her voice croaked and she coughed. 'I believe I can manage.'

'Shall I pass you a towel?'

'I am not yet ready, thank you. I have not finished washing.' Truth be told, she had yet to begin.

'I shall ask again, in that case. Would you like me to wash your back for you? I can avert my eyes, if it will make you easier.'

'I don't...' Felicity's voice failed.

'You don't trust me? Very well.'

There was a rustle and a muffled grunt behind her. Felicity risked another glance over her shoulder. Richard held her gaze as he tugged his neckcloth from around his neck. *Oh, my goodness. Surely he is not...?* He closed the door and held the neckcloth out, grinning.

'Here. You can tie this around my eyes so I cannot cheat.'

A squirm of heat snaked from the pit of her belly to the juncture of her thighs and she felt her nipples harden. Heavens. If the mere thought of him being close to her naked body could prompt such a reaction, how would it feel to lie together?

The water sloshed around the bath as Felicity sat up. She hugged her knees close to her chest. 'Very well.' This time, her voice squeaked. From a frog to a mouse, she thought wildly, clamping down the urge to laugh, certain it would sound hysterical were she to allow it to escape.

Richard shrugged out of his coat, and knelt by the bathtub, presenting his back. He lifted the neckcloth to cover his eyes and then reached behind his head to offer the ends to Felicity. She grasped them and tied a firm knot. He swivelled round to face her, and rolled up his sleeves. Felicity eyed his hair-roughened arms with hungry fascination. They were sinewy and lightly tanned—so different from her own pale, thin limbs.

'Hand me the soap, Felicity.'

His voice was husky. He reached out, palm up, and Felicity gave him the soap. Then he groped for, and found, her back and she saw his lips stretch into a sensual smile. Excitement spiralled through her body and her heart pounded as he began to stroke, his hand gliding over her wet, soapy skin.

'So very delicate,' he murmured, running one finger down her spine.

Her lids drifted shut as Richard lathered her back, fingers spread, palm flat and gentle as he traced her ribcage around, under her arm, until the tips of his fingers rested against the gentle swell of her breast.

'Relax.' The whisper danced across her moist skin, raising gooseflesh.

Relax? How could she relax? She wanted…she needed… she did not know what she wanted, aware only that her mind was at war with her body.

She heard him move, and his lips were on her hair. They traced a path to her ear and, with the tip of his tongue, he outlined the shell before soft lips nibbled at the lobe. Her head tilted, and he trailed warm, open-mouthed kisses down her neck to her collarbone as his hand slid across her torso, brushing the sensitive skin beneath her breasts.

The urge to lie back was strong. Was she really about to succumb to his seduction so readily? But why should she not? If her body could take pleasure in his lovemaking, why should she not relax and enjoy it? It did not mean she must relinquish her heart.

Her sigh murmured as she relaxed back, her thighs parting of their own volition. He could not see her. He had all the experience. Let him teach her of the pleasures of the flesh.

'Give me your hand.'

He pressed a kiss to her palm before washing her arm from wrist to shoulder, his touch gentle, mouth firm with concentration. As his hand moved across her chest, Felicity closed her eyes. He soaped each breast in turn, kneading. Her back arched, pressing into his touch, an unusual sensation tugging deep inside. Long sweeps of his hand soaped down the side of her body, along her ribcage, over the jut of her hip and down the length of her thigh. She drifted in a sensual haze, aware only of his touch, as he raised each leg in turn to soap them before lowering them back into the water. He lifted her foot, stroking the instep until her foot arched. Each toe in turn was enveloped by warm lips, and sucked gently.

A breathy groan sounded loud in the quiet of the room. Hers. Felicity tensed.

'Sssssshhhhh, relax.' The soothing murmur hung in the air and her body responded.

A large hand circled her stomach, the pressure increasing fractionally each time it neared the triangle of curls at the apex of her thighs. Her need climbed. His hand drifted up again, skimming around her breasts, barely touching the peaked, aching nipples. Despite the cooling water, Felicity's blood pumped hot. Then he took one nipple between finger and thumb and rolled it, gently tugging. Desire streaked through her, setting her blood aflame, and she shifted restlessly.

His lips were on her face again, feathery, butterfly-light kisses caressing her skin as his hand slid over her belly again to slip between her legs, caressing and probing the swollen folds. Her body arched, pressing into his touch. He stroked, and she whimpered.

Then Richard leaned towards her. 'Kiss me.' A request, not a demand.

Dreamily she half-rose from the water and met his lips. Soft, searching, sensual, his kiss inflamed her further. It was exquisite but it was not enough. Not nearly enough. She wanted passion. She *needed* passion…and she needed… need.

His need.

She wanted him to feel the same urgency that gripped her. She cupped his face in her hands and took control. He started in surprise, then responded and deepened the kiss, his tongue sweeping between her parted lips. She wound her arms around his neck, urging him on wordlessly. One arm swept around her, half-lifting her, moulding her wet, naked body to him.

The fine lawn of his shirt did nothing to shield her from the heat of his skin. Felicity tangled her fingers through his hair, her fingertips exploring the solid strength of his skull.

She hesitated over the knot in the neckcloth that still covered his eyes, but she did not loosen it. She felt a strange kind of power, being naked with this man, this stranger, with him unable to see. She need not feel shame, or doubt, or inadequacy. She could just enjoy. For the moment.

Her thighs opened wider as his fingers caressed and stroked the sensitive flesh between. Her head fell back as she abandoned herself to the sensations that whirled and intensified inside her until she felt she would shatter if she didn't move, and shatter if she did. She trembled as hot lips nibbled the delicate skin of her neck then froze momentarily as Richard's finger circled her entrance and dipped inside. *Goodness.* His finger slid full length inside her, withdrew, and was joined by another and Felicity abandoned herself to pleasure.

As his fingers began to move Felicity kissed him again, clinging as she urged him on. His tongue and his fingers joined in rhythm, driving Felicity on, spiralling ever higher. He pressed lightly with his thumb and she gasped, the sound swallowed within the joining of their lips. All thought suspended as her spiralling passion wound tighter and tighter. She reached and reached, yearning, straining.

'Let it come, sweetheart.' The whisper barely registered but the gathering, squeezing sensation at her very core climbed…building…building…until it peaked, exploding in wave after pulsing wave of pure ecstasy.

Strong arms swept her out of the water and Felicity was dimly aware of being cradled like a baby as Richard stood up. Her eyes stayed tight shut as she clung to his neck. He was moving—striding—across the room. His eyes could no longer be covered. Even as the final waves throbbed at her core, she shivered, cringing, as her mind caught up with reality. A door clicked open then banged shut.

A peep through her lashes confirmed they were in her bedchamber. The bed loomed large, dominating her restricted view. What would he do now? She could barely take in what had just happened to her. She had never imagined—how could she?—such ecstasy could exist. And now…would he want to take his own pleasure with her, straight away? She had a vague idea of what would happen—shortly before she died, Emma had confided her shame and heartbreak at having been seduced and abandoned by the man she loved. Nausea mushroomed from Felicity's chest into her throat. She swallowed convulsively, banishing all thoughts of her sister, focusing her attention on to her husband.

Chapter Fifteen

Richard moved again and heat from the flames caressed her skin. Slowly, he released her, her damp skin clinging to the fabric of his shirt as her toes stretched for the floor. He steadied her, his warm hand splayed between her shoulder blades. Then she felt the sweep of a towel across her shoulders and around her back: enveloping her, swaddling her, shielding her from his gaze. She forced open her eyes. He was smiling down at her. Her belly performed a twisty loop and her mouth flooded with saliva.

'Felicity Joy.'

His voice was a deep, comforting purr. He removed the pins, one by one, from her hair until it flowed loose. He swept her hair from her face, then bent to kiss her still-tingling lips. Her legs quaked and her knees sagged. He chuckled, scooped her up and placed her in one of the chairs by the fire.

Only then did Felicity see the tray of food on the table next to the chairs.

'You must be hungry,' he said, sitting in the other chair. 'I know I am. Come, let us eat.'

'I thought…I thought…'

'There is no hurry, sweetheart. We have all night.'

Felicity's stomach swooped again, and the flesh between her legs pulsed in an echo of pleasure.

'You have much to get used to, and I wish to discover what pleases you.' He reached for a plate, and selected a pastry. He leaned forward and held it to her lips. 'Taste, tell me, help me to learn.'

Does he mean the food, or...? Nerves jangling, she bit into the pastry, and buttery sweetness flooded her mouth: honey, almonds, and a hint of cinnamon.

'Mmmmm.' She savoured the sweetmeat as Richard popped the remainder in his own mouth.

They sat by the fire and ate their fill of the bread and cheese, delicate pastries and fruit, washed down with wine. Felicity began to relax, the mundane activity of eating distracting her from what was to come. Eventually, Richard sat back with a sigh, glass in hand, and gazed into the flames. Felicity took the opportunity to study him as the firelight played across his features. He was so very handsome. She felt as though she were in a fairy tale, the handsome prince having whisked her away from her humdrum life. But this was real life, and soon... As though he could hear her thoughts, Richard switched his attention to her, his eyes penetrating, a half smile playing around his sensuous lips.

'Have you had enough to eat?'

'Yes. Thank you.'

'Some more wine?'

Felicity held out her glass, and he filled it, then stood, holding out his hand. As if in a dream, Felicity placed her hand in his. He led her to the bed and took her wine glass, placing it on the bedside table.

He smoothed her hair from her face and pressed warm lips to her temple.

'I will snuff the candles. You get into bed, and we will drink our wine together, you and I.'

He swept the bedcovers down before crossing to the fireplace to snuff out the candles. Felicity released her grip on the towel and slid into the bed, pulling the covers right up to her chin. The room now in semi-darkness, lit only by the fire, Richard rounded the bed and began to undress. That chest. Broad, tantalizingly sculpted, dusted with dark hair.

He reached for the buttons on his trousers. She groped blindly for her wine glass, hand trembling as she raised it to her lips. The bed dipped as he sat on the edge then bent forward to finish taking off his trousers, his broad back smooth, muscles rippling. Her blood raced around her body, heart thundering in her ears, nipples tight and aching, the flesh between her thighs yearning for his touch.

She put her glass down and reached for him.

A hair's breadth from the skin of his back, she hesitated, registering the heat of his body as it warmed her palm. *Should I? Will he be shocked? Disgusted?* The wine made her bold. She splayed her fingers, and placed her hand on his back. He stilled. She waited.

'It's all right to explore, Felicity Joy.' His back vibrated with the deep rumble of his voice. 'I certainly intend to explore you.'

Her insides quivered. Her fingers trickled down his spine. He did not move. Emboldened, she knelt; crept a little closer; swept both hands up the solid planes of his back until her fingers curved over his shoulders. She kneaded with her thumbs.

'Aaaaaahh, that feels good. You have magic in your fingers, sweetheart.' He stretched his torso, rolling his shoulders.

How had he pleasured her? His neck. Shuffling closer still, until the tips of her breasts brushed his back, she pressed her lips to the side of his neck. Musky maleness flooded her senses. She was rewarded by a deep shudder and a quiet groan. She took his earlobe into her mouth and sucked. Then nipped.

'Ooh. You little…'

Laughing, he turned his head. His lips were inches from hers. Warm, wine-scented breath fanned her skin, raising a *frisson* of pleasure. She closed the gap, pressing her lips to his, reaching for his chest. Rough hair teased her fingertips as she stroked, fascinated by the difference between his skin and hers. She played with his nipple, and he moaned, deep in his chest. She slicked her tongue over his lips: they parted, tongues met, entwined, withdrew, touched again.

He swung round, took control, cupping her head as he eased her down. He lay beside her, half covering her, as he deepened the kiss. His arousal pressed into her thigh. Felicity closed her eyes, concentrating on *what* was happening rather than on *who* was stoking this wonderful, exciting, glorious maelstrom of need. Every other sense was on heightened alert. She luxuriated in his scent: spicy, musky, arousing; the texture of his hair-roughened skin as he moved over her; the moist heat of skin against skin; every inch of her—caressed by skilled fingers and questing tongue—a thousand times more alive than ever before.

'Touch me, sweetheart.' His voice was ragged, urgent with need.

She reached, marvelling at the silken skin that slid over his hot, solid length. She closed her fingers, heard his intake of breath, squeezed. His hand covered hers, guiding her even as long fingers penetrated her most intimate place. She arched, whimpering, and then he moved, covering her, easing her thighs wider. She felt the nudge at her entrance, and tensed.

'Ssssshhh. Relax. It might hurt this first time, but not for long. I promise.'

A steady push, and she stretched, and stretched until she could take no more. He was too big, she was too small, how…?

'Richaaaard.'

Her protest lost in a cry as he forged into her, the pain sharp, but brief. He lay still. Impaled, she waited. Then he began to move, and the yearning ache grew and grew, radiating out from the place they were joined until every muscle in her body strained to reach the pinnacle that seemed forever just beyond her reach.

Frantic fingers clawed at broad shoulders. Lips kissed and teeth nipped at every inch of skin within reach. Legs wrapped, and held, urging him on. He took her mouth in a searing kiss as he reached between them, and stroked. She flew over that pinnacle in a glorious burst of ecstasy that cascaded through her, shaking her to her core.

He began to move faster, penetrate deeper. Cool air washed between them. She cranked open a weighty eyelid. He was braced up on corded arms, eyes closed, his face a mask of concentration until, with a primal roar, he reached his release. She felt his seed empty into her and he collapsed on to her, rolling a little so as not to crush her, panting. They lay together, his leg straddling hers, arm across her waist. Felicity—tired, sated, content—could have stayed like that all night.

'Are you all right?' His breathing had slowed and he caressed her cheek as he spoke.

'Yes. Of course.'

What should one say, at a time like this? His question dissolved her pleasant haze of exhaustion as the sun disperses early morning mist. Words formed in Felicity's head, but were dismissed as too trite or too grateful; gushing, even. One could hardly thank one's husband for… She bit at her lip. Was there an etiquette for such an occasion? She felt awkward and unworldly and stiffened, her eyes screwed shut.

'Felicity. Look at me. Please.'

She did. Read the compassion in his eyes, but also the laughter that lurked in the background. Well, mayhap he was justified in finding her amusing.

'There is no need to be embarrassed. Not with me. What we have just done is natural. It is meant to be enjoyable. For us both.' He smiled, lines radiating out from the corners of his eyes. He kissed her on the forehead, then in one swift movement, he got out of the bed, and turned to tuck her back in. 'You sleep now. You must be exhausted. I will see you in the morning.'

The bed felt very big, and cold, and empty. Felicity wished he had stayed.

Chapter Sixteen

Felicity awoke with a start. It was early, judging by the light creeping around the edge of the curtains. She lay in bed and relived the day before, fingers twisting the gold band on the third finger of her left hand.

Married.

Well, and was that not what she wanted: a home of her own and a family? Richard was not quite what she had bargained for, but he was what she had. If she only thought of him as a means to an end, surely she could keep her heart safe?

She quivered with the memory of their lovemaking, and her hand crept between her thighs, where her flesh was still tender. Excitement flitted through her veins and her heart leapt at the thought of seeing Stanton...Richard...again.

Determinedly, she settled her thoughts, crushing the bud of happiness attempting to unfurl in her heart. This would never do.

Once she was with child he would continue with his interests and leave her to hers. That was their bargain. She must protect her heart. If she could ensure that intimacies such as last night remained in the bedchamber...would that not suffice?

It would not be easy.

In need of distraction, she threw the covers back, tucked her feet into her slippers and wrapped her shawl around her. Her bedchamber was huge, with three tall windows spaced along the wall opposite the bed. She drew open the curtains to let the light spill in but did not linger at the window. She would explore the gardens of her new home later. Her home. It was strange, knowing she would be living here, yet knowing so little about the place or the people who lived here, not even her husband. A shiver spread across the surface of her skin and she hugged her arms around her body, pulling the shawl tight around her shoulders.

There was a light tap at the door, and it opened to admit a maid, carrying a wooden box.

'G'morning, milady; I'm sorry your fire wasn't lit ready for you.' She cast an anxious look at Felicity.

'Don't be troubled, I did wake very early. What is your name?'

'Tilly, milady.' The girl, round-faced and pink-cheeked, bobbed a curtsy.

'Well, Tilly, when you have finished here, could you send up some hot water, please? I should like to get dressed.'

'Of course, milady.'

Finally alone—fully dressed and ready to face her new life—Felicity paused with her hand on the door handle, butterflies dancing around inside. She turned back and drifted around the room, examining sundry objects, before stopping by the window. In the garden below, a man was raking leaves from the vast expanse of lawn. Beyond the grass, the contours of the land dipped to reveal a glimpse of blue. A lake. The butterflies settled. She could not skulk upstairs all day. A pleasant walk to the lake would be her reward for braving breakfast.

About to turn from the window, a movement caught her eye: Richard, dressed in riding clothes, was striding along the path towards the house. He glanced up, and Felicity jerked away from the window, her pulse skittering as her breath caught.

Stupid! Why dodge out of sight as though you've been caught in some wrongdoing?

She peered out of the window again, but Richard was no

longer in sight. Hands clasped to her chest, Felicity gazed unseeingly at the view as she willed her heart rate to slow. If he had seen her, she must go downstairs. He would think her a complete ninny if she remained closeted up here. Still she dallied, until a peremptory knock forced her to open the door.

Richard stood outside. He brought with him the smell of outdoors, fresh and tangy. He was hatless, his dark brown curls windswept. His skin glowed and his eyes sparkled.

'Good morning, Felicity Joy. I trust you slept well and are fully refreshed?'

His rich baritone did strange things to her insides. She remembered the times she had sneaked a sip of brandy from her father's decanter after a cold ride. Richard's voice spread through her with a similar intoxicating warmth. Images of the night before flooded her brain and she felt her cheeks heat.

'Good morning, Lord St…Richard.' Her voice came out as a breathless squeak.

Richard grinned. 'I've just returned from my morning ride. Have you breakfasted yet?'

'No. I…I was just about to…to—'

'In that case, would you care to join me for breakfast in the parlour? Unless you prefer to take breakfast in your room, as my mother does?'

She straightened her back, striving for calm.

'Yes. Thank you. I should like to join you.'

Richard patted her hand as she took his arm to go downstairs. 'Don't worry; you will soon become accustomed to your new home.'

At least he seemed to understand how awkward she felt in this strange house. Not a guest, but not yet at home.

The food was laid out on a sideboard for them to serve themselves. Richard helped himself to thick rashers of bacon and eggs and placed it in front of the chair at the head of the table, big enough to seat eight. A second place was set at the opposite end, and Richard pulled the chair out for Felicity. 'Would you like coffee?'

'Yes, please.' Felicity set down her plate, with its slice of toast and boiled egg.

Richard poured them both coffee, sat down and began to eat.

'I always seem to eat twice as much when I'm down in the country,' he remarked. 'It is the fresh air and the exercise. I like to ride before breakfast as a rule, as long as the weather isn't too inclement.'

He paused, his eyes on Felicity. Heat erupted and her skin tingled. Would she ever become accustomed to him?

Richard watched his new wife surreptitiously as they breakfasted together. Her eyes glued to her plate, she picked half-heartedly at her food.

How little I know of her. Who is she, behind the mask? What are her interests? Her dreams? Her fears? Why was she so reluctant to accept me? Was it a ploy, to pique my interest, or was...is...there some deeper reason?

His jaw set. *Why plague yourself with such questions? Did you not merely require a wife who would fit in with your life? You have no need to know the whys and the wherefores.*

He focused on his bride. 'Do you ride, Felicity?'

Her amber eyes came alive. 'Oh, indeed I do. I love to ride. Do you have a lady's mount in your stables?'

'Not at present: my mother has not ridden for many years. Do you have a favourite animal at Bath, or at Baverstock? I can send a groom for it, if it would please you?'

'Unfortunately, no. The mare I used to ride became permanently lame, and I was forced to retire her to Baverstock. Then my stepfather...' resentment soured Felicity's tone '...declined to meet the stabling costs for another horse. He believed hiring a job horse was sufficient should I wish to ride out with friends.'

It was something he could remedy very easily; something to make his new wife happy. 'I shall instruct Dalton to find you a suitable mount.'

'I'm sorry…Dalton?'

'My head groom.'

'I see. Thank you.'

Silence reigned once more.

'If you would like it, I will show you around the house and gardens today. It will help you find your bearings.'

What had happened to his intention to spend the morning with Elliott, inspecting the estate ledgers to ensure his bailiff had overseen estate affairs properly in Richard's all-too-frequent absences? One more day would not hurt, however, and it would be a worthwhile sacrifice to help Felicity settle into her new role and become accustomed to him. She had reacted like a startled fawn when he had entered her bathroom last night. Covering his eyes had been inspired; she had relaxed and responded, revealing her hidden passion. He would hate to have a wife who was indifferent to or—even worse—disliked the marital act.

'I do beg your pardon, my dear. I'm afraid I was wool-gathering.'

He had completely missed Felicity's response to his offer.

'I said "thank you but that will not be necessary". You no doubt have important duties. There is no need for you to trouble yourself—I shall ask Mrs Jakeway to give me a tour of the house and, as for the gardens and grounds, I shall be quite content to explore them on my own.'

Chapter Seventeen

Richard placed his knife and fork on to his empty plate, biting back an irritable retort.

'I have put the day aside especially for you, Felicity.' A touch inaccurate, perhaps, but at least he had made the gesture. Whereas *she*… 'I thought we would spend it together.'

A flick of her eyebrow spoke volumes. 'We have a marriage of convenience, Richard. There is no need for pretence.'

'Pretence? Is it so wrong to wish for a comfortable relationship?'

'Comfortable? Oh, no, of course it is not. But may we not be comfortable without living in one another's pockets?'

Why did those words chafe? The uncomfortable conclusion was that although he did not wish his marriage to change *his* way of life, he had—hypocritically—assumed he would be the centre of his wife's world.

'I have annoyed you. I am sorry. That was not my intention. I wished to reassure you I will not be a wife who expects or desires your constant attention. That was not our bargain. I am accustomed to relying on my own resources for entertainment.'

Bargain? Richard expelled his breath in an audible huff. 'The fault was mine. I made assumptions. I wish only to ensure we have a contented marriage.'

'As do I. I promise I do not refuse your company out of churlishness. I simply wish to ensure you do not spend time with me from a sense of *duty*.'

How to respond? Their marriage had only taken place because of his sense of duty. Had that same sense of duty prompted his offer to show her around Fernley?

In his mind's eye he saw Felicity in her bath, felt again her silky skin, heard her soft sighs. His blood stirred. His new wife might not be as buxom as his usual preference, but her pert, springy breasts had excited him every bit as much as fuller, pillowy mounds had ever done. And those lean thighs…her taut belly…her enthusiastic responses…

He studied her face, animated with discussion, her eyes shining with sincerity.

'I promise I will never do that,' he said. 'I will summon Mrs Jakeway to show you the house.'

The morning sped by. To Felicity's reeling senses, it seemed Mrs Jakeway left no corner of the huge house unvisited and no history of the Durant family untold. Who would have thought touring one house could be so exhausting?

Mrs Jakeway opened a door leading off an upstairs landing and ushered Felicity through into a long, narrow, portrait-lined room. 'The gallery—the family are all in here.'

Felicity bit back a sigh, anticipating a long story to accompany each portrait, but as they stopped before the very first painting, the door at the far end of the gallery opened.

'There you are.' Richard strode the length of the gallery towards them. Felicity fixed her attention on the portrait, willing her fluttering pulse to steady. 'Thank you, Mrs Jakeway. You may return to your duties.'

'Yes, thank you, Mrs Jakeway. You have been most informative.' Felicity smiled at the housekeeper then said to Richard, 'It is a magnificent house, but I had no notion of how big it is. I feel as though I have walked miles.'

Richard laughed. 'You will be ready for some refreshment, then, to replenish your energy.' He held out his arm, and she took it with some relief. 'I am pleased you approve of your new home, Felicity Joy.'

She gritted her teeth against the tremor that sped through her at his deepening tone. *Felicity Joy*, indeed.

'Oh, I do,' she said. 'Your mother has the most exquisite taste; everything is beautifully decorated and furnished.'

'You must feel free to make any changes you wish, especially in your own chambers,' Richard said. 'Whatever you wish for, Felicity, you may have.'

Whatever I wish for...? Hmmph. 'You are most generous, but I have seen nothing yet I would care to change.'

They strolled along the dim gallery. Felicity cast around for a subject to break the silence.

'Your mother—'

'Will be moving to the Dower House in the very near future.'

That had not been what she was going to ask. 'You do not appear very...well, very close.'

A bitter laugh was quickly bitten off. 'You might say that. My mother has never hidden the fact she would have preferred my brother to succeed to the title.'

'Your brother?' Felicity searched her memory. 'I had forgotten. He was older than you, was he not?'

Richard indicated a portrait of a youth with a much younger boy. 'By eight years.' The youth was a serious-faced lad with the same brown, wavy hair as Richard. 'That is Adam and me as children. For a long time, my parents gave up hope of having more children. Then I came along. Adam was always the favourite. My parents were inconsolable when he died.'

'How could they be otherwise? He was their son.'

Richard shot her a dark look, then strode on. Felicity trailed in his wake, her mind spinning. They had the death of a sibling in common then.

At the door leading from the gallery to the upstairs landing, Richard paused. 'My father died four months after

Adam. He lost all interest in life. I was barely seventeen when I inherited the title, a position I never expected. Nor desired.'

His knuckles shone white on the door handle. He started when Felicity tentatively touched his hand. 'You suffered two grievous losses in a cruelly short time. I do understand. I lost my father when I was fourteen and then my sister, Emma, two years later. She was only eighteen.'

'Eighteen. So very young.' Richard lifted his hand to her cheek. 'You must miss her.'

'I do.' Felicity's throat tightened. 'It was…' She paused. She could not divulge Emma's disgrace, or her mother's culpability, or her own guilt at the anger she still harboured towards her mother. After Papa had died, her mother had been inconsolable. Following her year of mourning, however, she had launched into a round of gaiety and parties, with the excuse of Emma's come-out. But Mama had become too intent on her own needs and pleasures, and her naive and innocent daughter had paid a heavy price.

Determinedly, Felicity buried those memories. 'It was a dreadful time, as it must have been for you and your poor mother after Adam and then your father died.'

'After the initial shock, my mother coped admirably, as she always does. She did not allow…' Richard fell silent. 'Well, that is of no import. Come. Let us go and eat and, afterwards, if you will allow, I should like to show you round the gardens.'

She choked back her instinct to refuse, mindful of that glimpse of pain when he spoke of his family. 'Thank you.'

He smiled, and Felicity's pulse quickened. She spun round and headed for the stairs. As they descended, Lady Stanton was crossing the marble-floored entrance hall. Glancing up, she stopped. Richard's features were set in grim lines and, eyeing the dowager's haughty demeanour as they neared the foot of the stairs, Felicity felt a moment of sadness for them both. Two people, bound by blood and by common grief, should find succour in one another. All she could read here was resentment, in Richard's case, and indifference in his mother's; although…there was a glimmer of fear in her mother-in-law's eyes whenever she looked at her son that Felicity could not understand. What did she fear?

A footman held the door, and they sat at the table where luncheon—a selection of cold meats, bread and butter, pickles, salads and fruit—was laid out.

The dowager helped herself to a slice of beef. 'Did you find the Countess's suite to your liking, Felicity?'

'Thank you, yes. It is most agreeable.'

'I moved out of there when Richard's father died, into my current bedchamber.' Her gaze flicked towards Richard. 'I have sent the servants over to the Lodge to prepare.'

'The Lodge?' Felicity looked from her mother-in-law to Richard and back again.

'Fernley Lodge is the Dower House. Mother will move there now we are married.'

'We shall have to discuss which servants I may take with me, or do you wish me to hire new people?'

'Not at all, Mother. You may take your pick. I shall hire any replacements I need.'

'You will be happier with familiar people around you, I am sure.' Felicity ignored her mother-in-law's haughtily lifted brow; she was part of this family now; she would not sit quietly when family—and household—matters were discussed.

'Speaking of servants,' the dowager said, switching her focus to Felicity, 'I must insist you hire a lady's maid without delay. It is completely unacceptable—'

'It is in hand, Mother,' Richard interrupted. 'I have sent a message to Truman in Winchester to find suitable candidates for me to interview.'

'I should prefer to select my own maid.' Felicity pretended she did not notice the outraged stare of the dowager or Richard's amusement at her interjection.

'Then so you shall,' he replied.

'Thank you.'

'You are most free with your opinions,' the dowager remarked.

Richard's eyes were fixed on her, a distinct challenge in them. She pressed her lips together. *Start as you mean to go on.*

'I apologize if you think I speak out of turn, Mother,' she said, 'but I am, am I not, the Countess of Stanton? I am mistress of this house now, and I therefore believe I am entitled to express my opinion.

'What do you say, my dear?' she added, directing a searching look at Richard, who laughed.

'I have no objection to you expressing your opinions, Wife,' he said, 'just as long as they concur with mine.' The twinkle in his eyes confirmed he was teasing.

'I shall try and bear that in mind, Husband,' she murmured, narrowing her eyes at him before focusing on her plate once more.

Chapter Eighteen

This is what happens when you allow sympathy to overthrow your good intentions.

Felicity sat in a secluded arbour overlooking the lake, resentment scouring her brain. She had discovered the spot on her solitary exploration of the gardens and grounds. Her *husband* had been so easily dissuaded from spending time in her company, she could almost laugh. She had only accepted his offer to show her the gardens because she felt sorry for him. Well, maybe she'd been a *tiny* bit flattered he had confided in her about his brother's death and—possibly—she had been foolish enough to hope…but no! She was deluded. This neighbour…some crony of Richard's—she was so cross she could not even recall his name—had called on his way into Winchester, and Richard had jumped at the opportunity to accompany him, with no thought for her or for his promise.

Why so angry? You refused his company only this morning. Surely you are not already infatuated with him after only one night of passion?

She resumed her march around the lake. It was too cool to sit for long: dark grey clouds scudded across the sky, playing hide-and-seek with the sun much as her anger flirted with images of their lovemaking from the night before.

Richard had behaved in perfect accord with their bargain. Was that not what she wanted from their marriage? She should thank him for not encouraging her silly, missish longings.

She completed her circuit of the lake, and made her way back, to explore the flower gardens.

But...if only he had not been so tender...so loving... so—seemingly—*appreciative* last night. Her thoughts, as she wandered, sparked a myriad of unwelcome emotions. Surely this intensity...such pleasure...such ecstasy...would not—*could* not—last? In time, their lives would settle into the humdrum. Their paths need not cross during the day and, at night, Richard would visit her bed and service her until they had produced enough children to secure the earldom. He would then leave her alone. Unromantic, maybe, but those sentiments were exactly what she had planned for her marriage and exactly what she needed to bring her down to earth.

Why, then, did she feel so wretched?

She returned to the house to consult with Mrs Jakeway. The sooner she occupied her mind with the everyday matters of running of the household, the better.

'I've appointed a lady's maid for you. She arrives next week.'

Felicity froze in the act of setting a stitch. Slowly, she looked up at Richard, newly returned from Winchester, a satisfied smile on his lips.

'You agreed I might select my own maid.'

'Yvette comes highly recommended, Felicity. She will make you an excellent maid.'

Of all the high-handed... Felicity bit her lip and bent her head to continue with her embroidery.

'Truman told me—'

'Who is Truman?'

'He is my man of business in Winchester. I needed to consult him over additional staff for Fernley Lodge and I mentioned your need for a lady's maid.'

'I see.'

'I met the girl. She is in need of employment and her references are impeccable. Dalton will collect her on Tuesday. I am certain you will approve of her.'

Is she pretty? The words stole uninvited into Felicity's thoughts, her father's penchant for comely maidservants still fresh in her memory even after all these years. She concentrated fiercely on her stitching. 'I reserve the right to refuse her.'

She glanced up. Richard was frowning. 'Do you not trust my judgement, Felicity?'

Start as you mean to go on. 'I do not know you well enough to answer that. Staff appointments, however, are part of *my* jurisdiction and the matter of my personal maid is of particular importance to me, as you might imagine.'

'Very well. I ask only that you reserve judgement until you have met Yvette. I am certain you will like her.'

Richard watched Felicity push the food around her dinner plate with a distinct lack of enthusiasm. As far as he could tell, not a morsel had passed her lips. She had withdrawn into herself; was she fretting about the night to come? With his mother present, he could say nothing to ease her uncertainties.

'Is the food not up to your usual standards?'

Felicity's head jerked up at his mother's question.

'It is delicious, Mother, but I am afraid I am not very hungry. Please do pass my regrets to Cook,' Felicity added, directing her comment to Trick, who stood to one side of the room, 'I should not wish to cause any dismay in the kitchen. The fault is not with the food.'

'Well, really, Daughter. Why should kitchen servants care about your appetite, pray?'

'Mother.'

His mother ignored Richard's warning, her attention on Felicity, their gazes locked. A mental image arose of two fencers, each on the alert for any hint of vulnerability in their opponent. Richard sipped at his wine, settling back to await the victor.

'It may well be they would not be concerned about my lack of appetite,' Felicity said. 'But I, you see, *do* care that their work should not go unacknowledged. If I cannot express my thanks by eating the results of their labour, it costs me nothing to pass on a few words of reassurance.'

His mother stiffened. 'Well!'

Silence reigned. He could almost hear the wheels spinning in his mother's brain.

'I suppose there is no harm in it,' she eventually conceded. 'You are sending such a message only because it is your *wish* to do so, and not under any sense of obligation to the lower orders.'

First round to Felicity.

'I will move to Fernley Lodge as soon as the servants have made it ready,' Mother said, 'but I shall leave Trick and Jakeway here. You will need them to maintain the standards to be expected in a house such as Fernley Park.'

'That is most generous,' Felicity said. 'Do you not agree, Richard?'

'Richard? Why do you not use your husband's title? He has been Stanton since his father's death fifteen years ago.'

'Richard specifically requested that I call him such, Mother. And I know you will agree a wife should always obey her husband.'

Richard bit back a smile as his mother inclined her head, indicating her approval. He detected the mischievous glint in Felicity's eye and the laughter that warmed her voice, nuances that passed his mother by.

'I am sorry we will have so little time to become acquainted,' Felicity said.

'Fernley Lodge is barely half a mile distance, Daughter. You may walk over and visit me whenever you are at home.'

'And you, Mother, will be most welcome to visit us here at Fernley whenever you choose,' Felicity said promptly. 'Is that not so, Richard?'

'Indeed.'

Dare he hope to forge a better relationship with his mother, now he was wed? It was hard to remember the time—before Adam's death—when their bond had been warm and relaxed. He had tried to excuse her rejection but, over the years, his understanding had withered away, stunted time and time again by her condemnation of him.

'Besides,' he added, 'even if Mother were to remain longer at Fernley, we will not be here.'

'Will we not? Are we going away? You said nothing about a journey this morning.'

No, he had not, for he had only that very minute decided. He had racked his brains for ways to help Felicity adjust to her new life...to him. He recognized her skittishness around him, despite her efforts to conceal it. She appeared to believe that reducing the time they spent together—as per their bargain—was the answer. He begged to differ.

'It was to be a surprise,' he said smoothly.

It had occurred to him, as they talked about Fernley, that she would become more quickly accustomed to him—and to the idea of being his wife—in a more intimate establishment.

And he knew just the place.

'I have a small fishing lodge in the Welsh Marches. We will leave after Mother has moved to the Lodge,' he said. 'On our honeymoon,'

'*Honeymoon?*' Two bright patches of colour stained Felicity's cheeks.

'Honeymoon. The lodge is isolated, surrounded by beautiful countryside. It will give us time to get to know one another.'

There was a prolonged silence. Richard watched as various expressions swept Felicity's face.

She cleared her throat. 'If we are to go away, might I request we visit London instead?'

Chapter Nineteen

'*London?* For our honeymoon?' Any other bride would have been overjoyed at such a romantic setting as a fishing lodge on the River Wye.

'I…yes, if you please. I would welcome the opportunity to visit Westfield again.'

'Westfield? What is Westfield, pray?' the dowager interjected.

'It is an orphan asylum and a school for destitute children.'

'And you were involved with such a place as an unmarried woman? Shameful.'

Mutiny gleamed in Felicity's eye.

'It is hardly shameful, Mother, to help those less fortunate than ourselves,' Richard said. 'If it is your wish to go to London, Felicity, then we shall. I am interested to visit Westfield myself, and it will be an opportunity for you to have some new gowns made.'

'Thank you.' She flashed a smile in his direction. 'It is a very respectable establishment, Mother, run by Mr Peter Whittaker and his wife, Jane. You must not fear I shall run the family name into disrepute.'

His mother rose to her feet. 'If you have finished your meal, Felicity, we shall retire to the salon and you may tell me more about this place. We shall leave Stanton to his port.'

Richard had no wish to remain there alone, but he acquiesced, as he so often did in response to his mother's edicts.

She was his mother, after all, and he had no intention of quarrelling with her over what was, to her, an inviolable custom. Once she had removed to the Lodge, he would establish his own customs. He stood as the ladies left the room.

His mother's voice floated back through the still open door. 'Now, would that be the Hertfordshire Whittakers?'

Richard eyed the two women in his life with mounting frustration. Somehow, in the time he had taken to visit the kitchen and arrange for a few tempting morsels and some wine to be laid out in Felicity's bedchamber, his wife had persuaded his distant, disapproving mother into a genuine interest in her work with the orphans.

'Your mother,' Felicity had informed him with a sunny smile as he sauntered into the salon, ready to persuade her to retire early, 'made her début with Mr Peter Whittaker's mother. Is that not a coincidence?'

The tea tray came and went and still Felicity lingered, seemingly oblivious to his hints. Did she genuinely not realize he was longing to take her to bed?

Finally, he stood up. 'If you will excuse us, Mother, I am very tired and wish to retire.' He held out his hand. 'Come, Felicity.'

His wife's flaming cheeks spoke volumes. He caught his mother's amused glance at Felicity and felt a jolt of disbelief.

Amusement? From his mother? How was she so relaxed in Felicity's company, yet so stiff in his own? She had only known Felicity one day. It was as though a guard had been lowered in Felicity's company and yet, in his, that guard was constantly and insurmountably in place. He dismissed his stir of resentment with impatience.

'It is time I retired too.' His mother rose to her feet. 'Goodnight, Felicity; Stanton.'

Richard grabbed Felicity's hand and tugged her to her feet as his mother left the room. He could feel her trembling.

'Look at me, Felicity.' She did, her amber eyes round, the gold flecks in her irises reflecting the candlelight. 'I thought you enjoyed our lovemaking last night? There is nothing to fear, and no need to be embarrassed.'

A spark of…something…flashed in her eyes and her chin tilted up. 'I am not afraid.' She leaned forward, coming up on to her toes, and pressed her lips to his. 'I am not afraid.'

He swept her into his arms, lifting her with ease, deepening the kiss. Slender arms wrapped around his neck as he nudged the door open with one foot. A footman on duty in the hallway stared stonily ahead as Richard mounted the stairs, Felicity still cradled in his arms, their lips fused together as their tongues entwined.

He kicked the door of the bedchamber shut behind them, having dismissed the waiting maid with a jerk of his thumb. His blood was up, heart hammering, as he deposited Felicity on the bed and ran his fingers up her leg, stroking past the bare skin of her thigh to the moist heat at her core as he tugged down her neckline, exposing one small, firm breast, and sucked her nipple deep into his mouth. A gasp, cut short, inflamed him further.

Slow down. He wrenched away, shrugging out of his coat and discarding his neckcloth before approaching the bed again.

Felicity remained as he had left her. Spread-eagled, skirts rucked up to reveal smooth, slender thighs. His eyes roamed her body, lingering over her tiny waist, her heaving breast, the peaked nipple still glistening, to her face. Eyes glinted through half-closed lids as a pink tongue tip slaked across parted lips.

Little minx. With a growl that vibrated through his entire body, he launched himself on to the bed.

'Do you hunt, Lady Stanton?'

Felicity eyed her questioner. Lady Rowling was the local

squire's wife—a handsome brunette with dark flashing eyes. Felicity disliked her already, seething all through dinner as her hostess had monopolized Richard, seated to her right, and ignored the vicar on her left. The newlyweds, together with the dowager and some other neighbours, had been invited to dine with Sir Timothy and Lady Rowling.

'No. I love to ride, but the hunt is too fast and furious for me, I'm afraid.'

'Oh, I love to hunt. You do not know what you are missing. Why, we have had many a splendid run, have we not, Stanton?'

'We have indeed.' Richard had joined them, the gentlemen having returned to the ladies after the port. Felicity felt his hand settle at the small of her back, sending shivers dancing up her spine.

Lady Rowling sidled up to Richard. 'Do you recall that hedge, the last time we were out? The rest of the field queued for the gate, but we were not so cowardly, were we? Thor is such a fine animal—he flew that hedge, and my Duchess followed on his heels.' She laughed, showing—in Felicity's opinion—teeth reminiscent of a horse: long and yellowing. 'My Duchess would follow your Thor anywhere, I do believe.'

Felicity gritted her teeth at such blatant flirtation, but before she could think of a suitable riposte, they were joined by Sir Timothy and Richard's mother.

'Then I must urge you to exercise better control over her,' Sir Timothy said. 'She is a fine animal, but she does not have Thor's scope. He is magnificent, Stanton. I should like to see him pitted against my Brutus in a race across country.'

'Name the time and place,' Richard said promptly. 'Your Brutus won't see our heels for dust.'

The dowager swayed, the colour leaching from her skin, before she visibly rallied, saying, 'I do wish you would not,

Stanton. Think of the danger…your responsibilities. You have your wife to consider.'

'Oh, I am certain Lady Stanton can spare her husband for so short a time,' Lady Rowling said. 'Why, you would not care to interfere with your husband's pleasures, would you, my dear lady?'

What could she say? She had no more wish to see Richard risk his neck than her mother-in-law, but neither could she stand against him publicly so soon after their marriage. The challenge in Lady Rowling's eyes settled her response.

'I have no wish to curtail my husband's activities,' she said.

The squeeze of Richard's hand at her waist almost made up for the daggers in her mother-in-law's eyes.

'Saturday?' Sir Timothy said. 'We'll do a circuit of the parish, starting and ending here.'

In the carriage on the way home, the dowager berated Richard. 'The animal is unpredictable. You'll be thrown and injured. Even killed. You never consider the risks… you will get yourself killed. Like your brother.'

'His name was Adam. Why can you never call him by his name?'

Felicity heard the faint hitch in the dowager's breath. She reached in the dark, and clasped her hand.

'Please, Richard. Your mother is upset.'

'Have you *seen* Thor, Daughter?'

'Why, no.' She had seen little of her husband during daylight hours. Following their bargain.

'He is so huge, so strong—'

'I can handle him, Mother. You need not fear I will die before I do my duty and provide for the estate.'

Bony fingers dug into Felicity's palm at those bitter words.

'I am sure Mother did not mean…'

The carriage had pulled up in front of Fernley Park. Felicity's words faded as Richard flung open the door and jumped out. As he handed her down, he hissed in her ear, 'You do not know what you are talking about. I have lived with this since my father and brother died. It is *all* she cares about—the succession.'

He turned to help his mother from the carriage and into the house. Felicity followed thoughtfully.

Chapter Twenty

The following Tuesday Felicity made her way to Richard's study, having been informed by Trick that his lordship wished to see her. She had woken late and breakfasted alone. Richard had, according to Trick, been up since the crack of dawn. How did he find the energy? She was exhausted after a night of the most... She felt her cheeks bloom and, conscious of passing servants, forced her thoughts away from the night before.

She hesitated outside the study door. Raised voices sounded from within.

'She is totally unsuitable.'

'We must agree to differ in this instance, Mother. Yvette is a most experienced lady's maid.'

'Yvette. And French, too,' the dowager added in tones of disgust. 'And her *appearance*—'

'The decision is for Felicity to make.'

'No lady would countenance such a creature in their employ. I am astonished Truman had the effrontery to present her.'

'I reviewed all the available candidates. She was the best by far.'

'You should spare Felicity the distress of meeting such a woman.'

Richard's voice grew clipped. 'Yvette possesses all the necessary skills for a superior lady's maid.'

Does she, indeed?

'She has excellent credentials.'

Hmmph. No doubt she has.

What was so special about this Frenchwoman that Richard was so very eager to employ her? She was no doubt beautiful and flirtatious, as Frenchwomen were known to be. Felicity determined to dislike her on sight, and to send her back to Winchester and ask for some good, solid English girls to be presented for her approval.

She squared her shoulders, rapped on the door and walked in.

'Ah, Felicity. Yvette has arrived, for the post of lady's maid. She is in the parlour, if you would care to come and meet her?'

Richard urged her to the door, his hand warm at the small of her back. A shiver danced across her skin at his touch, further annoying her. She had her righteous indignation to maintain, she had no wish to be distracted by memories of the night before.

'Stanton!' The dowager's peremptory command stopped them in their tracks. 'I insist you forewarn Felicity about—'

'There is no need. Felicity is not a child to be protected.'

His hand urged her onward. Suspicion swelled. Would he try to coerce her into accepting this Frenchwoman? He would find she was made of sterner stuff than he imagined if he thought she would meekly submit. At the parlour door, Richard cupped her chin and looked into her eyes.

'All I ask is that you employ an open mind, Felicity.'

Felicity held his gaze, staring into deep brown eyes as open and honest as she could wish for. Was he really so false? All guileless innocence on the surface whilst hatching plans to bring a doxy into the house under the guise of a servant?

She stalked into the room.

A woman stood by the fire, her back to the door. She wore a plain black dress, her hair tucked neatly out of sight under a straw bonnet; medium height with a narrow back and arms so thin the sleeves of her dress hung in folds. She turned, head high, as Felicity entered.

Felicity bit back her gasp, quickly schooling her expression. So this was Yvette, the Frenchwoman she had mentally accused Richard of having designs upon. Her mind whirled as she rethought Richard's motives, shamed by her suspicions. This would teach her to judge. Not an attempt to introduce a pretty maid into the household—quite the opposite. Her husband climbed several notches in her estimation.

She studied Yvette's face as she crossed the room to greet her. Two scars, one above the other, marred her left cheek. The higher, longer one—silvery pink—curved from her mouth—where it puckered her top lip—to her temple, just missing the corner of her eye. The second, shorter scar angled across her jaw. The effect was exaggerated by her cheekbones, stark above hollowed cheeks. Dark shadows smudged her eyes, which were green and watchful, a hint of defiance in their depths. It was impossible to ascertain her age—she might be five-and-twenty or she might as easily be twenty years older. Those eyes certainly gave the impression of a long, eventful life.

'Good morning,' Felicity said, before Richard could perform any introductions. 'I am Lady Stanton.'

The woman curtsied, bowing her head. 'Good morning, my lady. I am Yvette Marchant.'

French accent. Not too strong. Well modulated. Yvette looked up again at Felicity and then her gaze flickered uncertainly towards Richard.

Poor thing. But pity was no reason to employ someone. Richard was watching intently. Was this a test? Is that why he hadn't warned her? To gauge her reaction? To see if she reacted in horror, with a scream, averting her eyes from Yvette's scars? Mayhap that should infuriate her but it actually intrigued.

Felicity smiled at Yvette, and gestured towards a chair.

'Please, take a seat, Mademoiselle Marchant. Will you tell me about yourself?'

The green eyes exuded pride and defiance. This was a woman who had been hurt and—evidenced by those hollow cheeks—she was a woman in dire straits. Was she as experienced as Richard had claimed? But he was no fool, to take on a maid with no skill to attend to his wife.

'Where are you from?'

'I was born in Paris, milady. I came to England when I was seventeen years old.'

'To escape the troubles?'

Yvette nodded. An *émigrée*, then. There had been many during those horrendous times in France.

'I see. Do you have experience as a lady's maid, *mademoiselle*?'

'But yes, or his lordship, why would he have brought me here to you? I was the lady's maid to Lady Ashcroft until the last year, when she died.'

Lady Ashcroft—a mental image of the baronet's wife arose: always immaculately dressed and *coiffured*, skin glowing, even at her advanced age.

'I have the reference.' Yvette held out a couple of sheets of paper. Her hand trembled. 'Milady wrote them for me when she was ill. Sir Humphrey, he gives me the letter, too. He has no need for lady's maid now. He lives now in the country all the time. He is, I think, not well either. He misses milady.'

Felicity took the papers. They were creased and smudged in places, as though they had been handled many times.

'Have you worked since Lady Ashcroft died?'

Yvette's shoulders dropped as a quiet huff of expelled air revealed she had been holding her breath. 'No. I have… this.' She gestured at her face. 'You do not say so, but you see it. No lady likes a maid they cannot look in the eye.' She stood, and held out her hand for her references.

'Wait. Please.' Felicity clasped Yvette's outstretched

hand. 'I would never reject you merely on account of your looks but, equally, I would not employ you *because* of them either.' She was conscious of Richard's scrutiny, but he maintained his silence. The decision was hers. 'I wish for a maid with skill, *mademoiselle*. I knew Lady Ashcroft, although not well, but I recall she was ever beautifully turned out…oh!' She laughed. 'Now I have made her sound like a horse, have I not?' A muffled snort sounded from the vicinity of the door, where Richard stood. 'Please, *mademoiselle*, be seated again whilst I read your references.'

Yvette sat, and Felicity read both documents. As she suspected—for Richard would not have presented Yvette unless he was impressed—they were glowing.

She smiled at Yvette. 'Welcome to Fernley Park, *mademoiselle*.'

'You will call me Yvette,' the Frenchwoman pronounced, pure delight shining in her eyes, 'for that is my name.'

After Mrs Jakeway had taken charge of settling Yvette— for her worldly belongings were packed into a valise she had brought with her—Richard said, 'Am I forgiven for bringing only the one applicant for you to interview, Felicity?'

'Indeed you are, although I wonder whether Yvette might regret taking the position when she sees what unpromising material she has to work with.'

Richard frowned, then strode across the room, taking her by the shoulders.

'Do not belittle yourself. You are the Countess of Stanton. You have the correct number of arms and legs, eyes and ears, do you not? Your body works as you wish it to work, and you are unscarred, unlike poor Yvette. If you do not judge her by her appearance, why do you judge yourself? You have a good heart and a bright and enquiring mind. And…' his eyes bored into her '…you are an attractive, passionate, vital woman.'

As his head lowered, sick fear clutched Felicity even as

her blood heated and her treacherous lips parted, ready for his kiss. This was not their bargain. Lust was urging him to kiss her. Nothing more. She felt it too, that lust. But already her heart skipped a beat whenever she saw him, or heard his voice. She must confine their intimacies to the bedchamber, where they belonged, or she would be lost. During the day, all she required was polite co-existence.

About to claim her lips, Richard hesitated. His eyes searched hers. 'What is it? What is wrong?'

Felicity tore from his grasp. Oh, she wanted him. But how would she survive when—as was inevitable—he turned his attentions elsewhere? Her bed would feel deserted and cold enough but if she had become accustomed to his attentions during the day as well, that would be too much to bear. She dragged in a breath, hardening her heart even as she stretched her mouth into a smile, holding her courage against his stormy expression.

'Nothing is wrong, Richard. You are right, I should hold myself in higher esteem. You do not need to kiss me to bolster my confidence. Your words were more than adequate. Thank you.'

She hurried from the room, willing her legs to stop shaking.

Chapter Twenty-One

Two days later

Richard grabbed Felicity's hand as she reached for the door handle.

'Why?'

'Why what?' Felicity tugged her hand free.

Richard paced the library, hot anger surging through his veins. He came to a halt in front of his wife. 'Did I wed twins? You are a different woman by night and by day. I cannot fathom you.'

He had come into the library, and Felicity had been seated by the window, reading. He had smiled; made small talk; invited her to walk with him by the lake. She had been cool, monosyllabic, polite as she had rebuffed his every overture. Then he had reached to stroke her hair and she had flinched from him. *Flinched.* What did she imagine he might do?

She had stood up. He had taken her in his arms, but she had ducked, evading him, and made for the door. Which is when he had grabbed her.

He studied her expression. 'What are you afraid of?'

'Nothing. I am not afraid. We have a bargain.'

'And my part of that bargain is to leave you entirely to your own devices all day every day?'

She nodded.

His teeth clenched so hard he feared they might crack.

'Very well. There is no need for you to go. I shall leave you in peace.'

He stormed into his study and strode to the window where he stared unseeingly at the view, his temper still simmering. His bride was an enigma. They had been wed a week and, by night, she was passionate, willing and generous: all soft gasps and breathy screams. But, by day, she held him at arm's length, shunning intimacy and shunning, it seemed, friendship and companionship too. Was it merely lust she felt for him? But, if so, where did that lust disappear to as the sun rose every morning?

Her confidence in her appearance was low—thanks to her mother—but she discouraged any attempt to bolster her self-esteem. Was he too impatient? Expecting her to change overnight, when she had spent many years seeing herself through her mother's eyes?

Women! Who could understand them?

Exasperated by his circling thoughts, Richard strode for the door. He was in dire need of fresh air and physical exercise and he needed to keep Thor fit for the race on Saturday.

Felicity sat in the library, her restless fingers drumming a tattoo on the arm of the chair as her equally restless mind pondered her marriage. What was she to do? It would be so easy to accept Richard's attentions and intimacies, but it would be all too easy to become accustomed to them. They had no meaning to him, despite his anger—they were empty words and empty gestures calculated to smooth the path of their marriage of convenience. He was being kind. Nothing more.

She had only to remember her mother, and poor Emma, to know what pain and despair lay ahead if she failed to protect her heart. It would be easier once in London, with more distractions. If she could just hold her nerve until she was with child, mayhap she could survive with her heart intact.

The telltale bustle of arrival in the hall roused her from her brooding. Visitors—just the thing to take her mind off the conundrum of her marriage. It was not long before a knock at the door announced Trick.

'My lady, his lordship's cousin, Mr Durant, has arrived. I have shown him into the salon.'

Richard's cousin? She had no recollection of meeting a Mr Durant during her rare forays into society.

'Thank you, Trick. Where is Lady Stanton?'

'She is in her sitting room, my lady. I have sent Peter to inform her.'

'And do you know where his lordship is?'

'He went out riding a little over an hour ago.'

'Thank you, Trick.'

No doubt out on Thor again. She had now seen for herself the spirited stallion, and could understand her mother-in-law's fears for Richard's safety, but he seemed to delight in the challenge of mastering the animal.

When Felicity entered the salon, Mr Durant greeted her with a twinkle in his eye and a wide smile. 'I take it I have the pleasure of meeting the new Lady Stanton?'

'You do indeed, Mr Durant. I am pleased to welcome you to Fernley Park.'

He was around Richard's height—six foot—but there the resemblance ended, for Mr Durant was as slender as a whip, with blue eyes and fair, curly hair. He extended an exaggerated leg and bowed low.

'I am delighted to make your acquaintance, my lady.' He glanced past Felicity and his grin widened. 'And my dear aunt—you are well, I hope?'

The dowager swept past Felicity and Mr Durant and sat, ramrod straight, in her favourite chair by the fire. 'Good afternoon, Mr Durant. I do not believe we were expecting you, were we? To what do we owe the pleasure of your visit?

'Mr Durant is a *distant* cousin,' she added, looking at Felicity.

Uncomfortable with her mother-in-law's frostiness, Felicity said, 'Welcome to Fernley Park, sir. I look forward to becoming better acquainted. Am I to understand you are a friend of Richard's as well as his kinsman?'

'I like to think so and, as we are now cousins—albeit *distant*—I beg you will call me Charles.'

'I have no objection,' Felicity said, warming to him. 'And I would be pleased if you will reciprocate and call me Felicity.'

'Indeed I shall. I can see we shall get on famously, Felicity. My cousin is a fortunate man.'

Felicity sat on the sofa. Charles immediately sat beside her.

'You were about to enlighten me as to the reason for your visit, Mr Durant,' the dowager said.

Charles appeared impervious to the dowager's inhospitable tone. 'I was knocking around town at a loose end, dear Aunt, and thought I'd pay my favourite cousin a visit. Nothing whatsoever,' he added, with a surreptitious wink at Felicity, 'to do with my eagerness to inspect his new bride, I do assure you.'

Felicity returned his infectious smile as two maids entered the room carrying trays laden with tea and cakes.

'I am sorry Richard is not here to welcome you,' Felicity said to Charles. 'He is out riding, but I expect him to return very soon.'

'Yes, so I was informed, on that crazy stallion of his. And I hear he is racing it on Saturday.'

Felicity tried to ignore the squirm of apprehension in her belly at the thought of that race.

'I do wish you might do something to curb Stanton's penchant for taking risks, Felicity,' the dowager said, in a faint voice.

'I beg you not to fret, dear ladies,' Charles said. 'The stallion is highly strung, but Richard is an excellent horseman. I very much doubt he will come a cropper.'

'I am all gratitude for your unwavering faith in my abilities, Charles—' came a dry comment from the doorway '—but I fear neither my mother nor my wife are likely to be reassured by your words.'

Chapter Twenty-Two

Richard had tried to shake himself free of his unaccustomed fit of despondency with a fast and furious gallop on Thor but as soon as he turned for home his frustration with Felicity's inconsistent behaviour had resurfaced with a vengeance. She had been reluctant to wed him from the first and, despite the 'bargain' of their marriage, her rejection hurt.

He entered the salon, cheered by the news of Charles's arrival, only to hear his cousin inadvertently fuelling the fears of Mother and Felicity over that blasted race.

'Stan.' Charles leapt to his feet and hurried across the room to clasp Richard's hand. 'You must believe I had no intention of scaring the ladies… Oh, you know me, Coz—my mouth runs before my brain at times.'

'Worry not, Charles, they were both in a fret about it before ever you arrived. It is good to see you.'

'I am relieved to hear you say so. I did wonder…with your so recent nuptials…if I am in the way, you only have to say.'

'You are welcome, Charles. I see you have made Felicity's acquaintance.'

'I have, and we have been getting along famously, is that not so, Felicity? Oh, do not take offence, dear fellow. I begged your lady's permission before making free with her name.'

Richard glanced at Felicity, whose eyes were firmly fixed on Charles. His temper flared.

'My wife is nothing if not accommodating.'

Ah. Now he had her attention. Her amber eyes clung to his face, then travelled slowly down to linger on his clenched fists. Swearing silently, he loosened his fingers.

'I trust you enjoyed your ride, my dear?' Felicity turned to Charles before Richard could respond, continuing, 'A vigorous ride is so very soothing if one is feeling a trifle out of sorts, would you not agree, Charles? Oh, not that I am suggesting for one moment that Richard was in any way out of temper, of course.' Guileless amber eyes turned on Richard. 'It was merely an observation.'

'My ride was exactly how I expected it to be. I find consistency in all things so very essential. Do you not agree, my sweet?'

Felicity lifted her chin. 'I find consistency overrated, Husband. It can so easily result in *ennui*, don't you find?'

Richard felt his mouth twitch and his prickly temper slowly subsided.

'I am not certain I followed that exchange, Coz,' Charles said, in a peevish tone. 'No doubt I shall, in time, become accustomed to interpreting such pointed asides. Although why you married couples needs must talk in riddles quite escapes me, I am sure.'

'It does not escape me,' the dowager said, tight-lipped. 'Quarrelling within earshot of others is most unbecoming. I am surprised at you, Stanton. I suggest you apologize.'

'Oh, no, Mother, it is I who should apologize,' Felicity said quickly. 'I am afraid I provoked Richard beyond endurance earlier, and I am sorry.'

'And I too, my dear.'

'And now we are all friends again, might I ask what time dinner is served?' Charles asked. 'I'm famished.'

'Well, *really*.' Richard's mother rose. 'You too, Mr Durant, could do with a lesson in good manners. I shall rest in my bedchamber before dinner.'

'Well?' Charles looked from Richard to Felicity and back again. 'Do you intend to enlighten me about dinner, or must I beg?'

'*This* is an abomination, milady.'

The words jolted Felicity from her reverie. She stared at Yvette.

Abomination? 'I beg your pardon?'

'This, milady.' Yvette marched across the room to the wardrobe and flung the door wide with a dramatic flourish. 'It is an abomination.'

Felicity sank on to a nearby chair. She had been preoccupied with Richard—it took her a few minutes to disengage her thoughts and concentrate on Yvette's words, and then a bubble of amusement lodged in her throat. She should be offended and take Yvette to task for her impertinence, or her lack of respect, or whatever else her mother-in-law would find to deplore in her maid's behaviour, but Felicity was, instead, diverted. The Frenchwoman was undoubtedly passionate and sincere.

'What, precisely, do you find to be an abomination, Yvette?'

'All of it.' Yvette flung a dismissive arm towards the open wardrobe. 'What are you to wear for dinner tonight, milady?' Yvette turned tragic eyes towards Felicity. 'There is a *guest*. And when we go to London? This?' She snatched out a white muslin dress and flung it on the bed. 'This?'

'Yvette!'

The maid stopped in the act of dragging another dress from the wardrobe.

'I am happy that you care about my appearance, but please understand that I have worn those same garments for some time now, and I have survived, have I not?'

'Ah, but, milady, then you did not have me. I have the reputation.'

Felicity bit back a smile. 'What are your objections to my clothes, might I ask?'

'The colours, they are *mal*. They make you—how you say, sickly. Your lips, your cheeks, they go *bleu*. You need the strong, the jewel colours, to make your skin alive.'

'Well, in time, Yvette, I shall purchase new dresses, and I shall rely on your help. But, in the meantime, I am afraid I have no choice but to continue to wear my existing gowns.'

Yvette continued to grumble as she helped Felicity dress for dinner. She arranged her hair, brushing it thoroughly then twisting and pinning it up in a way that softened and framed her face rather than accentuating the sharpness of her features.

'I make the lotions for your skin, it will be soft and smell delicious, for your lord, and he will not be angry with the bills from the modiste. And your hair—with my own recipe I will make it glow with the health. You will see, milady. You will not regret employing Yvette.'

Her fingers suddenly stilled on Felicity's hair. 'I have the idea, milady. You will wait there.'

The maid flew from the room. As Felicity waited, her thoughts turned yet again to Richard and, as if the thought had conjured up the man, a soft knock at the door heralded his arrival.

'I thought to escort you down to dinner, Felicity,' he said, sauntering into the room, starkly handsome in his evening clothes, his brown eyes appraising her. He held out a jewellery case. 'By way of an apology for my behaviour, and a token of my esteem.'

He opened the lid, and Felicity gasped. Guilt flooded her. She did not deserve gifts. She would try to find some middle ground in their everyday dealings.

'They are beautiful, Richard. Your mother—?'

'Never wears them.' He placed the case on the dressing table in front of Felicity. The ruby-and-diamond necklace and matching eardrops, cushioned on white velvet, glowed blood red and white-hot in the candlelight. 'They are part of the Stanton collection and, therefore, yours to wear whenever you please. If you wish to have any of the jewels reset, you need only to say. Some of the styles are too old-fashioned for today—they would swamp your delicate neck.'

Tingles raced through her as long fingers feathered the side of her neck.

One black-clad arm reached over her shoulder and lifted the necklace from the box. 'Allow me.'

The flesh between her thighs leapt in response to his deepening tone. Her teeth sank into her lower lip.

He bent to fasten the catch.

The hairs on the back of her neck rose as his warm breath played across her skin and, in the looking glass, the quickening rise and fall of her chest was emphasized by the glowing jewels. His face appeared over her shoulder, reflected next to her own as he rubbed his freshly shaved cheek against hers.

'You smell lovely,' he murmured and a delicious sensual awareness washed over her skin.

His head tilted and a warm tongue trailed up the side of her neck to her ear. Gentle teeth nibbled. Then he reached for the eardrops and hung one from her lobe. He nibbled his way around the nape of her neck to her other ear. Shivers raced up and down her arms and she trembled as her nipples grew hard and her bones turned soft.

'There.'

She could remain still no longer. She rose to her feet, and turned. Straight into his arms.

'It is dark outside, Felicity Joy,' he murmured, his lips inches from hers. 'It is our time.'

He claimed her lips with a deep-throated 'mmmm' that made her bones melt.

Chapter Twenty-Three

⁓⁓⁓

The door opened but, before he released her, Richard put his lips to Felicity's ear.

'Later…'

That seductive promise whispered across her skin and reverberated deep in her soul, setting her senses aflame. She clung to him, a moan escaping her lips. Strong hands steadied her. She sucked in a deep breath before turning to a beaming Yvette, who had returned carrying a deep red Chinese silk shawl.

'Tallis, she did not tell the untruth. She said the rubies.' Tallis was the dowager's personal maid.

Yvette bustled towards Felicity to wrap the shawl around her shoulders, oblivious to Richard's perplexed frown. Felicity ducked her knees to look in the mirror. She had never worn this colour before. Her skin in the candlelight looked warm and alive, her eyes sparkled back at her, her cheeks were becomingly flushed…or was that the result of Richard's kiss?

'What has Tallis to do—?'

'Milady needs the colour, milord. Her dresses, they are all…' Yvette hesitated, lips pursed. 'They are *pah*.'

'And I find I am none the wiser. Felicity…?'

'Yvette seems to think that my entire wardrobe is…unsuitable.'

Richard stepped back and perused Felicity, head to toe.

'I like you in that colour, Felicity Joy. But, still…Tallis?'

'I beg for her help,' Yvette said. 'I ask her for the coloured shawl to suit milady, and she tells me about the rubies. *Bon.* You will not disgrace me tonight, milady.'

'No, I will not, Yvette. Thank you.'

On their way to the dining room, the memory of their quarrel still weighing on her mind, Felicity searched for a neutral subject.

'Why does your mother so dislike Charles? I can see he might not be her idea of the perfect gentleman, but he *is* a family member, and a guest.'

'He is not merely a cousin, Felicity. He is, until our son is born, my heir. He is not, you may have surmised, the steadiest of fellows and I am afraid that goes for his attitude to money as well.'

'So her objection to him is *what* he is rather than *who* he is?'

'Indeed, although I could not with any honesty claim Charles is the sort of young man who would ever gain my mother's approval.'

Dinner was quiet, the dowager's brooding disapproval casting a shadow over the conversation, and the men subsequently lingered over their port. When they eventually joined the ladies in the salon, Felicity sat at the pianoforte and sang and a warm glow filled her at the heat in Richard's eyes as he watched her.

'Later...'

His promise echoed through her mind, a delicious tremor of anticipation snaking through her, as the dowager bade them goodnight and retired. Richard and Charles were sprawled on facing sofas, discussing hunting. Felicity, next to Charles and facing Richard, caught his eye as she stood.

'If you will excuse me, I am tired,' she said. 'I, too, will bid you goodnight.'

Both men stood, and Richard took her hands, pressing a kiss on her suddenly overheated skin.

'Goodnight, my dear.'

In bed, she waited. And waited. Finally, when the clock on the mantel read three o'clock, no longer able to keep her eyes open, Felicity snuffed out her candle and tried to sleep.

Richard buried his head under the bedclothes at the knock on his bedchamber door. His head thumped in rhythm with his heartbeat, which was entirely too loud for comfort.

'Come back later, Simson,' he gritted out. Even talking was an effort. Why had he allowed Charles to keep him up drinking so late?

'It isn't Simson. It's me.'

The bed dipped on one side and the sheet was slowly pulled back. Richard screwed his eyes shut against the light and groaned.

'Here. Drink this. My father used to swear by it.'

He cranked open one eyelid. A glass, filled with some noxious-looking substance, wavered in front of his eyes. He levered himself up into a half-sitting position.

'What is it? It looks foul.'

'Oh, it is. But it will settle your stomach and help with your headache,' Felicity said in a far-too-cheerful voice.

'If I drink it, will you leave me in peace?' He reached for the glass, willing to try anything to ease his pounding head.

'Don't sip at it, swallow it in one,' Felicity warned as his lips found the rim of the glass.

He tipped his head back, braced himself, and gulped the thick substance down. 'Urrgggh.'

He glared at Felicity, perched on his bed neatly attired in a white muslin morning gown, her hair pinned up. 'What time...?' He peered at the clock. 'Twelve o'clock?' He groaned, dropping his head back to the pillow.

'Charles has been up these past two hours.'

'He is accustomed to late hours and an excess of brandy. I gave up that particular weakness some time ago.'

'How do you feel now?'

Richard took inner stock. 'Better.' His guts were no longer roiling and the drumroll in his head had softened. 'What was in that?'

'It is better you do not know.'

Richard fumbled for her hand. 'Thank you. I hope you did not stay awake waiting for me last night?'

'Oh, no. I was quite exhausted. I was asleep almost before my head touched the pillow.'

Had she not missed him at all? The uncertainties that had plagued him after her rejection yesterday reared their heads again. Well, if that was how she wanted their marriage to be, who was he to deny her?

By the time Richard was fit to face the day, both the dowager and Felicity had eaten luncheon and only Charles was in the dining room, his plate still piled high.

'I came back for a second helping, Coz. Talented cook, your Mrs Pratt. I can recommend the pork pie. Help yourself.'

'Thank you, Charles. You are most generous.'

'Oh, don't mind me, Coz,' Charles said, waving his fork airily, 'you know I ain't one to stand on ceremony.'

Richard selected a slice of bread and some ham. His stomach lurched as he contemplated the pie, and he decided to pass.

'I am, as ever, delighted to see you, Charles, but I should warn you that Felicity and I leave for London very shortly. You are most welcome to stay longer, however, if there is a particular reason for you to be out of town?'

Charles laughed, quite unabashed. 'The duns aren't beating down my door quite yet, Coz, although a monkey wouldn't go amiss.'

'I paid off your debts last year, Charles. What happened?'

'Now, don't go all poker-faced on me, Stan. A fellow has to live.' Charles fell silent, eyeing Richard hopefully.

'One hundred, Charles, and no more.'

Charles grinned. 'Can't blame a fellow for trying. No, truth be told, I couldn't contain my curiosity any longer. You've set the *ton* on its ears with your marriage, don't you know? The gabble-mongers are in their element with the news the Elusive Earl has been leg-shackled at last and the air is rife with speculation about the speed of the wedding and the relative obscurity of the bride.'

Richard felt his forehead bunch and lower. 'It is no one else's business.'

'Couldn't agree more, dear chap,' Charles said, with a lift of his fair brows, 'but you must have been prepared for rumours to fly about.'

He had not.

'I should hate you to think I have come to spread gossip,' Charles continued, around a mouthful of pie, 'but I thought you should be aware of what is being said.' He lowered his voice, leaning closer. 'The latest *on dit* is that she entrapped you.'

'What the…!' Richard snapped his teeth against a curse. 'I am not in the habit of being forced to do anything against my inclination.'

'Oh, *I* know that, Coz. I believe the gossip is fuelled by your wife's age, and the fact she has been out for…*ahem*… several years. I'm ashamed to admit I could not quite bring the lady to mind, so I determined to come and see the truth for myself.'

Richard tensed as his pulse pounded. How dare *anyone* speculate about his wife in such a way?

'She is delightful,' Charles rattled on, 'but not…if I might venture…*quite* in your usual style. Love match, was it?'

His knowing tone and the mischief in his blue eyes goaded Richard, whose head was starting to hammer once more. 'Love? Love is for fools. Ours is a marriage of convenience. I have neither time nor inclination for more. Now, if you will excuse me, I have business to attend to.'

He strode from the room, Charles's amused, 'Didn't touch a nerve there, did I, Coz?' floating after him.

In the hall, Felicity was heading for the stairs.

'Felicity, wait.'

Richard searched her shuttered expression. Had she overheard his words to Charles? Did it matter? She had not overheard anything she did not already know.

On a whim, he said, 'Would you care for a turn around the garden?'

Her gaze slid from his. 'Not now, Richard. I have promised to go through the linen stores with Mrs Jakeway. And don't you have business to attend to?'

So she had heard. He watched her disappear up the stairs. Why had he even bothered to try? Why should he care? Love was a game for fools. Felicity had the right idea—stay aloof. That way you couldn't get hurt.

Clamping his teeth shut against the headache-induced nausea that swelled, he spun on his heel and marched into his study.

Chapter Twenty-Four

The next day was Saturday, the day of the race between Richard on Thor and Sir Timothy Rowling on Brutus. The course had been agreed, stewards placed at strategic points along the parish boundary and all gates along the route opened. The riders must pass each steward, but could choose to jump any hedge rather than divert through the nearest gateway.

Felicity, who had prayed for rain, cursed the cloudless sky as Charles drove her to Rowling Manor in time for the start of the race. Charles had ridden the course with Richard the previous afternoon, and described the course in frightening detail as he drove. Already sick with nerves, Felicity's mood was not improved when the first person she saw when they arrived was Lady Rowling, clinging to Richard, who had ridden over that morning.

'Do not worry, dear Lady Stanton, I have taken good care of your husband and ensured he is well nourished in preparation for his exertions.'

'Thank you.' *Why don't you concentrate on your own husband?* Her jealousy of the other woman appalled Felicity. If seeing him with Lady Rowling sparked such emotions, how would she cope in London, where he would be surrounded by women even more beautiful? Felicity frowned. It would seem her husband had already taken residence in her heart.

Richard extricated himself from Lady Rowling, grabbed Felicity's hand and drew her to one side. 'I am very pleased you came, Felicity. I know you do not approve, but there is no need to look so worried. I promise I shall return safe and sound. Thor is much fitter than Rowling's nag.'

'That is what concerns me,' Felicity said. 'You appear to believe you—and Thor—are invincible. What if—?'

'Stop! You have been paying too much attention to Mother.'

'She is distraught. I do not believe she will rest until this nonsense is over.'

'Nonsense? Did you expect me to reject the challenge? Trust me. I will return in one piece. You do not see Lady Rowling worrying over *her* husband's ability.'

No, indeed. She is too busy dancing attendance on you. 'I do not doubt your skills, Richard. I just do not understand why you needs must take such risks.'

'Now you *sound* like Mother. I'm a grown man. I know my abilities and my limitations. You should trust me not to take unnecessary risks.'

The whole race is one unnecessary risk. But she had said as much as she dared. He was clearly not listening. She watched, heart in mouth, as Dalton legged Richard up on to Thor, who wheeled round, ears flat. Richard settled him with a few words but both horses remained on their toes, sensing the atmosphere.

'Once they're off, there's a viewpoint up the hill where we can see most of the course,' Charles said in Felicity's ear. 'We will go up there, and you will see what a fine horseman you married.'

From the hill, they watched the two horses gallop neck and neck across fields, down lanes and through woodlands. Felicity was proud of Richard's undoubted skill as he handled the powerful stallion but, every time they faced a hedge, her heart froze until they landed safely on the other side. Towards the end of the course, it was clear Brutus was tiring and, before the last hedge, Sir Timothy steadied him, trotting through the gateway and lifting his hand in a good-natured salute as Richard and Thor disappeared towards the Manor.

'Shall we go and congratulate the victor?' Charles handed her into the curricle.

They drove up to the Manor in time to see Lady Rowling congratulate Richard with a kiss.

Shafts of pure jealousy speared Felicity. 'Charles. If you do not mind, might we say "congratulations" and then leave? I should like to set Mother's mind at rest.'

'Of course, if that is what you want.' Charles raised his voice. 'Congratulations, Coz. I never doubted you could do it.'

Richard, still red-faced, hair sweat-dampened, rounded the curricle to Felicity's side, his eyes searching hers. 'You look as tired as I feel.' He lifted her gloved hand to his lips. 'I told you I would be safe.'

Felicity forced a smile, conscious of Lady Rowling watching. 'You did indeed. Well ridden. I will see you at home later.'

'You must not take such women to heart,' Charles said as they took the road home. 'Richard has more sense than to be entrapped by such as Lady Rowling, I assure you. She is determined to fling herself at him, but she only succeeds in making herself look foolish.'

What could she possibly say to that?

Charles did not seem at all put out by her silence. Instead, he rattled on, 'Stan's not known as the Elusive Earl for nothing.'

'Elusive Earl?'

'They name him such in the clubs because he is discreet to the point of secrecy. In fact, there is a wager in the Book at White's as to the identity of his current mistress.

'Hoi, steady there!' He switched his attention to the horses, jibbing at a fallen branch on the road ahead.

Felicity absorbed his revelation, breathing deeply until

she was sure she had her emotions on a tight rein. Fortunately, Charles was preoccupied with the horses until they settled once more into a steady trot.

'What was I saying? Oops, my wretched tongue running on again. I should not mention the Betting Book to a lady, should I?' He laughed. 'They'd drum me out if they knew. Men's business, don't you know. Do not, I beg of you, mention this to Stan.'

That she could promise.

Chapter Twenty-Five

Ten days later

Felicity gazed from the window as the carriage pulled up outside Stanton House, in Cavendish Square. Richard, dressed for riding, top boots polished, riding whip in hand, appeared at the door, having driven to town in his curricle, with Charles. Felicity had managed to mask her hurt at his choice. She liked Charles, but she resented the way he had monopolized Richard's time.

Richard's words rang again in her ears: *'Love? Love is for fools. Ours is a marriage of convenience. I have neither time nor inclination for more.'*

How true that observation. As soon as there was an alternative to her company, he had become the Elusive Earl again.

Can you blame him? You rejected his every overture, even before Charles arrived.

'Welcome to Stanton House, Felicity.'

Still that cool smile as he handed her from the carriage. Despite it being safer in every way for her heart, she could not but regret the polite distance between them.

'Your house is very imposing.'

'*Our* house. It will be more suited to a family home than to a bachelor's residence, that is certain.'

Family? Not only had Richard avoided Felicity during the day since Charles's arrival, neither had he visited her bed at night. She had contrived to keep busy, allowing little time to think, but at night the minutes and the hours had stretched, mocking her futile efforts to banish him from her thoughts.

'You are going out?' *Is he going to see* her?

'I'm sorry to rush away, but I am sure Mrs Carter, the housekeeper, will show you around. I have some pressing business to attend to.'

'There is no need to apologize.' Felicity swallowed painfully. 'I am sure I will have plenty to keep me occupied.'

Who is she? How might I find out?

Her stomach screwed into knots. There was little hope of Richard returning to her bed whilst they were in London,

'I am sure you will.'

Richard smiled as he surveyed the street, his eagerness tangible. Felicity battened down her emotions and pasted on a bright smile.

This is how my life is to be.

'Will you be home for dinner?' she asked. She forced her imagination away from Richard's likely activities that afternoon and concentrated on her plan to visit Westfield tomorrow.

I wonder if Dominic is back in town.

'Of course. I will see you later.' Richard lifted her hand before she understood his intentions, stripped off her glove, and pressed warm lips to her skin. She fought not to snatch her hand from his grasp. 'I shall look forward to dining *à deux* with my wife. This is meant to be our honeymoon, after all, even though it has been delayed. I must confess, although Charles is good company in small doses, his constant rattle does weary one after a time.'

'You have not the excitement to be back in London, milady?'

Felicity started. She had pleaded a headache, postponing her tour of Stanton House with Mrs Carter, forgetting Yvette would be in her bedchamber, unpacking her trunk.

She put a hand to her forehead. 'I have the headache, Yvette. Could you finish that later? I wish to rest,' she said, even as her inner voice berated her for allowing Richard to overset her.

Other women accepted the realities of their husbands' hedonistic lives.

How many, though, are like Mama, hiding their distress and boredom behind bright smiles?

Felicity refused to descend into despondency. She had forged an interesting life before her marriage—despite the disapproval of some—and she would continue to do so. She was not—could not possibly be—in *love* with her husband. She enjoyed their lovemaking, and she had missed it over the past week or so, but that was not love.

Yvette folded down the bedcovers and waited to help Felicity disrobe. A glance at the maid's face gave Felicity pause. The Frenchwoman had not given up, despite her disadvantages. Felicity had learned something of the deprivations of Yvette's life since the death of her former employer. Shame niggled at her own self-pity when she enjoyed so many of the advantages and privileges of her class.

'My headache has eased,' she said to Yvette. She glanced at the ormolu clock on the mantelpiece. Four o'clock. 'Let us go for a walk in the park. The exercise will refresh us both after the journey.'

'You wish to be seen with *me*, my lady?' Doubt laced Yvette's tone.

'It is customary for a maid to accompany her mistress if she wishes to go out alone, is it not?'

Mutely, Yvette touched her cheek.

Felicity chose her words carefully. 'Yvette, *I* have no qualms, as long as you will not be uncomfortable. I should much prefer your company to that of a maidservant I do not know.'

Yvette huffed aloud, then bustled to the wardrobe. 'Me, I am uncomfortable only to be seen with the lady not dressed to her very best. This makes my skills look poor. You will wear the new walking gown.'

Their delayed departure from Hampshire had given Felicity the opportunity to have some new dresses made up in readiness for their visit to London. Yvette brought forth a round gown of sprigged-primrose muslin, a pomona-green spencer, and a matching bonnet and, studying the result in the mirror, Felicity blessed her new maid's unerring eye for colour and style. She was still no conventional beauty, but the colours gave her skin a healthy glow and, privately, she did believe she looked quite striking.

The first person she saw in the park was her husband, astride a dapple-grey gelding, beside a smartly dressed woman riding a stunning light grey. Behind them were Cousin Leo, Dominic and another woman. Jealousy flared.

So this is his pressing business—riding in the park. I suppose I should be grateful he can spare some of his precious time to dine with me tonight.

Felicity waited as Richard and Dominic peeled away from the group and trotted over to greet her.

Chapter Twenty-Six

'Felicity. I had no expectation of seeing you here. I made sure you would need to rest after the journey.'

He looks uncomfortable. Who is that woman? Is she his mistress? Is that why he has not introduced me? Or is he ashamed of me?

'I felt the need for fresh air.' Felicity's temples began to throb. She forced a smile for Dominic. 'I hoped I would find you in town, Dominic.'

Dominic leapt from his horse and pulled the reins over its head. 'It is good to see you, Fliss.' He slipped into using the name he had used since childhood as he offered her his arm to lean on. 'With your permission, Stan, I shall walk with your wife.'

Richard tipped his hat. 'With pleasure, Avon. I shall see you on the next circuit, my dear.' He wheeled his horse round and trotted off to catch up with the others.

'Who is that woman?'

'That? Oh, no one in particular. I'm pleased you are back in town, Fliss. I hope you mean to visit Westfield soon. There's a problem.'

He had definitely changed the subject. Felicity's stomach hollowed. Had her nightmare begun already?

'What is the problem?'

'It's Millie. Do you remember her?'

'Of course. She went to work in Viscount Radley's household, did she not? Is she ill?'

'Not ill. She has been turned off for loose morals.'

'Oh, no! Is she with child?'

Dominic nodded. 'She refuses to name the man. Thinks he loves her and will stand by her. It appears to have been one of Radley's intimates rather than one of the other servants though.'

Unrequited love. These poor, deluded girls who believe a man's attentions equated to love. Like Emma, although at least she had not been with child.

'Do you think he will provide for her and the child?'

Dominic halted, looking at her with raised brows. 'Do you?'

They walked on, Dominic's horse plodding behind them.

'There are places, I have heard.'

Dominic might be four years her junior, but he gave her a look reminiscent of his father, and his tone was disapproving. 'What have you heard?'

Felicity's involvement with Westfield had opened her eyes to much of life outside the confines of high society. 'There are charity places, like Westfield. For unmarried mothers.'

'My lady?'

Felicity turned at Yvette's interjection. 'Yes, Yvette?'

'I interrupt, I apologize. But I know of such a place. There is a lady, she is a…how you say…a patron.'

'Who? Do you know her name?'

'I do not, but this house is in Cheapside. My friend went there. They were kind to her.'

'Dominic, would you escort me to Westfield tomorrow, please?'

'Of course. I'll call for you at two. Take care you are ready, mind, for I—'

'Yes, do not say it,' Felicity interrupted, laughing. '*Don't keep your cattle standing in the cold.*' How typical of Dominic to worry about his horses catching a chill if she should dare to keep him waiting. 'I shall be ready for you at two.'

* * *

Richard tapped at the door dividing his bedchamber from Felicity's, and entered. She was already in bed—despite the earliness of the hour—her plaited hair draped over one shoulder. She closed her book, placing it on the bedside cabinet. He could gain no clue of her feelings from her expression. Was she pleased to see him? Indifferent?

'You are quite recovered from the journey, I hope?'

'Thank you, yes. I am sorry I did not join you for dinner tonight. I dare say I would have been wise to rest this afternoon instead of walking in the park. I was quite done in when we returned.'

'It is of no matter. It is more important that you take care of your health. Did you manage to sleep?'

'I did. And Yvette brought me supper on a tray earlier, so I have eaten as well.' She looked him and up and down. The tip of her tongue moistened her lips. 'You look very smart, Richard. Are you going out?'

Was that a hint of disappointment in her tone? There was a gleam in those amber eyes of hers that stirred his blood. He sat on the edge of the bed.

'I am going to my club,' he said. It was the truth, if not the whole truth. 'I did not think you would mind, as you are indisposed.'

She bit into her lower lip. His pulse quickened. It had been a week...more...too long... He swayed closer. '*Do* you mind, Felicity Joy?' He lowered his head, aiming for her cheek.

She turned her head.

Their lips met.

She was all hot, writhing passion in his arms as their tongues duelled. Frantic fingers tugged at clothing, threaded through hair, sought out sensitive places, tweaking and caressing. His jacket was pushed from his shoulders, his immaculate neckcloth pulled loose and discarded. Small hands splayed across his chest, drifting ever lower.

He reached between them and pushed down the bedcovers, kicked them free, reached for her nightdress, tugged it to her waist. The smooth nakedness of her thighs inflamed him further, and he fumbled for the fall of his trousers, only to find her fingers there already, deftly unbuttoning, delving within to release him, stroking and squeezing.

He moved over her, feeling her moist readiness, revelling in the wanting in her half-lidded eyes as she captured his gaze.

'Now.'

This was no supplication. It was a demand. One he was happy to obey. Scented skin, warm and silky, filled his hands as he cupped peachy buttocks. She opened for him, clamping her legs around his hips. All he wanted, all he could think about, was to be inside her. Hot, wet, welcoming, he entered with no finesse, no delay, and she gasped her pleasure as she stretched to take him, and then clenched fiercely around him as he moved in urgent rhythm.

Fast and furious, they came together, her scream almost drowned out by his triumphal shout. He collapsed on her, chest heaving, sweat beading his brow and upper lip, his brain tumbling in an attempt to catch up. He had come to her bedchamber to make sure she was not ill, to say goodnight. Not to make frantic, passionate love with his wife. He had exhibited no more control than a callow youth. As his breathing slowed and his pulse steadied, he eased his weight from her.

She whimpered, wrapping her arms around him, pulling him down, kissing his ear, whispering, 'I have missed you, Husband.'

Chapter Twenty-Seven

'And I have missed you, too, Felicity Joy.'

Richard sought her sweet lips and kissed her, slowly and thoroughly, until she began to shift restlessly beneath him again.

He reached between her thighs, stroking and circling, until she arched beneath him, small cries of pleasure tearing from her lips. Pushing the neck of her nightgown aside, he sucked one nipple deep into his mouth, flicking the swollen bud with his tongue.

'Richaaaaard.' Her scream trailed into silence punctuated only by gasps as her body bowed, pushing her hips against his hand. Then one final drawn-out cry, followed by her sigh of pleasure.

He took her lips in a long, soothing kiss. She smiled sleepily, lids drooping, lips still moist from his kisses. He straightened her nightgown and tucked the covers round her shoulders. She roused.

'Are you still going out?'

'I am. It is too early for me to sleep. I'm meeting Leo at White's.'

The purse of her lips struck at his heart, and at his conscience. It would take little persuasion for him to stay, to take her in his arms and to drift off to sleep together. He had missed her and he, too, was weary. But he had a visit to make that could not be postponed.

'Sleep well, sweetheart.' He kissed her cheek.

Felicity turned over and snuggled down with a deep sigh. 'I wish you would stay.'

Her words were slurred with fatigue and Richard had to strain to catch them. The urge to stay hovered, tempting, but he banished it with a silent growl. He was in danger of falling under his own wife's spell, and that would never do. Too much dependence on another would end in pain. His parents had taught him that.

He stroked the damp tendrils from Felicity's face and bent to brush her cheek with his lips. He had not lied, other than by omission. He had every intention of going to White's first, to meet friends, to hear the latest political intrigues and to play a hand or two of cards. But he would not stay long, for he had another, more important, visit to make.

Harriet. As he tied a fresh neckcloth, casting an eye over the rest of his clothing for creases, he pondered his former mistress. He owed her an explanation, face to face, about his abrupt ending to their arrangement. She had been an ideal lover—totally discreet, good company, and a pleasure in bed—and he hoped they could part on good terms.

After a pleasant few hours at White's, Richard elected to walk the short distance to Harriet's house in Sackville Street.

'Good evening, Stevens,' he said as he entered the hallway and handed his hat, gloves and cane to Harriet's butler.

'Her ladyship is expecting you, my lord. She is in her private sitting room.'

Richard entered Harriet's sitting room—which adjoined her bedchamber and was the scene of many of their passionate encounters—wishing she had chosen a more neutral setting.

'Good evening, my dear.' He crossed the room to where she lounged on her green-and-cream-striped *chaise longue*, and kissed her outstretched hand. 'You are in good health, I trust?'

He selected a chair that provided some distance between them.

Harriet pouted her full, pink lips as she patted the upholstered seat by her side. 'Are you not going to sit here next to me, Stanton?' She paused; the silence stretched. Then she shrugged. 'I can see by your expression that you have not, after all, had a change of heart. This is truly the end of our *affaire*, then?'

'It is.'

Harriet's lids drooped, concealing her thoughts, but her firmed lips hinted at her disappointment.

'I am sorry for the manner in which I informed you of my marriage. I have come to explain in person.'

'There is little need for further explanation.' Harriet's tone and words held no hint of chagrin. 'You have wed and you do not wish to continue our arrangement—at least, for the time being.'

Richard frowned. 'Do not labour under any misapprehensions, Harry. I have no intentions of continuing with any arrangements outside my marriage, until…'

He hesitated. He could not voice his intentions because, all at once, he was no longer entirely certain what they were. At this moment, he had no thought of bedding any woman other than his wife. He felt his frown deepen. He had never delighted in bedding as many women as possible. He had always preferred to have a mistress: one woman to be faithful to, until the *affaire* ran its course and he was ready to move on.

He had not considered the years ahead when he had so blithely decided to wed. There would be no clean break in the future: if he became dissatisfied with Felicity—or she with him, he realized, with a lurch in his gut—there would be no moving on. He would remain married.

Dark-fringed, violet-hued eyes regarded him teasingly. 'Until…?'

Richard stood abruptly. 'I have something for you, Harry:

a token of my appreciation.' He delved in his pocket, withdrawing a small square box. He had visited Rundell & Bridge that afternoon, and selected a pair of amethyst-and-diamond earrings for Harriet.

Harriet opened the box. 'Oh, Richard. They are beautiful.'

'I am pleased you like them.'

He had said all he wanted to say. There was no point in lingering.

Harriet looked up. 'I am sorry to lose you, Stanton. I hope we may still be friends?'

'I hope so too, Harriet. Goodnight.'

In the hall, Stevens handed him his hat, gloves and cane. Richard bid him goodnight and headed out into the night. He turned towards Cavendish Square, lighter-hearted now he had seen Harriet.

The sudden rush of feet alerted him.

He spun round, raising his cane. Two men, armed with clubs, were upon him. He jabbed the cane, two-handed, into the attacker to his left, who doubled over with a *whoosh* of breath. Switching the cane to his left hand, Richard bunched his right into a fist, watching as the second man swung his club. Richard dodged back, then leapt in close, aiming a short jab at the ruffian's nose. He felt the satisfying crunch and squelch of connection as a cry of *'Oi, there!'* reached his ears, followed by the welcome sound of a nightwatchman's rattle.

The world went black.

Chapter Twenty-Eight

Felicity awoke and stretched luxuriously, still enveloped in the afterglow of their lovemaking. If only Richard was asleep next to her. That wave of lust…it had swept him along too. It had been more than she had dared to wish for. Seized with an urge to see him, banishing the doubts that threatened to overrule her heart, she leapt out of bed and ran barefoot to the adjoining door. Sudden shyness caused her to open the door quietly, and only just wide enough to pop her head through.

Richard's bedchamber was empty, the bed already made. She closed the door and rang for Yvette. Richard must be at breakfast. It was barely ten o'clock. Surely he would not have gone out already?

Barnes, the butler, materialized in the hall as Felicity walked downstairs.

'Is his lordship at breakfast, Barnes?'

'I do not believe his lordship has arisen yet, my lady.'

She fought to conceal her dismay. Had he not returned last night?

'I make no doubt he was out late and is now catching up with his sleep,' she said, lightly.

'Indeed, my lady.' Not by so much as a flicker did Barnes hint that he knew any different. 'Breakfast is laid out in the back parlour, if you would care to follow me?'

Various dishes—tantalizing aromas scenting the air— were displayed on the sideboard. The table was set for two. Neither place setting had been disturbed.

'There is no need to remain, Barnes. I will serve myself.'

Barnes bowed. 'Very well, my lady.'

Had Richard gone straight from her bed to that of his mistress? Sweat prickled Felicity's spine as she recalled asking him to stay. At least she hadn't begged. Had she? She had been half-asleep: a dangerous state, for was that not the time the truth was most likely to be revealed? When the weary brain did not censor the words spoken? Was she developing feelings for Richard, despite her avowal to keep her heart safe?

She bit half-heartedly into a slice of toast and butter. It tasted of sawdust. She pushed her plate aside, and drank her chocolate, then shoved her chair back. That was enough soul-searching. She would not become a victim of love. By the time she had changed and was ready to go out, shops would be opening their doors for business. She would browse the linen drapers with Yvette and, later, she would visit Westfield with Dominic. It promised to be a busy day: precisely what she needed. There were far worthier causes on which to expend her energies than an errant husband.

In her bedchamber, Felicity contemplated her reflection in the pier glass between the windows. Mayhap she was no beauty, but Yvette had helped her to see she could look better. She fingered the curls that framed her face. Her hair was already glossier, with the use of the honey rinse Yvette had concocted. And her skin almost glowed, the rosewater-and-almond-oil lotion Yvette mixed proving more effective than the Bloom of Ninon de L'Enclos her mother swore by. If her husband preferred the bed of his mistress, she would not become embittered. She would channel her energy into her own life and interests, and learn to merely co-exist with him.

The closed door between her bedchamber and Richard's taunted her. With a muttered curse, she flung across the room and threw it open. She froze on the threshold. The room was still, mockingly, empty. But the bed…was she going mad? The bed that had been so neat and smooth was now rumpled and crumpled, a head-shaped dip in the pillow.

At the knock on her bedchamber door, Felicity hastily shut the linking door, her head whirling. Had she imagined it? No, she knew she had not. And that could only mean that Richard had not slept here last night, and that his servants were protecting him.

'I shall wear the ivory walking dress with the rose pelisse,' she said to Yvette, in no mood for anyone to dictate anything to her. 'And when I have changed, please fetch your cloak and bonnet. We are going shopping.'

Felicity and Yvette, accompanied by Thomas the footman to help carry their purchases, spent a pleasant few hours strolling the length of first New Bond Street, and then Old, examining the variety of goods displayed in the shop windows. About to turn for home, Felicity was accosted by a familiar voice.

'Good morning, Lady Stanton, or should I say "afternoon" as it is, indeed, past noon.' Felicity turned to greet Charles Durant, who was bowing before her. 'Might I offer you my arm?'

'Good afternoon, Mr Durant. You may indeed. We are about to turn for home.'

'That is indeed fortunate, for I happen to be heading in that direction myself.' He crooked his arm for her. 'Is Stanton at home?'

'I cannot be certain, sir. I have been out these past two hours or more.'

'No matter. I can always wait. Or mayhap he is at his club again. I saw him there last night, but he did not linger. Two hands of cards is all, and then he needs must rush off. One can only assume he had a more pressing engagement at home,' he added teasingly.

Felicity swallowed the bile that flooded her mouth.

After a beat or two of silence, Charles said, 'I trust you have spent a pleasant morning?'

'I have indeed.' Felicity indicated Yvette and Thomas, both laden with packages. 'As you see, I have been thoroughly seduced by the contents of the shop windows.'

'They have served their purpose, then.'

Felicity raised a brow.

'The shop windows, of course: the shopkeepers display their wares in the hope of enticing passers-by into their emporia to spend. And, lo and behold, you have obliged. One buys with one's eyes in the first instance. Payment soon follows.'

'That is most profound, Mr Durant.'

'Oh, please, call me Charles. You did so at Fernley.'

'Charles, then, though I must take care to revert to Mr Durant when in company.' They crossed into Cavendish Square from Henrietta Street. 'I have no wish to incur the censure of the *grande dames* of the *ton* so early in my marriage.'

'Have you not, Felicity Joy?' a deep voice said behind them. Felicity's heart leapt, as though it might beat its way free of the cage of her ribs. 'And what, might I ask, have you been up to, to risk such censure?'

Chapter Twenty-Nine

$\mathcal{O}\!$

Richard had walked up Henrietta Street, unnoticed, behind Felicity and Charles, who were deep in conversation. Anger had flared, shocking him with its intensity. Why should the sight of Felicity on another man's arm cause such emotion?

Possessiveness. What's yours is yours. Hasn't it always been thus?

He forced a calming breath. Charles was his friend and his cousin. This was a new situation for him, and it had provoked unexpected feelings. In time, he would adjust to having a wife.

Before he could hail them, Felicity laughed at something Charles said, glancing up at him. Why could she not be so easy around him? Why was she so guarded?

Except in bed. Perhaps he should be thankful she left her inhibitions at the bedchamber door. His mind drifted back to the night before, to the willingness of her soft, yet lithe, body in his arms. What would she do—how might she react—if he were to seduce her in the middle of the day? The idea excited him, despite the dull ache at the back of his skull.

At the sound of his voice, Felicity had stiffened and her expression, when she faced him, was wary, in stark contrast to her easy manner with Charles.

'Good afternoon, Richard.'

She failed to meet his eyes, but tucked her hand willingly enough in the crook of his arm after he and Charles exchanged greetings. As they continued around the square, the thump in Richard's head grew more insistent. Perhaps it had been unwise to walk home from Harriet's house, where he had been taken after the attack last night. He had thought the fresh air might do him good.

Richard glanced down at Felicity. 'And where have you been this morning, Felicity Joy?'

'I came upon her in Bond Street,' Charles said, before Felicity could reply. He gestured to the two laden servants walking behind. 'Your lady wife has been busy spending your fortune by relieving the merchants of their wares.'

'I am pleased you have occupied your time in such a pleasant manner, my dear. I understand you are promised to Avon later today, to visit Westfield.'

'Yes, I am looking forward to it.'

'I thought I might come with you, if you do not object?'

'There is no need, Richard. It will no doubt bore you beyond endurance, and I shall be quite safe with Dominic.'

'I am sure you will.' Richard hid his irritation behind his polite rejoinder. 'However, I am curious about the place. I hope, therefore, you will indulge me by allowing me to accompany you.'

'But of course, if that is your wish.'

Her reluctance grated.

'Thank you for your company, Charles,' Felicity said, as they arrived at Stanton House. 'Would you care for some light refreshments?'

'I would indeed. Now I come to think of it, I *am* peckish.'

Richard thrust aside his exasperation. It appeared Felicity would do almost anything to avoid spending time alone with him.

After having eaten their fill, they moved into the drawing room. Felicity was waylaid by Barnes in the hallway and Richard took the opportunity to tell Charles about the robbery the night before.

'I was hit with a grappling hook.'

Charles winced. 'Painful. Did they steal much?'

'Enough. They took last night's winnings. I was lucky the night watchman came around the corner when he did. He sounded the alarm and the cowards ran off. I was taken to a nearby house to recover.'

Harriet's house. He must pray Felicity never got wind of *that* particular fact.

'I've hired an investigator to make enquiries. He'll start down at the docks. It seems logical, given they used a grappling hook.' He heard a noise by the door. 'Hush, not a word to Felicity, mind. I do not want her troubled.'

'Coz! Soul of discretion, don't you know.'

Felicity entered the drawing room, a card in her hand. 'It is an invitation from Lord and Lady Plymstock,' she said. 'Their ball is tonight, and they beg our attendance.'

'It would be a feather in Lady Plymstock's hat if you made your first appearance as a married couple at her ball,' Charles said. 'Shall you go, do you think?'

'Yes,' Richard said.

'But—'

'The sooner we become old news, the better, Felicity. People will soon find something else to gossip about.'

'I shall hope to see you there,' Charles said, as he took his leave.

When he had gone, Felicity said, 'I must go and change my clothes, ready for our visit to Westfield.'

'Wait a moment, Felicity.' Richard followed her to the door.

She had opened it and he reached across her and pushed it shut. The scent of violets tantalized his senses. He moved closer, trapping her between his body and the door.

'What...? Richard...?'

Richard lifted her chin with his finger, forcing her to meet his gaze. 'What is wrong, Felicity Joy?'

'Nothing...nothing is wrong...I just need to...'

He silenced her with his mouth, angling his head, softening his lips. 'Mmmmmm. I have been waiting to do that. Do you not like to kiss me, Felicity Joy?'

'No. I mean, yes. I mean, not now. D…Dominic will be here very soon. I must change.'

He nuzzled at her neck, mouthing at her soft skin. 'You taste and smell delicious. I will help you change your clothes. Go upstairs and send Yvette away.'

A sharp intake of breath met his words and his wife turned rigid in his arms. 'It is not appropriate,' she said sharply. 'Not when a visitor is expected at any minute.'

Richard released her.

She looked up at him, hesitated, lifted one hand to his cheek.

Then she was gone.

Chapter Thirty

A familiar tremor raced down Felicity's spine. Richard had settled one warm hand at the small of her back as they entered Peter Whittaker's study at Westfield, Dominic having disappeared into the schoolroom as soon as they arrived. Would she ever be able to control her reaction to such casual intimacies? The touch meant nothing more than common courtesy to him, but to her…every nerve in her body screamed its awareness of him, triggering a yearning deep inside her body, and her heart.

She wanted him.

Desperately.

She must resist.

A weary smile crossed Mr Whittaker's face as he rose to greet them. New lines had appeared on his face in the months since she had last seen him and his hair had noticeably thinned.

'Good afternoon, Mr Whittaker,' she said. 'It is good to see you again.'

He crossed the room, with hands outstretched. 'Good afternoon, Lady Stanton. I was exceedingly happy to hear the news of your marriage.' His gaze slipped sideways to Richard.

'Mr Peter Whittaker, this is my husband, Lord Stanton—my dear, Peter Whittaker.'

'I am honoured to meet you, my lord. I do hope you will not raise objections to Lady Stanton continuing her support of our school? I cannot tell you what a boon she has been to us these past few years.'

'I am interested to see what good works you do,' Richard replied.

He did not reassure Mr Whittaker, and Felicity realized anew how much power he held. He could prevent her further involvement with Westfield, if he chose, despite his reassurances on the night of their betrothal.

'Might I show you around our establishment, my lord? It is not large, but we do our utmost for the children in our care.'

Richard motioned for Mr Whittaker to lead the way.

'Where do you find the children?' he asked as they left the study.

'Sometimes the magistrates will recommend a child to our care, if they judge a child who comes before them to be capable of redemption. Sometimes they come from the Foundling Hospital. If we can bring them up to be useful members of society, able to earn their living, then we consider our duty done.'

'Finding such children is never a problem. The problem is in choosing which ones are in most urgent need,' Felicity said.

'I understand from my wife that you seek employment for these children, when they reach a suitable age?'

'We do, my lord; we apprentice them with local tradesmen, or we place them in households as kitchen maids and boot boys. It is then up to the individual child to work hard to better themselves. I do not believe we would place half the number of children without the invaluable help of her ladyship and Lord Avon, for they have contacts where I have few.

'Come.' He opened the door to the schoolroom and waved Felicity and Richard through. 'The children are at their lessons. They have an hour of reading and an hour of writing every day. We do not presume to make scholars of them, but I believe it is important for every man and woman to have the ability to read the Bible and to sign their name at the very least.'

'Most enlightened, I am sure.'

Richard's enigmatic comment gave Felicity no clue to his real thoughts. His subsequent silence unnerved her as he stood in the wood-panelled schoolroom, taking in the scene before him, attracting surreptitious glances from the children. Dominic crouched by a young boy's stool, pointing to his slate, murmuring in a low voice.

Jane Whittaker, smiling uncertainly, hurried over to be introduced.

'I never imagined the next time I saw you, you would be a married lady,' she said, eyes anxiously searching Felicity's. 'Are you happy?' she added in a whisper as her husband explained more of the workings of Westfield to Richard.

'Yes, of course.' Felicity had no wish to elaborate. 'Might I speak with Millie, Jane? Dominic has told me of her circumstances.'

'I shall bring her to the study.'

'If you will excuse me,' Felicity said to Richard and Mr Whittaker, 'I must talk to Millie.' She briefly explained Millie's situation to Richard. 'I know you cannot keep her here, Mr Whittaker,' she added, 'but rest assured I will find a place for her.'

'Thank you. It will be a weight off my mind. I should hate to see the poor girl forced into the seedy existence that awaits many of these silly creatures who cannot resist temptation.'

Felicity bit her tongue against a surge of fury. Why did everyone assume such events were the sole fault of the female? She knew how persuasive and silver-tongued men could be in order to get what they desired. And the gullible girls—like her beloved Emma—were left to pick up the pieces of their broken hearts.

Millie, pale and slightly built, was in the study with Jane.

'Will you not name the man responsible, Millie?' Felicity asked.

'He said I mustn't or he won't love me no more.'

Felicity closed her eyes, hearing Emma's voice, stubbornly voicing the exact same sentiments eight years before. 'Does he know you have been turned off?'

A tear trickled down the side of Millie's nose as she shook her head.

'You do know you cannot stay here, Millie?'

'But where will I go, milady? I got nowhere else to go.' Panicky hands clutched at Felicity.

'Hush.' Felicity put her arm around Millie. 'There is a house for girls like you and I shall try to place you there. But you must face facts, Millie—this man does not even know you are in trouble. And you need to understand he is unlikely to stand by his word even if he does find out.'

Sobs racked the girl's slight frame. 'Oh, milady, but I love him. He said he loved me.'

Of course he did.

'It is a harsh lesson you must learn, Millie. Men—*some* men—will say anything to get what they want. Come, dry your tears. We will not see you on the streets, whatever happens. But I would urge you to tell me this man's name.'

And what would you do then? He would laugh in your face. She's expendable: a servant, with no family.

Sheer frustration over Millie's plight churned inside Felicity. The girl would be judged a hussy and beyond redemption by most people. Looking at her blotched face and swollen eyes, Felicity silently swore not to abandon her. She would not allow Millie to sink to the same depths of despair as Emma.

Nausea choked her as the image of her sister's body, lying broken on the flagstones, filled her mind's eye. Emma had died without ever naming the man responsible for her ruin. Scandal had been averted, of course. Suicide was a criminal act as well as a sin against God. Her death had been declared a tragic accident. Felicity knew the truth, however—as did her mother. She dug into her heart for forgiveness for her mother, who had failed to protect Emma. Her foolish, selfish mother, who was now more than half-convinced that the story they had concocted about Emma's death was true.

'Well, Fliss?' Dominic demanded, once they were on their way back home. 'What will you do about Millie?'

'I shall visit the house Yvette told us about, and see if they have room for her.'

Richard, sitting next to Felicity, stirred. 'I will escort you; you are not to go there unaccompanied.'

'Thank you. I admit I should not like to go without a male escort. I had intended to ask Dominic if he might accompany me this afternoon, but I am sure he has more interesting pursuits planned.'

'It is rather late to go today, but I shall hold myself at your disposal tomorrow.' Richard's voice was weary. Glancing at him, Felicity saw him touch the back of his head, wincing as he did so.

'Do you have the headache, Richard?'

'No. The merest twinge, that is all.'

Why won't he meet my eyes? What is he hiding? Suspicions over his whereabouts last night churned her stomach.

'Well, I must say I'm grateful to you, Stan,' Dominic said. 'Helping the children is one thing, but I can't say I'm eager to get embroiled in this other business. Besides, you'll be better placed than me to curb Fliss's enthusiasm for lost causes.'

'Dominic!'

'Sorry, Fliss, but you know it's true. Especially after—' He stopped abruptly as Felicity glared at him. 'Well, you know what I mean.'

'I confess that *I* have no idea what you mean, Avon,' Richard said. 'Pray enlighten me.'

Felicity thought quickly. She was not ready to confide in Richard about Emma's disgrace.

'Dominic merely means I was determined to help at Westfield despite my family's objections.' It was no lie. She had been unwavering in her effort to find some purpose to her life. 'You heard for yourself how Mama and Farlowe feel about the subject.'

'I did indeed. An encounter I should not like to repeat in a hurry. Your forbearance in the face of such antagonism does you credit, my dear.'

Chapter Thirty-One

The Plymstocks' ball was a success. Meaning, Richard thought, with an exasperated sigh, that it was a crush. Since their arrival, he and Felicity had been the centre of attention, every guest wishing to congratulate him and to claim acquaintance with Felicity, who was in high spirits. Her peacock-blue silk evening gown shimmered in the candlelight and a matching ribbon threaded through the shining ringlets framing her smiling face

'You look lovely,' he had said, as he escorted her to their carriage earlier. 'I can hardly believe the change in you.'

She had laughed, sounding delighted. 'You should thank Yvette: she instinctively knows what will suit me. I bless the day you found her, Richard. Thank you.'

As they waited in line to be greeted by their hosts, however, she had gone quiet, clearly on edge.

'What is wrong?'

He'd had to stoop to hear her low reply. 'There is nothing wrong. I am perfectly happy, thank you.'

So subdued, of a sudden. He had noticed her eyeing the other ladies queuing alongside them. Was she still so unsure of her appearance? He had slipped his arm around her waist and squeezed, intending to reassure her. She'd jerked away. He'd felt the frown gather on his forehead. The ups and downs of her moods were a mystery to him, and he brooded over her behaviour, unable to find any logic for her mercurial changes.

Now, whatever had worried her on their arrival had been

put aside. She was sparkling, her manner easy as she conversed with the people around her and it was his turn to be on edge as he battled his unexpected compulsion to thrust away every young buck eager to write his name on Felicity's dance card. A visceral reaction, deep in his gut.

What's mine is mine, he mocked himself silently.

He masked his dismay behind his customary urbanity. Inside, he was restless. He felt...vulnerable—a feeling as unaccustomed as it was unwelcome.

She did not want to marry you. It's better not to care. Keep your guard up.

'Greetings, Coz.' Richard started at the voice in his ear. 'Your wife is in fine form, I see.'

'She is indeed, Charles.'

'It makes one wonder why she shunned society for so long,' Charles murmured, *sotto voce*.

'Meaning?'

'She was telling me of her interest in that school. I cannot help but wonder if—' Charles stopped abruptly.

Richard felt the growl begin deep in his chest. 'You wonder if...?'

'Oh, nothing, Coz. Ignore me, I beg you. It was merely... her interest in children...pure speculation, and an atrocious gaffe on my part. Not for the world would I pay attention to such scandalous rumours and, if I hear any such, I shall be sure to put a halt to them, you can rely on it. Never fear, Coz. You have me to watch your back.'

Fists clenched, Richard battled to keep his hands off his cousin. He knew Charles was a rattle, and prone to 'slips of the tongue', although he had never been entirely certain if such slips were innocent, or a deliberate attempt to stir trouble.

'I should be obliged if you would do that, Charles. And you may rest assured: if I should hear any such scurrilous tittle-tattle attached to my wife's name, I shall have no hesitation in dealing with the culprit. Do I make myself clear?'

Charles grinned. 'Eminently, my dear fellow. Sentiments exactly as I would expect of a doting husband. I shall make sure I pass on…'

'Cha-a-arles.'

Charles's blue eyes widened. 'Was that a growl, Stan? I am merely assuring you of my support. No need to take offence with me, old chap.'

'You will not speak of this to anyone else, unless they mention the subject first. Is that clear enough? I will not have my wife's name bandied about. Under any circumstances.'

'Of course not, Coz; as if I would. Very fond of Felicity, I assure you. Now, with your permission, I shall go and make my bow.'

Richard glared through narrowed eyes as Charles sauntered through the group surrounding Felicity, and bowed. Felicity's face lit up, and she handed him her card. Charles scribbled his name. Richard strode forward to take his place by Felicity's side. The sparkle left her eyes, although her smile remained in place.

'They are forming the set for the first,' he said. 'You have not forgotten you are promised to me, my dear?'

'Of course I have not forgotten.'

The change was subtle. He doubted anyone else had noticed that hint of reticence in her manner. He stroked one finger down the stiff length of her spine, tracing tiny circles. He heard her sharp intake of breath, felt her relax.

That was better, though he still could not help but contrast her caution around him to her behaviour with others.

Chapter Thirty-Two

~~~~~~

Felicity suppressed the desire that shivered through her at Richard's touch.

Is *she* here? Is she watching?

She skimmed the crowd as Richard led her to the dance floor. This growing obsession with the identity of his mistress was painful but she could not help it. He had already spent their first night in London with her. After bedding his wife for the first time in over a week he had slunk away like a…like a *thief*. Well, she would not allow him to steal her heart. Or her newfound and burgeoning self-respect. She was happiest when she was surrounded by others, and when she could forget her conjectures about Richard and his mistress—who might be here, smiling in Felicity's face whilst all the time… She thrust away her thoughts, cramming her speculations about *that woman* to the darkest recesses of her mind.

True, he had appeared to be the perfect, attentive new husband since their arrival at the ball but she could *feel* his underlying tension. She conjured up a smile as the musicians struck up the familiar strains of a Scottish reel. If Richard could put on a mask for others, then so could she.

This is torture.

Felicity had danced the two first with Richard, responding to his comments with light ripostes. Her hand had then been claimed by a succession of partners, with whom she had exchanged the usual pleasantries even as her skin had prickled with the awareness of her husband's heavy-lidded scrutiny from the side of the room. He had danced with no other. Felicity was both relieved and rattled by this. As she danced down the set, she caught his eye. Her bones almost dissolved at the heat in that glance.

'You are quiet, Felicity.' Charles was her current partner.

'It is Richard,' she whispered, as the steps of the dance brought them together. 'He is not dancing. Do you think he is bored?'

'I am sure he is not bored. He did mention a headache earlier today, but I am certain he is more than content to be here with you.'

The dance parted them. Felicity glanced again at Richard, still smouldering at the edge of the floor, brushing off any attempt to engage him in conversation. His attention was still focused on her. Desire coiled deep within her, and she missed her step.

'Steady.' Charles gripped her hand and tugged her into the correct formation. 'Do not allow Richard to unsettle you. I'll wager he'll claim your hand as soon as you have a dance free.'

Felicity continued to dance by rote, options bouncing around inside her head. Her feelings for Richard were growing stronger. The thought of him with another woman hurt. Were her attempts to protect her heart in vain? Which path should she choose to follow? Should she continue to keep him at arm's length, and risk pushing him into *her* arms? Or should she fight? Try to win his love?

Even the thought of the latter seemed ridiculous and doomed to failure. But was the first option any better? After only three weeks of marriage she could finally empathize with her mother. She had found it was nigh on impossible to deny your heart.

You will not feel affection or love for this man.

She could almost laugh at her naivety. Unless the man in question was cruel or disgusting—a man one could never respect—it would be hard indeed to share the intimacies of the bedchamber and not feel some tenderness for him. And Richard was neither cruel nor disgusting. He was kind, and thoughtful, and strong, and capable. And the most handsome, the most utterly desirable man here tonight.

But he had a mistress. What chance did she, Felicity, have?

As much chance as any woman, if you will but believe in yourself.

She danced on. New partners came and went until, about to embark upon a country dance, a large hand grabbed hers.

'Excuse me, Cheriton. Might I borrow my wife?' The rich, velvety baritone slid like warm honey through every fibre of her being. She threw an apologetic smile over her shoulder at Cousin Leo, who stared after them, eyes creased with fans of laughter. Felicity felt her face flame as Richard led her from the dance floor and headed purposefully for the door. In the hall, he turned to her.

'You look tired, Felicity Joy.'

She searched his face, reading the strain around his eyes, the weary lines bracketing his mouth, the furrows on his brow.

'Is your head still aching, Richard? Charles said—'

'Charles says too much. No, I do not have a headache.'

'Then what *is* troubling you?'

'Nothing. I am merely concerned you are doing too much.'

His effort to smooth his expression was not lost on Felicity. He put his lips close to her ear. 'I cannot wait to bury myself inside you tonight.'

As a distraction, it worked. Her belly clenched and her bones turned pliable. She moved her head, so his lips brushed her cheek.

'I am—quite suddenly—exhausted,' she said, with a tremor of anticipation. 'Would you mind very much, my dear, if we go home?'

* * *

He dismissed Yvette as soon as they reached Felicity's bedchamber. As the door closed behind her, Richard framed Felicity's face, his kiss slow, sensual. She drifted dreamily as his fingers dealt with the row of buttons fastening her gown. She squirmed closer, pushing his jacket from his shoulders. In no time, his upper torso was bare and her corset had joined her gown in a pool by their feet. Felicity splayed her fingers against his warm, muscular chest then pressed her chemise-clad body hard against him, digging into his muscular shoulders as he stroked up her thigh.

He deepened the kiss as he grasped her buttocks and lifted her. She wrapped her legs around him, clinging tight. He tore his lips from hers and strode to the bed, lowering her to the mattress, and prised her arms from around his neck.

'Look at me, Felicity Joy.'

Felicity cranked open one eyelid, the heat of lust flooding her as he unbuttoned the fall of his evening breeches. He was magnificent. And she wanted him.

'Now.'

He laughed. 'Patience, my sweet.'

She reached for him, and he backed out of reach, shaking his head, a wicked glint in his eyes, a teasing smile on his lips. As she scrambled from the bed, he dodged around to the far side. He leant forward, his fisted hands propped on the mattress.

'Do you know what I want, Felicity Joy?'

Confused, Felicity shook her head. His lips stretched in a slow, sensual smile.

'I want to see you naked.'

Her heart stopped. Lurched. Then raced into a gallop. His hands had caressed every inch of her body, as had his lips. But for him to look at her...to *see* her...

Richard straightened, his naked body exposed: erect; enticing; edible.

She wrapped her arms around her waist, trembling as his eyes pinned her to the spot.

'There is nothing to fear. I know your body. I know its feel, its contours, its strength. I have taken pleasure in your body, as you have taken pleasure in mine.' He sat on the bed and beckoned. 'Come here. Please.'

Her feet obeyed before her mind could raise a protest. She rounded the bed and stood in front of him. He tugged her closer, between his knees. He lifted her chin with one finger until she was looking in his eyes again. She suppressed a quiver: it was as if he knew her deepest fears. Her darkest secrets.

'May I?' His hands were on the hem of her chemise. Brows raised, he awaited her reply.

She nodded, her eyes snapping shut as she felt the cool of the air caress the skin of her thighs, her buttocks, her back. She lifted her arms, and the chemise was gone. Her protection had vanished. Her screen—behind which she could fool herself and her husband she was a desirable woman with the abundant curves men desired—was no more. Time froze. Behind the blankness of her eyelids she waited for the axe to fall. The only sound, above the soft crackle of the fire, was Richard's breathing. Quickening. A quiet groan, and then a mouth closed around her nipple as gentle hands slid to either side of her waist and caressed her hips and bottom.

'So delicate,' he murmured as he nuzzled first one breast and then the other. 'You have no idea how desirable you are, sweetheart.' He lifted his head. 'Look at me, Felicity Joy.'

She did. His eyes were dark and hot, penetrating deep into her soul, firing her blood. Desire flared and licked along her veins as he stroked her thigh, down, around, and up…up… Felicity threw her arms around his neck as she pressed her mouth to his, flicking her tongue against his sensual lips. He lifted her, splaying her legs as he lowered her on to his lap, filling her. Lips caressed lips, tongue caressed tongue. Hands gripped at her waist, lifting and lowering, and she caught the rhythm, rolling her hips, stroking her aching nipples against his hair-roughened chest, taking control.

Then he lifted her, laid her back on to the bed and settled between her open thighs.

'Look at me, Felicity Joy.' The third time of asking. His whisper was hoarse. Almost a plea. She opened her eyes, and he captured her gaze as he slowly, slowly entered her again. 'I want you to see me; to know this is me, inside you.

'It will only ever be me.'

He began to move.

Chapter Thirty-Three

Felicity stood in the hall of Stanton House at ten o'clock the following morning, wondering what Richard was planning. In accordance with his instructions—relayed by Yvette—Felicity was dressed for riding. She wondered what her husband was up to.

Trick opened the front door. The faint sound of hooves from outside grew louder, and then stopped as Richard appeared from the direction of his study, smiling.

'Good morning, Felicity.' He urged her towards the open door with a hand at her waist.

She walked through into a bright, sunny morning and gasped in delight. Dalton stood in the road outside at the head of Richard's huge dapple-grey gelding, Gambit, and *the* most elegant light grey mare, complete with side-saddle. The mare whickered and pawed the ground. She shook her head, sending her silvery mane rippling over her neck.

'Oooohhhhhhh.' Felicity took a hesitant step towards the mare, who lifted her head and regarded Felicity with an intelligent eye.

'Felicity; meet Selene.'

'Selene?'

'You can change her name if you wish. Selene was the goddess of the moon in Greek mythology.'

'No. It is perfect for her. She is *beautiful*. Where did you find her?'

'Do you recall our meeting in the park on Monday?'

The day of their arrival in London. Felicity pictured the

scene: Richard riding alongside a woman on a grey horse. She had barely noticed the animal, her suspicious glare on its rider. Shame began its slow ascent from the pit of her stomach.

'Dalton heard she was for sale and I had arranged to see her in the park that afternoon,' Richard continued. 'Do you like her?'

'I *love* her.' *I don't deserve her, after those horrid suspicions.* 'She is beautiful.'

Felicity held her hand out. Selene stretched her neck and snuffled at Felicity's palm. Felicity moved closer still and rubbed gently under her chin, then smoothed her hand down Selene's neck.

'Thank you. I could not have wished for a more perfect gift.'

Felicity glanced at Richard as they rode side by side through the park gates. Pride swelled: he was so handsome, and he sat Gambit as if he was born in the saddle. *'It will only ever be me.'* She quivered at the memory of those words. He still had not stayed the whole night in her bed, but last night he had fallen asleep in her arms, and she had lain awake, reluctant to miss the moment, watching him. She must have drifted off eventually, for she had no memory of him leaving but, waking in the early hours, she had reached out and felt only chilled linen.

She had risen from her warm nest and tiptoed across the room to peep into Richard's bedchamber, ignoring her stab of shame at snooping. The flood of relief when she saw him in his own bed—sprawled spread-eagled on his back, sound asleep—had been overwhelming, as had her urge to climb in beside him, and run her hands over that wide expanse of bare chest. Instead, she had crept back to her own lonely bed and spent the rest of the night dozing fitfully.

Last night had given her hope. Could he be persuaded to love her, or was she fooling herself?

'How does she feel?'

She reached to pat Selene's neck. 'Wonderful. Her mouth is beautifully soft and she is as responsive as I could wish for.'

'Let's try her paces.'

They eased into a trot and Felicity gasped. Selene's trot was as smooth as riding in a well-sprung carriage. 'It is like floating.'

'I am glad you like her: she looks superb.'

His eyes lingered a moment on Felicity. She knew she did not do Selene justice. Yvette had been brutally blunt—her old black riding habit drained her of all colour.

'The new riding habit I ordered has not yet been delivered.'

Richard reached across for Selene's rein, drawing both horses to a halt. 'Why did you say that?'

Felicity bit her lip. Could he not have let her remark pass without comment? She did not want to engage in this conversation.

'You jumped to the conclusion that I found you wanting, did you not? Did last night teach you nothing? I was actually thinking what a fine seat you have.'

'Oh.' Felicity forced herself to meet his eyes. 'I am sorry.' She widened her lips in a smile. 'Thank you for the compliment.'

He held her gaze, then shook his head. 'You hear the words I say, but you do not listen, do you? You listen to that nagging voice in your head that says you are not good enough: not worthy of my esteem, or my compliments.'

His esteem? Was that all?

That instinctive reaction solved her dilemma: she would fight for his love, for that was what she desired above all else.

Esteem was a start. Love was the goal.

The conversation had become too challenging for this early in the morning. Without volition, Felicity's fingers squeezed the reins as she nudged Selene up to the bit with her leg. With the smoothest of transitions, the mare launched into a canter from a standstill. Within seconds, Gambit was alongside. Richard grinned at her.

'You win, my dear. Lecture over. Let us enjoy our ride.'

As Richard shrugged into his coat of green superfine, he contemplated that afternoon's visit to the house for fallen women with grave doubts. At least he would be with Felicity to—as Avon so eloquently put it the day before—'curb her enthusiasm for lost causes'. And to keep her safe.

Why was she so determined to help Millie? The girl's plight had clearly touched a nerve. Charles's hint that Felicity had given birth to an illegitimate child popped into his mind…might others wonder the same? It mattered not—*he* knew Felicity had been a virgin when he bedded her.

Yvette sat on the box with the coachman, Chivers, to point the way as they drove to Cheapside. Their destination was a tall, narrow, unremarkable house in the middle of a row of identical tall, narrow houses, its front door opening directly on to the street, which was noticeably more run down than most of the surrounding streets. Richard looked around in distaste. The carriage had already attracted the attention of young lads and loiterers.

'Drive around the streets a few times, once we are inside, Chivers, I doubt we shall remain above ten minutes.'

Richard rapped on the door, which was opened by a woman of around forty summers, greying wisps escaping her cap.

'Oh!' Her hands flew up, trying in vain to tidy her hair. 'I did not expect visitors.' She eyed them uncertainly.

'Good afternoon,' Richard said. 'I am Stanton, and this is my wife, Lady Stanton.'

The woman bobbed a curtsy. 'Mrs Tasker, milord, milady.'

'Might we come in, Mrs Tasker? There is a matter we should like to discuss with you.'

'Yes, of course.'

She stood back and indicated a door on the right of the dark hallway. Somewhere upstairs a baby wailed. They went through into a small but clean parlour. Felicity glanced at Richard, who gestured for her to continue.

'I shall come straight to the point, Mrs Tasker. I am a patron of the Westfield School and Orphan Asylum, which provides education and training for orphans and destitute children and then finds work for them when they are old enough.

'One of our former girls has found herself in…in…*difficulties*.' A blush stained Felicity's cheeks. 'I understand you provide a haven for girls in such circumstances. Is that correct?'

'Well, it is and it isn't, milady. You must understand that I take my orders from the lady who owns this house and provides the funding. We help girls who have fallen from grace under certain circumstances. We do not take in girls who have behaved immorally.'

Richard could not help but ask, 'By definition, have they not all behaved immorally?'

Mrs Tasker folded her arms. 'Some girls have no choice, if you take my meaning, milord. Some *gentlemen* think nothing of abusing their position of power over these girls.'

'Indeed, and they swear to a love they do not feel, in order to take advantage of unworldly girls,' Felicity said, with a bitterness that had Richard's eyebrows shooting skyward. So vehement over the circumstances of a girl she barely knew? There *must* be more to her interest than concern for one servant girl. 'And that is precisely the case poor Millie finds herself in. She was placed in the household of a gentleman and it appears a house guest persuaded her of his love. He, naturally, is long gone and she has been turned off because of her condition.'

Mrs Tasker frowned. 'It sounds like the type of case that will interest my employer,' she said, 'but I will need to speak to her first. If she agrees, we will find the room.'

'What is the name of your employer? Might we consult with her directly?' Richard glanced at Felicity as he spoke, and she nodded her approval.

'That is an excellent idea. Won't you give us her name please, Mrs Tasker?'

'It is Lady Brierley,' Mrs Tasker said. 'Do you know her?'

Chapter Thirty-Four

Richard had suffered plenty of blows to the gut whilst sparring in the ring, but never had he struggled so to draw breath. *Harriet?* This house was *Harriet's*? And now here was a tangle, with Felicity so keen to help Millie, she was bound to want to speak to Harriet. His mind reeled with the implications.

'I confess I am not acquainted with her ladyship,' Felicity said. 'Stanton?' She turned her enquiring amber gaze on him.

'We have been introduced.' His voice rasped. He coughed to clear his throat. 'With your leave, I shall call upon her and put Millie's case.'

'I shall accompany you,' Felicity declared. 'I am certain we will have much in common. I am interested in her work here, and I should like to see if I can help.'

Richard cursed silently. He stood up. 'Come, my dear. We must not delay this good lady any longer. Good day, Mrs Tasker, and thank you for your help.'

Once in the carriage, and under way, he said, 'I did not wish to say this in front of Mrs Tasker, but I should prefer you not to become involved with Lady Brierley and her charity, Felicity.'

'You raised no objections before.'

'I thought your intention was merely to find somewhere safe for Millie. You must consider your reputation. It is not acceptable for you to associate yourself with such women.'

'If it is good enough for Lady Brierley, I do not see why…'

'Lady Brierley is not a suitable…' He paused. He could not bring himself to lie by smearing Harriet's reputation. This was not her fault. 'Suffice it to say, I should prefer you not to pursue an acquaintance with Lady Brierley. I will deal with this matter myself.'

Felicity's lips thinned. 'I should prefer to pass my own judgement on Lady Brierley. She must possess some redeeming qualities if she is prepared to help those less fortunate than herself. There are many in society—and I should know, for I have come across much prejudice from them over the years—who consider themselves pious and good Christians, but their actions do not support that view.' Her amber eyes impaled him. 'Yes, they—you *all*—attend church services on a Sunday, but as to helping the poor and weak, as the Bible teaches…*well*.'

'We shall discuss this further at home, Felicity.'

Yvette was travelling inside the carriage for the journey home and he had no wish to argue with Felicity in front of her. He was unused to opposition—he was master of his life, of his world. Felicity, the compliant wife he had bargained for, was anything but. She had her own agenda, her own opinions, and she was unafraid to voice them.

Am I too autocratic? Do I really want a wife who meekly obeys my every whim and demand?

In this instance, he had no choice. He consulted his fob watch. Half-past three already. Time was stampeding away from him. He must mollify Felicity, and then he must visit Harriet. He must nip all this nonsense in the bud before it got out of hand.

Felicity stalked ahead of Richard into the front salon at Stanton House, stripping off her gloves. He closed the door behind them.

'I insist you yield to me in this matter, Felicity.'

'What, precisely, is your objection to Lady Brierley?'

'Is it not enough that I have voiced my opposition to the acquaintance?'

Felicity—her mouth already open to argue—hesitated. She bit at her lip, then crossed the room to stare from the window, which looked out on to the square.

'I have no wish to be perverse. Can you not at least give me a valid reason for your objection?'

Her tone was conciliatory. Surprised, Richard moved to stand behind her. He cupped her shoulders, relief warring with guilt in his heart. Although he was no longer involved with Harriet, the prospect of his new wife and his former mistress becoming friends—a distinct possibility—was unthinkable. Mayhap in time—when his marriage was more settled—it would not feel so *perilous*.

'I cannot. I am sorry, sweetheart, but I will not insult the lady other than to repeat my distaste for any social intercourse between you.'

Felicity had removed her bonnet on her way through the hall, and her pinned-up hair exposed the back of her neck: vulnerable, inviting. Without thought, he leaned towards her and pressed his mouth to her soft skin. Her tremor vibrated through his fingers and he slipped one arm around her waist, pulling her back against the full length of his body.

Even as he kissed her neck, he was braced for her rejection. But she did not stiffen, or pull away. Instead, her head tilted to the side, allowing him free access. She wrapped her arm over his, caressing his fingers as a quiet sigh escaped her. He explored her neck and ear as she leaned into him.

All too soon, however, she straightened, her head snapping upright. 'Oh, no!'

Richard followed her stare and bit back a curse. Despite the veil covering her face, the lady alighting from a carriage in the street outside was instantly recognisable. A maid climbed out behind her, and assisted the wilting figure of Lady Katherine Farlowe to the front door.

* * *

Felicity ran into the hallway.

'Mama. What is wrong? Where is Mr Farlowe?'

Lady Katherine sniffed, followed by a hiccoughing sigh. Recognising the signs, Felicity clutched her mother's arm and steered her towards the salon.

'Barnes, would you fetch a glass of ratafia for my mother, please? And ask Mrs Carter to show Wilkins—' she indicated her mother's maid '—to the Yellow Bedchamber.'

Footmen were already hauling trunks in through the door. Felicity cast an anxious glance at Richard. What would he make of this intrusion? She wavered between regret at the interruption, and profound relief. It was all very well deciding she would fight for her husband's affections, but the speed of events had given her no time to mull over the consequences of that decision. One touch of his lips, and she had melted. Would his affection—his love—be conditional upon her submission to his decree in all matters? She found it hard to believe that would make for a contented marriage; at least, not for her. His edict about Lady Brierley, for instance; such high-handedness was untenable. He'd offered no reasonable explanation for his disapproval.

As soon as the three of them were alone in the salon Mama threw back her veil and flung herself into Felicity's arms, wailing. Felicity guided her to the sofa, murmuring soothing words. Barnes brought the ratafia in, and immediately withdrew. Richard had remained silent throughout, standing with one arm propped along the mantelshelf.

As Mama's sobs subsided, she allowed Felicity to coax her to sip her drink.

'Come, now, Mama,' Felicity said, patting her hands. 'I wish you will tell us what is wrong.'

'Oh, Felicity. My life is over. I am undone. How could he do such a thing? And with Verity Godalming, of all people. I thought she was my friend.'

'He? Do you mean Mr Farlowe?'

A fresh paroxysm greeted Felicity's words. Richard stirred from the fireplace. He wore the expression of a man wishing to be anywhere but there.

'If you will excuse me, my dear, it would appear you have much to discuss. I will be in my study if you have need of me.'

Felicity wished it was possible for her to beat such an elegant retreat, and then immediately castigated herself for her uncharitable thoughts. Her mother was in distress.

Yes, but she will not listen to your advice. She will end up making excuses and will accuse you of casting Farlowe as the villain.

Gradually, her mother related the whole story of her stepfather's *affaire*—'Quite blatant, Felicity, I assure you. Everybody in Bath knows'—with her mother's friend, Lady Godalming.

'I have left him, my dear. I left him a note, telling him I was coming to you and dear Stanton. But he has not come.' Tragic eyes, brimming with tears, turned to Felicity. 'I made sure he would catch up with me on the road. I even instructed John Coachman to drive slowly. But he did not come.' Another sob burst forth and she pressed a lace-edged handkerchief to her lips.

Felicity put her arm around her mother, resigned helplessness churning her insides. She had done all she could to prevent their marriage, but her mother—in the exhilarating throes of early love—would not listen to reason. There was nothing she could do now other than support Mama through the next few days—or weeks, she thought, with an inner shudder—until Farlowe arrived. And arrive he would, of that she was certain. Farlowe knew exactly where he was best off. He would arrive, with sweet words and whispered excuses and deep regrets, and Mama would allow him to coax her round. And they would return to Bath and their life together. Until the next time.

Bile rose up to burn Felicity's throat. What would happen…how might she react…if…when…Richard? She could not finish the thought. Richard was a better man that Farlowe, that was undoubtable. But he had a man's urges, and their marriage was one of convenience. They'd made a bargain. There was no love on either side.

She had been on the brink of softening, but her mother's arrival revived all those reasons as to why she must continue to protect her heart.

Chapter Thirty-Five

Richard was standing at the window of his study when Felicity sought him out, having persuaded her mother to go to her bedchamber and rest.

'How is your mother?' He turned to face her but otherwise did not move.

'Resting. I'm sorry for her unannounced arrival. I hope you do not object, but I've told her she might stay until she is reconciled with Mr Farlowe.'

Felicity remained by the door, her hands behind her back, gripping the door handle. The room gaped like a chasm between them. A fleeting wish that he would come to her and take her in his arms was swiftly banished. That intimate moment between them in the salon might never have happened, their disagreement over Lady Brierley looming large again in her thoughts.

'Of course she must remain with us. She is your mother. Is it likely she will receive Farlowe when…if…he arrives?'

'Oh, I am certain of it.' She could not disguise her bitterness. 'And I have no doubt he will come for her. Eventually.'

Richard's eyes narrowed. 'And you, judging by your tone, disapprove. You would rather see your mother permanently estranged from her husband?'

'No, I cannot wish that. I do wish, however, she had never met him.'

'Because then you would not have been forced to marry me?'

Her heart contracted painfully. 'That is not what I meant.'

'But it is true, however.'

In three long strides, Richard was in front of her, lifting her chin, searching her eyes as his head lowered. She jerked her head aside before his lips could touch hers. Richard stilled before, very slowly, straightening.

'I am going out.' His voice was devoid of expression. 'You have not forgotten we are promised to the Davenports for dinner tonight? Or should I send our apologies?'

'No, there is no need to cancel. Mama has already requested a light supper in her room tonight. She fears she will not be fitting company and raised no objection when I explained we were dining away from home.'

After he had gone, Felicity sank into the chair at Richard's desk. The chasm she had sensed upon entering the study had remained as vast even when Richard was standing right in front of her. What would their future be?

She was jerked from her thoughts some time later by a knock at the door. Barnes entered. Surreptitiously, she swiped a tear from her cheek, castigating herself for being a ninny.

'Mr Durant has called, my lady. Are you at home?'

Charles—a friendly face to divert her, exactly the remedy she needed.

'Thank you, Barnes. Please inform him I shall be with him shortly, and ask the kitchen to send up a tea tray, but do pour a glass of Madeira for Mr Durant if he would prefer it.'

Alone again, Felicity smoothed her hair back and pinched at her cheeks to give them some colour. Several deep breaths later she was ready to face him.

Charles sprang to his feet as she entered the drawing room, his grin lighting up his face.

'Cousin Felicity, your very obedient servant.' He sketched a bow.

As she approached him, his smile faded to a frown. 'Is anything amiss?'

Felicity felt her lips quiver, and Charles blurred.

'No, nothing,' she said. What was wrong with her? She had never been a weepy sort of female. She felt a sob build in her chest, and hurriedly crossed to the sofa. 'Please, sit down.'

She indicated a chair by the fire, which Charles ignored, sitting on the sofa by her side and taking her hand.

'Do not think you can fob me off with such a feeble denial, Felicity, for you are clearly upset. Is it Richard?'

Felicity snatched her hand from Charles's grasp as the door opened to admit a maid with the tea tray. After she had gone, Charles brewed the tea and poured a cup for Felicity. Her hand trembled, and the cup rattled loudly in its saucer. Her mind whirled.

'It is my mother,' she said, before sipping at her tea. 'She arrived today for a visit, and…' She hesitated. How could she explain why her mother's arrival had so beset her? She had backed herself into a corner.

'And Richard disapproves of this visit?'

'No. It is not that. He is… Oh, I do not know, Charles. I dare say my mother's arrival has unsettled me. And Richard and I…' She really should not discuss their disagreement with anyone, but this could be her opportunity to find out. 'Charles, are you acquainted with Lady Brierley?'

'I am. Why do you ask?'

'You remember I told you about Westfield, the school I am involved with?' Charles nodded, and Felicity went on to tell him about Millie, and about the house in Cheapside. '…and I need to understand why Richard is so against our meeting,' she concluded. 'Can you enlighten me?'

'She is a widow and is universally received, to my knowledge. Might Richard simply have changed his mind about your involvement with this Millie?'

'Then why would he not say so, instead of raising suspicions about Lady Brierley's character? It makes no sense. Charles, will *you* introduce us? Please? I only wish to meet her and to discuss Millie. If Richard still disapproves, I shall not pursue the acquaintance.'

'Well, I'm loath to go behind Richard's back, but I really cannot see any reason why you should not be introduced. Are you invited out tonight?'

'Yes. We go to the Davenports' ball, and we dine with them beforehand.'

'I, too, have an invitation, although not to dine. I shall invite Lady Brierley to accompany me to the ball.'

'I hope you do not object to my confiding in you, Charles? I am not comfortable either, arranging this against Richard's wishes, but he was so…so…*intransigent* that I cannot believe he will change his mind and he would not give me *any* reason why he was acting in such a way.'

'It will be our little secret, Felicity.'

Richard dashed into Stanton House to find Felicity, dressed in amber silk, waiting in the hall.

'I am sorry I am late, my dear. I was delayed.'

He had been to see Harriet, to persuade her not to offer Millie a place at the house in Cheapside. A complete waste of time. First, Harriet had kept him kicking his heels in her salon for ages. And then she had flatly refused to comply with his wishes. Although he *should* acknowledge that, in his haste to persuade her, he might have sounded a touch dictatorial.

'Why do you imagine,' she had said, 'that *your* dislike of your wife and me becoming acquainted is of more importance to me than the future of a fourteen-year-old girl in such need?'

Put like that, he had no answer.

Then, to compound his problems, Harriet's butler announced Mr Durant's arrival, begging a word. He had been compelled to skulk in the salon until Charles had been shown into Harriet's parlour. Conscious of the lateness of the hour, he had then driven his curricle home at breakneck speed, causing Dalton to gasp aloud more than once.

Richard paused, one foot on the bottom stair, looking back at Felicity. 'I like that dress,' he said. 'It suits you very well.'

Felicity blushed and a sudden image surfaced from the night before, her slender body naked and flushed as she rode him. He stifled the urge to haul her upstairs there and then. Who would have thought when he contracted to wed Lady Felicity Weston that she would stir his blood quite so effortlessly? The nights, he could not deny, were sublime.

'Thank you,' Felicity said, 'but, truthfully, you should thank Yvette. She is very talented at making a silk purse out of—'

Richard strode back to confront her. 'Do not dare to finish what you were about to say,' he said through gritted teeth. 'We have had this conversation before. It is time you stopped denigrating yourself. Look at me, Felicity.' She tilted her head up, amber eyes dark and wary. 'You have beautiful eyes, wonderfully tempting lips…' he brushed them with his own, registering her sharp intake of breath. He lowered his voice and put his lips to her ear '…and the most seductive body I have ever known.'

Felicity jerked free. 'You should hurry,' she said. 'We will be late.'

Richard bit back his anger and took the stairs two at a time. Every effort to bind them closer together was rejected. It should not bother him. It was what he had wanted in his marriage—a wife who did not cling to him or interfere in his life. The sooner she got with child the better. Mayhap then she would settle down and become the compliant, agreeable wife he had bargained for. And he could return to his sporting pursuits without guilt.

Is that truly what you want? What about love?

Love? Where had that ridiculous notion sprung from?

He slammed into his bedchamber, where Simson was waiting to help him dress for dinner.

Love was for fools. You love someone, and you lose them. Adam…his father…even his mother…oh, she was still of this world, but she did not love him as she had loved his father and brother, that was abundantly clear. No, it was far safer not to love.

Chapter Thirty-Six

Later that evening, Richard wandered into the card room at the Davenports' house. He had danced the first with Felicity, and he had marked her card for the supper dance, but her card was now full and he had no desire to dance with anyone else. He perused the occupants of the room with little enthusiasm, selected the most promising of the tables, and sat down.

Two hands of loo later he excused himself and strolled back to the ballroom. He froze on the threshold, cursing silently at the sight of Felicity and Harriet, deep in conversation, on the far side of the room. *What the...?* Had he known Harriet was attending tonight he would have stayed to keep an eye on Felicity. To keep them apart. He strode across the dance floor, ignoring the exclamations and complaints of the dancers. As he reached the other side, two pairs of eyes—one wary yet defiant, the other apologetic—contemplated him.

'Richard.'

Did her voice tremble? Good. She should be worried. Did I not expressly forbid...?

His thoughts slammed to a halt. One thing he did understand about Felicity: she would do her duty, and what she believed to be right, even in the face of his disapproval. If he had given her a good reason why she should not meet Harriet, she might have accepted it. But he had not because he could not, and now it was too late.

'Charles was kind enough to introduce me to Lady Brierley,' Felicity said. 'I believe you already know her?'

Richard hauled in a deep breath. If he wasn't so furious, he would laugh. Could this be any more farcical? 'Yes. Indeed I do. Good evening, Lady Brierley. How do you do?'

'I have remained tolerably well since last we met, Lord Stanton. Felicity has been telling me about a young girl in need of help.'

Felicity?

'Yes, and Harriet has most generously said that Millie may move in tomorrow. Is that not splendid news?'

Harriet? They're already on first name terms? Richard's heart sank. Anything he tried to do now could only worsen matters.

Conscious of those two pairs of eyes watching, he cleared his throat. 'Splendid news indeed.'

'Evening, Fliss…I mean, Lady Stanton; Lady Brierley.' Dominic joined them, bowing to the ladies. 'I believe this is my dance?'

'Oh…yes, indeed, Dominic.' Felicity smiled at him and placed her hand in his. 'If you will excuse me?' She looked from Richard to Harriet, then back again.

'Of course.' Richard watched Felicity chatter happily with Dominic as they took their place on the dance floor. Would she *ever* be that relaxed with him?

'I like her, Stanton.' Harriet's soft-spoken words grabbed his attention.

'You must not pursue the acquaintance.'

'So you said this afternoon. And I shall give you the same answer I did then. I choose my own friends. You have nothing to fear—Felicity will never find out about us from me although, if you'll take my advice, you will tell her the truth.'

'Why would I do that?'

Harriet shrugged. 'It is my experience that truth will out in the end,' she said. 'It is your decision, however.'

'Indeed it is. Thank you for your advice, but I'm sure you will understand if I choose not to follow it. Tell me how you came to be involved with fallen women, Harriet.' He had not thought to ask when he saw her earlier. 'I believe it is not common knowledge?'

'No, it is not. And I have no wish for it to become so.'

'But why these particular women?'

'They are not just any fallen women. They are the poor souls who, by virtue of their need to work for a living, find themselves unable to reject the advances of their masters. And, if they are unfortunate, those same masters turn them away when they get with child.' Her violet eyes blazed. 'Such behaviour is despicable. I am appalled by the sheer numbers of girls soiled in that way. Including, I am ashamed to admit, two of my own maids when my husband was still alive.'

'Brierley seduced servant girls when he had you? I find that hard to believe.'

'He liked them young. They were not willing bed partners. I could not prevent him, but I could repair some of the damage he caused.'

Richard's opinion of Harriet climbed a notch.

'Would you care to dance?'

'I would love to. It will make a pleasant change to dance together without fear someone might guess our secret.'

'Indeed. You did not mention you were coming here tonight.'

'You did not ask. However, that was Mr Durant's purpose in calling upon me—to invite me to accompany him. If it will make you easier, I *did* try to dissuade him from introducing me to your wife when I realized his intention.'

'I thank you for that, and I am pleased we parted on good terms, Harry, but I should still prefer you not to become too friendly with Felicity.'

'It is a pity we cannot always achieve our heart's desire, is it not, Richard?'

Afterwards, Richard watched as Felicity danced with, and charmed, a succession of young men, and he pondered the discontent rumbling deep in his gut. Was it just possessiveness, or was his wife beginning to get under his skin? Whatever it was, it made him…tense.

Charles joined him. 'Surprised to see you dancing with the lovely Lady Brierley earlier, Stan.'

Richard stiffened. 'Why surprised?'

'I was given to understand you did not like the lady.'

'By whom, might I ask?'

'Your good lady wife. When she begged me to—'

'Begged you to what, Charles?'

Charles flushed, clamping his mouth shut.

'Now, let me guess. Did she, by chance, *beg* to be introduced to the lady in question?'

'Now, Stan…'

'And, despite knowing I disapproved, you went right ahead and contrived an introduction. Am I close?'

'I only meant to help.'

'Damn you for a meddling fool, Charles. Did it not occur to you I had a very good reason not to want the two of them to become acquainted?'

As soon as the words left his mouth, Richard could have bitten off his own tongue.

'Stan! No, do not tell me! Lady Brierley? You lucky, lucky dog! Stanton prevails where all others fail!'

Richard swore silently, viciously.

'I have no idea *what* you are bleating about, Charles.'

'You and Lady Brierley. Oh, this is priceless.'

Richard grabbed Charles by the arm and hauled him into the hall, currently deserted.

'Listen to me, Charles. I can see what idea you've got into your head, but it is *not true.* Do you understand? If you *ever* breathe a word of this to anyone, you will not only ruin the lady's reputation but you will upset me. Greatly. Do I make myself clear?'

Charles grinned. 'Eminently, my dear fellow, eminently. Never fear. I would not for the world upset either of you, you know that.'

Richard eyed him, unconvinced. Maybe Charles would not upset him deliberately, but Richard knew only too well how Charles often spoke without thinking. He could only hope his cousin would soon forget all about their conversation.

'What is so very urgent that it could not wait until the end of the ball?'

Felicity waited until the carriage was under way before challenging Richard. He had announced they were leaving immediately before supper. She had seen his anger when he spoke to Charles. Had he discovered she had inveigled an introduction to Harriet? She would not apologize for it. They had similar interests, and Felicity had relished every minute of their conversation, but it appeared their friendship was—for whatever reason—unacceptable to Richard. The tension in the carriage was palpable. His tension. He was like a wild animal on the prowl.

'I thought you did not care for society parties?' he said.

'That is no reason for such an abrupt exit.'

The carriage halted outside Stanton House. Once in the salon, a seated Felicity watched as Richard paced the room, occasionally thrusting his hand through his hair.

Attack is the best defence.

'Why do you not like Lady Brierley?'

He halted. His eyes narrowed. 'I do not dislike her.'

'Disapprove then. I noticed your *disapproval* did not preclude your dancing with her.'

'It would have been ungentlemanly to leave her standing there, after you went off with Avon.'

'You were angry with Charles for introducing us.'

'I'm angrier with you for persuading him to do it.'

'I had no choice. You would not offer a good reason why

I should not meet her. I ask you again—why do you not like Lady Brierley?'

His jaw set, lips a thin line. Felicity felt her frown gather.

'What are you not telling me, Richard?' She held his gaze. Read his frustration as his brow lowered. It was clear he was unused to having his decisions questioned. Felicity was equally clear in her own mind, for the sake of their future together, that she was entitled to understand *why* his decisions were reached.

'This conversation is at an end. I am going out. Goodnight.'

No kiss. No kind word or softened glance before he strode from the room. Felicity's heart sank all the way to her toes. If she had thought she could cajole or even force her husband to take her into his confidence, she had been badly mistaken.

The distance between them gaped wider than ever.

Chapter Thirty-Seven

Felicity rounded on her mother. 'Please, Mama, tell me it is not true.'

Lady Katherine's mouth set in a mutinous line. 'Do not take that tone of voice with me, Felicity. Why should it not be true, pray? Mr Farlowe does not owe Miss Bean anything.'

'But you promised you would take care of Beanie.' Tears choked her voice as Felicity paced the room.

'Tsk. She is a servant. Anyway, I dare say she will be very content, living with her niece in Bristol.'

'A niece she barely knows, who has four children squeezed into a tiny cottage, and a husband who works in the shipyard. How did you suppose they would manage when an elderly, half-blind relative was delivered to their doorstep? Always assuming, of course, that you did not expect poor Beanie to travel to Bristol on the stagecoach?'

'Would someone care to enlighten me as to what is going on?'

Felicity spun round. Richard was at the drawing-room door, brows raised. Her first thought was how drawn he looked.

It was three weeks since Lady Katherine had arrived on their doorstep; three weeks since Felicity had met Harriet; three weeks in which their attempts at communication had grown more stilted by the day.

Mama's constant laments about Farlowe continued to fuel Felicity's fears for her own future and her friendship with Harriet was a festering wound between her and Richard, his disapproval turning any talk of Westfield or the house in Cheapside into an argument. He had spent more and more time away from home.

'It matters not, Richard. It was something and nothing.'

He directed a sceptical look at her.

'That is correct, Stanton. Felicity is always creating a drama out of humdrum events. There is nothing to be—'

'I believe I heard Beanie mentioned? She was your maid, I seem to remember, before we married.'

Felicity bit her lip and nodded.

Richard switched his attention to Mama, who returned his look with wide-eyed defiance. 'Miss Bean will be more comfortable with her own family than remaining with us.'

'And are those your sentiments, Lady Katherine, or those of your husband?'

Mama's cheeks blossomed pink.

'I recall a promise given by you to Felicity, on the day of our wedding—a promise to take care of Beanie.'

'It is not my fault. Miss Bean raised no objection.'

'How could she possibly object? How could she stand up to my stepfather? She is frail and half-blind. You were supposed to protect her from him.' *Like you were supposed to protect Emma.* A sob bubbled up her throat and escaped her lips. She clamped her hand over her mouth and turned to the window, desperate not to cry.

A hand touched her shoulder. 'Hush, Felicity.'

How long was it since he had called her 'Felicity Joy' in that special way…the deepening voice…the delicious shiver of anticipation it elicited? They were more than ever like two strangers, living in the same house.

Unrequited love.

'We will find Miss Bean,' Richard said. 'There is plenty of space at Fernley, or there is a vacant cottage in the village she can have, if she prefers. You can ensure her well-being for yourself.'

Relief flooded her. 'Truly? I can go and find her and bring her home?'

'No. *I* shall go and find her. After I have escorted you and your mother to Fernley Park.'

'But—'

A long finger tilted her chin. Dark brown eyes drilled deep into her soul. A flutter of arousal reminded her how much she missed his nightly visits. Only once had he come to her since the Davenports' ball. He had not stayed afterwards: he had dressed again, and left the house, leaving her heartsore and suspicious and desperate. She longed to feel the comfort of his strong arms around her.

'No "buts", Felicity. You must be at Fernley to help Beanie settle in.'

'Of course.' She must write to Harriet, explaining the change of plans. Mayhap returning to Fernley would help mend some of the distance between her and Richard. And it would take him away from that harlot of a mistress; help to soothe the fearsome jealousy that seized Felicity whenever he deposited her at home after an evening out and went straight out again, leaving her to listen to her mother lament the fickle nature of men.

'Where does Miss Bean's niece live?' Richard asked Mama.

'Oh, in Bristol somewhere.' Lady Katherine waved a dismissive hand. 'John Coachman will know. He took her there. You see, Felicity. There is no harm done. Dear Stanton will ensure Miss Bean is taken care of.'

Felicity closed her eyes, willing the retort that battered at her lips to remain unsaid. Mama was...well, Mama. Felicity should have known that promise to take care of Beanie would last precisely as long as it took Farlowe to object to the arrangement. Mama's only aim in life was to agree with her husband in the vain hope she would become as essential to his happiness as he was to hers.

'It is not Richard's responsibility, Mama, but—' she smiled at him '—I thank you for making it so.'

'We will leave at ten tomorrow morning,' Richard said.

Richard stirred and stretched, easing his stiff muscles, as the carriage finally turned in at the gates of Fernley Park. He was alone in the carriage, Felicity having joined her mother for the second half of the journey, after they had stopped for refreshments at the White Hart in Bagshot.

He did not blame her. The atmosphere in their carriage had been thick with words unspoken. He gazed out of the window at his familiar home. Maybe here, without all the distractions of town life, he and Felicity might grow closer again. They had appeared on the verge of a new understanding, just before her mother had arrived and Felicity had met Harriet, but since then they had once more become strangers. He could not deny his share of the blame. He had thrown himself into his old way of life—visiting his club every day, boxing at Jackson's, fencing at Angelo's, shooting at Manton's—seeking any distraction so he did not have to address the complex swirl of emotions his wife provoked within him.

He alighted at the same time as Lady Katherine's carriage pulled up behind. A footman hurried to open the door, and Richard handed first Felicity and then her mother from the carriage. Felicity avoided looking at him, merely murmuring her thanks.

'Mama is not well,' she said as they entered the hall. 'If you do not object, I will see her settled and then I shall retire myself. I am very tired, and it is late.'

'I have no objection.'

He was tired too. There was a decanter of brandy in his study with his name on it. A couple of drinks and a good night's sleep was what he needed. He had another long day ahead of him tomorrow, travelling to Bristol to find Beanie.

Lady Katherine clutched at Richard's arm with urgent

fingers. 'Stanton; you must instruct the servants to inform me *the minute* Farlowe arrives.'

Richard patted her hand. 'You may rest assured they will do so.'

Lady Katherine's maid helped her to the stairs, where Mrs Jakeway waited to show her to a guest room.

Felicity flicked a glance at Richard. 'Mama is concerned my stepfather will arrive at Stanton House and not know where she has gone when he finds the knocker removed from the door.'

'Barnes will tell him soon enough. Always supposing Farlowe has enough nous to enquire at the tradesmen's entrance.'

Was that a glimmer of a smile? It was gone in a flash, and he could not be sure.

'Goodnight, Richard.'

He watched her walk up the stairs, struck by the weariness of her movements.

'Welcome home, my lord. Is there anything you need?' Trick was at Richard's shoulder.

A compass capable of navigating a female's mind?

'No, thank you, Trick. It is good to be home.'

Richard went to his study and sat at his desk, but could summon no enthusiasm for the mound of correspondence awaiting his attention. Instead, he leaned back in his chair and pondered his wife and their marriage.

An image arose: Felicity, turning from him, rejecting his advances. She had been reluctant to wed him from the first. Was her pleasure in their coupling a cynical ruse? Once she got with child, would she turn from him as unequivocally in the bedchamber as she did the rest of the time?

Papa. Mother. Felicity. They have all rejected you. Stay strong. Don't weaken. It will only cause more pain.

He swallowed past the lump constricting his throat.

It was safer not to care.

Chapter Thirty-Eight

Three days later Felicity dropped her embroidery and rushed outside at the sound of Richard's return. She had missed him more than she would have thought possible, and not only because the effort of keeping the peace between his mother and hers had proved exhausting. For two ladies who disagreed on almost every issue, their insistence on exchanging daily visits was incomprehensible to Felicity.

She drank in her husband's tall, muscular frame as he climbed from the carriage, his brown hair tousled, his expression…she peered closer. Her spirits plummeted. He looked livid: his brows almost meeting across the bridge of his nose, his lips a tight line. Did he regret his impulsive offer to travel to Bristol for the sake of her old nurse?

When he saw her waiting, his scowl lifted. A fraction. 'Good afternoon, Felicity.'

His voice was a deep, reassuring rumble, enfolding her like a warm blanket. Felicity felt her own expression relax into a smile. Whatever had annoyed him, he did not blame her. Her resolution to heal the divide between them grew.

'I am pleased to see you, Richard.'

His brow twitched. 'Well, I am pleased that you are pleased,' he said, and smiled. 'And there is someone else here you will be pleased to see, no doubt.'

He leaned back into the carriage and Felicity could hear him murmuring. Then he straightened, and lifted a frail figure to the ground.

'Beanie…' Felicity wrapped her arms around the elderly

lady '…I am so happy to see you. You must be tired after your journey. You will stay here for a few days to recover your strength, and then we shall decide where you would like to live permanently.'

'Oh, my lamb.' Wrinkled hands cupped Felicity's cheeks. 'I am so pleased to see you.' She lowered her voice. 'You have a good man there, my dear. Not like your poor mama.'

She half turned towards the carriage as she spoke. Movement caught Felicity's eye as Quentin Farlowe's tall, rangy form sprang from the vehicle. One glance at Richard confirmed the cause of his bad mood.

'I say, this is an impressive pile, Stanton. No wonder you can offer pensioners homes for life. Good afternoon, Felicity.'

'Farlowe! My darling, you have come for me at last.' Lady Katherine tumbled from the house and launched herself at her husband. 'Oh, I have missed you so. Come. You must be exhausted. I shall instruct Jakeway to make up the room next to mine.' She turned to Richard. 'It is most fortuitous you had to go to the West Country, Stanton, for now all has been resolved most satisfactorily, has it not?'

Felicity watched her mother and Farlowe disappear inside the house, then glanced at Richard's frowning face. 'I will talk to Mama, and ensure they leave tomorrow.' She hesitated, suddenly shy. 'Thank you for fetching Beanie. I must go and settle her, but I am *very* pleased to see you.'

The following morning Felicity sat in her private sitting room, staring from the window at the overcast sky as she twisted her handkerchief in her hands. What was wrong with her? She was constantly weepy, with no energy or enthusiasm for anything—as grey and dull as the weather outside.

Her pleasure at Richard's return had been short-lived. Between keeping the peace between her mother and the dowager—who had been invited to dine with them—and between Richard and Farlowe, she had been exhausted by bedtime. As she climbed the stairs, she had tripped and, had Richard not been behind her, might have fallen. He had swept her into his arms and carried her upstairs, placing her gently on the bed.

'You look exhausted. Get some rest. I will see you in the morning,' he had said, before leaving her to Yvette's care. How she had longed for him to return. To take her in his arms and hold her; to reassure her that they would resolve their problems.

At a tap on the door, she straightened and swiped at her eyes.

'I wondered where you were hiding, my lamb. I hope you do not mind me coming in?'

Beanie hobbled towards Felicity, a small brown book in her hands.

'Of course not, Beanie. Did you sleep well?'

'Oh, yes. Like a babe in arms. Such a comfortable bed, after…' Beanie pursed her lips, shaking her head. 'No, I will not complain. Jeannie was so kind to me. It is not her fault they have so little room.'

'No, indeed.' A tide of shame washed over Felicity. What right did she have to sit there moping, when there were women like Jeannie, struggling their way through life? 'Sit down, won't you, Beanie?' She patted the sofa next to her.

'Thank you, my dove, but I only came to give you this.' She held out the book.

Felicity eyed it. 'What is it?'

'Emma's diary.'

'Her *diary*? I did not know she kept a diary. Where did you find it? How long have you had it?'

'I saved it for you. Your mama, she told me to burn it, when we found it.'

Felicity's hand trembled as she reached for the diary. 'What does it say? Have you read it?'

'You know I cannot read well enough for that, my lamb,

and your mama… It upset her too much to finish it but she
told me it was about *that* summer. That is when I decided I
must save it for you. I thought *someone* should know Emma's innermost thoughts.'

'You did the right thing.' Memories flooded back. Desperate, heart-wrenching memories. Felicity's throat ached
and the book blurred as she stroked the fine-grained leather
cover.

'Why did you not show me this before?'

'I could not. Your mama said it was *detailed*, and you
were so young and innocent. I hid it away and I forgot about
it, until I packed my things to go to Bristol.' Beanie laid her
hand briefly on Felicity's head. 'I hope I have done the right
thing by giving it to you now. I know I should not like to re-
live that time, but I thought it important for you to read it.'

After Beanie had gone, Felicity read Emma's diary, stopping frequently to mop her eyes and blow her nose. Her sister's words brought her to life in a way no mere memory
ever could, and Felicity suffered the pain of losing her all
over again.

She was staring numbly out of the window, the diary
clasped in her arms, tight to her chest, when Richard walked
in.

'Felicity, there you are. It is time…' In two strides, he
was by her side, kneeling down, clasping her hands. 'What
is it? What is wrong? Are you unwell? Shall I send for the
doctor?'

Felicity gulped, then forced a laugh. A doctor could not
cure what ailed her. Part of her wanted to curl into a ball and
never think about Emma and the agony of her loss again;
another part of her…*that* part raged and fought and rattled
the bars of the cage around her heart. It longed to break free:
to talk about Emma—her disgrace and her death—and to
try to make sense of it all.

'I am upset. Not unwell.'

'Is it Farlowe? Tell me, for—stepfather or no stepfather—

it would give me the greatest pleasure to plant him a facer before they go.'

How could she tell him? But how could she not? Her emotions swirled and whirled, dizzily fast. She must talk to someone. Her mother? Impossible. Beanie? It would be unfair to resurrect such painful memories. Could she trust Richard? His face swam before her: concerned, kind. He had never been anything but kind.

Her husband. They were bound together, were they not? Surely he would not sully Emma's name by revealing her scandal and her sin to the world?

Chapter Thirty-Nine

'Felicity, if you do not tell me what is amiss, I shall send for the doctor.'

Felicity took an audible breath. 'Beanie gave me this.' He noticed for the first time the book she clutched. 'I did not even know it existed.' She sounded dazed.

Richard took the book, turned it over in his hands, opened it.

'It's a diary. Whose is it?'

'My sister, Emma's.'

Emma. All he knew of Felicity's sister was that she had died after her first Season.

'What did she write to upset you so?' He read the first entry. It began with a date in March 1802. He flicked through the pages, all written in the same neat, feminine hand. It was three-quarters full, ending in the December of the same year.

He sensed Felicity's eyes on him. 'Read it. That last entry.'

Some of the words were faded by tears that had been shed as they were written. There were fresh splodges on the page. Still damp.

I cannot go on. There is no hope left. He will never return to me now. He is gone. All the light and the colour have gone from my world. I pray to God to forgive me and to watch over my beloved family. I am sorry.

'She killed herself?'

Felicity nodded. 'Herself…and her baby.'

'She was with child?'

Felicity moaned as fresh tears poured down her face. 'I didn't know. She didn't tell me. She went up to the roof and…and…' Her voice trembled. 'I…I found her… Oh, dear God!'

Her hands flew to hide her face. Richard gathered her into his arms, rocking her and stroking her hair as scalding tears soaked his shirt. Suddenly, she stiffened and pushed away.

What now? Am I now not allowed to comfort her when she is in distress?

'Urrrgh.' Hand clapped to her mouth, Felicity shot up from the sofa and through the door into her bedchamber.

Richard followed. She was leaning over the basin on the washstand, heaving. His arm around her waist, Richard supported her until she finally stopped retching, then dipped a cloth into the jug of water on the stand and wiped her face. A glance into the basin revealed no solids.

'Have you not eaten this morning?' He picked her up and laid her on the bed, hitching his hip to sit on the mattress facing her, stroking her hair back from her ashen face.

'I could not face breakfast.'

'Have you been sick before?'

'I was sick yesterday, after breakfast.' Her eyes rounded. 'Do you think…?'

He pinched her chin, smiling at her incredulous expression. 'Do you not know? When were your last courses?'

Her face fired red. 'Not since before we left for London. Oh! How wonderful, if we are to have a baby already.'

Wonderful? Yes, but… Richard studied Felicity. *Will she now withdraw completely? At night as well as during the day?*

Her eyes darkened. 'I do not want to tell anyone. Not yet, until we are certain. And not my mother… Not now.

Not so soon after reading Emma's diary…it brought it all back, so vividly.'

'We will say nothing before they leave. You can write and tell her your news when you are ready.'

'I tried so hard not to blame her for failing Emma. If only she had chaperoned her, as she should have done.'

And yet, despite Lady Katherine's neglect and Felicity's anger, there was still love in their relationship.

Regret wormed its way into Richard's thoughts. Neither Adam's death nor his father's had been his mother's fault but, somehow, there was this awkward gulf between them. Words left unsaid; emotions left unexplored.

Suicide.

The word revived all the horror and pain of Papa's death. A sin and a crime. To be hushed up at all costs, and never spoken of again.

'My father also committed suicide.' He had not intended to blurt it out, but the words were out there now, tainting the air. He studied his hands, clenched in his lap. 'He could not bear to live, after Adam died. I always regret…' He paused. His innermost fear. Could he reveal it?

'You regret…?' Soft-spoken words; delicate hands—warm—covering his.

His thoughts spilled in a rush. 'He lost one son. But he had another. And I could not make up for his loss. I was not good enough for my father to want to live.'

The words were out there, in the open, screaming of his failure as a son. He had let his father down. Voicing that failure had exposed his vulnerability. He was a man. How could he be so weak?

'Oh, Richard.' The mattress dipped as she knelt up. Her arms enfolded him, comforting, and her soft cheek rubbed against his. 'I'm sure that is not true. People…in grief… they sometimes behave…they do things they would not do if their minds were not overset. Like Emma. Another day, maybe even another hour of that day, and she would not have jumped. But, in that split second…it was the only way she knew to be free of the pain.'

Richard scrubbed his hands over his face, then wrapped his arms around his wife.

'Thank you.' He mulled over what Felicity had said. He was comforted by her support but she did not know the whole. It was not only his father, but his mother too. The way she had withdrawn from him. No matter what he did, he had never been good enough for her. But that was his cross to bear. He would not burden Felicity.

'Will it distress you to tell me more about Emma? In her diary, she writes of a man. How did she meet him? Who was he?'

Felicity drew a shaky breath. 'Until today, all I knew was she had fallen in love with a man who seduced her with promises and lies and then deserted her. She says in her diary that she wrote to tell him she was with child, believing he would return to her. He never replied.

'So young, so foolish, so blindly *trusting*. Believing the strength of her love would conquer all. Just like Mama. Stupid! Stupid!' A fresh wave of tears shook her. 'And now… the diary…*still* she is protecting him. She does not name him. Not once. "M" she calls him.'

'Where did she meet him?'

'At a house party, the summer after her first Season.'

'How on earth did he get close enough to a young innocent to seduce her? What was your mother doing? I presume she was chaperoning Emma?'

'She was meant to be. Mama does not always show good judgement of others.' Her voice hitched. He could feel the effort it took for her not to break down again. 'Poor Emma. I never knew she was with child. I thought she killed herself because he broke her heart.'

'Your poor sister.'

'She was not a bad girl.' Felicity wriggled free of his embrace, anxiously scanning his face.

'I do not condemn her,' Richard said. 'Your mother, however—'

'I have tried so hard not to blame her but, deep down, I do. I always have done. And then I feel guilty, for thinking of my own mother in such a way. Oh, I do not expect you to understand.'

But he understood only too well. He had tried to be a good son, but the pain of knowing his mother could never love him as much as she'd loved Adam had driven them apart. And if his own mother could not love him...

A tap at the door, and Yvette came in, her eyes apologetic. 'Beg pardon, milady—' She got no further.

'There you are, Felicity.' Lady Katherine brushed past Yvette with a barely concealed grimace of distaste. 'I do declare you are the most thoughtless girl alive when it comes to your family. We have been waiting this age to leave. Dear Farlowe has come all this way to take me home, and you needs must leave him kicking his heels awaiting your convenience. And you, Stanton...' she wagged her finger at Richard. His temper simmered '...I thought you came to fetch Felicity and here you are, making love to your wife instead of attending to the needs of your guests.'

'We are coming now, Mama,' Felicity said.

How did she remain so calm in the face of such provocation? Renewed respect for his wife's strength of character warred against his longing for Felicity to stand up to her mother's tyranny. For that is what it was. What child could withstand the mental onslaught of a disparaging parent without starting to believe that criticism? That Felicity had grown into such a kind, thoughtful and caring young woman gave witness to the goodness of her heart.

He held out his arm for Felicity and they followed her mother down the stairs.

Chapter Forty

It was a relief to wave goodbye to Mama and Mr Farlowe as their carriage rumbled down the drive of Fernley Park. And a *profound* relief that she had not voiced the rage burning inside.

Richard's incredulity had eased Felicity's guilt for that rage, and had allowed her to view the full extent of her mother's failure in her duty to protect Emma, whose beauty had inevitably attracted male attention of the worst kind. She had been flattered into falling in love and, with no one to stand sentinel, she must have been as vulnerable— and as innocently unaware—as a newborn fawn circled by hungry wolves.

'Come…' Richard's arm wrapped around her waist, and she leaned into his embrace '…let us go indoors. You must be cold.

'Trick?'

'Yes, milord?'

'Please bring some tea and something to eat to the salon. Her ladyship is hungry.'

Felicity opened her mouth to protest, but remained silent as Richard's arm tightened on her waist. When Trick was out of earshot, he murmured, 'It is possible you have two mouths to feed now, Felicity. You will oblige me by not starving yourself. If you are unable to face large meals, at least promise you will try to eat little and often, to keep up your strength.'

* * *

A few weeks later, Richard's insistence on cosseting Felicity to an almost excessive degree was driving her to distraction. He had even sent for the family's London physician, despite it being too early for Sir Roger to be able to fully establish that Felicity was with child. Her symptoms were, however, consistent with that condition.

'I will be perfectly safe on Selene,' she protested, when he came upon her in the stables, about to ride to the village to visit Beanie in her new cottage.

'I will order the carriage. Sir Roger—'

'*Sir Roger* advised me to take light exercise and to get plenty of fresh air. He *said* it would help my appetite.'

'That is a low blow, Felicity Joy, knowing I worry about how little you eat.'

Felicity Joy. Her heart leapt. It was a long time since he had called her that. Longer even than he had remained absent from her bed. Did he believe he would somehow damage the baby if he lay with her, or was there another reason for his lack of interest? Felicity had, with much blushing, asked Sir Roger if the baby would be hurt, and he had been most reassuring. But she had not yet plucked up courage to tell Richard.

And now, he appeared to want to ban her from riding Selene until after the baby was born.

'Do you not trust my common sense enough to believe I would never put myself or our baby in jeopardy?'

'If you should fall—'

'I will *not* fall. Have you so little faith in my ability as a horsewoman?'

His brow remained furrowed. 'I cannot spare the time to escort you. What if—?'

'I do not need your escort, Richard. Selene is completely trustworthy and I shall have a groom with me. I promise the most I shall risk is a slow canter—no galloping and no jumping. I am as concerned as you are for the baby's welfare, but I cannot stay cooped up for the next seven and a half months.'

'I shall teach you to drive,' he said, his frown clearing. 'Then you will not feel so penned in.'

'Well…I cannot deny it is a skill I should like to learn, for I have never driven anything apart from Boxer, our old cob, before…but that is a separate issue. I enjoy the exercise I get on horseback, so I should like to continue riding until it becomes uncomfortable.'

'Very well.' Richard heaved a poor, put-upon male sigh. 'But *please* promise you will take care. You, Harry…' the groom straightened from tightening Selene's girth '…are you accompanying your mistress to the village?' Harry nodded. 'Woe betide you if any harm befalls her, then.'

Harry grinned. 'She'll be safe with me, milord.'

'She had better be. Hold the mare steady, will you?'

Harry moved to stand at Selene's right shoulder, holding the reins with one hand and steadying the saddle with the other.

Strong hands settled at Felicity's waist. She had barely thickened, but she gratefully dispensed with her corset whenever possible. His intake of breath and the widening spread of his fingers suggested Richard had just discovered that fact. She looked up to see almost-black eyes boring into hers. She gasped when he pulled her closer, his thumbs brushing the underside of her breasts. Under her habit her nipples tightened into hard buds and arousal fluttered deep inside. Then, before she quite knew what was happening, she was in mid-air, being swung into the saddle.

Harry went to fetch his own mount, and Richard held the mare as Felicity hooked her right leg between the pommel and the second horn of the side-saddle, and found the slipper stirrup with her left foot. Selene fidgeted and fussed beneath her until she gathered the reins and settled her.

'Ride carefully, my dear. You carry a precious cargo.'

How can I forget? She watched Richard stride away

from her, down the path towards the house. The width of his shoulders strained at the centre seam of his jacket and accentuated his narrow hips as his long, muscled legs, sheathed in tight breeches and gleaming topboots, covered a yard or more of ground with each pace. She swallowed a sigh as she arranged the skirts of her new olive-green riding habit.

Her husband hardly seemed to notice her presence these days, unless it was concerning the baby. Their days had settled into a humdrum existence of running the household for her and overseeing the estate for him. At least, if he did teach her to drive, they would spend more time together. Always supposing he did not delegate that chore to Dalton or one of the other grooms.

She had hoped their shared confidences about Emma and Richard's father might draw them closer, but it appeared to have had the opposite effect on Richard. He had grown more distant, not less, much to Felicity's frustration. He had flatly refused to discuss his father's suicide, or his feelings about it, and he had become adept at avoiding her company. Except, she thought, with an inner *hmmph*, when he deemed her in danger of risking her health, or that of the baby.

Cast around as she might for a solution, the only one to come to her was one she was unwilling to take. The thought of taking the initiative and visiting him in his own bedchamber brought her out in a cold sweat.

What if she took the risk, and he still did not want her? What if her fears were proved correct and, now he had got her with child, he had no further use for her until his heir was born? There was no longer any need for him to fabricate any interest in her or any pleasure in her company. Cold dread settled in the pit of her stomach. Was she doomed to follow in her mother's footsteps after all?

As soon as Harry was mounted, Felicity nudged Selene into a trot and they clattered out of the yard. She could do little about her feelings for Richard—whatever they proved to be—but she determined then and there never to sink into despondency.

Mayhap the promised driving lessons would bring them closer together?

Felicity's mouth set in an uncompromising line.

'What is wrong?' Richard indicated the pony and gig standing patiently in the yard. 'George is very docile. He—'

'When you offered to teach me to drive, I assumed it would be a pair. I already possess the skill—if that is what it is—to drive a pony and gig.' Narrowed amber eyes glared at him. 'I expected a challenge.'

'But you are—'

'*If* you say—once more—"but you are with child, my dear", I swear I shall scream.'

Dalton, at George's head, was studying the sky, whistling through his teeth. Richard took Felicity by the arm and marched her out of the stableyard to a nearby bench.

'Sit!'

She did, averting her head and sticking her nose in the air, two bright spots of colour staining her cheeks.

He hovered a moment, then sat beside her. A little too close, their upper arms touching. He could not risk shifting away. It would be too blatant. But to be touching her, so close he could smell her violet fragrance and, beneath that, her own unique, woman scent… He gritted his teeth.

'How often have you driven, Felicity? And how recently?'

She stilled, holding her breath. Then slumped. Glanced at him through her lashes. 'Not often. Not recently.'

A grudging admission as delicate fingers plucked at her skirts. Richard tamped down the urge to take her hand, the old uncertainties plaguing his gut. Ever since he had confided in Felicity about his father, and exposed his deepest fear that he was not good enough for his father to want to live, the old wounds of vulnerability and inadequacy—wounds he had believed long healed—had reopened. A single crack in his outer shell of strength and confidence, a crack that was raw and bloody, and deeper than he had ever realized.

'It is not like you, to fly up into the boughs so readily.'

'No. I'm sorry. I…' She paused. 'No, you're right. I'm sorry.'

What had she been going to say? He wished she had not stopped. He studied her, head bowed. He hated this awkwardness…the things unsaid between them. What was she thinking? Why could he not take the risk, and talk to her of the things that mattered? She was a good woman. She would not reject him, like his parents.

Would she?

She rejected you before. Many times. She only married you because she had no choice. The devil riding his shoulder, on constant alert, raked him with its spurs. It ensured he never forgot; never weakened.

He loathed this indecisiveness, this cowardice. It was not like him. Why did he feel so vulnerable with Felicity? He buried any urge to expose himself further. Risking another rejection was a risk too far.

'*If* you had allowed me to explain,' he said, cringing inside at the pomposity of words that revealed nothing of the doubts plaguing him, 'you would know that George is merely the starting point. We will progress to a pair, you have my word.'

He knew what he wanted.

She was his wife. She would be the mother of his children. But that was no longer enough. He also wanted her as his friend and his companion. As his lover. He wanted her on his side. No…he wanted them to be on the same side. Partners.

The question was: what did she want?

Chapter Forty-One

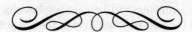

When the winter weather permitted, Felicity's lessons continued, and she began to cherish the time she spent with Richard. They chatted about the weather, the scenery, the estate, mutual acquaintances…any subject, in fact, that could not be construed as personal.

After a few days of driving the placid George, Felicity walked into the yard to find a large bay gelding harnessed to the gig. She received an inkling of the test to come as she manoeuvred horse and gig out of the yard gate.

'Get over, Trusty.' The horse seemed intent on scraping the gig against the gatepost. Thankfully, they exited the gate without damage to either gig or post.

'Well done.'

A sideways glance revealed Richard's fists relaxing.

Felicity drove Trusty down the lane at a spanking trot, whip ready in her left hand as the horse revealed a tendency to drift towards the nearside. 'Whoever named him Trusty has a sense of humour,' she said. 'Is that why I am driving him today? To see if I can cope with a less obliging animal than dear old George?'

'Indeed. For if you cannot control a wilful sort like Trusty, how will you cope with two?'

'So you intend to send me out with *two* wilful animals in the future? You do surprise me.'

Richard laughed. 'Not deliberately. But you know what flighty animals horses can be. If one imagines he sees a monster in the hedgerow, his mate will almost certainly see two. If you can anticipate Trusty and his tricks, then we will take a pair out tomorrow.'

At last. If I prove I can handle Trusty, then I can drive a pair.

Felicity started to get Trusty's measure as they bowled along the lane through the estate. She checked him as they approached the gateway leading to the track through the woods that would bring them out on to the Whitchurch road, where the traffic provided a better challenge.

'Steady, now, lad,' she called as Trusty, true to form, fought to cut the corner. She breathed a silent sigh of relief as they drove through the centre of the narrow gateway without mishap.

'Oh, well handled.'

She glowed at Richard's praise and sent Trusty along the track with a flick of the whip. Suddenly, a pheasant flew from the undergrowth with a clatter of wings and a raucous cry and Trusty jerked his head into the air. His powerful hindquarters bunched, then propelled him forward.

Bracing her feet against the front of the gig, Felicity struggled to regain control. Richard threw his right arm round her, pulling her into the side of his rock-hard body as he reached across with his left hand to take the reins.

'No! Let me…do…it.'

The hand withdrew. Surprised, she risked a sideways glance. One brow lifted as Richard caught her eye. 'He's… all yours…Felicity.' His voice jerked in rhythm with the rocking gig.

Trusty, ears flat to his head, charged blindly on. Felicity was conscious of Richard, next to her, poised to take over if necessary but if she did not prove herself now he might never let her drive again.

She fought to stay calm until Trusty's wild pace slackened and she could bring him to a halt. Richard tied the reins off, jumped down and held his arms out for Felicity. As her feet touched the ground, her knees buckled and she was only saved from landing in an ungainly heap by Richard's strong arms around her. He clasped her tight, his chin resting on her head. She leaned into him, inhaling his familiar, masculine scent: comforting and yet arousing.

All was still; all quiet now save for their harsh breathing, and the thunder of Richard's heart in her ear. Somewhere, a thrush sang, rousing Felicity. She wriggled to loosen Richard's embrace.

'Thank you.' She leant back to study him, hands braced against the solid wall of his chest. He was pale. A vertical slash divided his brows whilst his lips were so tightly compressed they were barely visible.

'What are you thanking me for?'

'For trusting me.'

'Trusting you with Trusty, eh? You did well. Are you all right?'

'Yes. And you?'

'Yes. No thanks to…' His head swivelled and he stared back along the path. 'Wretched pheasant.'

'No wonder poor Trusty bolted. It startled me too.'

'Poor Trusty?'

With a single quirk of his brow, Richard indicated his opinion of the horse. Then he stilled. He cupped Felicity's chin. Desire licked through her veins as she stared up into his darkening eyes. His head lowered. He hesitated, searching her face, his mouth scant inches from hers. With an impatient inner huff, Felicity slid her fingers through his hair and crushed her lips to his. She wanted him. She was weary of tiptoeing around him, fearing he did not desire her. His eyes revealed the truth: at this moment in time, he wanted her. She would deal with any regret later.

Richard's arms slid beneath her cloak, enfolding her as the kiss deepened and she pressed against him, the evidence of his arousal hard against her belly. As their tongues tangled, his hands slid around her waist and up the sides of her ribs. He tore his lips from hers to murmur huskily, 'No corset, Felicity Joy?' before reclaiming her mouth. Pure lust sizzled through her as he unbuttoned her jacket and caressed her breast through her linen shirt. She reached between them, unfastened his breeches and closed her hand around him: hot, silky skin sliding over engorged flesh. She stroked and he growled, deep in his throat, pulling her skirts up, and up again to her waist, exposing her.

A long finger slid between her aching, swollen folds and she pushed against it, frantic for more, her cry of pleasure swallowed by his kiss.

Then she was in the air, her legs tightening around his hips as he entered her. Still coupled, he turned to trap her against a tree. He was quick, hard, demanding. She urged him on, meeting each thrust, clenching around him. Frantic for release, she wound tighter and tighter until she shattered, throwing her head back, her cry echoing in the still December air, drowning his deep cry as he pumped his seed into her.

His forehead rested against hers as they stilled, panting. Felicity closed her eyes. He was still inside her, softer now, her legs still tight around his hips. Warm lips caressed her lids, trailed down her nose to kiss its tip.

'Why have you stayed away from me?' The words were out before she could stop them. She kept her eyes tight shut.

'I…when?'

'At night.'

Silence. She peeked through her lashes. He studied her, frowning. Her courage faltered. If only she could unsay those words.

'You must be uncomfortable.'

He supported her as he stepped back from the tree and slowly lowered her to the ground. She did not meet his eyes as she rearranged her clothing.

'Felicity?'

Reluctantly, she looked at him; took heart at the hint of vulnerability in his expression.

'Do you mean…that is, I thought, now you are with child, you—' He spun round and strode over to a nearby sapling which shook as he thumped it. His shoulders rose and his back broadened as he sucked in an audible breath. 'I have been trying to respect your wishes.' He strode back to face her. 'You seemed unhappy with my attentions, other than in bed, and I thought you only welcomed those as you were keen to get with child.' Deep brown eyes bored into hers. 'Was I wrong?'

She tamped down her embarrassment at discussing such intimate details. He was her husband, if she could not discuss such matters with him, then with whom?

'Yes. I would like it if we could still…' Her face burned. 'That is, I would like it if you would continue to visit me at night.'

He lifted her chin. 'Only at night, Felicity Joy?'

No. I want you to love me. Always.

An image of her mother, hopelessly yearning after her father and, now, her stepfather, swept into her mind, followed by Emma, in despair over a man she had trusted, who had heartlessly abandoned her. They would go back to London in February. He would go back to his mistress. She hardened her heart. 'I think it is for the best.'

'Why?' His eyes seared into her, scrambling her thoughts. 'What are you afraid of? Is it because of your sister?'

'It is not only her.'

He gripped her shoulders. 'Not only Emma? Who else? Why does this barrier between us feel insurmountable? Your mother? Is it her?'

Felicity wrenched away from him. 'It is how I feel. It is what I want.' Every nerve in her body was strung tight, every muscle rigid.

The silence hummed with tension. She refused to look at him, staring fixedly down the track, back the way they had come.

'Very well, if that is how you feel, I shall not ask again.'

Richard strode over to the gig. 'It is time we went back,' he said, and waited to help Felicity aboard. What else could she have said? She had no words to explain. Her feet dragged as she walked towards the gig.

'Richard?'

'Felicity?'

'I am sorry. I—'

He almost threw her up into the vehicle and leapt in after her, gathering the reins.

'Get up, Trusty.' He slapped the reins on Trusty's broad back, his lips tight as he glowered at the track ahead.

Chapter Forty-Two

Mid-January, 1812

As Richard crossed the hall, he glanced up at the staircase. Felicity, dressed in a woollen walking dress that clung provocatively, was walking down the stairs. His breath caught at the tantalizing sight. He never tired of caressing the gradual changes to her body—her ripening breasts and the gentle swell of her belly. Her condition was not yet obvious, except to him, who knew and revelled in every inch of her.

'Are you going out for a walk, my dear? I should be happy to provide an arm to lean on,' he said, as she had reached the foot of the stairs.

'Thank you, Richard, but I am to call upon your mother. I am persuaded you will find it tedious beyond measure and, as you see, Yvette is to accompany me.' She gestured behind her to where her maid had followed her down. 'Besides, I see you are dressed for riding and I make no doubt you will enjoy such exercise far more than walking at my slow pace.'

His wife was consistent, he would give her that. She had said she would not welcome his attentions during the day, and she had kept to her word. Despite his efforts to convince himself it was for the best, the terms of their marriage were eating away at him. Angry words, he knew, would get him nowhere.

He bowed. 'Enjoy your outing, dear. I shall see you later.'

Ten minutes later, Richard waited, tapping his whip against his boot, as Dalton saddled Thor.

'You'll be wanting someone to accompany you, milord.' Dalton voiced it as a statement, not a question.

'No. I shall ride alone.'

Dalton paused in his task. 'He's very fresh, milord. Mebbe—'

'Are you suggesting I cannot handle my own horse, Dalton?'

The groom stiffened before buckling the throat lash.

'Forgive me, Dalton, I should not have snapped at you. I am in no mood for company. There is no need to worry about my safety.'

'Very well, milord.' Richard closed his mind to the doubt in the groom's tone.

Dalton held the stallion as Richard mounted and Thor threw his head up in reaction to the weight on his back. As the horse's muscles bunched beneath him Richard grinned in anticipation of the ride to come. It would take all of his concentration to settle the horse—exactly what he needed. He rode Thor out of the yard, using seat and legs to drive him up to the bit and encourage him to drop his head.

The strains of the day drained from Richard as they trotted along the track leading from the stables down to the river meadows a mile away. Once down in those broad, flat fields—through which the River Fern flowed—he would give Thor his head and shake the fidgets out of them both with a long gallop. Despite his intention to focus his full attention on Thor, Richard's mind continued to meander, his body reacting instinctively to the stallion's antics as he boggled at rustles in the hedgerows and shied around puddles.

Why was he so restless? Why did he feel as though something constantly hovered beyond the reach of his understanding?

He should be content: his mother was now settled at the Lodge and Felicity was with child, yet she continued to welcome him to her bed. A tremor shuddered through him at the thought of the spine-tingling satisfaction he found in his wife's arms night after night. She oversaw his household in a calm and uncomplaining manner and she *appeared* content with her life, yet… No amount of teasing or probing by him had yet uncovered any chink in her outer shell. He hated that Felicity would not confide in him.

Trust. He longed for his wife to trust him. He wanted… *needed* to be the centre of her world, the most important person in her life.

They reached the gate at the end of the track, and he stretched down to unlatch it. As it swung open, Thor bounced into the meadow, snatching at the bit.

Richard laughed, his spirits lifting. 'You know what's coming, don't you, old fellow?'

This had been a favourite ride since his boyhood, when he and Adam would race their horses, jumping over the numerous ditches that drained the fields above into the river, then riding home, happy and exhausted, through Fernley woods. Despite the age gap, they had been close. Until… His spirits dived again, like a swallow in flight.

He nudged Thor until he breasted the gate shut, then reached down to latch it. He felt those powerful haunches bunch under him as Thor tried to wheel round, anticipating the gallop. Richard sat deep, holding the stallion between hand and leg, heading for the river at a slow, collected canter. The decision to gallop would be his, and his alone.

As they reached the bank, lined with trees, he reined to a halt to admire the sun glinting on the river and the sound of the river rushing past. He sat and watched for several minutes, enjoying the moment, aware of half a ton of quivering horseflesh between his thighs. Then he turned Thor and pointed him downstream. The big horse needed no further encouragement, catapulting into a gallop, the ground a blur beneath his pounding hooves. Richard felt his lips stretch into a wide smile as they flew over familiar ditches, the wind in his face blowing his troubles away.

At the far end of the meadows they slowed to a canter, a trot and, finally, a walk, both heaving for breath. Here, a tributary joined the river. It was too wide to jump and the sloping banks were too high and unstable to negotiate, so a footbridge—around fifteen feet long and strong enough for a horse and rider—had been constructed. Once over the bridge, there was a quiet lane to cross into Fernley woods, towering majestically up a steep slope before levelling out.

The way home.

Thor jibbed at setting foot on the bridge.

'Come on, lad. I know you don't care for it, but you've done it before.'

After some urging, including firm encouragement from Richard's heels and a tap with the whip, Thor ventured on to the narrow bridge, ears flat to his head. He jibbed again at the halfway point and an inkling of danger struck Richard.

Too late.

The wooden structure sagged and tilted with an ominous crack. Frantic hooves scrabbled for purchase on the wet boards as Richard kicked Thor on, hoping they might, by some miracle, reach the opposite bank before the bridge gave way. The stallion made a valiant attempt to respond, lurching forward, his front hooves almost home even as his hind legs slipped over the side of the bridge. He hung there for a few seconds, giving Richard precious time to kick his feet free of the stirrups and throw himself clear of the falling horse. He landed with a thump, on his back, in the freezing water.

Remorse needled Felicity as she took tea with her mother-in-law. It had been so very hard to resist the heat in Richard's eyes as he watched her come down the stairs, but she had forced herself to deny his company.

She was a coward. She did not want their marriage to continue like this but, whenever she was on the verge of relenting, the thought of his mistress stopped her. Her dread was all too real that, once back in London, Richard would forget her and once again plunge back into his old life. She must not become reliant on him or his presence.

Other than their continuing driving lessons—she had by now graduated to driving a pair—she had become adept at avoiding any but the most fleeting of interactions with Richard.

Except at night.

A tug of anticipation deep inside recalled the passion and ecstasy she experienced night after night at his skilful touch.

A gentle cough returned her with a jolt to the present, and to her mother-in-law's cool appraisal.

'Oh.' Felicity felt her blush build up once more. 'I am sorry.'

The dowager patted her on the knee. 'Ladies in your condition are known to be prone to a little absentmindedness.'

The dowager had been delighted with the news of Felicity's pregnancy, and she and Felicity had become ever closer over the past weeks. Richard's relationship with his mother, however, had continued to be fraught.

'It will be dark shortly,' Felicity said eventually. 'I should—'

A sudden flurry of activity in the hall—raised voices and running footsteps—prevented her from finishing her sentence. A glance at the dowager revealed a face leached of colour.

'Wait there, Mother. I will see what is amiss.'

Richard—skin whiter than the neckcloth swathing his head, his clothes soaking wet—sat on a chair in the hall whilst a footman tugged at his boots. The butler and various other servants hovered nearby.

'I am perfectly well, I tell you, Davis,' Richard said to

the butler. 'There is no need for the doctor. Send for Dalton immediately, will you? Thor is in need—'

'Never mind your horse.' Felicity dropped to her knees beside him. His hand was freezing. 'What on earth happened?' She reached to the cloth wrapped around his head, and he flinched. Then she saw the blood and her stomach roiled. 'Davis,' she said. 'Send someone for the doctor. Immediately.'

'Yes, my lady.'

'Hold hard there, Davis.' Richard glared at Felicity. 'What do you mean by—?'

'You have an injury to your head. I cannot be certain you are capable of making rational decisions, so I have done it for you.'

Their gazes clashed, a storm brewing in Richard's brown eyes.

Chapter Forty-Three

Felicity held her breath, determined to stand firm. Richard held her gaze for what seemed like an age until, suddenly, he smiled. It was like the sun appearing from behind thunderclouds.

'Very well, Felicity Joy. Davis?'

'Milord?'

'Tell Dalton to come here first, before he sees the horse.'

'Dalton? But he's a groom.'

'He's patched me up many times, Felicity. I'll not have that quack from the village anywhere near me, and anyone else is too far away.'

'Very well.' Dalton was a man of sense, he would very soon say if he thought Richard in need of a doctor. Felicity touched his cheek. 'What happened? Were you thrown?' She was always apprehensive when Richard rode the lively stallion.

'*Thrown?*' Disgust coloured his tone. 'No, I was not *thrown*. The bridge gave way as we crossed. We landed in the stream and had to wade along the river until the bank was low enough to climb out.'

Felicity's imagination embroidered his spare tale with horrific images. 'You were fortunate Thor did not…' Her blood ran cold. She probed Richard's ribs as she scanned him for injuries. At his bellow of pain, she snatched her hands away. '*Did* he land on you? Were you crushed?'

Richard hacked out a laugh, which merged into a cough which, in turn, merged into a groan. Felicity sat on her heels, hardly daring to touch him in case she caused any damage. Eventually, he gasped, 'Do I…look crushed? I rolled… clear…pleased to say. Ribs…damnably sore. This was… nearest place.'

'I am so glad I was still here. Here, let me help, can you stand?' Felicity slid her hand under his arm, then hesitated before she tried to help him to his feet. He had begun to shiver violently, and she did not like the sudden greyish cast to his skin, or the roll of his eyes.

She beckoned to two male servants. 'Help his lordship upstairs immediately. He needs to be dried and kept warm.' Davis came hurrying back along the hall. 'I think a measure of brandy would be welcome, Davis, if you have such a thing. And you,' she addressed one of the maids, 'go to the kitchen and ask Cook to send up hot water and a tea tray, please.'

Richard's arms were draped over the servants' shoulders, and their arms linked together around his back. Felicity could see the effort he made to take some of his weight on his own legs, which alternately buckled and straightened.

'I will go ahead of you and—'

A moan caught Felicity's attention. The dowager had emerged from the drawing room and stood, visibly trembling, her eyes riveted on her son.

'No, you go ahead. I will be with you shortly.' Felicity scanned the hall, and spied the worried-looking housekeeper hurrying from the rear of the house. 'Mrs Norton—' she called, as the men began their slow climb up the stairs, half carrying Richard, whose head lolled alarmingly '—her ladyship is taken ill. Please ask Cook to prepare another tea tray for the drawing room and ask Tallis to attend us there.'

Anxiety clawed at her as she hurried to the dowager's side. As she put her arm around her Felicity registered, for the first time, her physical frailty. Her erect stance and unyielding manner gave the impression of strength but, in reality, there was little flesh covering her bones.

She settled the dowager in a chair by the fire then drew up a footstool, sat on it, and chafed her bony hands, which were as chilled as Richard's. Thinking of her husband triggered an urge to be with him, but she could not leave her mother-in-law until Tallis—her maid—arrived.

'Richard will be all right, Mother.'

Those dazed eyes settled on Felicity's face. 'I could not bear to lose him, too,' she whispered.

'You won't. He is strong; he will recover in no time, you'll see.'

She believed it—she *had* to believe it.

What would I do...? What if...? No. He is strong. He managed to walk this far. He is bruised and exhausted.

'We will *not* lose him, Mother.'

'The Stanton men, they all die before their time.' The dowager shuddered, grabbing Felicity's hand, nails cutting into her flesh. 'I thought him improved...you have been good for him. He has always been like his father...and his brother...worse, even...seeking out excitement...getting involved in anything and everything dangerous...oblivious to the risks...' She moaned, rocking back and forth. 'If anything...if he should—'

'He will not—'

'I should have told him.' Tears tracked down the dowager's pale cheeks, dampened her bloodless lips. 'Now it is too late...'

'What should you have told him? It is not too late, Mother. Please, try to stay calm. Richard will not die.'

Please, God. Oh, where is Tallis? I need to see him...to take care of him.

'I only did it to protect his memories of his papa—'

'Milady?' Tallis rushed into the room, followed by a kitchen maid carrying a tea tray.

The dowager released her grip. 'Go to Richard, Daughter. He has need of you.'

Richard? That was the first time Felicity had heard his mother call Richard anything other than Stanton.

'Take good care of him, please. And let me know…let me know…'

'I will let you know how he is as soon as I can.'

The dowager smiled, although her lips trembled. 'Thank you, dear.' She straightened in her chair with a visible effort. 'I pray you will forgive my moment of weakness. It was the shock. Tallis, you may sit with me while I drink my tea, and then I shall go to bed.'

Felicity pondered her mother-in-law's disjointed words as she climbed the stairs. What had she not told Richard? He already knew his father had shot himself—what could be worse than that? Of one thing Felicity was certain: Richard was wrong to believe his mother wished he, and not Adam, had died. Her mother-in-law cared very much for her second son, despite her constant criticism. And she was terrified of losing him.

Her trepidation as she entered the bedchamber was unfounded. Richard sat in a comfortable armchair by the fire, a blanket tucked around his legs, as Davis dabbed gingerly at the blood in his hair. As Felicity entered, Richard's head snapped round, knocking Davis's hand aside. She crossed the room and peered at his scalp where the gash—a good three inches long—continued to ooze blood.

'Felicity, where have you been? Can you *please* stop this imbecile from fiddling with my head? It stings like the… that is, it's very sore.'

Davis cast a reproachful look at Richard.

'He is only trying to help,' Felicity said. 'But I do not think you can achieve much more, Davis—you have done an excellent job of cleansing the wound. If you have a clean pad to cover it, Dalton will soon tell us if any stitches are required.'

She bit back a smile at Richard's barely audible *hmmph*.

A tea tray was on a nearby table. 'Have you had a cup of tea?'

'I've had some brandy.'

'Then I shall pour some tea for you, and sweeten it well, for it is said to be beneficial in cases of shock.'

'I am not in shock. I am angry. I could have lost Thor.'

Felicity opened the tea caddy and spooned some leaves into the teapot, then poured in hot water to allow the leaves to steep.

'As I said before, you were fortunate Thor did not crush you.' She stirred the pot as she willed her voice not to tremble. 'Is he injured?'

'Not seriously, thank goodness. Bruised and scratched, but nothing broken. I need to examine that bridge tomorrow and find out why it gave way.' Richard sipped at his tea and Felicity was relieved to see his colour improve. 'I am sure I recall an entry in the ledgers showing it was repaired last spring. I need to speak to Elliott.'

'You are unlikely to be fit enough to ride tomorrow,' Felicity said. 'It is possible you have broken your ribs.'

Richard glowered at her. She smiled in return. It would be what it would be, and no amount of willing it otherwise would change it.

'Where were you?' he asked. 'I thought you were behind us but you disappeared.'

Felicity glanced round. Davis was occupied on the far side of the room. 'I was with your mother. She was very disturbed, so I waited with her until her maid could attend.'

'Hah. No doubt petrified I'd die before we have our heir.'

'That is unfair. She was much shaken. She cares about you, more than you realize.'

'I do not—'

'Hush.' Felicity laid her fingers against his lips. 'Trust me. She cares.'

Their gazes fused. His tongue flicked against her fingertips and her pulse stuttered. At the sound of a knock, she snatched her hand away just as Dalton walked in.

After examining Richard, Dalton stitched his scalp and strapped his ribs. 'It don't appear no worse'n a bump, far as I c'n tell, milady.'

'You may address me, Dalton,' Richard said irritably. 'I am perfectly rational, you know.'

'Nor do the ribs look to be broken,' Dalton continued, 'but I reckons a couple're mebbe cracked. They're like to be sore awhile. You'll need to rest up a few days, milord.'

'I shall return home in the morning,' Richard said. 'I've things to attend to, and I need to inspect that bridge.'

Dalton raised his brows. 'You know best, milord, I'm sure. All I know is cracked ribs is very painful an' takes time to mend. They'll be a sight worse by morning, you mark my words. I'll take a look at the bridge tomorrow and report back.

'Now then, Simson's on his way and he's bringing arnica for your bruises. If that's all, I'll go and see to Thor.'

After seeing Richard settled in bed with Simson to watch over him, and reassuring her mother-in-law that Richard was not lying at death's door, Felicity ate a solitary supper before retiring. After Yvette left, she tossed and turned, sleep evading her as she relived those terrible moments when the dowager's fears had awoken the possibility she might lose Richard.

She clasped her belly protectively. What would the future hold? She saw now, with absolute clarity, that her life was in danger of becoming a self-fulfilling prophecy. If she continued to push Richard away, the result would be the kind of life she feared above all else.

But their lives at Fernley Park were one thing, London was quite another. What would happen when they returned in February as planned? What of Richard's mistress?

Chapter Forty-Four

Next morning, Richard roused sleepily, began to turn over, and catapulted awake.

'Aaaaargh.'

The pain in his side spiked before easing to a throb. Memories of his fall flooded back: the split-second realization that Thor might crush him, his frantic efforts to scramble clear; the terrible certainty that Thor was dead, until his legs began to thrash about. Tentatively, Richard probed the clipped area at the back of his head, the stitches scratching at his fingertips. He massaged his temples.

'How do you feel?'

The delicious scent of violets surrounded him as Felicity leaned over him, forehead puckered in enquiry, plait dangling, a shawl wrapped around her shoulders. Her hands clutched the shawl below her breasts, doing little to cover the burgeoning mounds revealed above the lace-trimmed neckline of her nightgown. He forced his attention to her face. Her lids were heavy as she stifled a yawn.

'How long have you been here, Felicity Joy?'

Her eyes skittered from his scrutiny as she perched on the side of the bed. 'I couldn't sleep.'

'How long?'

'A few hours. I wanted to be here in case you needed anything.'

'Simson was here. There was no need for you—'

'I sent him to bed. There was no need for us both to stay.' She paused. 'I wanted to be with you.'

Warmth flooded his body. 'Did you miss me, Felicity Joy?'

A blush spread from her neck to her cheeks but she held his gaze and nodded. 'I was afraid…that is, there was a moment, yesterday, when I thought…' Her chest heaved, his eyes drawn to her breasts as a bee to nectar. She was still small breasted, but pregnancy had added to their lushness. Saliva flooded his mouth, and he swallowed, silently cursing his sore ribs.

'You thought…?'

She pleated and repleated the fabric of her nightgown. 'It forced me to consider how I might feel if anything should happen to you.'

Moving carefully Richard reached to cover her hands with his. They stilled.

'And how might you feel?'

Tears sheened her eyes. 'I could not bear it. I realized… how very glad I am that I married you.'

'Come here.' He gave a little tug and she moved closer.

He stroked her soft cheek then hooked his fingers around her nape. She leaned down willingly, bracing her hands on the pillow either side of his head, lips—soft, pink, alluring—parting. She hesitated, and then brushed his mouth in a sweet kiss before sitting back again.

'More.'

She laughed down at him. 'You will not thank me if I get carried away and bump your ribs. I can think of nothing more likely to cool your ardour. We can wait.' Her amber eyes darkened as she swept his lower lip with her thumb. 'We have our whole lives ahead of us.

'Are you hungry? Would you like breakfast sent up?'

'No.' Richard winced as he sat up and eased the covers down. 'That is, I am hungry, but I wish to get up and eat breakfast downstairs. Will you ring for Simson?'

'Do you think you should…?'

He was already on his feet. 'You *are* a little worrier. It

was only a tumble. I promise I will be sensible about resting. Ah, Simson, that was quick. Thank you. I am going downstairs for breakfast. Will you help me on with my banyan?'

As they ate breakfast, Tallis came in. 'Begging your pardon, my lord, but her ladyship wishes you to attend her in her sitting room when you have finished your breakfast.'

Richard lowered his forkful of eggs as Tallis left the room. 'I've been summoned. No doubt to hear a lecture on how—yet again—my penchant for risk-taking might have cleared the path for Charles to inherit Fernley and throw my mother to the wolves.'

Felicity frowned. 'That is unfair. Your mother was distraught: her only concern was for you. I do not believe any thought of the succession crossed her mind.'

A knot of resentment lodged in his chest. What did Felicity know? She'd not had to live all these years with the knowledge that his mother would rather it was he—Richard—who had died. He had barely existed in her eyes after his brother's death.

'Besides,' Felicity continued, 'as I am with child, Charles will not necessarily inherit Fernley.'

'And I can assure you I intend to live a long, healthy and—hopefully—happy life with you and our children.'

Felicity's smile wobbled. He pushed back his chair and beckoned.

'Come. We will go and hear what my mother has to say.'

'Me? Oh, I don't think your mother would expect me—'

'*I* expect you to be privy to our conversation, Felicity. You are my wife. I should like you to understand why my relationship with my mother is so troubled.'

His mother sat staring into the fire, her lips pinched and pale. When she looked round, Richard's lungs seized. She looked old, and grey, and…shrunken, somehow. How had that happened without him noticing? She lifted her hand to Felicity, who clasped it and stooped to kiss her cheek.

They have become so close. Why can neither of them be as relaxed with me?

Or me with them? He thrust that thought aside.

'Thank you for coming,' Mother said. '*Both* of you.'

A peculiar sensation of watching from outside himself settled over Richard as they sat down. This felt different to Mother's usual rant about needlessly courting danger. *Is she ill? Seriously ill? Am I going to lose her?* His throat thickened. He coughed, then dragged in a calming breath.

'How are you this morning, Richard?'

About to utter a dismissive, 'I am perfectly well', Richard paused. It was time for honesty. 'My ribs hurt abominably and I am bruised, but I will recover.'

'Good.' Mother stared pensively into the flames. 'I have to tell you something I should perhaps have told you many years ago. I make no excuses, although I did have good reason. But I promised God—when I prayed for your recovery—that I would tell you the truth. About Adam.'

In the sixteen years since his brother's death, Richard could probably count on the fingers of one hand the number of times his mother had spoken Adam's name aloud.

What truth? I already know everything.

'Richard was away at school when it happened.' Mother glanced at Felicity before returning her attention to the fire. 'It was a lovely autumn, and Richard's father and Adam went shooting.'

Richard shifted on the sofa. He knew what was coming. It had been an accident. Adam had been careless.

'They ran to tell me,' Mother continued. 'Oh, my dear, but I hope you never have to endure such agony.' She paused, her knuckles white as she visibly composed herself. Felicity slid from the sofa to kneel by the chair and hold her hand. 'Adam was already dead by the time I reached them. Shot in the back.'

'*What?*' Richard surged to his feet, barely noticing the agonising pain that shot through his torso. 'The *back*? Who—?'

'Your father.'

That stark reply hit him with the force of a knockout punch. The air left his lungs with a *whoosh* and he fought for breath.

Papa *shot Adam? No! It cannot be true.*

'No.' The word came out a croak. 'No.' He shook his head, trying to rid himself of the words, the image they evoked.

'It was an accident. Your father *pleaded* with me not to tell you the truth and I promised I would not. You idolized Adam, and Papa could not bear that you might grow to despise him.'

Richard scrubbed his hands over his face, struggling for composure. 'It was an accident. Why would I despise my father? He did not shoot Adam deliberately. Why did you not tell me the truth after Papa died?'

Mother sighed. 'I vowed to tell you the whole truth, and I shall. If it had not been for me, I believe your father would eventually have told you the truth. It was *I* who despised *him*, in those first months. In my grief, I blamed him for taking my child, my son, my firstborn.

'It is *my* fault Papa killed himself. If only I had supported him through his own guilt and grief. But, no.' She paused, and when she spoke again, her tone was bitter. 'No, I could barely bring myself to be civil to him. It was easier to withdraw completely and leave him to drown in his own misery whilst I drowned in mine.'

'You were mad with grief,' Felicity said. 'No one could blame you for reacting—'

'I blame myself. And what I didn't see, until it was too late, was that not only had I cut myself off from my husband, but also from Richard. By the time I realized, it was impossible to bridge the gulf between us.'

She struggled to her feet and went to Richard. Every muscle in his body was rigid as his brain tried to make sense of his mother's words.

'I was a coward, and I am so very sorry. Every time I thought to tell you the truth, I became petrified you would blame me for the loss of your father the way I blamed him for the loss of Adam. All I could do was try to protect you and keep you safe. You were all I had left, but the more I tried to curb your activities the more you resented me and so the gulf widened.'

'I believed...' Richard closed his eyes, sorting his thoughts. *Should I say this? Is now the right time?* A rational decision eluded him, but if he did not admit what he had held to be true these past fifteen years, it would continue to eat at him and the rift between them might never be healed. 'All these years, I believed my father killed himself because I was not a good enough replacement for Adam; that he did not love me enough to want to live.'

'Oh, no! My darling son...' Her voice caught on a sob. 'I have been blind. And foolish. To think you believed that, all this time. Your father *never* thought that. He loved you both. Equally. We both did. But Papa could not live with his guilt.'

He felt her hands cup his face and he forced his eyes open. 'Yesterday, you looked so weak and pale. I have never seen you like that. I suddenly understood that if my worst fears ever came to pass, you might die and I would never have the chance to tell you the truth. I saw what I must do—what I should have done years ago. Can you ever forgive me?'

He pulled away and strode to the window. Angry clouds scudded across the sky, mirroring the thoughts charging around his brain. Trees bowed before the strengthening wind, their top branches whipping back and forth and, as the first raindrops spat against the glass, Richard turned to face his mother.

He was tempted—oh, so tempted—to vent his anger on to her: anger for deceiving him for all these years.

It is hardly her fault you believed what you did. You could have simply asked her.

I was a child!

Not so much a child at seventeen. And you have long been a man.

Even as he turned, he wasn't certain what words would come out of his mouth: angry words to lash out and hurt, or conciliatory words to heal?

And there was Felicity, in his path, amber eyes anxious and searching, hands on his chest.

'Think.'

The word was whispered so softly he barely heard it, but it was powerful enough to stay him for that split second whilst his rational mind fought with his gut emotions. Rationality won. He crossed the room and, in the end, no words were needed as he wrapped his arms around his mother and held her, feeling the sobs that shook her frail frame and blinking back the moisture in his own eyes.

Chapter Forty-Five

Early February 1812

They arrived in London on a grey February afternoon. Their visit would be brief, because of Felicity's condition.

'I confess I am disappointed we shall miss most of the Season,' Felicity said to Richard, lounging on the seat next to her, booted feet propped on the opposite seat. 'I had hoped to attend Olivia's coming-out ball.'

'Maybe we will still be here. Knowing Leo, he will ensure his daughter's ball is one of the first, and the best. Then he will sit back and enjoy watching the rest of the *ton* in their attempts to emulate his opulence.'

Felicity laughed. 'I can just see him "coming the duke", as Papa used to say.'

'You have changed, Felicity.' Richard lowered his feet to the floor and swivelled sideways to face her. Her pulse leapt, as it always did when he turned those velvety brown eyes on her. 'Five months ago, you would not have given a fig that you might miss the ball of the Season. Now...' he studied her '...now you have become a stylish society lady.'

'Thanks to Yvette.'

Richard cocked a brow. 'You give Yvette too much credit. You have developed confidence I never thought to see in you, but I believe you would have changed anyway. I hesitate to criticize your mother, but since you ceased to be influenced by her shallow perception of what is important in life, you have bloomed.' Gentle fingers drifted down her cheek, and she leaned into his touch. 'You are as lovely on the outside as you always have been on the inside.'

Rendered awkward by his praise, Felicity stared out of the window.

'Do not blush and turn aside, Felicity. Hold your head high. Be proud of who you are and what you have achieved.'

'Achieved? I have achieved nothing.'

'What about the difference you have made to all those children at Westfield? How many young women in your position concern themselves in the plight of orphans? To my shame, I never thought of such people either, until I met you. So you have changed my attitude too.'

He took her hand and raised it to his lips. Even through the fine kid of her glove, she could feel the heat of his mouth and, before she could think better of it, she leaned over and kissed him. In an instant, he clasped her to his chest and took possession of her mouth, his lips working their magic until she was lying prone on the seat, panting, with Richard atop her, his arousal pressed against her thigh.

'That,' he said, chest heaving, 'was most scandalous behaviour from a society lady, if I might say so, Lady Stanton. Mayhap I should rethink my appraisal of your character to that of an abandoned hussy.' He kissed her soundly. 'You once told me you were glad you married me. I shall return the compliment, and say I am very glad I married you. I think we suit very well.'

He sat up and rearranged his neckcloth, gazing out at the passing sights.

Still no words of love. Felicity tamped down her disappointment.

Since the dowager's confession, Richard and his mother had grown closer, step by faltering step. Felicity had found it hard to believe two people could drift so far apart over words they dared not say. She had vowed not to let unspoken words strangle her relationship with Richard in the same way. But it was easy to make that vow, much harder to put it into practice as, night after night, Richard made love to her and then left her bed.

The words 'I love you' died unspoken on her lips many times.

Was it so very important he should love her? He had said he was glad he had married her. Was that not enough?

She knew the answer before she finished formulating the question. No. It was not enough. She must live with it, but she would never stop hoping for more. Fear and doubt still gnawed at her confidence. What if he grew bored? She was under no illusions: she would be left to her own devices whilst he pursued his many other interests.

Loneliness loomed.

'What brings you to town this early, Stan?' Leo hailed Richard from a chair by the window of White's the following day.

'I might ask you the same, Duke,' Richard replied as they shook hands.

'Cecily *insisted* Olivia needs a hundred fittings before her ball,' Leo said, with barely concealed disgust. 'We've only been in town a couple of days and I've already had my fill of it. What's a man to do?'

'Hide in his club and leave the women to it?'

'Now why did I not think of that? And you?'

'Oh, Felicity was keen to visit that school of hers, and I need to visit Barker's. I've ordered a phaeton for Felicity from them and I want to inspect it before it's delivered. I'm also looking for a well-schooled pair, if you should hear of any. She's become quite skilled with the ribbons.'

'I'll keep an ear open. How is Felicity, by the by?'

Richard felt a wide smile split his face. Leo raised a brow.

'We weren't going to tell anyone yet but, as you were there at the conception of our marriage, I think it only right—'

'Hold hard, Stan. There are some things a man has to draw the line at. I point-blank refuse to be present at the conception of your heir.'

Richard stared, momentarily taken aback, then guffawed.

Leo beamed. 'I take it congratulations are in order? Felicity is well?'

'She's very well, but she tires easily so we won't stay in town long. Besides, I cannot be away from Fernley for too long. I've had to dismiss my bailiff.' Richard told Leo about his accident on the bridge and his subsequent discovery that Elliott had been siphoning funds from the estate by putting forged invoices through the accounts. 'I believed Elliott to be trustworthy—he's been with me years—but I won't make the same mistake with the new man.'

Felicity, meanwhile, had penned a note to Lady Brierley, informing her of their arrival in town. The footman sent to deliver the note returned with an invitation to take tea that afternoon. Harriet was her usual charming self, entertaining Felicity with the latest gossip. They arranged to visit Westfield together the following day.

The tea tray had been removed, and Felicity rose to her feet, saying, 'I fear I am monopolizing your time, dear Harriet. I must…'

The walls appeared to bulge and then recede, and Harriet's voice came as though from a great distance: 'Felicity? What is wrong?'

'I…I…' Felicity's legs turned to jelly. A hand gripped her elbow and she was eased back on to the sofa. She hauled in a deep breath, and the room steadied before her eyes. 'Oh, goodness, I am so sorry, Harriet. Might I take a few moments to compose myself?'

Harriet chafed Felicity's hand. 'You may take as long as you like, my dear. There, you have some colour back in your cheeks. Did you feel faint?'

Harriet skimmed Felicity's body. 'Ah,' she said.

Felicity sighed at the speculation embodied in that simple utterance. 'I stood up too quickly. It happens from time to time. Please promise me you will not tell anyone.'

'That you are with child?'

Felicity nodded. 'Richard and I agreed to keep the news secret until we return to Fernley. I long to attend Lady Olivia Beauchamp's come-out ball—the duke was my guardian, you know, and I have known Olivia all her life—but I cannot bear being an object of scrutiny. The sticklers would be alert for the merest hint that I should already be retired from society.'

'Your secret is safe, dear. Please, stay until you are completely recovered. Now, tell me all about your first winter at Fernley Park.'

One story led to another and, eventually, Felicity found herself telling Harriet about Beanie, and how Richard had gone to Bristol to find her, and bring her home. Her voice faltered as she recalled Emma's diary and, before she knew what she was doing, she had confided in Harriet about Emma, her seduction, and her suicide. Instinct told her she could trust the other woman, and it was a great relief to share her past with another female.

'I remember your sister—such a beautiful young woman. We attended several of the same house parties in the summer of…let me see…was it '02? Or '03?'

''02,' Felicity said. 'She was eighteen and was presented that spring.'

'Such a tragic story. Forgive me, but I thought at the time that some of those gatherings were unsuitable for such an innocent. In a way, I cannot be surprised at such an unhappy ending. Do you know who the scoundrel was?'

'No. She referred to him in her diary as "M". They first met at a house party in Hertfordshire but it seems they met at other parties too. I did not know she was with child until

I read her diary. I always believed she had been driven to suicide by grief because her lover abandoned her.'

I have allowed that belief to overshadow so much of my life.

'I must go, Harriet.'

It is time to make amends to Richard for my suspicions and my stubbornness.

Richard was kind, attentive and the most wonderful lover she could ever have imagined. She was in love with him, but did he love her in return? Or was their marriage still a novelty, to hold his attention until another woman caught his eye?

Unrequited love.

It was time to take the risk. It was time to say those words.

I love you.

Chapter Forty-Six

'What do you say, Stan? Can you bear to leave Felicity to fend for herself for a week or so?'

Richard leaned forward and topped up Leo's wine glass. The duke had called round with the news of a driving pair for sale by a neighbour of his cousin, who lived in Buckinghamshire.

'They should be perfect for Felicity; Rockbeare's cattle are always beautifully schooled.'

'It sounds too good an opportunity to miss,' Richard said.

'And the hunting in the area is excellent,' Leo added persuasively.

Richard sat back, considering the implications of being out of town for several days. The purchase was to be a surprise for Felicity, hence the cover of going hunting. He pictured her amber eyes lighting up and her joyous smile at having her own phaeton and pair. He would miss her, though.

'Why the hesitation?' Leo said. 'Can't stomach leaving Felicity for so long? I never thought to see you so in thrall, Stan. I thought you and I were as cynical as each other about love and matters of the heart.'

Richard forced a laugh. He had always believed that too. Lately, though…

'Love? I merely wish to keep Felicity happy and contented for the baby's sake.'

Disingenuous, perhaps, but he was in no mood to become embroiled in a discussion about love.

'Good afternoon, your Grace. You are well, I hope?'

Both men leapt to their feet at Felicity's words, Richard's stomach hollowing. *Did she overhear?* Her expression revealed nothing other than pleasure as she greeted Leo.

'I am very well, my dear,' Leo said as he sauntered over to Felicity and kissed her cheek. 'As are you, I hear.'

'I hope you do not object, sweetheart, but I told Leo our news yesterday.'

'Of course not.' Felicity smiled at Leo.

'Have you had a pleasant afternoon?' Richard asked as Felicity settled on the sofa and he and Leo returned to their chairs.

'Most enjoyable, thank you. I took tea with Lady Brierley, and we have arranged to visit Westfield tomorrow.'

Harriet? Richard could only hope she remained discreet. It would seem his wife and his former mistress were fast becoming friends. There was nothing to be gained now from trying to keep them apart. Why had he not admitted the truth to Felicity right from the start, as Harriet had advised? But at least no one else was aware of their connection. Leo, who knew most goings-on, had not batted an eye when Felicity spoke of Harriet.

'I am glad you will have some company whilst I am out of town.' At Felicity's look of enquiry, he continued: 'I'm going into Buckinghamshire, hunting, with Leo and one or two others.'

'Oh.' Felicity hid her disappointment well, but there was a definite tinge of it in her tone. 'Well, I shall miss you, of course, but you will enjoy the change, I make no doubt. Will your ribs—?'

'They will be fine.' An image arose of Felicity riding him the night before, after ministering to him with skilful fingers and lips. He had not protested. She had become quite the seductress whilst his ribs had been mending, and he had thoroughly enjoyed her attentions. A scorching glance from those amber eyes, and a pinkish tinge to her cheeks, told him that she was thinking the same. He would make it up to her tonight. His loins tightened at the thought and he propped one ankle on the opposite knee to conceal his arousal.

'I am pleased to hear it,' Felicity replied, dropping her eyes demurely to her lap as the tip of her tongue stroked her upper lip.

Little minx!

'Ahem.' Leo rose smoothly to his feet, voice bubbling with amusement. 'This is not the level of deference a duke expects from his associates, my dears. I am feeling decidedly *de trop*. I shall say my *adieux*, and I will see you first thing in the morning, Stan. Don't be late.'

As Leo left the room, Felicity said, '*Are* your ribs completely healed, Richard?'

'I should hardly arrange to go hunting if they were not.'

Such an innocent tone. Felicity narrowed her eyes at him. 'Last night?' He had claimed the soreness had returned, blaming the journey to town.

He shrugged. 'You seemed to be enjoying yourself.' His voice quivered as he bit back his grin, his brown eyes brimming with laughter. 'I had no wish to spoil—'

'Oh, you...you...'

He cocked a brow. 'Yes? Are you struggling to articulate your thoughts, my sweet?'

Felicity relaxed into the sofa, draping one arm along the back. 'Come here, Husband.'

Richard sucked in one cheek. 'I detect some sorcery at work but...is it retribution on her mind...or seduction? Hmmmm, only one way to find out.'

He rose with the lithe grace of a big cat, and prowled towards the sofa, taking his time. Her heart leapt at the intent in his dark, hooded eyes, then lurched into a mad gallop. Heavens, what had she started?

'The servants!'

Richard swerved to the door. He opened it, stuck his

head out and said, 'No one, under any circumstances, is to disturb us.' He shut the door and turned to face Felicity. 'Now—' his voice was at its silkiest '—where were we?'

His breeches revealed the extent of his arousal and Felicity's breath all but seized at the sight of her powerful, handsome husband.

Mine! At least... No! She batted the unhelpful and unwelcome doubt away as she rose to meet him and took him in her arms, tilting her face as his lips lowered to take hers.

Sometime later, sprawled on the sofa, cosily wrapped in Richard's arms as he dozed, her treacherous mind bombarded her again with doubts. She had heard Cousin Leo's comment about love and matters of the heart earlier, and she had paused to hear Richard's reaction. His words had stung, particularly after her earlier resolve. How could she say those words to him now?

Carefully, she moved her head and she studied his face: at peace with his world, dark lashes feathering his cheeks, brown hair dishevelled, sensual lips relaxed and slightly apart as his breath huffed in the quiet of the room.

Had he spoken the truth of what was in his heart? Was it likely he would have admitted he loved her when the duke's unwavering cynicism about love was common knowledge?

No. She did not believe he would, but still she did not quite have the courage to open her heart to him.

The following day, Felicity and Harriet visited Westfield. Felicity's childhood friend Jane Whittaker greeted them warmly, and they spent a pleasant afternoon helping the children with their lessons, discussing ideas both to raise money and to encourage more employers to take apprentices.

On the journey home, Felicity reflected on how pleasant it was to have a friend such as Harriet. Most other ladies of her acquaintance thought her eccentric for even bothering with the orphans. Jane also liked Harriet and the feeling appeared mutual. For the first time in her adult life, Felicity began to feel like she belonged.

'Are you and Lord Stanton going out tonight?' Harriet asked.

'No. I did not tell you, did I? He has gone out of town for a few days, with the duke. They are staying with the duke's cousin, in Buckinghamshire.'

'In that case, would you care to dine with me this evening, if you are not too weary? And, if you should care to join me, I intend to go to Cheapside tomorrow afternoon.'

'Thank you, Harriet. I am delighted to accept *both* invitations.'

The note, clearly scribbled in haste, was delivered to Felicity at breakfast the following morning.

Dearest Felicity

I regret to inform you that I must leave London for a few days to attend to some urgent business. I am sorry to cancel our visit to Cheapside, but I shall contact you upon my return to rearrange the outing.

Your friend

Harriet

Felicity read it again. What had happened between when she had left Harriet's house last evening and this morning? Self-pity loomed, but Felicity thrust it away, impatient with such selfishness. Rather she should feel sympathy for her friend, for good news rarely forced such an abrupt change of plans. She hoped it was not *very* bad news, for Harriet's sake.

Stanton House was too large and, somehow, less colourful without Richard's presence, and the days stretched dully before her. She called upon Cousin Cecily and Olivia, Cousin Leo's daughter, and the few other acquaintances in town this early, but was aware she was merely passing the time until Richard came home. He wrote to her once, and she broke the seal, hope burgeoning. She scanned the contents, praying for news of his return, only to subside at his words. After the first few days of indifferent scent, he wrote, the weather had improved and the hounds were running sweetly, so they had decided to stay a day or two longer. He hoped she would forgive him, and that she missed him as much as he missed her.

Irritated to have become so dependent upon him, Felicity forced herself to keep going out. She had heard nothing more from Harriet and could only hope she was all right.

'When is my cousin due to return?' Charles enquired one day, just over a week after Richard had gone away, as he escorted Felicity to Hookham's Circulating Library to exchange some books.

'I know no more than I did yesterday when you asked.' Felicity was immediately riven with guilt for snapping.

'I merely asked,' Charles said, with a lift of his fair brows and a touch of affront in his tone, 'because I understood you to say he went with Cheriton.'

'He did. Why do you ask?'

'Is that not the duke in his carriage over there?'

Charles indicated a carriage, bearing the Cheriton coat of arms, at the head of a line of vehicles trailing behind a slow-moving coal wagon.

'Yes, but...' Felicity peered closer. Charles was right. She recognized Leo's profile. 'Oh!'

'You will tell him I need to see him urgently as soon as he gets home?'

'I will,' Felicity promised, although she knew it would not be for a few days. She had only received Richard's letter the day before.

Suspicion reared its head. If Leo was back in London, where on earth was Richard?

Chapter Forty-Seven

Four days later, Richard finally arrived home. He sent Dalton ahead to instruct Felicity to be at the front door at three o'clock sharp. Dalton waited with her on the front step and, as the longcase clock in the hall struck the hour, a gleaming phaeton, drawn by a pair of chestnut high-steppers, swung around the square and came to a halt in front of Stanton House.

Felicity's interest, however, was reserved exclusively for the driver. Richard grinned down at her: rich chocolate eyes creased at the corners, lips parted to allow a glimpse of white teeth.

'Well, Wife?' he said, removing his hat before leaping to the ground with the grace of a cat. With a deep laugh, he swung her into his arms and kissed her soundly on the lips.

'*Richard.*' Felicity struggled to free her arms to push him away although, secretly, she was delighted with his show of affection, her heart full to bursting. 'What will people think?'

'That I am a most fortunate fellow, to be welcomed home with a kiss from my lovely wife,' Richard responded, with an aplomb that made Felicity giggle. He tugged her around so they were both facing the phaeton and pair. 'Well? What do you think?'

Felicity studied the phaeton—midnight blue with gold-painted trim—and the beautifully matched ponies. They were glossy chestnut geldings with eye-catching flaxen

manes and tails, identical white blazes, and four white
socks apiece.

'They are exceedingly handsome,' she said.

'A bit like your husband?'

'*Exactly* like my husband. What are their names?' She
felt Richard's eyes on her as she spoke, and she glanced up at
him. 'Oh, how I have missed you, my love.' The words burst
from her lips before she could think what she was saying.

'And I have missed you too, Felicity Joy. And their names
are Nutmeg and Spice, although you may wish to change
them.'

'Oh, no. It's unlucky, and I think their names are perfect.'

'And so, my sweet, are you. Come, let us go indoors.
Dalton, will you take care of these two, please?'

'Can I not drive them?'

'Not now, my sweet. I am weary, and I make no doubt
they are too; we have been on the road since yesterday. I
did not wish to hurry them. Besides, Dalton will be keen
to settle them into their new homes. We will take them to
the park tomorrow morning, I promise. Tomorrow morning, eleven o'clock.'

'Lord Stanton!' A man, dressed in an ill-fitting brown
suit, hurried across the road towards them.

'Turner, any news?'

'Yes, milord.'

'At last. You'd better come inside.' In the hall, Richard
said, 'I shall join you in the drawing room shortly, my dear.
This should not take long.'

Felicity hid her irritation at being dismissed. This Turner
had clearly brought news important to Richard and, therefore, it was important to Felicity. She paced the floor.

Before fifteen minutes had passed, Richard came in.

'You look pleased, Richard. I must presume Mr Turner
brought good news. Might I be allowed to share in it?'

Richard gathered her into his arms and nuzzled her neck. 'I should rather share something else with you, sweetheart.'

She wrapped her arms around his neck as her insides swooped but, despite the involuntary responses of her body, her mind still fretted over Turner and his errand. Why would Richard not tell her? His reaction had suggested news of some importance. She pulled away, tilting her head to study his expression.

'Is it a secret?'

A crease appeared between his brows, then relaxed as he huffed out a sigh. 'You are not going to let the subject drop, are you, Felicity Joy?'

'Should I? It sounded important, and you seem pleased. I admit I am curious, and I do not like feeling something is being kept from me.'

'Very well.' Richard led her to the sofa. 'It was…well, not quite a secret, but I did not want you to worry about it. I was set upon by…'

Set upon? The rest of his sentence was drowned out by the panicked clamour in Felicity's brain. 'Are you all right?' She twisted to face him, cupping his face between her hands. 'Are you injured? What about your ribs?'

Richard grasped her wrists and pulled her hands away from his laughing face. 'Calm down. It happened last time we came up to town.'

'Where? When?'

'I was attacked and robbed by three men in Sackville Street on our very first night in London in October. I hired Turner to investigate. He tells me there have been several similar attacks since. Evidently one of the waiters at White's has been passing information to the gang, telling them who had won at the tables, so they knew who was likely to have a heavy purse.'

'I wish you had told me.' Felicity stroked Richard's hair back from his brow.

'And what would you have done, Felicity Joy? Worried

on my behalf? Now, tell me how you have been spending
your time whilst I have been away.'

'Oh, the usual round of morning visits and walks in the
park,' Felicity said. 'And…oh, I nearly forgot. Charles is
very anxious to see you. He asked me to tell you *most particularly.*'

'I will speak to him tomorrow. I am going nowhere tonight. It is good to be home.' Richard cupped Felicity's face,
brushing his thumbs gently under her eyes. 'You look tired,
my love.' Heat swirled in the depths of his darkened eyes.
'I prescribe bed rest before dinner.'

Pulse quickening, Felicity leaned into his touch. 'I am
not so very tired, Husband, but I think a lie-down might
help restore my spirits.'

'Your spirits?'

'Mmmm.' She raised her lips to his. 'They have been
feeling neglected.'

'Are your spirits the only part of you suffering from neglect?'

Long fingers trailed down her neck to play with her neckline. Her pulse pounded as their lips met. She relaxed into
Richard's strength, his masculine scent pervading every
cell of her body: comforting, enticing, exciting.

He took his mouth from hers. 'I missed you too, Wife,'
he murmured, before claiming her lips again.

That night, Richard came to Felicity again, took her in
his arms and made love to her with such intensity she could
barely catch her breath. His lips and his hands caressed
every inch of her skin, his body moved over her and inside
her with such tenderness she had to blink back tears for fear
they might be misconstrued.

When she reached for him—to show her love for him the
way she always had, with her body—he pinned her hands
above her head and slowly, relentlessly, brought her to the
brink of ecstasy once more, driving her until she shattered

into a thousand million stars, and flew free, scattered into the infinity of the night sky.

'Richard...I love you!'

Richard rose up on his forearms, sweat glistening on his forehead. 'I love you, too, Felicity Joy.'

His deep voice reverberated through her as the tremors racking her body subsided and she drifted off to sleep in his arms, secure and content and loved.

Felicity awoke the following morning to the sun filtering through the curtains, still clasped in Richard's embrace, and felt her heart would burst with happiness.

He had become her whole world. Within her heart, her soul, her mind, there was only him. He fulfilled her, he completed her. He had become an intrinsic part of her, and she could not imagine how her life could be better.

Chapter Forty-Eight

'I'm sorry, Felicity, but we must postpone our drive until this afternoon,' Richard said as he came out of his study at eleven o'clock that morning and found her waiting in the hall. 'I have to go out on urgent business.' There was a letter in his hand.

'I am sure it cannot be helped, Richard,' Felicity said. She was disappointed, but it would not hurt to wait a little longer to drive Nutmeg and Spice. Nothing could spoil her mood today; she felt as though she could fly if she wanted to. She suppressed a smile. She had certainly flown last night.

After Richard had gone out, Felicity sent for Yvette, to go shopping in Bond Street.

As they left the house, a familiar figure approached.

'Good morning, Charles. What a pleasant surprise. I am just on my way out, as you can see.'

Charles tipped his hat and flashed a brief smile at Felicity before his gaze slid past her, to the front door.

'Good morning, Felicity. I hear my cousin returned yesterday. Is he in?'

Taken aback by his abruptness, Felicity said, 'I'm afraid he was called out on urgent business. I did tell him you wish to see him. Can I not help?'

'No. Yes. Oh, I don't know.' Charles swept the hat from his head and raked his fingers through his already dishevelled curls before replacing it again. He glanced at Yvette. 'Might I have a word in private?'

'Why, yes, of course, Charles. Shall we go back inside?'

'No. Thank you. This will be easier if we walk and talk at the same time. That way, I shall not have to read the disdain in your eyes.'

'Disdain? Oh, no, Charles. Why should I look at you with disdain?' His blue eyes were filled with worry. 'Please walk on ahead, Yvette. We shall be right behind you.'

'Thank you.'

Felicity took Charles's arm. His tension was tangible.

'Will you not tell me what troubles you? If I can help, you must know that I will.'

'I should not discuss such matters with a lady,' Charles muttered. 'Stan would have my guts if he knew, but I can wait no longer.' He fell silent, and Felicity waited. Eventually, he drew in a ragged breath. 'It's these debts. I don't quite expect you to understand, but I have borrowed against…against…'

'Against the expectation of the earldom, and all that goes with it?'

A sidelong glance revealed a flush on Charles's cheeks as he fixed his gaze on the pavement ahead of them. 'Put like that—so baldly—it sounds so very heartless.' He spun on the spot, clutching Felicity's hands. 'I have to…I am sorry to ask, but could you lend me some money? I wouldn't ask,' he added hurriedly, 'but there are some unpleasant coves after me for a debt, and I must pay them *something*.'

'Money?'

They began to walk again, crossing Oxford Street into New Bond Street.

'I wouldn't ask if I wasn't desperate. Richard refused me last time I came down to Fernley. It was a blow, I don't mind telling you. He'd barely notice such a paltry sum.'

'Lend? Have you *ever* repaid anything you have borrowed?'

Charles huffed a short laugh. 'No. I take your point. And I have changed, I promise you. I've been careful, I swear.

This particular debt…it is of long standing. Truth be told, I had forgotten about it, until the duns came knocking.'

'How much do you need?'

'Five hundred guineas should be enough.'

'I'm sorry, Charles, but I do not have that much at my disposal.'

'Will you talk to Richard? Please? Tell him this will be the last time, I promise.'

'You invest too much faith in my powers of persuasion, I fear, but I will…oh, *look*, there is Harriet. I did not know she had returned. Come, I should like to speak to her.' She called to Yvette, 'Please wait there, we will be back very soon.'

Felicity urged Charles across the road. A sweeping boy hurried to clear their path, and Charles tossed him a coin.

'That is most obliging of you, Charles, as you are so short of money yourself.'

'Oh, it was only a farthing. That barely counts as money, does it?'

And therein lies much of your problem.

'Harriet turned down here,' Felicity said, as they turned the corner of Brook Street. Time appeared to slow as Felicity's lungs seized. Harriet had stopped next to a waiting carriage, its door standing open. Richard stood close to her, gazing down into her face as she spoke earnestly, her hand on his lapel. As Felicity watched, Richard took Harriet's hand, lifted it to his lips, then handed her into the carriage. He climbed in behind her and slammed the door.

'What the…!' Charles trapped Felicity's hand in his elbow and towed her back around the corner.

She couldn't summon the strength to resist. *Richard?* And *Harriet?* The intimacy of the scene scorched her brain.

'Come, my dear.' They paused to wait for a break in the traffic to cross back to Yvette, waiting on the opposite side. 'I am sure there is a perfectly…they *are* old friends, after all.'

Old friends? Then why has neither of them ever said?

Aware she was clutching Charles's sleeve, Felicity loosened her grip.

'Old friends?' she asked lightly.

'Oh, yes,' Charles continued airily. 'Don't worry. I'm certain Richard must have ended their *friendship* as soon as he married you.'

Harriet was Richard's *mistress*? All Felicity's old doubts and suspicions charged to the fore. 'Urgent business,' he had said. That letter…from *Harriet*? Stomach churning, nausea crowding her throat, Felicity fought to keep control. What a complete and utter fool, to be taken in by their lies. She cringed when she remembered how she had confided in Harriet. Her husband's mistress.

When had Harriet returned to London? Had she been out of town with Richard? Felicity herself had told the scheming hussy where he had gone. Is that what he had been doing after Leo came back to town?

Oh, dear God…

'Steady on, Felicity. You almost fell then. I say, you don't look… Hoi! Girl! Drat it, what the blazes is that girl called?'

'Yvette,' Felicity whispered. She dredged up a memory. The attack he had told her about. In Sackville Street. Harriet's street. That was the night he had not come home, and the servants had lied to cover his absence. He had gone to visit Harriet. No wonder he had objected to Felicity becoming involved with the house in Cheapside.

Pain knifed through her, and she gasped, suddenly terrified for the baby.

'Yvette!'

Heads turned to see who was shouting. Charles's grip on Felicity's arm was painful, and she could feel his panic, but it helped clear her head. As the pain subsided, she forced her head high, gritting her teeth. She refused to provide fodder for the gossipmongers. The pain had not struck her womb, but higher. Her heart. Five months ago she would have scoffed at such a fanciful notion, but not now. Her heart was shattered. Every beat was agony.

Yvette hurried to join them.

'Quick, girl, your mistress is taken ill. I think she should—' he waved urgently at a hackney coach '—return home forthwith.' He handed Felicity up into the coach. 'Should I come with you?'

She shook her head. 'No. Thank you. Yvette will look after me. Charles?'

'Yes?'

'Please, not a word, about…about…'

He pressed her hand. 'I shall be the soul of discretion. Never fear.'

'Thank you. Oh, and Charles? About that other matter? Give me a few days, and I will see what I can do to help.'

'You, my dear, are an angel. Please, do not fret about… that.' He waved a hand in the general direction of Brook Street. 'I am certain there must be—'

'Yes! Thank you, Charles. Please ask the driver to drive on.'

'Milady?' A hand touched her shoulder, then stroked across her back.

Felicity pushed against the mattress, shuffling around into a sitting position.

'Is it the baby, milady?'

Felicity shook her head, not trusting her voice not to wobble and to set off a fresh bout of tears.

'Then it is, milord,' Yvette said. 'Tsk. If what you think, it is the truth, then he is not worth your tears. But, it is possible, *bien sûr*, that you have jumped to the conclusion, is it not?'

Yvette's words lingered in the air. If only last night hadn't been so perfect. She had been so happy, finally feeling secure in Richard's love. Now, not only had her husband and her best friend lied about knowing each other but, to discover they had shared a secret liaison out of town…so many emotions pounded at her heart and her brain that she barely knew what to think. One minute she wished she could die— *Oh, Emma, now I understand your agony*—and the next, murderous impulses charged through her mind and body until she had to restrain herself from racing to confront the lying, cheating, despicable pair.

How ironic, that this is the exact situation that made Mama leave Farlowe.

I will not run.

It had been her first instinct: to pack her bags and to leave, never to see Richard again. The very thought brought more tears to blur her vision.

How can I bear to face him?

You have faced worse, and survived. This, too, will pass. Protect your heart. Protect your baby.

She caressed her belly. Oh, yes, she would protect her baby.

Galvanized into action, she swung her legs off the bed. 'Yvette?'

'Milady?'

'Please help me to make myself presentable. I must go downstairs.' She would not skulk in her bedchamber. When Richard returned home, it would not be to a wet rag of a woman, but to a proud and strong lady who would never reveal her heartache.

Yvette poured water from the jug on the washstand into the basin, and wrung out a washcloth.

'And, Yvette?'

The maid turned. A glow of appreciation for the Frenchwoman's unwavering loyalty struck Felicity. 'Thank you for being here. I know I do not have to ask, but…'

'I shall not breathe the word, milady.'

Felicity forced her lips into a smile.

Smiles were something she must learn to fake. She felt as though she might never again produce a genuine one.

Chapter Forty-Nine

Before going downstairs, Felicity wrote a note to Charles, begging him to call upon her at four o'clock. She would take Charles when she drove her new phaeton and pair for the first time: she refused to spend even the shortest time driving in the park with Richard, making polite conversation.

Richard strode into the drawing room—where Felicity was industriously embroidering a set of cushion covers—at a little after three o'clock.

'Your business must have been important, to take until now,' Felicity remarked, glancing at him briefly before concentrating once more on her stitches.

'What, no greeting for your errant husband, my sweet?' A pair of Hessians entered Felicity's field of vision, and a finger nudged her chin, tilting her face until she had no choice but to meet his gaze. She struggled to hide her still-churning emotions. As he leaned down to kiss her she jerked away. His lips landed by her ear.

'Felicity? What is wrong?'

'Nothing is wrong. I have the headache.'

'I am sorry to hear it. I presume, therefore, you wish to postpone driving Nutmeg and Spice?'

Felicity inclined her head, not trusting herself to speak. She felt sick, until cold fury rose up to drown her guilt. Why should *she* feel guilt? She hardened her resolve.

'Have you had something to eat?' she asked, instead of answering his question, avoiding the outright lie.

'Yes. I ate at White's with Leo. He's been having family

troubles.' Felicity had no interest in the duke's problems. She had enough of her own. She stood up.

'I must go and lie down,' she said.

As she walked to the door, Richard stopped her with a hand on her arm. He tugged her round to face him.

'What is troubling you? And do not tell me it is nothing again, for I shall not believe you. What has happened? Why are you so *cold*? I should have thought, after last night, this daytime *aloofness* would be in the past.'

'Last night? I do not recall anything remarkable about last night.'

She almost quailed at the flash of fury in his eyes, but held tight to her nerve.

'You do not recall anything remarkable about last night?' He spoke through tight lips, his voice ominously quiet. Felicity swallowed convulsively. 'You said you love me. I said I love you. And you think that *unremarkable*?'

Felicity shrugged. It almost broke her heart to do it, but she conjured up that intimate scene on Brook Street. Felicity's heart had already been cleaved in two; the worst had already happened. This denial—this lie—could not possibly hurt more.

'Sometimes, one says things in the heat of the moment. Words are cheap, are they not? It is surely actions that speak the truth. Now, if you will excuse me?'

She tugged her arm from Richard's grip and left the room.

Lying...scheming...insensitive...women!

Woman, Richard amended silently, as he slammed his study door, following a curt 'I do not wish to be disturbed' to Barnes.

Well, she had certainly taken him for a fool. She'd had him believing every word and, all the time, she...

He stamped over to his desk, grabbing a bottle of brandy from a side table as he passed. He poured a measure and drank, grimacing as the brandy burned a passage down his throat. He held up his glass, squinting at the light from the window shining through the amber liquid. Amber. The same colour as her eyes. He slumped into his chair, chewing over her words...visualizing her expression...the scorn in her eyes. *Scorn*? Where had that come from? She had been distant before...but scorn was something new.

With a muttered oath, he straightened and pulled a pile of papers towards him. He needed distraction, and there was plenty of work to take his mind off his infuriating... frustrating...*incomprehensible* wife.

Three-quarters of an hour later, Richard was tilted back in his chair, hands linked behind his head, booted feet propped on his desk, having dealt with precisely one piece of correspondence. He couldn't concentrate, and it was all Felicity's fault.

'Words are cheap, are they not? It is surely actions that speak the truth.'

Her words echoed again and again through his brain. Actions? His actions? His *lack* of action?

Felicity had closed her mind to him again. He could *feel* her slipping from his grasp, and yet she refused to tell him what was wrong. Was he supposed to be a mind reader? Again, the thought surfaced that she had never been this shuttered, even in the very early days of their marriage. And lately, since his accident, they had been growing closer and closer. The future had shone with promise. With love.

What had happened since last night? Richard swung his feet from the desk. The chair legs crashed to the floor. Something must have happened to trigger this change in her. She hadn't withdrawn from him on a whim and, by God, he was going to find out precisely what that something was.

He took the stairs two at a time and thrust open her bed-chamber door without knocking. Empty. He ran downstairs again and checked all the reception rooms, ignoring the curious glances of the footman on duty in the hall. No Felicity. Anxiety and irritation now at war in his breast, he ran down the servants' stairs. Startled faces stared as he strode into the kitchen.

'Where is Yvette? I wish to see her in my study. Immediately.'

He did not wait for a reply, but returned to his study to await Yvette.

A knock at the door and Yvette entered, head high. He never ceased to admire the Frenchwoman for the way she faced life. He also admired how she was unafraid to speak her mind. She was never disrespectful—he would not stand for that in a servant—but she was forthright. It was that trait he needed now.

'Yvette. Come in and sit down, please.'

He waited as Yvette settled in the chair opposite. Yes. Something had happened, and Yvette was aware of it. He could see by the wary look in her eyes and the set of her jaw.

'Where is her ladyship, Yvette?'

Silence greeted his question.

'Well? Has her ladyship instructed you not to tell me where she has gone? Or do you imagine to somehow protect her by concealing her whereabouts?'

'She has not instructed me, no. She does not need another upset. It is important she is calm for the baby.'

'*Another* upset? Was she upset by something this morning? Was it because I cancelled our outing to the park?'

Nonsense. Felicity isn't petty. It has to be more than a fit of pique over a cancelled outing.

'No, it was not.'

'Then what happened? Something here, or did her ladyship go out?'

Richard fought to hide his growing exasperation, knowing any attempt to force information from Yvette would be met with stubborn silence. She would, however, respond to honesty.

'Yvette. I know something has upset her ladyship this

morning. She will not confide in me, but how can I put things right if I do not know what happened? Did she go out?'

Yvette sighed. 'I will tell you because you employ me. I am fond of my lady and I want her to be happy and she is not happy, no.'

Now we're getting somewhere.

'What happened this—?'

'No.' Yvette glared at Richard. 'I tell this in my way. My lady, she is in love with you but she is scared. Then today, I do not know what she see, but she see something and she nearly swoons and Mr Durant put us in a hackney and milady cried.'

Richard's stomach knotted. He longed to pepper Yvette with questions, but forced himself to go slowly. 'Mr Durant?'

'Milady and me, we go shopping and Mr Durant escorts us. But I am told to walk ahead so I do not know what he says, but he is worried about something.'

Money. Debts. Nothing new there.

'Milady sees the Lady Brierley going into Brook Street, and she follows her but stops on the corner.'

Ice-cold fingers clutched Richard's heart. He had met Harriet in Brook Street. What had Felicity seen? He pictured their meeting. Nothing there, surely, to cause such upset.

Apart from the fact you cancelled your outing with her to meet clandestinely with your ex-mistress?

Nonsense! Felicity does not know... His brain seized, then stuttered forward, inch by agonizing inch.

Felicity did not know Harriet had been his mistress. Felicity did not know Richard and Harriet had more than a nodding acquaintance. And yet...Richard had broken his promise to Felicity in favour of meeting Harriet. They had talked and then driven off together in his carriage.

But, still, was that enough to...why did she not just *ask* him?

Charles! Damned loose-tongued... Richard recalled their conversation at the Davenports' ball. It was possible. It was the only thing that made any sense.

'Thank you, Yvette. That will be all.'

He must talk to Felicity. Explain why he had met Harriet that morning and, he knew, it was time he told her the truth about their past relationship. No other woman mattered in his life. Only Felicity.

He was overcome with a sudden urge to find her. *Now*, to clear the air, to convince her of his love.

'Yvette!' The maid returned at his shout. 'You did not tell me where her ladyship has gone.'

'She has driven to the park with Mr Durant, milord.'

Of course she has. What else would his Felicity do but try to prove she did not care by continuing their plans without him? Spurred into action, he shouted to the footman to send to the stables for his horse and to tell Dalton he was to accompany him.

Richard set a spanking pace around the park, nodding to friends and acquaintances alike, but stopping to speak to no one. At last, on the far side, he spied his target. Defying convention, he urged Gambit into a gallop, overtaking the phaeton and pair before skidding to a halt in front of them.

Felicity pulled up Nutmeg and Spice and glared at Richard.

'What are you doing?' she hissed. Richard ignored her, his eyes fixed on his sheepish-looking cousin. He nudged Gambit around to where Charles sat.

'Out!'

'Now, steady on, Stan.'

Richard swung down from Gambit and tossed the reins to Dalton. 'Take them home,' he ordered, his eyes still on Charles who, after the very slightest of hesitations, climbed from the phaeton.

'Charles? Don't, I beg of you—'

Richard leapt aboard, taking the reins from Felicity's un-resisting hands. 'Say goodbye to Charles, Felicity.'

'I say…'

Richard clicked to the ponies. They set off at a trot.

'You won't forget that little matter we spoke about, will you, Felicity?' Charles's voice faded into the distance.

'Has he asked you for money?'

'Yes. Richard, why—?'

'I do not appreciate other men dunning my wife for money.'

The sharp intake of breath beside him warned Richard this conversation might not go as planned. Planned? Hell, he hadn't planned anything…had thought no further than finding Felicity, taking her in his arms and convincing her of his love.

Chapter Fifty

⸻

'And *I* do not appreciate other women making secret assignations with my husband.'

As soon as the words left her mouth, Felicity regretted them. What had come of her plan to keep her dignity and ignore Richard's behaviour? Did she *have* to blurt out the thing that was uppermost in her mind almost the second she saw him?

Richard reined Nutmeg and Spice to a halt on the side of the Row, and set the brake, twisting to face Felicity, who gritted her teeth and stared defiantly ahead.

'You saw me with Harriet.'

It was a statement, not a question. 'Harriet, is it now? It was always Lady Brierley before, whilst you were making a fool out of me.'

Felicity gripped her gloved hands tightly in her lap. As people rode and drove past, she was aware of their surreptitious glances.

'Neither of us has any desire to make a fool of you, my darling.'

Richard covered her clasped hands with his.

'I will tell you everything, and then I can do no more than hope you will forgive me. Not for anything I have done, but only for not admitting the truth when you first met Harriet.'

'I thought she was my friend.' A tear threatened to spill and Felicity snatched her hand from Richard's grasp to swipe at it.

'She *is* your friend. She is very fond of you, and has done more for you than you know.'

'*Hmmph.*' Felicity did not want this conversation. And she most certainly did not want to hear it here, in the park, in front of all these curious, prying eyes. 'I want to go home.'

Richard leaned closer, his voice low. 'First, we will have this conversation. *Then* we will go home.'

Despite her anger, a tug of awareness snaked through Felicity as his warm breath danced over her skin. She clamped her teeth tight, fighting her instinctive reaction.

'What I have to say, I will say now. And you need to hear it now, whilst you are upset and open and vulnerable. If I give you the time, I am too afraid you will rebuild those wretched fortifications around that stubborn little heart of yours, and I shall be marooned forever on the outside.'

She risked a sidelong glance. Dark-chocolate eyes burned into her. Afraid? Her strong, capable, confident husband afraid?

She inclined her head. 'Very well. It would appear I have little choice, as you are holding the reins.'

An apt metaphor for a woman's life: someone else always in control of the reins.

'Before I decided to wed, I was a single man. Harriet was a widow.' Gentle fingers caressed her nape. Shivers cascaded down her spine. 'We had an understanding—'

'An *affaire*!' Her squirming stomach made Felicity shift uneasily on the seat. 'You were in love with her.'

'Yes, an *affaire* and, no, I was never in love with her. Nor she with me. It was a mutually agreeable arrangement. I know how cold that sounds, but it happens, sweetheart. We satisfied each other's physical needs. Nobody else knew.'

'Charles knew.'

'He did not know. He guessed, and only very recently. I suppose I should be grateful he managed to keep that much a secret. If he had not, the entire *ton* would know by now.

As soon as we were betrothed, I wrote to Harriet to end our arrangement.'

'Why?' Felicity concentrated her gaze on his sensual, skilful lips. Had those lips caressed Harriet…? She shied away from the thought, miserably aware she was being unfair. She was an adult. People had *affaires*. She, of all people, knew that.

'Why did I end it?'

She nodded.

'I wanted to be fair to you, and I wanted our marriage to be content. I told myself I could always take another mistress later, after you were with child.'

Felicity stiffened. Tried to pull away from his touch. His arm wrapped around her, holding her still.

'I am being brutally honest with you, my love, because there must be no further misunderstandings between us. At that time, both you and I expected a marriage of convenience. I did not know what the future held. That is what I thought and how I felt then. It is not how I feel now.

'When we came up to town, that first time—on the very first night—I called upon Harriet. I presented her with a gift and we parted on amicable terms. That was the night I was attacked, and I stayed the night at Harriet's, in the guest bedchamber.'

'I know,' Felicity said.

'You know? How…?'

'I knew you hadn't come home that night…'

'But I sent instructions…'

Felicity felt a blush building in her cheeks. 'I looked into your bedchamber very early. I wanted…I wondered…I saw the bed was all made and yet, later, after breakfast, it was all messy and looked slept in. I suspected then you had spent the night with a woman, but I never dreamt it was…' Her voice hitched.

'But it was not, my sweet. At least, not in the way you mean.'

Felicity's brain whirled. His explanation made sense. She had begun to trust Richard, had ceased to believe he had a mistress. And yet…

'You did not return home with the duke…'

'He had to leave early, to deal with a family crisis.'

'Harriet went out of town at the same time. Was she with you?'

'Is that what's bothering you? You saw me meet with Harriet, and then recalled we were out of town at the same time? And thought the worst of both of us? Oh, dear, Felicity Joy. No wonder… I had not even thought, until this minute, you might imagine such a thing.'

He brushed an escaping wisp of hair out of her eyes, then dropped a kiss on her nose.

'At least this has solved my quandary.'

'Quandary?'

'Harriet wrote and asked to meet me, to discuss some information she had, and whether she should reveal it to you.'

Richard released Felicity to take a letter from his pocket. 'It's fortunate I still have this with me.' He laid it on Felicity's lap. 'This is the letter I received from Harriet this morning asking to meet me. Read it.'

Her hand twitched, but she did not touch the letter. 'No,' she said. 'Please. Tell me what happened. I want to trust your words. I do not want to live my life searching for either proof of your truthfulness or evidence of your guilt.'

Gentle fingers brushed across her cheek. Deep brown eyes fixed on her lips and she felt her body respond as her blood quickened.

'Very well. We met in Brook Street because Harriet did not want me to visit her at home, out of respect for your friendship. She said you told her about Emma.'

Misery squeezed Felicity's chest. She had trusted Harriet. 'That is true. I also told her where you had gone. I had dinner with her that night, and she made no mention of going out of town, but the next morning she had gone.'

'She only decided to go away after you left. She hoped to help you come to terms with Emma's death. She attended the same house parties as your mother and Emma that summer, and thought she could identify the wretch who seduced Emma.'

'Who is he? I want to see him. He must pay for what he did.'

'Steady.' Richard grabbed at Felicity as she turned to jump from the phaeton. 'He is not in London, which is why Harriet went into Kent, to see him. She did not tell you because she did not wish to raise your hopes if she was mistaken.

'And she told me of her discovery before telling you because of your delicate condition. She wondered if it might be better to wait—'

'Who is he?'

Richard sighed. 'Now you know this much, you must know the whole, I suppose. But understand this, Felicity Joy. There is no possibility of you going to see him. He is Sir Malcolm Poole.'

Sir Malcolm Poole? Try as she might, Felicity could not put a face to the name. 'I should like to—'

'Yes, yes—' Richard laughed, prising her fists loose '—you should like to kill him. I know that, my darling, but it won't be necessary. He is, at this very moment, paying a heavy price for his debauched lifestyle and is close to meeting his maker.'

'What did he say? About Emma?'

'He admitted to seducing her, but showed no remorse when told of her suicide, according to Harriet. The fellow has always been a rake of the worst kind—an out-and-out scoundrel. His kind live only for their own pleasure without thought of the consequences for their victims. He has been an outcast from polite society for many years now.'

'Was he...' Felicity felt her forehead pucker as her

thoughts spun and she strove to weave a coherent question from them '…was he an outcast *before* he met Emma?'

Richard gathered her against his chest. 'I'm afraid so.' His voice rumbled in her ear, deep and reassuring.

'Then that means…Mama…those parties…'

'They were no place for an innocent.'

A sob built in her throat. Harriet had said the same, and she had always suspected as much, but had given her mother the benefit of the doubt.

'Your mother… You must remember she did not take Emma to those places from malice.'

'No. I know. She was just selfish and thoughtless. As she still is. I *begged* her not to make me—' Felicity stopped with a gasp. How could she allow her mouth run on so?

'You *begged* not to have to marry me?'

Richard's voice quivered, and Felicity peeked up at him. Then straightened. 'You wretch!' She slapped at his chest. 'You are laughing at me.'

'No, no, I'm laughing at myself. At fate. I knew you were reluctant to marry me, but I could not fathom why. That only made me more determined to go through with it, hence the speed of the wedding. I did not want you to find a way out. Not only had you landed a bruising blow to my self-esteem, but I found myself eager to learn the truth of your reluctance.'

'And did you?'

'We worked that out together, Felicity Joy, did we not? When you read Emma's diary?'

'I suppose we did. When I knew the real reason for her suicide, I recognized my greatest fear was based on an untruth. Emma did not kill herself over unrequited love, but because she was with child and the man she loved had abandoned her.' She touched her belly. 'I do not believe that will happen to us, Richard.'

'Indeed it will not,' he said. 'I love you, Felicity Joy. I love every inch of you, inside and out.' He pulled her closer, tilting her chin. His warm breath feathered over her suddenly sensitized lips. 'Over these past few months I have fallen further and further under your spell. You fill my every waking thought and my every dream.'

His eyes darkened and awareness shivered through Felicity. She leaned closer.

'Well! Really!' The outraged female tones penetrated the sensual haze surrounding Felicity.

'Richard, no! What will people say?'

'I could not care less. All I care about is you.'

His lips covered hers, warm and seductive, as she melted into his embrace.

When they finally came up for air, it was to a smattering of applause. But they had eyes only for each other.

Epilogue

July 1816—Cheriton Abbey

'Back where it all began.'

Richard sprawled at his ease on a blanket, propped on his elbow as he gazed around with satisfaction. The Devon air was soft and sweetly scented. The melodious trill of sky-larks and the hum of bees working the nectar-rich clover in the meadow were punctuated by an occasional squeal of childish delight.

The duke had thrown a family party to celebrate the birth of his new baby. He had insisted Richard and Felicity also attend as they were—in Leo's words—family, too.

Felicity caught Richard's eye and smiled, and he felt the familiar squeeze of his heart. Even after all this time, he still wanted her.

And needed her.

And loved her.

He never stopped wanting her.

'It seems like another life entirely, does it not?' Felicity said, as she cuddled baby George close to her breast. 'Do you remember the very first time we met? On the stairs?'

'I do indeed. You were a naughty minx then and you're a scandalous minx now.'

Felicty's giggle tiptoed through his heart. 'Hush, Rich-ard. The children!'

'They are far too busy playing to worry about what their staid old parents are up to.'

Richard looked again, picking out their eldest, Emma, now four, and three-year-old Adam, Baron Durant of Fernley. His heir. And now—he regarded George with pride—the traditional spare as well. Life could not be sweeter.

Sarah, George's nursemaid, approached. 'Shall I take the baby now, milady?'

George had fallen asleep in his mother's arms, and barely stirred when Sarah lifted him, merely pursing his lips and frowning fleetingly. As Sarah carried him away, Richard made up his mind. He leapt up, grabbed Felicity's hands and tugged her to her feet. He studied her beloved face—amber eyes round with amused enquiry, soft pink lips parted on a breathless laugh.

'Felicity Joy…'

Her laughter faded. He tucked a stray curl behind her ear, and stroked her silky cheek before taking her hand again. The first time had been business. This was—undoubtedly—his heart's desire. He dropped to one knee, his gaze never leaving hers. Her eyes widened.

'…I love you more than you can ever know. You have made my life complete. Although I asked you once, and you accepted, and we are already man and wife…I ask you again. This time from my heart.

'Will you marry me?'

Felicity threw her head back and her laugh rang out across the meadow. 'I will, I would, every time!'

She tumbled to her knees, took his face between her palms, and kissed him.

* * * * *

SCANDAL AND MISS MARKHAM

To Mum

I like to think you would be proud.

Chapter One

Thea's head snapped up at the sound of wheels crunching across the gravel outside Stourwell Court.

Daniel!

Hope erupted through her…it had been five days since her brother had gone out one day and not returned. She leapt to her feet and hurried to the salon window. A glimpse of a curricle drawn by a pair of blacks set her heart racing, and she flung her embroidery aside, gathered her skirts and ran for the door. Across the hall and through the front door she sped.

Please. Let it be him.

Doubts nipped at her as she sprinted down the steps to the now stationary conveyance, but she ignored them. She could not bear to let that prayer of hope fizzle and die. She shut her mind against the evidence of her eyes as she reached the foot of the steps and hurried to the curricle.

'Daniel—'

Her eyes met those of the driver—a stranger—and she skidded to a halt, gravel spinning from beneath her feet.

'Who are you? Where is Daniel?' She raked the driver with her eyes and then switched her gaze to the horses. 'Those are his—'

Her jaw snapped shut and her cheeks scorched. 'Oh!'

Those doubts had caught up with her and knocked her flat. She bit her lip as sick disappointment flooded her, followed by the fear that had dogged her ever since her brother had failed to come home.

'I beg your pardon, sir. I mistook your horses for those of my brother's but I see, upon closer examination, they are not his.'

They were a pair of blacks, yes, but of far superior quality to Daniel's, and a groom—another stranger—perched on the back of the curricle. And besides...

Fool! Daniel didn't even take his curricle. He was on horseback.

And that had been her one ray of hope in this desperate mess, one that she clung to with all her heart: her brother had ridden away and not returned, but neither had Bullet, his grey gelding, whose homing instinct was powerful and who in the past had often carried his foxed rider safely home after a night spent drinking. Thankfully, though, Daniel had soon outgrown that wild behaviour.

And now Thea clung to her belief that whilst Bullet was missing, there was still hope.

The stranger appraised her with raised brows and she scowled back at him, irritated by the amused curl of his lips. She quashed the tug of attraction she recognised deep in her core. It was a very long time since she had allowed herself to be attracted to any man.

'Your brother being Mr Daniel Markham?'

His voice was deep and cultured—that of a gentleman born. Thea had been subjected to enough elocution lessons to recognise that aristocratic drawl. She studied the driver, from the brim of his tall beaver hat to the toes of his shiny boots. What business could a man like this have with Daniel? Suspicions swirled. Did this stranger have something to do with Daniel's disappearance? Daniel had been troubled before he disappeared, that much she did know. But, unusually, he had refused to confide in her.

'He is,' she said. 'And you are?'

He frowned, clearly put out by such a brusque demand. Well, Thea had more pressing concerns than a strange gentleman's sense of his own importance.

'I am Lord Vernon Beauchamp, here to speak to your brother.'

'A *lord*? What on earth do you want with *Daniel*?'

A muscle leapt at the side of his jaw. 'Bickling, hold the horses.'

He tied off the reins and the groom jumped down and ran to the horses' heads. Lord Vernon Beauchamp climbed in a leisurely fashion from his curricle and walked across the gravel to Thea, not stopping until he was so close he towered over her, radiating confidence and power. Thea set her jaw and stood her ground, refusing to be intimidated even though his commanding air and his raw masculinity rattled her from her head to her toes.

'I suggest that is a matter between your brother and me, madam. Am I to understand he is not here?'

'No, he is not.'

She glanced back at the house. No sign of her mother. Good…no doubt she was with Papa; she often read to him in the morning after he awoke. Heaven knew how much longer Thea could protect them from knowing the full truth of Daniel's absence. She looked up at Lord Vernon.

'If it concerns Stour Crystal, I assure you that I am perfectly able either to assist you myself, or to refer any query to the appropriate individual at the manufactory.'

'Stour Crystal?' Lord Vernon surveyed the frontage of Stourwell Court before looking back along the carriage-way, to the wrought-iron entrance gates in the distance. Thea bridled as she fancied she detected a slight curl of his upper lip as he stripped off his driving gloves. 'Your family manufacture lead-crystal glassware?'

'We do.'

And I am proud of it.

Her father had built the business from scratch, manufacturing some of the finest quality cut lead crystal in the land. *His Lordship* might have been born into the aristocracy but that did not give him the right to look down upon her. But with that defiant pride came the realisation that she had not offered her visitor the customary hospitality due a visitor. She had allowed her disappointment he was not Daniel to override her manners and that would surely only add to his lordship's low impression of her and her family. She bit back any further comment and moved away from Lord Vernon to smooth her hand over the haunch of the nearest horse. She smiled at the groom.

'He is hot,' she said, 'and you must be tired and in need of refreshment.' After the heavy rains of a week ago, the weather had turned unseasonably warm. 'Take the horses around the back—you will see the way to the stable yard and you may care for them there. Come to the kitchen afterwards. Cook will give you some food and something to drink.'

The groom waited until his master gave him permission—granted by a flick of the head—to proceed before leading the horses away. Lord Vernon, a look of irritation on his face, swished his driving gloves against his palm. No doubt he was unhappy at his groom and horses' needs being considered before his own: yet more evidence of his sense of entitlement. Mentally, Thea shrugged but she took care to conceal her scorn. She had neither the strength nor the heart to engage in a verbal sparring session.

'You, too, must be weary, my lord. Shall we continue this discussion indoors?'

As the scrunch of hooves faded, his lordship inscribed an arc through the air with his arm and then bowed.

'After you.'

Thea marched to the front porch, feeling much like a cat whose fur had been rubbed the wrong way, but she vowed to remain polite; she had no wish to reinforce his prejudices. The man had been neither rude nor derogatory, but—she pictured again that subtle curl of his lip—she knew how his sort viewed ordinary business folk who must work for their living.

She led him across the hall and into the study.

'Would you prefer ale or wine, sir?'

'Tea,' he said.

She was certain he was being deliberately awkward. Their aversion was mutual then. So be it. She had more pressing concerns than how some spoilt aristocrat viewed her and a handsome face and a manly physique meant nothing to a woman who had forsworn all men. She jerked at the bell and a footman soon attended.

'Bring tea for the gentleman, please, George, and a glass of Madeira for me. And some of Cook's fruit cake.'

As George turned to leave, Thea said, 'Is Mama with Papa?'

'She is, miss. Shall I inform her we have a visitor?'

Thea glanced at Lord Vernon, who had removed his hat to reveal a full head of auburn hair that curled around his ears. A little flutter deep in her stomach taunted her: perhaps she wasn't as immune to an attractive man as she thought. She wrenched her attention away from her treacherous body.

'No. That will not be necessary, George.'

'Very well, miss.'

Thea then sat in a chair by the window and gestured to a nearby chair.

'Please, take a seat, sir.'

She waited until he was settled, her thoughts whirling. She knew from past experience, through her dealings with other men, that he would be reluctant to discuss business with her simply because of her sex. If she were to learn the truth of his visit, she must try to annoy him into indiscretion and she knew the perfect way to aggravate him: men often found it hard to deal with females who were direct.

'Is it money?'

His brows lowered into a thunderous frown. 'Is *what* money?' His question almost a growl.

'Does Daniel owe you money? Are you here to collect on a debt?'

'I do not—' He snapped his jaw shut, abruptly cutting off his heated response. His eyes—an arresting shade of green that sparkled in the light of a stray sunbeam filtering through the window pane—narrowed. When he spoke again, his voice was level. 'Why should you jump to such a conclusion? Is your Daniel a gambler?'

Thea frowned in her turn. This man was clearly not to be easily manipulated.

'He is not.'

'Then I ask again, why do you jump to the conclusion I am here to collect on a debt?'

Thea shrugged, stood up and paced to the fireplace. She swung around, to see that her visitor had risen to his feet. She huffed a silent laugh. A lord and a gentleman, trained from birth in correct etiquette. When a lady stands—even a lowly born lady such as she—a gentleman, too, must stand.

'Please. Sit down.' She crossed the room to sit in her own chair and his lordship—with a supercilious lift of one brow—followed suit.

He folded his arms. 'I am waiting.'

His voice was soft. Almost menacing. Thea shivered at her sudden mental image of a wolf: crouching, watching, patient. She thrust aside that picture, silently castigating herself for such a fanciful thought. He was a man…a powerful lord, maybe, but a man none the less.

His question…what was it again? About debt. 'We are in business, my lord. I wondered if Daniel had overlooked a bill.'

His lips twitched. Thea searched his expression and felt her tension ease and her sense of foreboding lift as she realised he was trying not to laugh. No sign of a menacing predator now. She really must try to curtail her imagination.

'I cannot decide whether to be amused or offended that you could even suspect I am a debt collector,' he said. His smile now surfaced fully, his lips parting to reveal white, even teeth.

Heavens, he is a handsome devil.

She quashed that thought and dismissed the accompanying trip of her pulse.

'Might we, do you think, start this conversation anew and dispense with the suspicion on both sides?'

Thea inclined her head by way of reply. A truce would speed this meeting along and give her the opportunity to discover if Lord Vernon Beauchamp knew anything that might shed light on Daniel's disappearance.

George came in with the refreshments and Thea poured a cup of tea for her visitor before handing him the cup and saucer. He captured her gaze as he murmured his thanks, his deep voice vibrating through her. Then he brushed her fingers as she handed him a plate with a slice of cake. A whiff of cologne arose to tease at her senses: spicy, with notes of cinnamon. Musky and expensive. The resulting flicker of desire deep in her stomach exasperated Thea all over again.

She recognised his tactic. This was an attempt to use his charisma to wheedle information from her. He was a handsome aristocrat, experienced in the art of flirtation and accustomed to having his own way…well, he would soon find she was too shrewd to allow weasel words and admiring glances to fool *her*.

She had been burned before.

Never again.

Besides, she had neither the time nor the inclination to engage with him in this particular game. There was far too much at stake.

'I do not know your name.'

His statement startled her. 'But…of course you know my name. Daniel is my brother. I, therefore, am Miss Markham.'

He cocked his head to one side. 'But I did not know whether or not you were married, Miss Markham. For all I knew, you could be Mrs Wilful, or Lady Copper Curls.'

He smiled. Charmingly. A fan of crinkles formed at the outer corner of each eye. Thea raised her chin and directed a stern look at him.

'You were about to tell me your business with my brother, sir.'

Lord Vernon set his teacup and saucer on to a side table and settled back into his chair, his elbows propped on the arms as he placed his hands fingertip to fingertip beneath his chin.

'My business is with your brother. It is not proper that I should discuss it with you.'

'Because I am a female?' No matter how many times she was told she was unable to understand business matters, it became no easier hearing the same sentiment from yet another male. 'As I said before—my brother and I collaborate in our father's business. We do not have secrets.'

'And yet you have no idea why I am here.'

Thea swallowed past the painful lump in her throat. 'That is entirely different. I cannot be privy to your whims and fancies in deciding to call upon Daniel.'

'Whims and fancies,' he murmured. 'I cannot say I am

flattered at being thought a man subject to whims and fancies.' His expression hardened and again she was reminded that, beneath his urbane exterior, there lurked an altogether different beast. 'You boast there are no secrets between yourself and your brother and yet you are unaware it was your brother who wrote to *me* to request a meeting.'

'For what purpose?'

He raised a brow. 'Perhaps *you* can enlighten *me*?'

Thea shook her head and a lock of hair sprang loose to dangle in front of her eye. She clicked her tongue in irritation, swept the curl from her forehead and hooked it behind a hairpin, then sipped at her Madeira, her mind working furiously. This conversation was not going the way she intended. She was desperate to find out if this man had any information that might tell her where Daniel had gone.

'I have not the first idea why Daniel wrote to you. Was it connected with the business?'

'I can safely say he did not summon me to discuss a matter of business. The only knowledge I have of lead-crystal glassware is the quality of the liquid contained therein.'

'That comes as no surprise.'

Heavens! When will I learn to curb my tongue?

A muscle bunched in his jaw. 'And such a riposte is entirely predictable. You clearly suffer under the illusion that the idle aristocracy are fit for little other than frittering their fortunes away upon their own pleasures and depravities.'

She couldn't decide if she felt shame at having insulted him, albeit indirectly, or pride that she could stand her own against such a man.

'They are your words,' she responded, raising her brows. '*Your* interpretation of my expressed belief that you would have no knowledge of the manufacture of lead crystal. And I was correct.'

His lips thinned. 'Where is your brother, Miss Markham? When do you expect him home?'

She bit her lip.

'I do not know.'

Her stomach clenched into a tight, hard ball of fear. Unable to sit still, she rose to her feet and crossed the room to the desk. Daniel's desk. But there were no clues there. She had searched it thoroughly and there was no hint of where he had gone or what had happened to him. She fingered a contract that lay on the top of a pile of papers awaiting attention, that same all-pervading sense of dread crawling through her veins. This contract was important to Stour Crystal.

Would Daniel really just…go? Would he really be so negligent?

Of the business? Of her? Of their parents?

'I do not know,' she repeated.

Chapter Two

Lord Vernon Beauchamp eyed Miss Markham. Lines of strain bracketed her mouth and worry lurked in those huge hazel eyes—eyes that had sparked such fire at him only moments ago. In fact, all her fire had fizzled out… This was not merely a case of her brother not being at home this afternoon, of that he was certain. But alongside the worry in her eyes lurked caution. Maybe attempting to flirt his way into gaining her good opinion…her *trust*…had been a mistake.

He rose to his feet and approached the desk. She tracked his every movement, her wariness plain.

'Do not be alarmed,' Vernon said. 'Will you not sit down and tell me what has happened? There truly is no need to be suspicious of my intentions towards your brother. If it helps to reassure you, you should know that I have never before met Daniel and I know nothing more than he wrote in this letter.'

He reached into his pocket and produced the letter that Daniel Markham had penned, the letter that had prompted Vernon's journey into Worcestershire. Miss Markham subsided into the desk chair and took the letter, unfolding it to read. Vernon hitched one hip on the far corner of the desk. After a few seconds, she raised her gaze to his.

'The Duke of Cheriton? This letter is not addressed to you…is it?'

Vernon laughed. 'No, I am not a duke. Cheriton is my brother. He had every intention of writing to your Daniel with an invitation to call upon him to discuss his concerns, but I formed a sudden desire to visit Worcestershire and so I offered to travel up here to meet your brother myself.'

Leo—Vernon's brother—had recently married again and the bride's maternal aunt, Lady Slough, had set her sights on Vernon as a suitable catch for her daughter. Not that Vernon had anything against the chit, but Lady Slough sported all the finesse of a wild boar and he had decided that putting some distance between himself and the lady in question would be best for all concerned. He would not put it past Lady Slough to attempt a spot of entrapment.

Vernon had no inclination to enter the parson's mouse-trap. Not for a very long time, if ever. Leo already had his heir and spare—plus a daughter—from his first marriage, thus securing the future of the dukedom, so there was no absolutely no need for Vernon to wed. And why would he choose to give up his charmed life of a popular, wealthy bachelor? He wanted for nothing.

Except purpose.

He thrust aside that mocking voice, even though he was unable to deny that restlessness had also played its part in persuading him to travel up here to Worcestershire.

Miss Markham had continued to read her brother's letter, a frown knitting her forehead.

'Henry Mannington? Who is Henry Mannington?' Her voice was unusually deep for a woman and slightly gruff—quite at odds with her petite figure and luxuriant curls.

'You have never heard of him?'

She shook her head and two of those springy, copper-coloured curls of hers bounced over her forehead. She pushed at them absentmindedly, her gaze still fixed on the letter.

'No. Never.'

'He is not a friend of your brother's? A customer? A rival?'

'No. None of those. I *told* you,' she said, with a hint of sarcasm, 'I have never heard of him.' She paused, white teeth nibbling at her lower lip. Then she narrowed her eyes. 'But *you* know who he is. Or you would not have come all the way up here to speak to Daniel.'

Impressed by her quick uptake, Vernon decided there was nothing to be gained in concealing the little knowledge he did possess.

'Henry Mannington is a distant cousin of the Beauchamp family, but none of us has seen him or heard of him for several years. He is a classics scholar with a passion for exploring ancient sites and even as a young man he had no interest in socialising in our circle.'

'The upper ranks of society, you mean?'

There it was again. That hint of disdain in her tone, but recognisable for all that. Miss Markham clearly did not approve of the aristocracy.

'Yes.' He would neither apologise for who and what he was, nor feel guilty for it. Her prejudices were her problem. 'He is my age and we were at university together. Our paths have not crossed since then.'

Miss Markham thrust the letter back at Vernon. 'I cannot see how this will help me find Daniel.' She crossed her arms.

'*Find* him?'

Her cheeks reddened, clashing with her bright hair. Her lips compressed.

'How long is it since you have seen Daniel?'

For the first time her composure wavered, her nostrils

flared and her hazel eyes, fringed with thick, dark lashes, sheened.

'Come.' Vernon gentled his voice. 'You are upset. Tell me what has happened. I might be able to help.'

'I do not need help.'

'How long?'

'F-five days.'

Vernon checked the letter. 'Three days after this was written.' He re-read the missive. 'By its wording, Daniel had suspicions about Henry Mannington, but what manner of suspicions? It must be more than Henry claiming kinship with Cheriton, for that much is the truth and easily verified. And Henry is a decent chap, not the sort to become embroiled in matters dastardly enough to drive your brother to beg help from a peer with whom he has no acquaintance.'

Miss Markham stood up and resolutely smoothed down the skirt of the peach-coloured gown that skimmed her petite frame. The colour should have clashed with her hair, which was the colour of an autumn leaf, but the combination put Vernon in mind of the brilliant sunset of the evening before and he felt a smile tug at the corner of his mouth. She glared at him as he also rose to his feet. She really was a tiny little thing, barely reaching his shoulder. She put him in mind of a cornered kitten, fur fluffed up and claws out, ready for a fight.

'There is no need to stand every time I do,' she said, placing her fists on the desk and leaning on them. 'I am not one of your fine ladies, ready to take affront at imagined slights.'

'Maybe you are not,' Vernon said, quashing down the laugh that tickled his throat. That really *would* infuriate her. 'But *I*, you see, *am* a gentleman. And I therefore stand when a lady does. Whether *she* considers herself a lady or no. And…' he added, tweaking his neckcloth and smoothing the wrinkles from his sleeves, merely to irritate her and to see those remarkably fine eyes flash fire again '…as for taking affront, I quite see that particular emotion is alien to your sunny nature.'

He smiled at her scowl and her muttered imprecation. Fortunately, perhaps, he could not make out her exact sentiments. She was indeed a little hothead, hardly surprising with that head of hair. His own hair had reddish tones, but it was more of a dark chestnut colour than the fiery hue of Miss Markham's. He would warrant his temperament was less fiery than hers, too.

'Have you made enquiries as to your brother's whereabouts?'

'Yes… That is, I sent the grooms out to search the countryside around, but I instructed them not to make enquiries. Not yet. I did not want to raise a fuss only to find there was a simple explanation for his absence.' She sucked in a deep breath and his eyes were drawn to the swell of her breasts. 'They found no trace of Daniel or his horse. And so I waited. I kept hoping he would return. Or that he would write to me.'

'In other words, you have done nothing to find your brother. You shut your eyes to reality and simply hoped for the best.'

She flashed a look of daggers at him. 'I did not wish to stir up a wasps' nest of trouble for him if there was no need for it.'

'Trouble? Why should you suspect he was in trouble?'

She stared down at the desk, fingering the stack of papers in front of her. Then she subsided into the chair.

'He was preoccupied…*upset*…in the days before he went missing.'

Her voice was low and husky with a hint of vulnerability and it stirred within him a peculiar urge to protect her. To help. She was nibbling at her full lower lip, her tawny brows creased in a frown as she stared past Vernon, into the distance. Vernon tore his gaze from her mouth, disconcerted by the slow but undeniable tightening in his loins.

'I *knew* he was worried,' she said, 'and yet I did not make him tell me what was amiss. I allowed him to fob me off.'

'I doubt you could have compelled him to confide in you.'

Her gaze met his, a glint of humour in her eyes. 'Oh, I think I could, had I tried. I should have *forced* him to tell me where he was going.'

Vernon felt his lips twitch. 'You have piqued my interest, Miss Markham. How, pray, do you imagine you could have *forced* your brother to tell you?'

'I could have threatened to follow him.'

'And he would have believed you?'

'Of course.' She tilted her chin. 'He knows I never make empty threats.'

His lips twitched again, but he held back his grin. 'I shall have to remember that,' he murmured. 'Do I take it you are older than your brother?'

'Yes. By three years.'

'That explains much.'

Her brows snapped together. 'This—' Her lips tightened. 'I am doing it again. Allowing myself to be diverted, because I am scared… I fear…' She bent her head.

Vernon waited.

'You were right… I *have* been waiting. And hoping. But no more.' She pierced him with a fierce gaze. 'You have spurred me into seeing what I must do. I shall go myself and I shall make enquiries. I shall find out where he went, all those days when he was out for hours upon end, returning home to eat and sleep and then leaving again at first light. He must have left a trail. He would have been seen. He had to eat.' She was on her feet again, pacing. 'Oh! Why did I not go out that first day? Immediately? What a fool I have been, waiting at home like a…like a…*ninny*…when Daniel had need of me.'

'And where do you intend to make your enquiries?'

'Oh! I do not know.' She waved her arm as she paced, brushing aside his query as though it were an irritating fly. 'His usual haunts. The Nag's Head, in Stourbridge, for a start. He often went there for a drink in the evening. Someone there might know where he went. And they will know of other places he frequented.'

'The Nag's Head? A public house?'

She slammed to a halt, staring at him. 'Do not—' her voice throbbed with warning '—tell me I cannot go there because I am a woman.'

Vernon felt his eyes narrow. 'That is precisely what I *am* telling you. Such scandalous behaviour is completely unacceptable. Your reputation would be ruined.'

'Scandal! What do I care for scandal? My brother is missing and I must—'

'You *should* care about scandal. Your good name, once lost, will not be easily recovered.'

'We are not in your overprotected and rarefied world now, my lord. As I said before, I am not—'

'Not one of my fine ladies. Yes, you have already made that point.'

Her mouth set in a mulish line and the dogged determination upon her face reminded Vernon of his niece, Olivia, when told she could not do something she had set her heart upon. But Olivia was eighteen years of age. Miss Markham should…*must*, surely…have more sense.

He'd had enough of this, she was not thinking rationally. She must realise how dangerous such places might be and not only to her good name. He changed tack. Demanding her obedience would not work, that much he had already learned.

'Promise me you will not go haring off on such an ill-advised crusade.'

'But I must, for if I do not, who will?'

'Your father?'

She turned her head aside, but not before he recognised her anguish. 'He is not well. He must not be upset.'

'Other male relatives?'

She shook her head, freeing even more of those fascinating curls to bounce around her face. Her hair appeared to have a life of its own, the curls like flaming corkscrews.

'I am not a fool,' she said. 'I would not go alone. I would take a groom. Or even two. For protection. So, you see, there is no need for you to be concerned, or even to stay here any longer.' She tilted her chin. 'You said yourself you do not know Daniel and neither do you know the area. *You* would not know where to begin looking.'

Vernon eyed her with exasperation as he pondered the mystery of Daniel Markham's disappearance and how, if at all, it was connected to Henry. He should, probably, return to town and wait for Markham to make further contact. But…he considered that option. What was there to return to? Leo would be fully occupied with his new bride and, soon, most everyone would be leaving London to spend summer on their estates or in the seaside resorts.

There was little enticement there to lure him home in a hurry.

And here, in Worcestershire…his blood stirred. All kinds of emotions swirled within him and chief amongst them was intrigue. Not only was there a mystery to solve, but he was *needed*, whether Miss Markham admitted it or not. That thought gave way to another as he realised, with a sense of shock, that to be needed was a rare feeling in his life thus far. The Beauchamps were a close family, but he was not *needed*…he was just there.

The spare, of the 'heir and a spare' fame.

He had learned the lesson that he would always play second fiddle to his older brother as a young man on the town for the first time. He had fallen in love—or so he had thought—with the Incomparable of the day, but although Lady Pamela had happily flirted with him and even encouraged his attentions, she had made it perfectly clear she wanted a man with a peerage, not a duke's second son with a mere courtesy title. Had Leo not been married to his first wife at that time, she would doubtless have set her cap at him.

Vernon's heart had not been broken, although it had been bruised. It was his pride that had been battered.

He loved Leo and he loved his nephews and his niece but he had to admit he still found it hard to find his own place in the world. They ran many businesses in partnership—the estates, their horse-breeding enterprises, the mining interests in Cornwall and the coal mines in the north-east—but, with Leo being the older of the two, as well as the Duke, Vernon was outranked for ever.

He did not want to walk away from the mystery of Daniel Markham's disappearance. He wanted to be involved, to take action, to *help*.

'There is still the question of why your brother wrote to mine,' he said. 'You cannot expect me to leave without finding out how my Cousin Henry is involved and it is both senseless and unnecessary for you to risk either your reputation or your safety when I am better able to make the necessary enquiries. So, Miss Markham, I shall be your flagbearer: I shall visit the Nag's Head and make enquiries on your behalf. And—' he raised his voice as she opened her mouth…to argue, no doubt '—I urge you to remember that other men will tell me things they would not say in front of you.'

'What sort of things?'

He wagged his head at her, stifling another grin at her

clear frustration. 'You cannot possibly expect me to divulge such secrets, Miss Markham. Suffice it to say that I have a better chance of prising information from them than you.'

The tiniest wobble of her lower lip reminded Vernon that, however brave the face she presented, beneath it, she must be devastated.

'Do not despair, Miss Markham. I shall find Daniel.'

Hope lit her eyes and, having raised it, he was not about to dash it by voicing aloud the thought that followed: *Alive or dead, I shall find him.*

Footsteps clacked along the hall outside, getting nearer, and then the door behind Vernon opened. Miss Markham's expression blanked and she tensed.

'Dorothea.' A woman's voice. 'There you—oh!'

Vernon looked around. A middle-aged woman, her greying hair bundled into a cap, had entered the room.

'I beg your pardon,' she said to Vernon. 'I was not informed we had visitors.' Annoyance lent an edge to her tone and the look she cast Miss Markham—*Dorothea*—was…bitter.

Dorothea, meanwhile, had hurried around the desk, but halted before she got too close to the other woman. To Vernon's eyes, she appeared to stand at attention, her hands clasped at her waist, her fingers twisting together.

'Mama! There was no need to inform you of L… Mr Beauchamp's visit. He called in on a matter of business and is about to leave. I am sorry. Did you have need of me?'

This was her *mother*? Vernon looked from one to the other, wondering at those noticeable cracks in their relationship.

Mrs Markham gave a tight smile, but ignored her daughter's question.

'I trust my daughter was able to satisfactorily answer your queries, Mr Beauchamp? It is unfortunate my son should happen to be away from home at present. He is on urgent business, but Dorothea is familiar with every aspect of the manufactory.'

'She has proved most satisfactory, ma'am.'

'Good. Good.' He was clearly of little interest to the woman, for she turned her full attention to her daughter. 'Your father feels well enough to sit in his chair today, Dorothea, so I shall stay with him. Have a small repast sent up around noon, if you please. Now—' she flicked a glance at Vernon '—I must return to my husband, Mr Beauchamp. I am sure you will excuse me?'

Vernon bowed again as Dorothea walked with her mother to the door. There was no further exchange of words between mother and daughter. Mrs Markham left and Dorothea shut the door, muffling the tip-tap of her mother's rapidly departing footsteps. She turned to face Vernon.

'Mr Beauchamp?' He raised his brows. 'Might I ask why?'

'I do not want my parents to wonder why a lord is calling upon Daniel. I cannot allow them to be worried; they have enough to cope with. They believe Daniel is in Birmingham on business—that is another reason I asked the grooms not to spread the news that Daniel is missing, for it would be sure to reach the house servants' ears and they would tell my mother.'

'What is wrong with your father?'

'He had a stroke. Six years ago.' Her face twisted: grief, guilt. 'He cannot walk or talk properly. Mama devotes herself to him.'

'He must require a lot of care. Your parents are fortunate to have you here to help.'

'M-Mama says my visits agitate Papa; she d-discourages me from attending him.' For the flash of a second, a bewildered child stared out of those huge hazel orbs. Then it seemed as though a shutter closed and the brisk, efficient Dorothea Markham returned. 'Daniel took over the running of the business when Papa…when it happened. I help as much as I can, but now Daniel is missing and, somehow, your cousin is involved, and I—*Mannington*!'

Her voice suddenly rang with excitement and she captured Vernon's gaze, her eyes sparkling, sending a jolt of heat sizzling through his veins. He could barely concentrate on her words, so taken aback was he by his unexpected physical response.

'I recall… I am sure I have seen…'

She ran past Vernon to the desk, leaving a trail of floral scent wafting in her wake.

Roses. A summer garden. Quintessentially feminine.

She snatched up a handful of papers from the pile he had noticed before and began to leaf through them. After a few minutes she exclaimed in triumph, extracted a sheet of notepaper, and waved it in the air. 'It did not resonate with me at first, but then… I remembered.'

'May I see?' Vernon reached for the sheet of paper.

Her gaze flicked to his outstretched hand, but she made no move to hand it to him. 'I thought it was the name of a place,' she continued. 'It never occurred to me that Mannington was a person. At last, I have a definite clue.'

Vernon did not retract his outstretched hand, merely waited until she capitulated and handed him the paper.

'Thank you.' He scanned the sheet. It took no time at all, for there were only two words, separated by a pair of initials.

Mannington—R.H.—Willingdale?

Vernon frowned. 'What…or where…is Willingdale? And who, do you suppose, is R.H?'

'I have no idea.'

Silence reigned. A glance revealed Dorothea seemingly deep in thought as she leaned back against the edge of the desk, her arms folded as she gazed unseeingly past Vernon, a vertical groove between her brows.

Vernon reread the words written on the paper.

Willingdale… A village? An estate? The name of a person?

He was torn from his thoughts by a muffled whimper.

Chapter Three

Thea tried so hard to hold back her tears, but she simply could not. She dropped her chin into her chest, hand pressed against her lips as her sight blurred. To her horror a single tear plopped on to her bodice, leaving a damp splodge as the fabric absorbed it. Then another tear fell, and another. A large handkerchief was pressed into her hands. She dabbed at her eyes and forced herself to look up. The sympathy in Vernon's green eyes almost set her off again, but she gritted her teeth and cleared her throat.

'I am sorry. I was just thinking…if only I had paid more attention…'

'You must not blame yourself.'

Thea swallowed her bitter laugh. Blame herself? She had done nothing but blame herself for the past six years.

'Where is he?' The words burst from her. 'Why has he not even wr-written?' Her voice choked in her throat, and she buried her head in her hands. 'I fear the worst…' A sob broke free. Then another. 'B-but I must *know*. I c-cannot bear this…this *ignorance*. I f-feel so…so *alone*.'

Two arms wrapped around her and her head was pressed to a strong chest, the thud of his heart steady and reassuring in her ear. He held her, and stroked her hair, and she gave way to the storm of tears she had dammed up ever since the morning she had discovered that Daniel had failed to come home.

Finally the tears slowed, leaving empty shame at having succumbed to such womanly weakness. What must he think of her? Her breath hitched as she battled for control.

'Do not despair, Miss Markham.' Vernon's deep voice rumbled into the ear pressed against his chest, reverberating through her entire body. Words he had spoken before but somehow, this time, of even more comfort. 'You no longer carry this burden alone.'

Thankfulness and hope floated into her heart. Her need to confide, to have somebody on her side, was so strong it almost overwhelmed her innate caution. She felt torn: she wanted so much to believe him…to follow the instincts that told her she could trust him, but…he was a stranger. She could not be certain of what was in his heart.

As she grew calm again a single thought clarified in her mind. She cared not how she managed it but—if Vernon was going to search for Daniel—she was going, too.

'I am sorry,' she said, mopping her eyes again with his handkerchief, as she wriggled free of his arms. She blew her nose. 'I am not normally given to such displays.'

She crossed to the table near the window to finish off her glass of Madeira, then squared her shoulders and turned to face Vernon. It was time to stop moping and take action.

'Shall we discuss strategy?'

'Strategy, Miss Markham?'

The laughter lines at the corner of his eyes deepened although his lips remained perfectly straight. Thea scowled at this spoilt lord who clearly found her an object of fun.

'I have no need of strategy. With this information…' he picked up the discarded note from the desk, folded it and tucked it inside his jacket '…and a quick chat with your grooms, I have everything I need.'

He swung around and strode for the study door and panic swamped Thea.

What have I done?

'Wait!'

She had handed this stranger information that might help him trace Daniel, but could she trust him? What if he meant Daniel harm? This was happening too quickly. He might have decided *he* needed no strategy, but she needed time to think. To plan.

Above all, she needed reassurance that this man was precisely what he appeared to be: a charming, cultured gentleman. She recalled her fanciful notion that she had glimpsed a wolf beneath his surface: a wolf that watched and waited. What if he had a hidden agenda? What if he was like Jasper Connor who, for months on end, had duped Thea and her entire family into thinking he was something he was not?

Vernon had halted at her command and he slowly rotated to face her. He raised a brow, the epitome of aristocratic arrogance. An idea started to form in Thea's brain. If she could but delay his departure a short while…

'You will stay and have luncheon before you set out?'

'I thought time was of the essence?'

'It is. But a few hours will not make much difference. You must eat.'

Doubt—and masculinity—radiated from the man: his booted feet planted a yard apart, his arms folded tight across his chest, his lips compressed.

Inspiration struck. 'You cannot go to the Nag's Head dressed as you are.'

He glowered. 'What is wrong with the way I am dressed?' He unfolded his arms and took a pace towards her. 'I'll have you know this coat is by Weston. It is—'

'It proclaims you for what you are,' Thea said. She stepped closer, and held his gaze. 'A wealthy gentleman. Places such as the Nag's Head are not patronised by members of the aristocracy, but by ordinary men: businessmen, tradesmen, farmers. They will not speak openly to a man of your ilk. A stranger.

'Why don't you go to the stables and speak to the grooms,' she went on, 'and by the time you return to the house there will be food ready for you to eat and, after that, I shall find you something appropriate of Daniel's to wear.' She looked him up and down. 'You are of a similar height and build to him. His clothes will help you to blend in.'

That should buy her time to put her plans into place.

'Very well.' Vernon paused as he was about to leave the study. 'I just wish I could be certain Daniel's disappearance is connected to Henry Manning. If the two things are coincidental, I might end up on a wild goose chase.'

And that proves I am right to be cautious. If the two enquiries lead in different directions, I make no doubt Lord Vernon Beauchamp will go chasing after his cousin and consign poor Daniel to the Devil.

Vernon strode back to the house half an hour later, not much wiser about how he might discover what had happened to Daniel Markham. The grooms could not tell him who or what was Willingdale and nor did the initials R.H. mean anything. None of them had ever accompanied Daniel on his more recent daily excursions—although they confirmed Dorothea's story that her brother had been troubled—and nor could they offer any reason for this change in Daniel's behaviour. They were frustrated that they had been stopped from making enquiries—and Vernon had learned that was mainly due to Dorothea's concern that any worries about Daniel's welfare would damage confidence in Stour Crystal—and they had scoffed at the notion that Daniel had run up gaming debts.

'Mr Daniel ain't never been a one for gambling, sir,' the head man, Pritchard, had said. 'Not since his papa lost all their money. Both Mr Daniel and Miss Thea have worked too hard to save the business to put it at risk again.'

Mr Markham senior would not be the first man to gamble away a fortune, but Vernon's comment along those lines had resulted in a fierce denial that the money had been lost at the gaming tables. Pritchard had then clammed up, refusing to elaborate further.

Vernon had not pressed Pritchard, but had caught Bickling's eye and given him the nod before returning to the house, confident his trusty groom would winkle out the truth and pass the information on to Vernon later.

Dorothea—Miss Thea, Pritchard had called her, which was much less of a mouthful—must have been watching for him, because she appeared at a side door and beckoned him inside. He followed her along a passageway, eyeing her neat figure with appreciation, the smell of roses and summer teasing at his senses.

'I have laid out some clothes for you to change into,' she said over her shoulder, 'and there is food for you in here.'

She threw open a door that led into a shabby but homely parlour, the table laid with cold cuts, meat pies, bread, cheese and fruit, reminding Vernon of his hunger. The decor would have been the height of fashion a decade ago—in stark contrast with the ostentatious entrance hall and its grand staircase and even the more subdued but still luxurious furnishings in the study. Vernon recalled his initial scathing assessment of the well-tended surrounds of Stourwell Court as he had driven up the carriageway. The house—relatively newly built, with no passing architectural fashion left unsampled—had screamed *new money* to one familiar with the sprawling ancient Beauchamp family seat of Cheriton Abbey in the County of Devonshire.

Having learned of the family's financial loss and subsequent struggle, Vernon was unsurprised by the tactic he had seen many times in the past: a family on its uppers, putting what money they could spare into the public rooms where visitors were entertained in order to keep up appearances.

'Did you discover anything new?'

Thea came straight to the point as she closed the door behind them. Vernon was unsurprised—she had already impressed him with her directness, as well as her quick understanding.

'Only the names of some of Daniel's friends who drink at the Nag's Head.' He had no intention of revealing that the grooms had spoken of her family's past financial difficulties. 'Pritchard was of the opinion that Daniel had spent much of his time in Birmingham in the days before he went missing. He also reckons your brother called in at the Nag's Head most nights on his way home. So that will definitely be my first port of call.'

'Will you drive your curricle, or ride?'

'I had not thought that far ahead,' Vernon admitted. 'If, as you say, my clothing would excite interest, then no doubt my curricle and pair will as well.'

'A top-of-the-tree rig such as yours? I should say so,' she said, gravely, but with a twinkle in her eye. When she wasn't scowling she was an attractive woman. 'You may take one of Daniel's horses. They are perfectly decent animals, suitable for a gentleman of your standing.'

Vernon grinned. 'I am delighted to hear it. A man of my consequence cannot be too careful.'

He might as well pander to her opinion of him as a spoilt aristocrat.

'We had better eat.' Thea crossed the room to the table and picked up a plate. 'It will be more practical to go on horseback. We can take shortcuts across country—'

'We?' Vernon strode forward, grasped her arm and tugged her round to face him. 'What...? Oh, no. No, no, *no*! Definitely not. You are *not* coming with me.'

Thea's tawny brows snapped together, meeting across

the bridge of her freckled nose as she drew herself up to her full height. Which was short.

'You cannot stop me. Daniel is *my* brother. I *want* to come.'

Vernon stared down at her mutinous expression and heaved a silent sigh. He was hungry and he was anxious to set off, now he had a definite idea of where to start with his search. First he must deal with this hissing, spitting kitten.

Thea shrugged out of his hold, replaced her plate on the table with a crack that made Vernon wince and folded her arms.

'You cannot tell me what to do. I am going.'

Vernon squared his shoulders. 'Not with me you are not.'

'You cannot stop me.'

'You are correct. I cannot stop you going anywhere or doing anything you wish. But I tell you here and now…you will *not* do it with me. I shall return to London and you may never discover what has happened to your brother.'

Her eyes widened.

Good. That has shaken her.

'You would not do that.' Her voice lacked conviction.

Vernon lowered his own voice, injecting a silky menace into his tone. 'If you put me to the test, Miss Markham, I think you will find that *I* do not make empty threats either.'

Her lips thinned as she glared at him. 'What about your cousin?'

Vernon shrugged nonchalantly. 'I shall pay an investigator to track him down and report to me in London. What you choose to forget, Miss Markham, is that I have neither desire nor need to remain here in Worcestershire, or to embark upon a search for a man I have never met. I offered my services because it is unsafe for you, as a female, to go into the places on that list. Which, incidentally, is the exact reason you cannot come with me: *it is not safe.* I admit to some curiosity as to my cousin's involvement, but I shall not lose any sleep over it and you will do well to remember that.'

She hung her head, her eyes downcast. Vernon felt like an out-and-out brute, but knew he must not show any weakness for he had no doubt she would quickly seize upon it and, despite what he said, he really *was* curious to find out what had happened to Daniel Markham.

'So, are we agreed? I shall leave after I have eaten and changed my clothing and you, Miss Markham, will wave me goodbye.'

'Very well. I shall not insist on leaving with you.'

Her mouth drooped and he wondered if she were about to cry again. He had been certain that earlier bout was uncharacteristic. He could not abide women who cried at the slightest provocation, using tears as a weapon to get their own way. But, despite that, he still felt sympathy and also a little guilty, knowing how worried she was about her brother. He reached out and nudged one finger beneath her chin, tilting her face to his. Respect for her crept through him: she was dry-eyed and he was relieved at this proof she was prepared to listen to and accept his reasoning.

'Miss Markham, you must also understand that, quite apart from it being unsafe, it would also be entirely improper for you to accompany me. Your reputation would be in tatters.'

A gleam lit those huge hazel orbs and Vernon was disconcerted by the undeniable kick of his pulse and his sudden impulse to kiss her,

His awareness of her as an attractive woman rattled him into speaking more bluntly than he should.

'We have no idea what has happened to Daniel, but I know you are aware he could have met with foul play. It would be wholly irresponsible for me to allow you to be exposed to possible danger.'

She blinked and her cheeks paled, causing the freckles

that dusted her nose and cheeks to stand out in contrast. Vernon felt a brute all over again, as though he had kicked a puppy. Or—perhaps more fitting in Thea's case, given his earlier fanciful thoughts—a kitten. He released her chin and clasped her upper arms, bending his knees to look directly into her eyes.

'I apologise. I did not mean to shock you.'

Her throat convulsed as she swallowed. He had upset her, but she was struggling to conceal her emotions and his respect grew at the way she handled herself in such a horrible situation.

'Do not lose hope, Miss Markham.' He gently rubbed her arms, trying to buoy her spirits. 'There could still be a perfectly reasonable explanation for Daniel's disappearance.'

She huffed a disbelieving laugh, shaking her head, her curls bouncing. 'Such as? No, I cannot be hopeful. He would have written to us. He would not stay away without a word.'

Vernon released her and stepped back from the temptation of taking her into his arms again to offer comfort.

'He might be too ill to write,' he said. 'Or he has lost his memory. Or maybe he *has* written and the letter has been lost en route?' He paced the room and then returned to come to a halt in front of her. 'Whatever the reason, I shall discover it, but you must leave this to me. Do you understand?'

'I understand. Now, if you will excuse me, there are matters requiring my attention.'

'You will not join me?'

'I find I no longer have an appetite. Enjoy your luncheon, sir. Ring for George when you have finished eating and he will show you to Daniel's bedchamber to change your clothing. I shall see you before you leave.' She left him with a brisk step, leaving the scent of roses lingering in her wake.

* * *

After Vernon had eaten his fill, he was shown upstairs by George.

'I shall leave as soon as I have changed,' Vernon told the footman. 'Could you inform Miss Markham that I will see her downstairs in, shall we say, fifteen minutes?'

He wondered if Thea would come to see him off, or if she would stay away, sulking. No, he decided. Sulking was not Miss Markham's style.

George bowed and left. Vernon wasted no time in changing into the clothing that would help him to blend in. He donned the fawn-coloured breeches and the respectable linen shirt and neckcloth left on the bed. The boots, however, were too small. He eyed his Hessian boots and their mirror shine with regret as he realised there was nothing for it but to smear them with soil when he went outside, to dull the shine. A moleskin waistcoat and a brown jacket completed Vernon's transformation from a man of fashion into a respectable country squire.

He ducked to peer into the dressing-table mirror and ruffled his fingers through his hair. At least he would not present himself all neatly barbered at the Nag's Head and wherever else his enquiries might lead. His hair had needed a trim before he left London, but he had decided to leave it until his return. It was a touch long and unruly, but the less well-groomed his appearance, the less notice he would attract.

He rotated, studying the room: Daniel's room. Quashing down any guilt—he was trying to help, not snoop—he quickly searched through drawers and cupboards. Nothing. He must hope that someone at the Nag's Head could either throw some light on the reason Daniel had been riding to Birmingham on a regular basis—if, that is, Pritchard was correct that Daniel had been visiting the city—or that they might solve the mystery of what, or who, Willingdale and R.H. were.

A battered saddlebag had been left on the bed. Inside was a clean shirt and neckcloth, reminding Vernon that this mission might take several days. He slung the bag over one shoulder and, with one last look around, he strode from the room.

In the entrance hall, he waited. The scrunch of hooves on the gravel outside told him that his horse had arrived. He went out to find Bickling holding a dependable-looking bay hunter and sent him running back to the stables to retrieve Vernon's shaving kit and other personal necessities from his valise in his curricle. When Bickling returned, Vernon stowed the articles in the saddlebag as his groom filled him in on what he'd discovered about Mr Markham's lost fortune.

'Seems he raised funds against his business and invested them all in some non-existent scheme through this swindler who befriended the family and then vanished with their money,' he said. 'The stress caused Markham senior's stroke and, although Pritchard clammed up when I tried to get more from him, it seems this fraudster also had something to do with Miss Markham.'

'In what way?'

Bickling shrugged. 'The man's very loyal to Miss Markham. He wouldn't say more than the bastard took Miss Markham in, too, and that she's never forgiven herself. Blames herself for her father's stroke.'

Had he courted her? Had she fallen in love with him? That's what it sounded like to Vernon. 'Thank you, Bickling.'

'Are you sure you don't want me to come along with you, milord?'

'There is no need, I can take care of myself and, besides,

you'll be on edge the entire time if you have to leave my blacks in anyone else's care.'

Bickling was even fussier about Vernon's horses than he was, if that were possible. And he knew that Bickling would be forever saying 'milord', and that would mean no chance of staying discreet.

'I could always take one of the men from here, but they appear short-staffed already. I will be fine going alone, do not worry.'

'Very well, milord.' Bickling's glum face said it all.

Vernon glanced at the front door. Still no sign of Thea. He did not want to leave without saying goodbye so he went back inside. Immediately he heard hurried footsteps approaching from the nether regions of the house. Thea soon appeared, slightly breathless.

'Come with me,' she said. 'There is something you need to see.'

Chapter Four

Thea had to give his lordship credit: he followed her without question to the gunroom. Once inside, he turned a full circle, eyeing the rows of shotguns, rifles and muskets that lined the walls. The windowless room was illuminated by the three lanterns Thea had lit on her earlier visit. Somehow, with Vernon inside, the room seemed to have shrunk and Thea wrapped her arms defensively around her torso and stepped away from him, putting a little more distance between them.

Vernon tilted his head as he met Thea's gaze and those penetrating green eyes of his glinted as they caught the light. They felt as though they reached deep into her soul. She just prayed he could not read her thoughts.

'I trust you do not plan to hold me hostage down here, Miss Markham.'

His comment startled a laugh from her. The thought had crossed her mind. Not to hold him hostage, but to force him at gunpoint to take her with him—a crazy thought that she had dismissed the minute her whirling thoughts, desperate to find a way to go with him, had seized upon it. That crazy idea had, though, led to another plan.

Which was why she had ventured down here to the gunroom in the first place.

'Have no fear, my lord,' she said. 'None of these weapons is loaded. You are quite safe.'

'Then why are we here?'

'It occurred to me to wonder if Daniel was armed,' she said.

'Would he normally go out with a gun?'

'He had a blunderbuss that was always buckled to his saddle, in case of an attack,' she said. 'There have been a few robberies on the roads hereabouts, over the past year or so. Daniel said there has been an increase in vagrants wandering the countryside—former soldiers, he reckoned, although others like to blame the gipsies. But a blunderbuss is not a weapon he could carry in his pocket. Look—' she pointed to the table in the centre of the room '—I found that pistol case in the cabinet. It should have two muff pistols inside, plus the flask and balls. Firearms are Daniel's passion. He bought this case and pistols at an auction in Birmingham a few weeks ago.'

She tilted the case to show the single remaining pistol to Vernon. He whistled.

'So…your brother went out *expecting* trouble. Or even danger.'

'It would appear so, although I cannot understand why he would take that particular pistol. It is very small.'

Vernon moved closer as he peered at the contents of the case, his sleeve brushing Thea's arm, sending a tingle of awareness racing through her. She shivered in reaction, fighting the urge to leave the room. Her discomfort was unimportant…she must do this for Daniel.

'Small but deadly,' Vernon said. 'I should imagine he took it precisely because its size means it is easily concealed. I see he has several cases of duelling pistols…' He selected one case at random and opened it. He whistled again, lifting out one of the guns and sighting along the barrel. 'Manton's. A fine piece. But, too big to conceal and…'

'And what?'

He shot her an apologetic look and grimaced. 'Sorry. I was thinking out loud.'

'But, having begun to speak, you must now finish,' Thea said, irritation at her physical reaction to his proximity making her sharp.

She had no wish to be aware of him as an attractive man. Men were not to be trusted.

'I told you before,' she went on, 'I am not one of your fine ladies who needs mollycoddling. I have dealt with hard reality and survived. Please do not patronise me. Do me the courtesy of dealing with me as an intelligent adult, not a child.'

He sighed. 'Very well. I was about to say that a duelling pistol is not as handy at close quarters.'

Her stomach churned at his words, but she tamped down her fear. She had asked him and he had replied. She could not now blame him because she did not like what she heard. Besides, that was an interesting point to remember. She had already selected and primed a duelling pistol, ready to pack in her saddlebag along with her spare clothing. Daniel had other small pistols—she would take one of those along as well.

'I thought you should see this for yourself,' she said to Vernon. 'As you said, it suggests Daniel was expecting trouble when he left.'

Just speaking those words made her throat constrict with unshed tears but Thea forced her emotions to lie low, knowing she must keep a cool head if she was not to hinder the search for her brother.

'It is time to go,' she said, 'but there is also something else I must show you.'

Vernon raised a brow but, again, followed her unquestioningly. Up the stairs this time and along the upper corridor to the long gallery, where the family portraits hung and where Thea and Daniel practised fencing manoeuvres. The physical exercise had helped Thea to exorcise some of her anger and guilt after Jasper Connor had betrayed her and near bankrupted both Stour Crystal and her family.

Vernon headed straight for the portrait of Thea. 'It is a good likeness.'

For a second, admiration glowed in his eyes, but Thea ignored the answering tug deep in her core. She could not help but be aware of Vernon's allure. She'd wager there were ladies galore in the *ton* who regularly swooned at his feet, given one look from those green eyes, or one of his smiles, brimming with charm, but she was not interested. Not in Lord Vernon Beauchamp nor in any man. Being jilted at the altar tended to have that effect.

'That is not why we are here,' she said and led the way to the portrait of Daniel.

Apart from the portraits of Thea and Daniel, and an earlier one of Mama and Papa—painted before Papa had his stroke—there were only landscapes on the walls. Papa had harboured such grand dreams: dreams of building a dynasty, dreams of using his wealth to ensure his grand-children might be accepted into the ranks of the upper classes, dreams of this gallery being filled with portraits of the generations to come. Now it might all come to naught. Thea would never give him grandchildren and, if Daniel... She choked off that thought, afraid her precarious control would shatter again if she followed her fears to their natural conclusion.

'That is Daniel,' she said, feeling another lump form in her throat as she looked up at his strong, dark features. 'I thought it would help for you to know what he looks like.'

Vernon examined the portrait in silence.

'He has your eyes,' he said, eventually, 'but I see no further resemblance.'

'He gets his colouring from Mama, but he is tall like

Papa,' Thea said. They headed for the door. 'I get my red hair from Papa, but my height—or, rather, my lack of it—from Mama.'

Back in the entrance hall, Vernon picked up the saddlebag by the front door.

'I shall have to hope,' he remarked, regarding his reflection in a mirror with a grimace, 'that I do not meet anyone with whom I am acquainted. They will think I have run quite mad, dressed like this.'

Thea bit back her scathing retort.

'I shall write to let you know what I find out about your brother and how my cousin is connected to him.' A frown creased his forehead. 'I still find it hard to believe Henry has anything to do with your brother's disappearance. I have every hope of discovering the two things are unconnected.'

Which, again, proved Thea was right to follow him as she planned. If Henry Mannington was found to have no connection with Daniel's disappearance, Vernon would go chasing off after Henry and what chance then would Thea have of finding Daniel?

She followed Vernon down the front steps, where Bickling, his groom, held the reins of Warrior, one of Daniel's favourite hunters. Vernon swung into the saddle, raised his hand in farewell and set off down the carriageway at a brisk trot.

Thea watched until horse and rider disappeared from sight, then spun on her heel and raced up to her bedchamber. There was no time to lose. She had already told her mother she was going to visit a sick friend for a few days and Mama, as usual, showed little interest in Thea's activities; she had never forgiven her daughter for the disaster that had befallen their family.

Thea had also written to Charles Leyton, the manager

at Stour Crystal, to warn him he would not be able to contact either her or Daniel for a week or so. She hoped she would not be away as long as that, but it was best to err on the side of caution.

It was a relief to be taking action—she had been near paralysed with indecision until Lord Vernon's visit, afraid of the consequences should Stour Crystal's customers, or—God forbid—their rivals, learn that Daniel was missing. Uncertainty was bad for business. If she was responsible for spreading rumours and Daniel turned up unscathed, he would, rightly, be furious with her. She had caused enough trouble for the business six years ago. She could not bear to be the cause of more.

She had slipped across to the stables earlier, whilst Vernon was eating, and taken Malky—the groom who had taught her and Daniel to ride—into her confidence about her plan. He had not been happy but, in the end, he had agreed to saddle Thea's favourite mare, Star, with a conventional saddle so she could ride astride and to meet Thea, with Star, on the edge of the copse behind the walled kitchen garden, out of sight of both the house and the stables.

She changed hastily into the clothes she had kept from Daniel's boyhood, the ones she wore for their fencing bouts and for riding astride. She wondered whether or not she should take Malky with her. It would be the sensible thing to do, at least until she caught up with Vernon, but it would leave the estate short-handed at a busy time.

She examined her appearance in the mirror. She had bound her breasts to flatten them and had dusted fine ash from the fireplace across her skin, dulling it. She was dressed the same as countless young lads around the country, in jacket, shirt, waistcoat, breeches and boots. Her hair…she leaned closer to her reflection. She could pass muster as a lad during one cross-country ride—with her hair plaited and pinned and bundled into a cap—but would that suffice for a longer masquerade?

She reached for her scissors. It would grow again. She unpinned her hair and gathered it together. She swivelled her head from side to side as she gazed into the mirror, considering. Some lads had hair that grew to the nape of their necks, or even longer. She set her jaw. Time was wasting. She cut, hacking again and again at her thick hair until the bunch came free in her hand. She stared at it, lying limp across her palm, trying and failing to quash her distress.

It cannot be helped.

She pushed the hair under her mattress where it would not be discovered, and turned again to the mirror, biting back a cry at the sight that met her eyes. She pushed her fingers through her hair, fluffing it out—her curls more unruly than ever—then ruthlessly scraped it back and tied it with the length of twine she carried in her jacket pocket for emergencies. Her reins had snapped once, several miles from home, and since then she had always been prepared. Never had she envisioned using it for this purpose, however.

It is just vanity. Who cares what you look like?

Unbidden, Vernon's face arose in her thoughts.

Hmmph. She thrust his image aside. *He is a means to an end: finding Daniel. Nothing more.*

It was time to go. Malky would have Star ready by now. Thea cast a last look around her bedchamber, sucked in a deep breath to quell her nerves and picked up her saddlebag. A quick visit to the gunroom for pistols, powder and shot and then she would be gone. As she crept down the back stairs she prayed none of the servants would see her. Her stomach roiled all the way to the gunroom and for the entire time it took her to load the smaller pistol she had decided to take with her.

She slipped out of the side door and hurried along the path to the kitchen garden, following the outer stone wall around until she reached the far corner. Then she breathed a sigh of relief, knowing she was no longer visible from the house. She stood still, leaning back against the wall, feeling the sun's warmth, stored in the stones, radiating through her twill jacket, and waited for her nerves to settle. They did not. Her stomach continued to churn until she felt sick and she realised, with a jolt, that it was not the adventure to come that frightened her so very much but the thought of Lord Vernon Beauchamp's reaction when he discovered she had followed him. Contrarily, that thought irritated her, which then had the effect of finally grounding those butterflies fluttering around inside her stomach.

It was not *his* place to dictate her movements and it was not incumbent upon her to obey him. She was her own woman. Seven-and-twenty years of age. Intelligent. She had no reputation to sully—it simply was not important to her. She would never marry and she was long past the days when she worried about how many partners she might attract at the assembly room in Bewdley. Come to think of it, she could not remember the last time she had visited the assembly room. Losing everything, including a fiancé and, very nearly, her father had effectively put an end to all such frivolity. They had—both she and Daniel—put their heads down and *worked*, with no thought other than to pull the family back from the precipice of bankruptcy. They had teetered upon the brink of that chilling state for a very long time.

Those years... That lump ached once more in Thea's throat. She and Daniel had worked in partnership and they had not given up until the manufactory was safe. They had worked with Charles Leyton and the other men to develop new products that were now eagerly sought after by customers keen to decorate their homes and to display their wealth.

And now, when it seemed they could finally begin to breathe again, Daniel had vanished.

Thea pushed away from the wall. She could see Malky waiting, with Star and another horse, at the top of the opposite bank of the stream, on the edge of the trees. Gratefulness hummed through her. Malky clearly intended to accompany her and she saw now that was the best solution, at least until she caught up with Vernon. Her guise as a lad would protect her a little on the ride between Stourwell Court and Stourbridge, but not completely—a solitary youth might prove fair game for any manner of rogues on the road. She would believe that was what had befallen Daniel, but for the fact his horse had not returned: Bullet would always return to Stourwell Court. He had been foaled here.

She ran down the bank, jumped the narrow channel of water and hurried up the slope to Malky.

'Afore you say aught, miss, I'm coming with you and there's an end to it.'

Malky…he had taught her to ride. Solid. Dependable. Unflappable.

'Thank you, Malky.' Thea turned to Star, put her foot in the stirrup and was soon settled astride the spirited black mare. 'Just until we catch up with his lordship, mind.' Or, actually, before. Or his lordship would merely order her to return home with Malky. That would not suit her purpose at all. 'Let's go.'

They rode across country, taking the shortest route to Stourbridge, and Thea began to breathe a little easier at the knowledge they had made up time. Finally, they arrived at the outskirts of the town and they halted.

'I will be safe enough now,' she said to Malky. 'You should return home. No!' She held up one hand as Malky started to protest. 'You cannot come further. You are needed at Stourwell Court. I shall be quite safe... I intend to let myself be known to his lordship before nightfall. It will be too late by then for him to send me home.'

'And what do you intend to do while his lordship is inside the Nag's Head?'

'I shall go inside, too. It is a respectable enough inn. It will be an opportunity to find out if my disguise will stand casual scrutiny. You cannot deny it is better I begin here—in full daylight—than enter some low alehouse after dark when it is like to be filled with men in their cups.'

Malky sighed. 'I don't like you going inside such places, Miss Thea.'

'*Theo*, Malky. I told you, I am now Theo. And I must go inside or how shall I discover—?'

'I've bin in and out of such places all me life, mi—' He clamped his lips together with a scowl. 'You told me you were going to *follow* his lordship. You never said you'd be risking your reputation and worse besides by going inside such places.'

She touched his arm. 'You cannot stop me, Malky. You know me. You know how stubborn I can be.'

'Never a truer word,' he muttered.

'Must I order you home, Malky? You and I cannot ride into town together, or someone will recognise you and wonder who I am. Trust me... I will stay safe. I shall follow his lordship and, as I said, I shall make myself known to him before nightfall. He is a gentleman. He will protect me.'

'And that's another thing to worry about,' Malky muttered. 'His sort...they think nothing of debauchery and such like and you an innocent and all.'

'I am well able to protect my virtue, Malky,' she said grimly. 'You need have no fear on that score.'

After several more grumbles, Malky finally left her and Thea rode Star up New Street towards High Street and the

Nag's Head, her stomach twisting with nerves at what she was about to do and at the thought of Vernon's likely reaction when he discovered she had followed him. But then she thought of Daniel. She was doing this for him. And her nerves steadied as she left Star with an ostler and approached the door of the inn. She hadn't planned much further than simply catching up with Vernon and then tailing him, but she had faith everything would work out all right. She patted her pocket, feeling the reassuring shape of the pistol. She could take care of herself and, whatever might have happened to Daniel, she would make certain she, at least, returned home to her parents.

She followed a man in through the door and turned left, as did he, into a taproom. A sweeping glance took in the dingy walls and ring-marked tables. She watched carefully how the man she had followed in behaved. He slid on to a settle and caught the attention of a serving woman by the simple expedient of raising one finger. The girl brought him a tankard, presumably of ale or porter.

Thea took a seat in an empty corner, where she could take in the whole room and see the door at the same time. As the woman turned from the other customer, Thea raised her hand. The woman acknowledged her and soon delivered a tankard, setting it on the table with a bang that sloshed its contents over the rim. She scooped up the coins Thea had tossed on to the table with a brief grin that made Thea suspect her tip had been overly generous. Nevertheless, she breathed a little easier. The woman had barely looked at her and neither had the other customers.

She sipped her ale—wrinkling her nose at the bitter taste—and allowed her gaze to slide around the room, examining each occupant in turn. The taproom was not full, with around eight customers, including Thea and the other newcomer, and a man behind the bar whom she assumed was Perrins, the publican—she knew his name from occasional comments Daniel had made about the place. But there was no sign of Vernon.

Where is he?

On the heels of that thought, the door opened and in strolled Lord Vernon Beauchamp.

Chapter Five

There was a lull in the conversation as the men in the taproom eyed up this newcomer. There had been no such reaction when the other man and Thea had entered and she took heart that the other customers had taken her appearance at face value. One single glance confirmed the newcomer was Vernon, but his appearance, far from offering relief, wound Thea's tension a notch tighter as she kept her head bent and her attention on her drink. In her head, as she had planned her first venture into this alien world, she had entered the taproom and Vernon was already seated. She had not reckoned on him following her in. What if he sat at her table?

From the corner of her eye, she watched as he paused inside the door and swept the room, his gaze lingering on each man in turn before moving on to the next. She clenched her teeth as he scrutinised her, wrapping her fingers tightly around her tankard as she fought the urge to check that her hair was still tucked up inside her cap. The colour, surely, would give her away in an instant. After what seemed an age, Vernon's gaze moved on and Thea released her held breath as he sauntered deeper into the room, and selected a seat at a table with three other men. He looked every inch the gentleman he was, despite Daniel's clothing, and Thea sensed the sudden unease of the men he had joined. Even Perrins watched Vernon with suspicion.

'Good afternoon,' Vernon said.

His voice, well-modulated and…well…superior, carried around the room, prompting another pause in the various conversations. Now the immediate danger of him recognising her had passed, Thea began to enjoy herself. Vernon might be a lord, and the brother of a high and mighty duke, but he was out of his depth in this world. She fully expected the three men he had joined to finish up their ale and to leave, but they did not. Vernon reached into his pocket and extracted a pack of cards, looking around the table with his brows lifted in invitation. The men exchanged glances and nodded, and Vernon dealt the cards.

Perrins called across the bar, 'Mind you keep them stakes low, gents. I don't want no trouble in here.'

Vernon laughed. 'I have no choice but to keep them low, landlord. My luck has been out for too long, I fear. But I harbour hopes it is about to change.'

His smile encompassed his three companions, who appeared to perk up, exchanging eager looks.

They played cards for nigh on an hour, while Thea nursed her drink in the corner, growing steadily more indignant. She could hear their banter. Not once had Vernon mentioned Daniel. Or Henry Mannington. Instead, he fed them scraps of information about himself—none of it true, from what Thea knew of him—as he steadily lost, hand after hand. Then, he won a hand and, jubilant, he ordered a bottle of gin and four glasses. Thea could not fathom his strategy. Time was wasting. They needed clues. Why did he not just get on with it instead of throwing his money around? If *he* had experienced the dread of ending up in debtors' prison, he would not be so careless of his money.

Then, with the gin bottle half-empty—the level in Vernon's glass, she noted, had barely dropped—he said, 'That's it. I'm done, lads. You've cleaned me out. Landlord…what time do you have?'

'Half-past four,' Perrins called in reply.

'Half-past *four*, you say!'

His words slurred a little, but Thea did not believe he was in the slightest bit foxed. Vernon swore an oath that made Thea blush, then pushed himself unsteadily to his feet.

'Have I the wrong place, I wonder? I made sure he said to meet here at four.'

'Who're you meeting, then? Anyone we know?'

'Friend of mine. Daniel Markham. Business matter, don't y'know?'

He tapped one long forefinger against the side of his nose and winked at his companions, who promptly vied with each other to suggest other places Vernon might conceivably have arranged to meet Daniel. Thea found herself revising her opinion of his lordship and a grudging respect crept through her. Even the customers who had not played cards proffered suggestions. It seemed they all knew Daniel, but none of them appeared aware he was missing.

'No, no,' Vernon said, in response to each suggestion. 'They do not sound familiar. I'll know the name when you say it, I am sure. Perhaps…' He paused, staring at the table, frowning. He shook his head. Looked around at his companions. 'Maybe it was not in Stourbridge at all? Was it somewhere near Birmingham? Or in Birmingham itself?'

'It could well be,' Perrins said—the first time he had ventured a suggestion. 'He hasn't been in here for the last few nights—I dare say we'm not grand enough for him, now he's consorting with them nobs at the Royal Hotel.'

Royal Hotel! R.H!

Thea gripped the edge of the table to stop herself leaping from her chair, as Vernon pumped Perrins by the hand.

'The Royal! I remember! He *did* speak of the Royal—

that must be the place. Now, how could I have got it so wrong? But he definitely spoke of the Nag's Head as well— I must have confused the two.'

'He'll be long gone by the time you get to Birmingham,' one of the other men said. 'You might as well play another hand. He might call in on his way home tonight—it'll save you a long ride.'

'No…how far is it? Ten, twelve miles?'

'Nearer thirteen.'

'We had plans to meet up and spend the evening together. I cannot believe he will give up on me so easily. My horse is fresh. I can cover that in less than two hours. Now, I must make haste…only, before I go, does anyone know a place called Willingdale?'

His question met with shaking heads.

'A man called Henry Mannington?'

As further denials rang around the room, Thea became aware she was now the only customer not taking an active role in the discussion. She stood quietly and, when Vernon's attention was on Perrins, she slipped quickly and quietly from the bar. She did not wish to attract Vernon's curiosity, convinced she would not pass too close a scrutiny from those astute green eyes of his. She retrieved Star from the yard behind the inn, mounted and then waited around a corner for Vernon to emerge. He strolled into the street, still looking every inch the nobleman, surrounded by his customary aura of assurance and entitlement. The ostler must have been watching, for he soon appeared, leading Warrior, and Vernon mounted with a fluid grace that made Thea's mouth go dry. He was so very…*male*. She licked her lips to moisten them, irritated by her involuntary reaction. What was it about this man that touched her in ways no one else had ever done? Even Jasper. The man she had been going to wed, before he had left her standing at the altar.

She tore her thoughts away from that wretch. It had happened long ago. She was older and wiser now, and Jasper was dead—killed in a fire at a wayside inn—and buried. She would never...*never*...put her trust in another man, no matter how handsome his face and no matter what feelings he had aroused as he'd wrapped her in his arms and comforted her, his strong embrace reassuring, his heartbeat steady in her ear.

Thea gave Vernon a head start and then she followed.

By the time dusk began to fall, Thea was beginning to regret her foolhardy decision to follow Vernon. She was bored and she was saddle sore. Vernon appeared in no hurry to reach Birmingham and that irritated Thea beyond measure. Surely the sooner they reached the Royal Hotel the sooner they might discover what had happened to Daniel? She'd made the connection immediately, but had Vernon linked the Royal Hotel with R.H? Certainly he appeared unaffected by the sense of urgency that snapped at Thea's heels—he paused at every wayside inn they passed.

After following him into the second such inn—where, again, he quietly questioned the publican about Daniel, Willingdale and Henry Mannington—Thea realised that unless he was totally oblivious to his surroundings Vernon would soon notice a young lad shadowing his every move. So, of necessity, she'd remained out of sight as he had visited further public houses. She supposed she must be grateful he did not waste as much time as he had at the Nag's Head.

Now, as she rode Star at a discreet distance behind him, she was also hungry and thirsty and—

Thea straightened in the saddle, drawing Star quickly to one side of the lane they rode along. Vernon's form was indistinct in the distance as the light faded, but Thea could just make out two shadows—humped, awkward-looking creatures—moving swiftly parallel with the lane, on the far side of group of bushes from Vernon and his horse. Thea pushed Star into a trot, trusting that her mare's black coat and Thea's own dull clothing would render them invisible to any backward glance. The two—and she could now make out they were men, crouching as they ran—had overtaken Vernon, who appeared not to have noticed he had company.

She recalled all the recent reports of footpads in the area and she realised how reckless she had been in following Vernon in this way. Suppose it had been her they had spotted and now stalked? She had been blind to everything other than finding her brother. The gap between her and Vernon had closed. Without taking her eyes from the two men, she eased Star back to a walk and fumbled with the buckle on her saddlebag. She withdrew the duelling pistol, thanking God she'd thought to prime it in advance. She pulled the hammer to full cock and pointed it skywards. Even though she was a fair shot, she could not risk hitting either Vernon or Warrior.

There was a break in the bushes a few yards ahead of Vernon and the two men paused at that point, still hunched over. Thea could just make out they both held weapons— one short and thick, like a club, the other longer and very slim—and Thea prayed it was not a blade of some sort.

Vernon rode on at an easy walk.

It happened very fast. The two men erupted from the bushes. One grabbed at Warrior's reins as the other, thick club upraised, went for the rider.

Thea dug her heels into Star but, even as she yelled a warning, she saw Vernon's leg jerk sideways. His boot collided with his assailant's head and a scream of pain rent the air as the man staggered back, clutching his face, his club discarded. Vernon shot a swift glance behind him, in Thea's direction, before launching himself from the saddle at the second man, who had come alongside Warrior, still clutching his reins. Vernon cursed viciously as the man jabbed his stick at him. Thea hauled Star to a halt, leapt from the saddle, and ran towards the struggling men, pistol in hand. She stopped a few yards away, pistol still pointing into the air.

Vernon threw a punch, catching his attacker on the jaw with satisfying crack. As the man staggered back, Vernon shot another glance at Thea.

'Don't stand gawping, lad. Guard the other one.'

Thea gulped and pointed the pistol with a shaky hand in the general direction of the first assailant, still moaning on the ground, blood pouring from his nose. Vernon stalked after the second attacker, who was stumbling backwards, his eyes riveted to the menacing figure that followed. He gripped his stick—which Thea could now see had been sharpened at one end—with both hands, pointing it at Vernon. A movement from the man on the ground then secured Thea's attention and she saw no more, but the cries and the curses coming from two men behind her suggested they now grappled and finally, unable to bear the suspense, she glanced round. Vernon, his hand clutched to his side, was bent over, but there was no sign of his assailant.

Vernon's head lifted and she felt the force of his gaze upon her. 'Look out!'

Desperation leant an edge to his shout, but his warning was too late. A solid mass thumped into Thea from behind, knocking her aside. She stumbled, desperately trying to stay on her feet and to keep hold of the pistol, her stomach clenching tight as bile rose to choke her throat.

By the time she steadied herself, the two assailants were disappearing amongst the bushes by the side of the road, one man's arm draped across the other's shoulders as he was dragged along. She aimed her pistol at the bushes, following the rustling sounds, using her left hand to steady her shaking right one.

'Leave it!' That voice brooked no disobedience.

Thea lowered her arm, gulping with relief that she would not have to use the firearm, although she would have fired had she been forced to. What if those ruffians had not run away? What if Vernon had been incapacitated? The enormity of her decision to follow him in this way suddenly hit her. And now…she realised how likely it was Vernon would see through her disguise and her relief seeped away to be replaced by fear at the thought of facing him. He would not be happy. She sucked in a breath.

'Thank you.' Vernon's attention was still on the spot where the two men had disappeared into the bushes. 'I am in your debt.'

In the spot where they stood, where trees overhung the road, the light had all but gone. Thea kept her face averted from Vernon and muttered, 'Glad to help.'

Vernon crossed slowly to Warrior and reached into his saddlebag, keeping a wary eye on the surrounding bushes. All sounds of the men's retreat had faded away, but Thea still breathed a thankful sigh when Vernon withdrew his own pistol. At least they were both now armed and ready for anything.

'How far is Birmingham? I need a bed for the night.'

Thea pointed ahead. 'Two or three miles.'

He grunted. 'I'll stop at the next inn. There must be another between here and the town.'

Vernon rubbed his hand across his jaw, the rasp of whiskers against his palm reminding him of the long, weary day behind him. He shoved his foot into the stirrup and hauled himself up to the saddle. He was knackered even before those two had jumped him, but now… He pressed his hand to his side and winced. That bastard had caught him with his stake, but he was sure it hadn't punctured anything vital. When he had first become aware of the two figures lurking in the undergrowth, energy had flooded him, banishing his weariness and helping him to fight them off. But now that that unnatural surge had dissipated and all he wished for was a hot meal and a comfortable bed. He hoped the next inn would be a decent place. Some of the places he had stopped at since leaving Stourbridge had left much to be desired.

Vernon glanced round at the lad, riding a little behind, out of Vernon's direct line of sight. He was not the talkative type and that suited Vernon very well, but he was aware how fortunate it was that the lad had seen what was happening and come to Vernon's aid. He wondered idly if the boy was local…that was a very fine mare he was riding. Vernon frowned, staring at the road ahead as suspicions stirred. Such a quality, fine-boned animal was an unusual choice for a country lad. He glanced back again. The combination of the dim light and the lad's cap pulled low over his eyes rendered his face all but invisible.

They had ridden into a village and around a curve in the road. There before them was a small inn, the Bell, set between a churchyard and a row of neat cottages. Vernon could just make out the church itself, set back from the other buildings, its square tower silhouetted against the night sky.

'Do you know anything about this place?'

The lad shook his head.

'No matter,' Vernon said. 'Go in and see if it looks respectable, will you, lad? I'll hold the horses. Oh, and enquire for the local constable, while you're there, will you?' Once he left the saddle he feared it would be more than he could manage to remount. 'I must report that attack—I was informed earlier there has been a spate of such incidences in the area. I make no doubt the constable will be interested in the information, especially as one of those men looks unlikely to go far.'

The boy merely grunted by way of reply and did as he was bid as Vernon clenched his teeth against the pain in his side and battled the urge to slump in the saddle.

The boy soon emerged, with a couple of men. He nodded at Vernon, who took that to mean the inn was acceptable. He slid to the ground, relieved he need ride no further.

'I'm Joseph Deadly, constable here,' the taller of the two men said. 'What's been a-happening?'

Vernon told Deadly how the two men had jumped him.

'I'll wager it's them gipsies that set up camp by the woods. They often come through this time of year, picking up odd jobs, and we allus seem to get a spate of thievery and such like when they're around.'

Vernon recalled Thea's earlier remark, that Daniel had suspected former soldiers of local attacks rather than the gipsies commonly blamed. His immediate impression of his two attackers meant he was inclined to agree with Daniel.

'I am not sure you are correct, Deadly,' he said. 'Whilst gipsies are not unknown for petty thieving, the ones I've met in the past have not struck me as violent men, unless they perceive themselves under threat. The men who attacked me appeared more like vagrants.'

Deadly shrugged. 'One and the same thing, as far as I can see. You say one of them's injured, sir?'

'He is. I suspect my boot in his face will leave a visible clue to identify the culprit.'

Several men had by now joined them outside the inn, tankards in hand.

'Any volunteers to come with me and pay them gipsies a visit?' Deadly said.

A chorus of enthusiasm met his words and Vernon's heart sank. He hoped he hadn't been the instigator of a lynch mob. Still, that was for the constable to control.

'Never fear, sir,' Deadly added, clapping Vernon on the shoulder and making him wince, 'we'll go to the scene first and scout out from there. But, you mark my words, it'll be them gipsies.'

'Before you go…' Vernon tossed his horse's reins to the

lad—who had shrunk back into the shadows—and then took the constable to one side to tell him about Daniel Markham's disappearance. 'Will you make a few enquiries, but discreetly, please? Mr Markham's family do not wish his disappearance to become common knowledge. He was riding a light grey horse. I also need to know if you have any knowledge of Willingdale or of a man called Henry Mannington. You may attend me here in the morning, if you will, to let me know if you have any news for me and to tell me if you've had any luck in tracking down my attackers.'

Deadly touched the brim of his hat. 'Very good, sir.'

Vernon was relieved to call a halt to his enquiries, even though his original intention had been to reach Birmingham and the Royal Hotel that night. He felt in his gut that the Royal Hotel would hold the clue he needed to unravel what had happened to Daniel Markham.

He turned back to Warrior. The lad who had been holding him had gone, leaving the horse's reins weighted with a large stone. Vernon frowned. He had wanted to thank him properly. He looked along the street and there, in the distance, he could just make out the lad riding away on his black mare. His body screamed at him to let the lad go, but his suspicions about the quality of the horse, coupled with the lad's reluctance to look Vernon in the eye and his lack of conversation, set warning bells jangling in Vernon's head. Then he recalled the lad's pistol. How many country lads like him would own a *duelling* pistol?

Is he a runaway?

And those few words decided him. His nephew, Alex—Leo's youngest son—had run away only a few months previously, and Vernon remembered the worry and the grief of the entire family as they had imagined the worst. And then there was Thea—her anxiety over her brother's disappearance had touched Vernon as he saw how bravely she tried to shield her parents from the knowledge. The thought of another family going through the same horror of not knowing what had become of their loved one made the decision for him: he could not allow the lad to ride off into the night without at least trying to discover his story.

Vernon clenched his teeth and, sweating with the effort, hauled himself into Warrior's saddle. He put his hand to his side again, reaching inside his borrowed moleskin waistcoat, feeling the sticky warmth of blood. He inhaled—he should get it seen to, but then the boy would be long gone and, if he *was* a runaway, Vernon would have lost his only chance to help.

He set Warrior into a trot, biting back a gasp as the gait jolted him and pain scorched across his ribs.

'Damn,' he muttered, beneath his breath. 'Let's get this done,' and he dug his heels in.

Warrior broke into a canter—a smoother pace but still agony to Vernon. He hooked his left hand under the pommel and forced his thoughts away from the pain and on to the lad. As they neared the black mare, the lad glanced back and, for a moment, it seemed as though he would take flight. He did not, however, but reined to a halt and waited, staring fixedly at his horse's mane.

'Why did you leave?' Vernon said as he pulled his horse round in front of the mare.

'Need to get home.'

There was something about that gruff voice...but it hovered just out of Vernon's reach. He watched the boy as he studiously avoided meeting his gaze.

'And where is that?'

A cough took Vernon unaware. Pain forked through him and he sucked an involuntary breath in through his teeth. The boy's head jerked upright and he stared through the darkness at Vernon.

'Are you hurt?'

'Merely a scratch,' he gritted out. 'You left before I could thank you properly.' He fumbled in his pocket, pulled out a half-sovereign. 'Here. I am—'

Vernon bit off his words. The boy had reached out for the coin, muttering *Thanks*, and something about that disgruntled, near-sarcastic tone of voice jogged a memory. He did not stop to think about it…about how unlikely it was…he nudged his horse closer to the dainty black mare and took hold of her reins. The fresh scent of roses assailed his senses.

It cannot—

In one swift movement he snatched the cap from the boy's head. Even though it was too dark to see the colour, there was no mistaking the spring of the curls that tumbled about her forehead, nor the delicate oval of her face, nor the plump softness of the lips that formed a silent *Oh!* of horror. Vernon lifted his gaze to meet a pair of large, startled eyes that he just knew were hazel in colour.

'What the bloody *hell* do you think you are doing?'

Chapter Six

Thea shrank from the utter fury in Vernon's voice, the blood stuttering through her veins. She said nothing. There was nothing she could say. The only sound was of the early stirrings of nocturnal wildlife rustling in the still evening air. She suppressed a shiver. She was unafraid of the dark, but she could not begin to guess how Lord Vernon Beauchamp might now react. She had not trusted him to concentrate on finding Daniel, but had never stopped to wonder about her own safety if...*when*...he discovered her presence.

A growl sounded, muted at first, as though contained deep within him, but it grew and grew until, with a hasty gesture that made Thea flinch, Vernon snatched his hat from his head, thrust his other hand through his hair and then, swinging his right leg over Warrior's neck, he jumped to the ground and strode away. After a dozen paces, he stopped and then hunkered down, his head hanging.

Thea chewed her lip. It was too late to ride away. He knew it was she and therefore she had no choice but to face him. She dismounted and approached the still figure. His breath came in hoarse rasps and, with a flurry of concern, she recalled that fight and his earlier hissed intake of breath.

'Are you injured?' She dropped a timid hand on his shoulder.

'I *said* it is but a scratch.'

He stood and Thea staggered back several paces as he towered over her. He held up his hands, palms facing her, in a gesture of peace.

'It is all right.' There was still a hard edge to his voice, but that raw anger had softened. 'I might be furious, but I have never in my life offered violence to a woman and I am not about to start now, no matter *how* tempted I am to put you over my knee and spank you.'

Thea gasped, but shock soon gave way to her own anger. 'You cannot dictate my movements, Lord Vernon. You are neither my father nor my brother—'

'Thank God for that small mercy.'

'And I do not answer to you.'

'Again, thank God. I can think of nothing worse than being responsible for a little firebrand such as you.' He heaved a sigh. 'Except, of course, I *am* now responsible for you.'

'You are most certainly not responsible for me. I am a woman grown. An adult. And a perfectly capable one at that.' Thea moved closer to him, stretching to her full height and thrusting her face as close to his as she could manage. 'I am responsible for myself. It is nothing to do with you.'

He huffed a laugh of disbelief. 'Then…' he put his hat back on and started back towards the horses '…I shall leave you to it, Miss Markham.' She heard him chuckle as he walked away. 'Dorothea! Dotty is more like it. Yes, that is it.' He spun to face her, continuing to move away, walking backwards. 'Dotty by name, dotty by nature.'

Thea swallowed down an urge to cry. She would not give that brute the satisfaction. She crossed her arms over her chest and turned away, staring fixedly back down the road. She would not turn back until she heard him ride off. *That* would show him how little she cared.

I do not need him. I have money, so I can stay in inns. I have my pistols and I have my wits about me.

Silence reigned. All she could hear, once more, was the sound of night-time creatures moving through the undergrowth. No creak of a saddle as he mounted. No horse's hoofbeats fading into the distance. But she would not look.

'You…' the voice came from directly behind her, making her jump '…are the most wilful woman it has ever been my misfortune to meet.'

Her pulse settled and a warm glow settled deep inside her. For all her bravado, she had dreaded being left alone on a strange road now darkness had fallen.

'What is your plan? Where did you think to spend the night?'

She faced him. She hadn't really planned…at least, not in such detail. She had trusted in her own ingenuity to work out those minor inconveniences when the time came.

'I *planned*…' she stuck her nose in the air '…to stay at inns overnight. That is what they are for, after all.'

'An unaccompanied female, staying in such places?'

'There is no need to sound so very…*scandalised*. I told you before that I am not one of your delicate society misses, fit for nothing other than being dressed in fancy clothes and doing as they are told.'

The man standing in front of her snorted with laughter.

'*What* is so funny?'

'You should meet the females in my family, if that is what you believe. My sister, my new sister-in-law, my niece: they are not women to meekly do as they are bid without question.'

'Then you should be more than comfortable with the notion that *I* am capable of making my own decisions. Besides, it may have escaped your notice, but I would not be staying in inns as an unaccompanied woman, but as a youth. See? Scandal avoided. Not even you recognised me, until now. Tell me, what gave me away? I shall need to know if I am to escape detection as we continue searching for Daniel.'

'Continue…? Oh, no. You are not coming with me. You are to go home. Right now. You have seen how dangerous it is on the roads. I cannot allow—'

'One: as I said before, it is not your place either to give or to withhold permission. Two: it is now dark and I am not so foolish as to ride all the way home, on my own, at night. Who knows what scoundrels I might meet? Not to mention Mr Deadly and his bloodthirsty band. Three: I cannot wait meekly at home, waiting for news of Daniel. I have had five days of that. Five days of doing nothing other than hoping for the best, as you yourself said. I need to be doing something. *Please*. Allow me to help.'

'But—'

'No one will find out I'm not a youth, I promise.' He was wavering, she could tell. She pressed home her advantage. 'Tell me what gave me away and I'll make sure it does not happen again. Besides…' she stepped closer '…you need someone to watch your back. I proved that, earlier.'

Vernon huffed a sigh.

'What gave me away?'

'Your voice. Specifically…' he tilted her chin up until their eyes met '…the irritatingly hoity tone in which you said your thanks when I gave you that coin.'

Thea bit back a grin. She *had* taken offence at that typically aristocratic gesture towards a lesser mortal who has done them a service. She had not met many as high-ranked as Vernon, but she recognised the type.

'Then I shall ensure I am suitably humble in the days ahead.'

'And,' he continued, 'I have yet to come across a youth

who smells quite as...*enticing*...as you.' His voice lowered. 'You smell of flowers—like a garden in midsummer.'

His deep tone did peculiar things to her insides.

'Then I shall neglect to wash myself for a few days,' Thea said. 'We cannot have you too...er...*enticed*, now, can we?'

A muffled snort of laughter gave her encouragement.

'What say you?' she said. 'Are we partners?'

'Partners? Hmmm.' He shook his head. 'I just know I am going to regret this, but...very well.'

'Yes!'

'I insist on one condition, though.'

'Which is?'

'You remain in disguise, every minute of every day. You must think of yourself as a youth—no missish airs and graces, no maidenly protestations and most definitely no tears or swooning. You will be my nephew.' Thea caught a flash of white as he grinned. 'I shall be your Uncle Vernon Boyton.'

'Boyton?'

'One of my brother's minor titles. We use it occasionally when he doesn't want to travel as a duke, with all the pomp that can entail. So, Master Boyton, what name shall we—?'

'Theo,' Thea said, before he could come up with some totally unacceptable name. 'Daniel calls me Thea, so—'

'Not Dotty? I am disappointed.'

'So,' she went on, through gritted teeth, 'Theo will be perfect.'

'I shall endeavour not to forget. Now, I don't know about you, Dot—*Theo*! I *do* beg your pardon—but I am starving. Shall we return to...what was that village? Harborne, that is it...and have something to eat?'

When they reached the Bell they rode around the back to the stable yard where an ostler scurried out of the stables to take the horses. Vernon tossed him a coin in that careless, aristocratic manner that had so irritated Thea earlier. If he had ever known the fear of losing everything, he would not be so unthinking in tossing a coin.

'Take care,' Vernon murmured, as they returned to the front of the inn. 'We must not discuss your brother yet. Wait for when we are alone.'

Those words prompted a flutter deep inside Thea's stomach. *When we are alone...* For a few glorious moments she savoured those words, until common sense intervened. They were taking part in a masquerade. He was of a completely different world to her and, besides, had she not sworn to herself that she would never again look twice at *any* man?

She sneaked a sideways peek at Vernon as they arrived at the front door.

He seems *trustworthy*.

But, then, so had Jasper: handsome and smooth-talking on the outside, concealing deceit and greed and downright cruelty.

The innkeeper greeted them and passed them on to the care of his wife when Vernon requested bedchambers for himself and his nephew.

'I've got joining chambers available, sir, but that'll be no problem for you and the young sir there,' Mrs Topping said as she led them up the stairs.

She showed them into a large room and lit two lamps with a tinderbox from her apron pocket. A huge bed dominated the centre of the room. Mrs Topping held one lamp aloft and ushered Thea to a door in the corner, through which there was a box room with a tiny window and a narrow single bed. There was no outer door, she noted uneasily, just the door into the main chamber.

'These will suit us very well, Mrs Topping,' Vernon said. 'I shall be able to keep close tabs on young Theo here.'

He reached out and, before Thea realised his intention, he tweaked her ear.

'Ouch,' she squealed, rubbing at her ear.

'Oh, dear. That voice of yours will not behave, will it, nevvy?' Vernon said, with a wide grin. 'One minute low, the next squeaking like a girl. You'll be relieved when it's finally broken for good, I dare say. At least then you will *sound* like a man.'

Thea glared at him, still rubbing her ear. He was relishing this, the wretch, and she wondered how many more jokes he would enjoy at her expense.

'Dinner will be ready in half an hour, sirs, if you care to come down to the parlour then,' Mrs Topping said. 'The maid will be up directly with warm water for you.'

After she had gone, Vernon sat on the edge of the double bed in the outer chamber and bounced a couple of times.

'Hmmm, yes, perfectly adequate,' he said, before swinging his legs up and stretching out full length upon the mattress.

Thea averted her eyes and hurried into the smaller room, feeling her cheeks heat as a devilish chuckle followed her.

'Be so good as to send the girl in with the water when she comes,' she snapped, before slamming the connecting door.

She sat on the bed, slumping despondently as she registered quite how sparse and unforgiving the mattress felt under her buttocks. She had not anticipated being at quite such close quarters with Vernon. Neither had she envisaged being stuck in a tiny hole of a bedchamber with the only way out through *his* bedchamber. She must endure for tonight—to demand better accommodation would only risk revealing her disguise—but if Lord Vernon Beauchamp imagined she would accept such arrangements in any of the nights to come, he might think again.

Tomorrow morning, she would be laying down some rules.

She lay back upon the bed, wriggling to try to get comfortable. Then the murmur of voices and the click of a door closing catapulted her to her feet, to wait for the maid to bring her water through. There was silence from the adjoining room. Thea crept over to the door and put her ear to the wood. There was no sound for the longest time and then…a grunt, followed by a gasp and then the splash of water being poured. She waited, but all she could hear was the slosh of water in a basin and the occasional hiss, as of air being inhaled sharply through gritted teeth.

Impatient to know what was happening and when she, too, might expect some water, Thea tapped on the door. Lifting the latch, she inched it open.

'Are you decent, my lord? Is it safe to come in?'

'Decent *and* safe?' He chuckled, setting her teeth on edge. 'Now there's a question. Yes, you're safe enough, Theo, my lad. My tastes never did run to boys.'

Thea thrust the door wide and stalked into the other room. 'Where is my…*oh!*'

A wide expanse of hair-dusted chest met her gaze. A ripple of…*something*…undulated through her, stealing her breath, and she wrenched her gaze from Vernon, mentally scolding herself. She had seen Daniel's bare chest numerous times, as well as the workers in the fields at harvest time, so why did *his* chest affect her so?

'I wondered what had happened to my water,' she said.

'The maid only brought the one jug. She said she was bringing another *for the young master* straight away. She would think it strange if I allowed you to have the first jugful.'

He was right, but that did not soothe Thea's ruffled feelings. She faked indifference as she scanned the room although all she wanted to do was to feast her eyes once more on Vernon's magnificent torso, with its sculpted muscles, wide shoulders and the tantalising trail of hair that narrowed as it disappeared into his breeches…

Her thoughts stuttered to a halt.

Vernon had dropped his shirt and, as her gaze alighted on it, Thea gasped and swooped on the garment, snatching it from the floor. She shook it out and held it up to the light of the lamp.

'You're bleeding! Why did you not say?'

Vernon—one arm raised above his head as he dabbed at his side with a washcloth—snorted.

'What would've been the point of that? There was nothing could be done about it before and I am dealing with it now. Besides, I did tell you.'

'You *said* it was a scratch.' Thea hurried over to him. 'Let me help.'

She ducked under his raised arm and took the washcloth from his unresisting hand. She wrung it out in the water and turned her attention to the gash across his ribs.

'It *is* a scratch. The knife must have glanced off a rib,' Vernon said. 'Look—'

He indicated one end of the gash, at the front of his torso, about three inches below his left nipple. Thea's mouth went dry at that fascinating flat disc, so different to her own.

'It started here and then glanced away, and around my side. Bit of luck it didn't go in deep.'

He twisted from the waist and Thea saw the long gash became shallower as it followed the curve of his ribcage. Vernon's arm was still raised and, when Thea glanced up, she had to batten down a peculiar compulsion to stroke the soft chestnut-coloured hair that grew underneath. Her heart hammered in her chest as his musky scent surrounded her, but the realisation that Vernon was entirely unmoved by their proximity—concentrating solely on his wound—gave her the strength she needed to ignore her erratic reactions.

She began to cleanse the wound, which had stopped bleeding, aware that infection could be a problem.

As if he'd read her mind, Vernon said, 'I asked the maid to bring up a length of bandage and a glass of brandy.'

'Good,' she said. 'It will sting, of course, but that is preferable to an infection of the blood.'

'Sting?' That one word was infused with horror. 'My dear Dotty, the brandy is to drink. I am in dire need of a tonic.'

Thea pursed her lips, aware he was deliberately provoking her by calling her Dotty. She could only hope he would soon tire of the sport if she did not react.

At that moment there was a tap on the door and the maid came in, carrying a jug, a glass containing amber liquid and a strip of cloth. Thea reacted quickly, reaching the maid before Vernon had even turned around.

'Thank you.' She took the glass and bandage from the maid. 'If you could put the jug in the other room, please?'

Vernon had tilted his head and was watching Thea closely, his eyes narrowed. She held his gaze. He needn't think he could intimidate her so very easily. She needed him fit and well if they were to find Daniel, and that meant— like it or not—the brandy was going on his wound. The maid emerged from the inner room.

'Thank you…er…?'

The maid bobbed a curtsy. 'Janey, sir.'

Vernon smiled at her, bringing a rosy blush to her cheeks. 'Thank you, Janey.'

Hmmph. Flirting with the maid in front of me. He's only doing it to annoy me.

Vernon's smile widened as he caught Thea's eye. The maid left the room, closing the door behind her, and Vernon held out one hand.

'I'll have that, thank you,' he said.

Thea wrapped both hands around the glass, holding it

tight against her chest, and shook her head. 'You can drink brandy any time. This is needed for medicinal purposes.'

He prowled across the room towards her. Her pulse quickened, and she retreated to the far side of the bed.

'Precisely,' he said. 'And it will fulfil its medicinal function from the inside. In my belly.' He rounded the end of the bed.

'No. Listen...'

She was trapped. There was nowhere to go other than across the bed itself—impossible while holding a glass of brandy. Why hadn't she thought this through before challenging him? He neared her with every step, that bare chest of his filling her vision and turning her insides into a mass of jelly.

'Well?' he queried, silky smooth. 'You asked me to listen.'

'If there is any left, you may drink that,' she said.

'After a cloth has been dipped in and out of it?' He shook his head. 'I think not. Try again.'

He halted in front of her, but made no move to take the glass. Her legs trembled—and not with fear—as she searched her mind desperately for something...*anything...* to say to persuade him. Her gaze, she realised, was still locked on to his chest—so close, so tempting—and she forced herself to look up at his face. Where she caught, and recognised, the roguish glint in his eyes and the twitch of his lips. She frowned.

Vernon threw his head back and laughed uproariously. 'Your expression,' he gasped. 'It was a delight. You did not really believe I would wrestle the glass from you by force?'

He spun round and crossed the room to stand by the lamp. Thea remained still.

'But...' she said. 'You...'

'Come.' He beckoned her. 'Come and do your worst.

Of *course* I ordered the brandy to cleanse the gash, foolish girl.'

Fuming silently, Thea walked over to him. Before she could say anything, though, he reached out and cupped her chin, tilting her face to his.

'You are entirely too gullible, my dear Dotty.' He pinched her chin gently before releasing it. 'We are going to have to toughen you up, if you are to pass muster as a youth. Teasing and ribaldry are all part of the disguise.'

He lifted his arm again, and passed Thea a handkerchief. 'Here. Use this. It is clean.'

Thea moistened the handkerchief and dabbed at the cut, repeating the process until the entire length had been treated. Throughout, Vernon remained silent, only the occasional flinch betraying the sting of the spirit.

'There. It is all done,' Thea said.

She fetched the bandage from the bed, where she had thrown it when Vernon began stalking her. Vernon raised both arms and challenged her silently with a raised brow. Thea narrowed her eyes. He was entirely too cocky. She would not give him the satisfaction of knowing how rattled she was by being here with him half-naked. She moved closer and reached around him to pass the bandage behind his back. Heat scorched her skin as she momentarily pressed her cheek to his chest. She forced herself not to react, but calmly brought the bandage around and tied a half-knot to hold it in place. Then she walked around him several times, wrapping his torso—and those fascinating slabs of muscle that caught her eye every time she passed in front of him—until the gash was covered and she could tie off the bandage.

'There. Now I must go and have a wash and put on some clean clothes, or we shall be late for our supper.'

'Wait.'

A hand grasped her shoulder before she had taken two

steps towards the door in the corner. She faced him, raising her brows in enquiry. He reached out and ruffled her hair.

'What *have* you done?'

His soft query, the underlying sadness in his voice, brought a lump to her throat as she recalled her hurried shearing of her locks. She tried to smooth her hair, knowing the attempt was futile.

'It is nothing. It will grow again.'

His lips tightened momentarily. 'It is a mess.'

He then captured her gaze and a teasing glint lit his eyes. 'I refuse to be seen in the company of a youth with such a dreadful haircut,' he said, 'particularly when that youth claims to be a relative of mine.'

He strode to his saddlebag, rummaged around inside, and then turned to reveal a pair of scissors in his hand.

'Oh, no.' Thea backed towards the interconnecting door, shaking her head. 'No, no, no. I refuse to allow you near me with those.'

Vernon followed her, gaining on her. 'I cannot possibly make a worse fist of it than you already have,' he said. 'Joking aside, Dotty…it looks utterly appalling. Come… I shall only tidy up the ends a little. They are so ragged *anybody* could guess you have cut your hair yourself. Do you really want to draw such attention to yourself?'

Put like that, what could she say? With a silent sigh, Thea stalked across to a wooden chair and sat down. She closed her eyes and folded her hands tightly in her lap.

A comb began to tug through her curls, snagging on tangles. She kept her eyes screwed shut as Vernon worked quietly and methodically. Then there was a pause and he lifted one curl, raising a shiver that raced across the surface of her scalp. She clamped her lips together as she heard the metallic snick of the scissors. Each time he fingered another curl her skin grew increasingly sensitised and the heat rose from deep inside her to flush her chest, neck and face as she battled to remain motionless on the chair.

By the time he murmured, 'There. All done', she was a quivering wreck.

She did not look into the mirror. Nor did she pause to look at the hair on the floor. She sped through the door between their bedchambers and closed it softly behind her, leaning back against it as she fought to calm her breathing.

Chapter Seven

'You were in the taproom of the Nag's Head when I came in,' Vernon said.

He waited until their food had been served in the parlour of the Bell before broaching the subject that was on his mind. Ever since they entered the inn, and he had seen Thea properly, by the light of the lamps, he had been plagued with the mystery of where he had seen her before, dressed as a lad.

'You were sitting in the corner, nursing a tankard of ale, and you did not join in the conversation once. When I got up to leave, you had already gone.'

'That should prove I can pass unnoticed.'

Thea, sitting across the table from Vernon, kept her attention on her plate of stew. She had been subdued—withdrawn, even—ever since they had come downstairs: speaking only when spoken to directly, reluctant to hold a decent conversation. And he thought he knew why.

He shifted in his seat as his body reacted to the memory of that haircut. He'd had no choice but to trim her hair after she had left it such a raggedy mass, but he had not anticipated the…*intimacy*…of doing so: the soft, heavy curls between his fingers, her tightly closed eyes and her full lips—so near, so tempting, so *inviting*—the sound of her breathing, loud in the hush of the bedchamber…

He'd wager Thea had been as affected by the unexpected sensuality of that haircut as he had been. But now…this silence…it was hard to stand. It gave him too much time to think.

He could always tease her again, provoke her until her eyes flashed with fury and her temper flared. But teasing, too, felt perilous… He could not rid his mind of the knowledge that, under that male costume, was a flesh-and-blood woman and teasing between a man and a woman could so easily turn into something…*more*.

He would keep this businesslike. 'Do you not wish to decide our plans for tomorrow? To discuss how we might trace Daniel?'

Her head jerked up, her eyes huge.

'Of *course* I wish to discuss him.'

The pain in that husky voice of hers did strange things to him. It was not pity, although he did feel sympathy for her, but, strangely, following his earlier thoughts, it did not provoke the urge to tease but the opposite. It brought forth the desire to comfort and to protect—a feeling he had only thus far in his life felt in relation to the members of his own family. Why did he feel such responsibility for her? It had been her decision to come along, after he had particularly told her to wait at home for news. It was her decision to dress—quite outrageously—in a youth's clothing and to chop her hair off in that barbarous way. She was, as she had pointed out, an adult capable of making her own decisions.

Was it merely the fact she was a female? He huffed a silent laugh, imagining her fury if he was unwise enough to voice *that* particular thought aloud.

'We should speak to the innkeeper about Daniel and ask whether he can recall him visiting this inn,' Thea went on.

'I have already spoken to him,' Vernon said. 'Whilst you were washing.'

He'd had to get out of his room, after she had blithely informed him she would change into clean clothing for the meal. His imagination had run riot—he could not help but wonder what she had done with her breasts. There was no sign of them, but he distinctly recalled them from earlier that day, in that sunset dress of hers. She must have strapped them down and he had begun to wonder if that hurt, and then he had fantasised about soothing the pain and plumping them up again…and he'd had to remove himself from her vicinity before his rakish tendencies overcame his good sense and he attempted to turn fantasy into reality.

Good God…she's not even my type, yet I was fantasising about her like a sex-starved lad.

'I gave my shirt to Mrs Topping to try to remove the bloodstain and to mend the rip,' he said, 'and I spoke to Topping then.'

She waved a dismissive hand at his explanation. 'What did Topping have to say?'

'Nothing. He cannot remember a man of Daniel's description; he did not know his name and he has never heard of Henry Mannington or of Willingdale.'

'Hmph. Well, at least you obtained the information more speedily this time than you did in the Nag's Head,' she said.

Cheeky little…

Vernon resisted the impulse to reach across the table and cuff Thea's ear. This masquerade was doing strange things to his head. One minute, he found it impossible not to think of the female body hidden beneath those clothes and the next he had almost treated her exactly as he might treat the impertinence of any young lad. He quaffed a quantity of ale, giving his temper time to subside.

'I am not certain what you expected this afternoon,' he said, capturing her gaze as he leaned across the table towards her, 'but—'

'I do not understand why you could not simply ask the questions and leave. You did so at the other inns you stopped at. You did not remain at any of those above ten minutes. We could be at that hotel in Birmingham by now if you had not been so…so…intent upon playing a part at the Nag's Head. This is not a play, my lord. It is real life. There could be a life at stake…' Her voice choked and she cleared her throat.

Vernon sat back, frowning. 'If you will allow me to explain.'

She shot him a smile of apology. 'Now I have angered you. I apologise. I did not mean to sound ungrateful.'

'I am not angry. I see why you reached such a conclusion, but I did not act in the way I did for my own amusement, but in order that I might learn the truth and not be fobbed off with shrugged shoulders and denials.

'Those men in the Nag's Head are not stupid. They knew I was an outsider, so it was of no use me pretending otherwise. I acted the part of a gentleman down on his luck… my atrocious gambling habit, don't you know.' He grinned at her and was rewarded by a faint smile in return. 'Such a man will always find a welcome in such public houses, but it takes time to build a rapport and it is necessary to earn a man's trust before asking questions. Had I gone in and immediately bombarded them with questions, they would have feigned ignorance even if Daniel was in the next room. Do not forget, those men *know* your brother. They would see it as protecting him. Taking time as I did may have been frustrating for you, but at least I left the place with some information.

'I did not need to behave with the same circumspection at the other inns because, as far as I am aware, Daniel is not a regular customer there.'

'But why bother to make enquiries at every single inn between Stourbridge and Birmingham? You are wasting time.'

'I disagree. We may now know that R.H. means the Royal Hotel, but that does not mean the answers we seek will fall into our laps the minute we walk through the door. We still need to know what or who Willingdale is and we need to know how Henry Mannington is connected with Daniel's disappearance. What we *do* know is that Daniel made this same journey twice a day for several days in succession. I take the view that, as we are passing, it is worth our while asking the pertinent questions. We do not want to be forced to retrace our steps, do we?'

She bit into her lower lip. Vernon averted his gaze and fixed it on his plate as his pulse kicked. This escapade might prove intolerable if they did not discover the truth about Daniel quickly.

'You are right,' she said. 'I had not thought it through. I am sorry.'

'There is no need to keep apologising.' Vernon indicated her plate. She had barely touched her food. 'Are you not going to eat?'

She pushed the plate from her. 'I find I have little appetite. It has been the same ever since Daniel disappeared.'

The dining room was empty apart from the two of them, the other guests having dined earlier. He reached across the table and covered her hand with his. It felt so tiny. The bones fragile. Again, the urge to protect welled up and he closed his fingers gently around hers.

'It is of no use to tell you not to worry, I know, but I promise we will find the truth. You must not starve yourself, though. Tomorrow will be a long and trying day and you cannot risk falling ill. You will need energy and strength. Even if you have no appetite, try to eat something. I have never known any lad who would not clear that plateful and ask for more so, if you wish to maintain your charade, please try to eat some more.'

Her eyes searched his. They were huge, luminous pools and he felt himself being drawn into their depths. He wrenched his gaze from hers and withdrew his hand.

'We will find out what has happened to Daniel and, God willing, we will find him safe and well,' he said, scraping back his chair. 'In the meantime, I shall go out to the stables and check on our horses and see if the grooms can recall seeing Daniel or his horse.' He smiled at her, adding, 'I never met a groom yet who paid more attention to a rider than his horse.'

He was rewarded with a fleeting smile and the sight of Thea pulling her plate back in front of her and picking up her spoon. Vernon quashed his guilt at leaving the table whilst Thea still ate. These were exceptional circumstances and, besides, if he did not soon put some distance between them, he did not think he could resist sweeping her into his arms and just holding her. Comforting her. And that he could not risk. He needed a dose of fresh air and some uncomplicated, masculine company, even if that was only the ostlers in a country inn.

Out the back of the inn, all was quiet. Vernon opened the door to the stable to be greeted by the contented sound of horses munching hay. He breathed deep of the soothing, familiar smell of horses, leather, saddle soap and hay. A man holding aloft a lantern emerged from a door at the far end of the row of stalls.

'Is aught amiss, sir?'

'No. I have come to check our horses are settled, that is all.'

They chatted easily about horses for a while, before

Vernon said, 'I believe a friend of mine has stopped here several times. He rides a light grey gelding, about sixteen hands high. Name of Bullet.'

The groom smiled around a mouthful of chewing tobacco.

'I remember him, sir. Good strong-boned piece of 'oss-flesh. He's called in here a few times—on his way to and from Birmingham.' He leaned closer to Vernon, and lowered his voice, 'One of the wenches here's a bit…you know, sir, a bit generous, shall we say?' He winked knowingly. 'The gent took to calling in to visit with her, if you see what I mean. Janey, she's called, if you've an interest in that direction yerself, sir.'

'Thank you.' Vernon had no such interest in Janey, but he would speak to her for she might hold a vital clue. His pulse quickened. He would find her after he'd finished with the groom. 'Can you remember the last time you saw him?'

The groom cocked his jaw, frowning. 'Lemme see. Last Thursday, it were. Ayuh, that was it. Thursday morning. I remembers, you see, 'cause that's the day the carrier calls in.'

Thursday. That was the day Daniel failed to return home.

'He did not call in on his way home that evening?'

'Not as I recall, sir.'

'Do you know a man called Henry Mannington?'

The groom shook his head.

'Thank you, you've been most helpful.'

Vernon slipped the man a coin. The groom took it and tucked it away with a nod of thanks.

'One last question—does the name Willingdale mean anything to you?'

'No, sir. Never heard of it.'

Vernon crossed the yard to the inn, choosing to enter through the rear door. As luck would have it, as he followed the passage that led to the dining room, Janey was approaching him from the direction of the stairs. Vernon continued towards her and halted just past the closed dining room door. He wondered if Thea was still inside.

'Janey,' he said, as the maid came closer.

She smiled and her hips appeared to take on a life of their own, undulating in a silent *come hither*. She did not halt until her breasts—squeezed by her corset into bulging mounds above her neckline—were a bare inch from his chest.

'Can I offer you anything, sir?' Her tongue played with her top lip.

'Information, if you please.' He kept his tone brisk, careful to offer her no encouragement. He had no wish to wake in the night to find her willing body slipping between his sheets. 'I understand you are…er…acquainted with a friend of mine, Daniel Markham?'

'Danny?' She pouted. 'He promised to bring me a present, but he never came.'

'When was this?'

She didn't hesitate. 'Last Thursday. He was going into Birmingham as usual, and he *promised* to br—'

'To bring you a present. Yes, yes, so you said.'

Vernon reached into his pocket and extracted a coin. A brief glance confirmed it was a crown—more than he intended, but the girl's eyes lit at the sight of it so, with a mental shrug, he pressed it into her palm. If it kept her sweet enough to answer his questions, it was worth it.

Too late, he registered the sound of the door opening behind him. As Janey ostentatiously slid the coin into the deep cleft between her breasts, Thea stalked past with a muttered 'Good night, *Uncle*.'

Vernon suppressed his sigh, knowing what she must think.

'That,' he said to Janey, more harshly than he intended to, 'is for information only. Is that clear?'

Her lips thinned.

Great. Now I have two affronted females to pacify.

He clasped Janey's arm and steered her into the dining room.

'I can't stay,' she said, twisting her arm free from his grip. 'Mrs Topping will be after me and I can't afford to lose my job.'

'Then answer my questions quickly and she will never notice you are gone.'

Damn it! Why did Thea have to come out at that precise moment? With an effort, Vernon tore his thoughts from Thea and back to solving the mystery of Daniel's disappearance.

'Did Daniel tell you why he went into Birmingham every day?'

Janey's eyes narrowed. 'Why do you want to know? Is he in trouble?'

Vernon held out his hand, palm up. 'You took my money—you answer my questions. If you won't, you can return it now.'

A flush coloured her cheeks. 'I only know he was searching for someone.'

'Who?'

'Are you him?' Her eyes widened. 'Are you this Henry he was so angry with?'

'No.'

'Promise?' Her voice trembled. 'I don't want nothing to do with him. Promise you're not him?'

'I promise. I am a friend of Daniel's and of his family. I want to find him to help him. Now, think, Janey, did Daniel say why he was angry with Henry?'

'It were about money, that's all I know. He saw him at a sale and he followed him, but he lost him. He were fumin' when he called in on his way home. *Fumin'.*'

'You knew Daniel before that day? How long have you known him?'

She shrugged. 'Couple of years. He took to calling in when he went into town, maybe three or four times a year. Until that day. He went up to Birmingham every day after that, looking for this Henry, asking questions about him.'

'Did he tell you what he found out?'

'Some,' she said. ''e found out where Henry stayed when he went to town—some hotel.'

The Royal Hotel! I'd bet my life on it!

'So he said he would go back every day until either he saw Henry again or until he found out where he lived and that when he tracked him down he was going to kill him.'

'*Kill* him?'

Janey nodded. 'He shook with anger when he talked about him. Said he couldn't talk 'bout it to no one but me. *That's* why he was going to bring me a present, 'cause I'm a good listener, I am.' She sniffed, her eyes welling with tears. 'But he never came back. Five days it's been.'

Vernon patted her shoulder. 'Thank you for your help, Janey. Off you go now, or Mrs Topping will be after you.'

'Thank you, sir.' Janey reached for the door handle, then hesitated. 'I hope you find him, sir. I hope he's not hurt. I was angry at him, thinking he'd lied to me, but now... I just hope he's all right.'

'I hope so, too,' Vernon said as he followed the maid from the room.

Janey disappeared towards the rear of the inn and Vernon stood irresolute in the passageway, eyeing the staircase leading to the floor above. He felt drained. His ribs were sore and his temper felt as though it balanced on a knife's edge.

And up there was Thea. In the adjoining room. Smelling of roses. And...annoyed with him all over again.

He could not face attempting to explain how what she

had seen transpire between himself and Janey was entirely innocent. With a huff of impatience, he spun on his heel and headed for the taproom. It was too early for bed, anyway. He needed time to sift through all he had learned.

And he needed a drink.

Chapter Eight

◦◦◦◦◦◦◦◦

Vernon woke the next morning with a thundering headache.

He'd spent a restless night and when he finally slept it was to dream fitfully of men lurking in the shadows who, as they emerged into the light, metamorphosed into women, who rubbed around him as he stood frozen to the spot, only for their fingers to sprout claws that raked him, time and time again. He startled awake more than once, sweating, his heart racing.

A little quiet reflection as the dawn light fingered through a gap between the curtains did nothing to ease his troubled mind for, even if what had awoken him *was* only a dream, the underlying worry that plagued him was very real: he was responsible for Dorothea Markham and for her safety. And he had no way of knowing what dangers might lurk ahead of them.

He finally awoke with the conviction that, somehow, he must persuade Thea to return to her parents and to leave him to search on alone for her brother. She would not be easily persuaded. Never had he come across a more stubborn female. Even the women in his family—always ready to challenge a man's authority—were not as tricky to handle. Further consideration, however, set him wondering if that was because they were primarily Leo's responsibility, as head of the family. Vernon had always—their whole lives—been second in command. It was the lot of younger brothers.

As for females who were not members of the Beauchamp family, neither could he recall any of them being so…contrary. Although—and this seemed to be a morning for self-doubt—his renown as a ladies' man could simply be due to his position. Many ladies were eager to impress a wealthy, titled gentleman who was considered a great catch.

He snorted at that last thought. He could never accuse Thea of trying to impress him…she appeared oblivious to his charms. Although, and a slow smile curved his lips at the memory, she was certainly not impervious to his chest. Or to his touch as he trimmed her hair.

The trouble was—he was not impervious either.

He thrust aside the sheet that covered him and swung his legs to the floor. All this thinking was getting him nowhere. He was not second in command now…it was time to get on with finding Daniel Markham.

He washed in the warm water in a jug on his washstand—water he could not remember being delivered to his room and, after dressing, he knocked on the door to the inner chamber. There was no answer and he popped his head into the room to find Thea gone. Unable to quash the terror that jolted him—an after-effect of the night's dreams, his rational mind insisted—he hurried downstairs and there she was, bright-eyed and glowing, clad in her boy's clothes, waiting impatiently for him to appear and eager to continue their journey.

She was altogether too chirpy for Vernon's aching head.

'You are too accustomed to town hours,' she said, teasingly. 'You were sound asleep when I came through your room.'

And the thought of her seeing him sleeping in his bed set

his senses all a-jangling, discordant and sharp. And now… he watched Thea from under lowered brows and through bleary eyes as she tucked into another round of buttered toast and sipped from her cup of chocolate.

Nothing wrong with her appetite this morning.

And another thought followed on its heels: he'd expected her to still be annoyed about seeing him with Janey, but it clearly wasn't bothering her in the slightest.

Which was good. Was it not?

'How is your che…your injury this morning,' Thea asked. 'You look as though it is causing you pain.'

'My chest?'

The light blush that painted her cheeks cheered him somewhat, proving she wasn't totally indifferent to him. Not that he was interested in her, of course.

'It is not my chest that pains me, but my head.'

And the minute he uttered those words he knew his error. The tinge of sympathy he had recognised in those hazel orbs vanished and she immediately became more businesslike.

'Did you discover anything new last night?'

Vernon swallowed his mouthful of eggs and then told her what he had learned from the groom and from Janey. Thea's eyes widened when he told her what Janey had said. As soon as he finished, Thea jumped to her feet, the scrape of her chair setting Vernon's teeth on edge.

'What are we waiting for? Come…' she was already halfway to the door. The woman really was like a lick of flame, darting around so a man could barely keep track of her '…we must make haste.'

'Stop!'

Vernon winced at the loudness of his own voice as it echoed through his head. How much had he drunk last night? He hadn't thought he was over-imbibing, but maybe the local ale was stronger than his customary brew. Thea paused with her hand on the door handle, her tawny brows raised.

'I need to speak to the constable first, to find out if they caught those two ruffians from last night.'

Thea waved a dismissive hand. 'They are not important. We must—'

'Of course they are important. You heard the constable, there have been other attacks. Who knows, they might even have attacked Daniel and left him lying somewhere, or knocked him on the head so he has forgotten his own identity. They might have important information. We need to know one way or the other before we go rushing off to Birmingham.'

'That is true. Let us go.'

The wretched woman was almost bouncing with enthusiasm, those preposterous curls of hers springing around her ears. In these unguarded moments, despite her attire, it was impossible to see her as a youth. She looked young and feminine and…a little adorable. Vernon tore his gaze from her and eyed his plate of congealing eggs. He pushed it away.

'First,' he said, as repressively as he could, his temples still pounding, 'we need to talk.'

She stilled. 'You are going to renege on your promise.'

'Promise? I do not recall promising you anything. You, on the other hand, did promise you would remain at home.'

'I did not.' She dragged out her chair again and sat down. 'I was most careful about my wording. I said, "I shall not insist on leaving with you." And I did not. I *followed* you.' She folded her arms across her chest and her chin jutted forward. 'I will not go home.'

Vernon sighed and pushed his chair back from the table. He leaned back in his chair and stretched his legs out, crossing them at the ankle as he crossed his own arms.

'I have told you what the maid said: Daniel was fuming

when he saw Henry and he was determined to track him down. Quite what poor Henry can have done to attract such ire I do not know, but you have to admit this is not a dispute for a woman to become embroiled in.'

'*Poor* Henry? It sounds very much as though I made the right decision to follow you. I can see whose side *you* would be on.'

'Side? Who is talking of sides? All I am interested in is finding the truth. And it will be easier and quicker if I do not have to be constantly worrying about you.'

Thea stuck her nose in the air and averted her face. 'I do not need anyone to worry about me. I shall look after myself. As I did last night and again this morning whilst you were snoring your head off.'

'I do *not* snore.'

'How do you know? You were asleep.'

He closed his eyes and drew in a long, steadying breath. 'The fact still remains that you are at risk.'

'Vernon…'

He felt her breath on his cheek. Smelled the roses. He opened his eyes. Thea was bending over him, her eyes boring into his.

'…I suggest you save your breath for the questions we need to ask,' she said sweetly. 'I am going to Birmingham, to the Royal Hotel. Whether that is by your side or riding three lengths behind is up to you.'

She straightened, her expression one of smug satisfaction.

'And if I do not go to Birmingham? If I return to Stourwell Court for my curricle and pair and then go back to London?'

He knew what her answer would be, but honour dictated he should not concede without some fight.

She arched one brow. 'Then I must go alone.'

Hell and damnation!

He knew when he was beaten. He stood, and gestured to the door. 'In that case there is nothing more I can say. But do not come weeping to me if you get killed.'

She beamed. Positively *beamed* at him. Wretched, *wretched* woman!

The constable called upon them at the Bell just as they were leaving, with bad news.

'We found neither sight nor sound of your attackers, sir,' he told Vernon. 'And you were right. It weren't them gipsies. They'd moved on and Farmer Whitton, he told us they left yesterday morning, so it couldn't have been them that tried to rob you.'

The constable sounded disappointed. Thea hoped he'd remember this lesson the next time he was quick to point the finger of blame at the gipsies. They were a familiar sight in and around the Stourbridge area. They came and they went, and the men carried out odd jobs and repairs and helped on the farms at harvest times, whilst the women sold pegs and told fortunes for anyone prepared to pay them a penny or two. She did not believe they would attack someone unprovoked.

They set off towards Birmingham in silence, Vernon's scowl an effective barrier to conversation. Eventually, however, his puckered forehead smoothed and his grouchy mood appeared to lift as he showed more interest in the countryside they rode through.

'I feared you had the beginnings of a fever from your wound,' Thea said, after Vernon had commented on the cascading song of a skylark that hovered overhead—a barely visible speck in the deep azure of the sky. 'We do not have the time for you to be laid up in bed.'

He raised a brow. 'You are all heart, Dotty.'

'Well, of course I did not mean I should not care if you

became ill,' she said crossly. 'I only meant that…well, as I said—there is no time.'

He laughed, then tipped his head up and breathed in, his chest swelling. 'The fresh air has made all the difference. I woke up with the headache. It is all but gone now.'

Thea had tried hard not to dwell on his likely activities after she had seen him with that maid last night. It had been a shock to see him pressing money on the girl and Thea had climbed the stairs with her heart weighed down with disapproval and…yes…disappointment. Now, knowing that he had been paying the maid for information left her feeling in a charitable mood and so she forbore to point out that the pain he suffered—in his head, at least—was self-inflicted and therefore barely deserving of sympathy. She glanced up at the sky…not a cloud in sight and the sun already high and hot. She tugged at her cap, pulling the peak to shade her face.

'It is fortunate the weather has improved,' she said. 'We had thunderstorms three days running last week—the air was so thick and heavy your headache would not have cleared so readily.'

'Fortunate indeed,' he agreed.

She felt his eyes upon her and kept her attention on the road ahead, sensing he had questions on his mind. She did not have long to wait.

'Do you mind me asking…why are you not married?'

Star skittered slightly as Thea tensed. She relaxed her fingers on the reins and the mare settled again. He had taken her by surprise, asking such a very personal question. She shrugged, aiming for nonchalance.

'It takes two to make a marriage. Why are *you* not married? I assume you are not?'

'No. I am not married. I doubt I shall ever marry.'

'How can you be so sure?' Yet, even as that question

left her lips she realised it was possible to be sure...*she* was sure, after all.

'I have no need to wed. And I enjoy my life too much to ever get tied down to one woman.'

'Then it sounds as though you have made the right decision,' Thea said.

'You have not really answered my question.'

'I was betrothed. Once.'

'What happened?'

'We decided we would not suit.'

Not for anything would she admit the reality: being left heartbroken at the altar whilst her parents' main concern had been about the money Papa had given to Jasper to invest on his behalf.

'And no one since?'

'Would you ask such questions of a lady from your own world?'

There was a brief silence. 'No,' he said, finally. 'No, I would not. But that does not imply a lack of respect. It is perhaps a result of the unusual circumstances in which we find ourselves.'

'I see. In that case...no, there has been no one since. I am not interested in marrying.'

'We are two of a kind,' he said with a laugh.

She glanced at him, tall and elegant in the saddle, every inch the gentleman despite the less than fashionable cut of his clothes.

'Hardly,' she said, with an answering grin. 'You are the son of a duke. I am the daughter of a glass manufacturer. We are far removed from one another in almost every way you may imagine.'

Lulled by warm weather, by the roll and sway of Star's back and by the rhythmic thud of the horses' hooves on the road, Thea found it easy to relax and chat, without paying much attention to what she was saying and before very long they were riding into Temple Row where the Royal Hotel stood opposite St Philip's Church and churchyard.

Thea's stomach churned as she perused the simple but elegant hotel, four storeys high, with a central portico. Did this building hide the secret of what had happened to her brother? That maid had said Daniel discovered a hotel where Henry Mannington stayed and Thea was certain this was it. And she had no doubt in her mind that Henry Mannington was responsible for Daniel's disappearance.

She and Vernon had already agreed to reserve rooms for that night, to give them time to question the staff about Daniel and about Henry Mannington. They halted next to a side gateway that led to the stable yard behind the hotel, and Thea jumped to the ground as an ostler hurried out to take charge of the horses. Vernon dismounted in a more leisurely fashion, perusing their surroundings: the church in its spacious churchyard in the middle of a large square surrounded by smart town houses and a school on one corner. Taking stock, Thea thought.

'Have our bags taken inside,' Vernon said to the ostler as he led the horses away.

'Yessir.'

'Should we not question him about Bullet?' Thea hissed.

'There is no need. Not yet.'

'Why not?'

'We already know Daniel has been here, so we need no confirmation that Bullet was in the stables. I shall talk to the grooms later, when they are not as busy.'

And with that, Vernon turned on his heel and began to walk away from the hotel, beckoning Thea to follow. She ran to catch up and grabbed his arm.

'Where are you going? We need to speak to the people in the hotel.'

Is he afraid of what we might discover about Henry Mannington? Is he genuinely interested in finding Daniel?

'Now we are here, I wonder if it is too big a risk for us to go inside together,' Vernon said. 'This...' he swept his arm around, including the hotel and the square in his gesture '...is a wealthy area and the hotel guests may very well include someone who will recognise me.'

'But I do not see why that should matter. You have as much right to go inside the hotel as they do.'

'Yes, but do you not see? If they know me, they will know Leo and they will know my *real* nephews, Dominic and Alexander. You, my dear Dotty, look nothing like either one of 'em.'

'I had not thought of that.' She bit her lip, thinking. 'Could you not say I am a friend?'

Vernon halted in the middle of the pavement, staring down at her with an unfathomable expression.

'No, that will not wash either. You look no more than fourteen years old. No one will believe we are friends.'

He means his reputation would suffer, being seen in company with someone like me.

She tamped down the resentment that swelled on the heels of that thought.

Not me...he means someone like Theo... I must not forget this is not me.

Vernon's gaze again swept the surrounding buildings. 'We must find you somewhere safe to wait whilst I make enquiries inside the hotel.'

'But...we agreed to stay here overnight.'

A rueful smile twisted his lips. 'I did not think it through. It will not work. We must stay elsewhere.'

I do not want to go elsewhere.

She *must* take an active part in the search for Daniel. She could not bear to be left to wait silent in a corner somewhere whilst Vernon went inside to speak to people who must have seen her brother on his visits to the hotel. Besides, how could she be sure Vernon would tell her everything he learned? What if he was told something detrimental about his cousin and he decided to hide it from her?

The only way to change Vernon's mind would be to come up with an explanation for her presence. As Vernon gazed around the square as though for inspiration, tapping his crop against his boot, ideas whirled around Thea's head.

'I have an idea,' she said, as her tumbling thoughts blended together to form a plan, 'but you might disapprove.'

Chapter Nine

Thea's cheeks grew hot under Vernon's scrutiny as his brows shot up in response to her statement.

'That will make a most welcome change, my dearest Dotty,' he murmured. 'It is, after all, so uncharacteristic of you to come up with an idea of which I might disapprove.'

Thea gritted her teeth against a caustic rejoinder, knowing any reaction would only encourage him to tease her further with that accursed nickname.

She caught the twitch of his lips.

And now he is laughing at me!

Silence stretched over several minutes as their gazes clashed. Thea pressed her lips tight, determined not to elaborate until he was ready to listen to her in a serious manner.

'Pray continue,' Vernon said, finally, with a sigh.

'Our story *could* be that you…or rather, that *I*…well… that Theo is your…' Thea lowered her voice to a whisper although there was nobody near enough to hear what she said '…your bastard.' Mortifyingly, her cheeks now scorched and she knew they must be an unbecoming shade of red. She fixed her gaze on a point beyond his right ear. She inhaled and allowed the remainder of her words to tumble out, finding it easier to refer to herself as Theo.

'I… *Theo*…knows you are his father, but he does not

know your true identity, but you support him and when you come to visit him and to take him out, you dress less fashionably so you do not draw attention and so that Theo does not guess you are really a duke's brother.'

'That…' Vernon said.

Thea looked up hopefully, her eyes searching his.

'…is an excellent idea.'

She beamed, relief flooding through her as she recalled her earlier suspicions. Surely, if he *were* untrustworthy, he would have raised objections to her plan.

'And,' Vernon added, 'it will provide an explanation for you if…when…we catch up with Henry Mannington. For he, too, will know you are not my nephew. However, for the sake of respectability when I reserve our rooms, you shall remain my nephew and I shall remain Mr Boyton. I do not imagine the Royal Hotel will actually approve of my…er…by-blow mingling with their other guests. We shall keep that story as a last resort.'

'By-blow?' Thea enquired innocently as they headed back to the hotel.

'It is slang for…oh!' Vernon broke off when he caught sight of Thea's expression. 'You little tease,' he said and reached out.

She braced herself for the twist as he took her lobe between finger and thumb but, instead, he tugged gently, and she felt an answering tug deep inside her core. Their gazes fused and her heart lurched as she saw the amusement fade from his eyes to be replaced by an inner fire as heat flared between them. Then fear reared up to overpower her sudden impulse to step closer and to accept his unspoken invitation.

I must never forget Jasper Connor. Men can't be trusted. And Vernon… Dear God! He's the son of a duke. I could never mean anything to a man like him.

She jerked her ear from his grasp. 'Ow!' She glared at him as she rubbed at her ear, taking refuge in anger.

'Do not pretend that hurt, you minx,' Vernon muttered. 'What are you—?'

'*I* am attempting to keep up the appearance of being your nephew,' Thea snapped. 'We do not know who might be watching.'

'Hmph.'

But a sideways glance showed he had taken her point and Thea breathed a little easier that she had averted that awkward moment.

They had by now arrived back at the hotel and they walked through the door into a large reception hall. A servant took their hats. Vernon nudged Thea and leaned down to whisper in her ear, 'It is fortunate I tidied up that unkempt mop of yours, is it not? At least if I do see an acquaintance you will not now shame me by being seen in company with such a ragamuffin.'

His teasing reinforced her conviction she had been right to quash the desire that had flared between them. He had shrugged her rebuttal away as though it were nothing. And no doubt it *was* nothing to him. He was totally unmoved, whilst *she*...the bindings around her breasts all of a sudden made it hard to breathe. Vernon's mention of that haircut revived the memory of how strangely intimate it had been and Thea suppressed a shiver as she recalled the effort it had taken to sit still whilst he moved around her, his body brushing against hers, his fingers threading through her curls, moving across her scalp. Never had she imagined a simple haircut could be so...so...*unsettling*.

'Fortunate indeed,' she hissed. 'For however would your reputation otherwise survive?'

A man dressed in a tailcoat and satin knee breeches approached, and bowed. 'Good afternoon, sirs. My name is Parkes, the concierge. Whatever your requirements, I shall use my best endeavours to fulfil them.'

'Good afternoon, Parkes,' Vernon said and Thea marvelled at the change that came over him. *No one* could mistake him for other than a highly born gentleman and yet just a few minutes ago he had been joking like a schoolboy. 'My name is Boyton. I should like two bedchambers, if you please, for my nephew and myself. I trust our bags have been sent in from the stables?'

'Indeed they have, sir.' Parkes clicked his fingers and a footman came running, scooping their saddlebags from behind a desk. 'I shall show you to your rooms myself, Mr Boyton.'

'Thank you, but maybe later? Young Theo and I are in dire need of refreshment after our journey. Have you a coffee room?'

'But of course.' Parkes bowed. 'This way, sirs.' He showed them through a nearby door into an empty room. 'I shall send the maidservant in with coffee.'

'Thank you. Before you go, Parkes…' Vernon selected a table by a window that overlooked the street and sat down, 'I had rather hoped to meet an acquaintance of mine here. Mr Henry Mannington. I believe he often frequents your establishment?'

'Mr Mannington? Yes, he is known to me, sir, but I have received no word of an impending visit.'

'That is a pity, for I have some business I most particularly wish to discuss with him. Do you recall his last visit?'

'It was last week some time, sir. Thursday? Friday? I shall have to consult the hotel register to be certain of the day.'

'If you would be so kind,' Vernon murmured.

As soon as the door closed behind Parkes, Thea said, 'Why do you ask only of your cousin? What of Daniel?'

Green eyes contemplated Thea, bringing heat to her cheeks. She squirmed slightly, then said, 'Well, you cannot blame me for…for…'

'For being suspicious?'

That is exactly what she meant, but put as baldly as that, it sounded…rude. Shame mixed with defiance. She had a right to challenge him, did she not? Otherwise, he would never explain anything of his actions to her and she would be left to trail in his wake in ignorance.

Vernon placed both hands flat on the table and sighed.

'I ask first about Henry because it is his patronage of this hotel that prompted your brother's visits. As I said outside…we already know that Daniel has been here and we know he was searching for Henry. We know that he has disappeared. Henry is our only link to what might have happened. Ergo…our main objective must be to track down Henry and to find out what he knows.' He glanced at the door, then reached across the table and touched cool fingers to Thea's cheek. 'There is no underhand motive, Thea. I promise.'

At a noise from the direction of the door, his hand slipped from her cheek. A maid carrying a tray set with a coffee pot and two cups entered the room, with Parkes on her heels.

Parkes came straight to the point. 'Mr Mannington was our overnight guest on Thursday of last week, Mr Boyton.'

Thursday! Thea forgot any embarrassment at revealing her suspicions of Vernon. *Daniel must have seen Mannington. Talked to him, possibly.*

She strove to mask her excitement in front of Parkes and the maid, who was preparing to pour their coffee.

'Thursday?' Vernon said. 'Now there is a coincidence. I believe a friend of mine was also a guest on that night. Mr Markham? Daniel Markham?'

Parkes paused, frowning in thought. 'No,' he said eventually. 'I am afraid I do not recall that name, sir.'

Thea's spirits plunged. *If Daniel did not come here, where on earth did he go?*

'I must be mistaken,' Vernon said in an unconcerned

tone. 'I thought he had visited here frequently in recent weeks. Now, if you will pass on Mannington's direction to me, Parkes, I shall call on him myself. He will not wish to miss this opportunity, that I can tell you.'

Thea's attention was caught by the rattle of china. She looked and the maid's knuckles were white on the handle of the coffee pot as she poured Thea's coffee. Thea leaned back in her chair and caught Vernon's eye, flicking her gaze to the maid. He nodded imperceptibly. So he had noticed her reaction, too. Thea's stomach tightened in anticipation.

'I regret I cannot oblige with Mr Mannington's direction, sir,' Parkes was saying. 'I only know that he lives on the far side of Worcester, towards Great Malvern. He has business interests in Manchester and the Royal Hotel is the perfect place for him to stay when he must travel north.'

'It is an ideal location,' Vernon said. 'Now, I must allow you to return to your duties, Parkes, but before you go, does the name Willingdale mean anything to you?'

The maid, on the verge of leaving the room, gasped audibly and Parkes beckoned her back inside.

'Well?' Parkes said. 'What do you have to say?'

The girl met Vernon's gaze with a boldness that made Thea itch to slap her.

'My name is Willingdale, sir. Alice Willingdale.'

I might have known. Thea did not trust herself to look at the girl, who she was now convinced was no better than she ought to be. Daniel had always been something of a flirt, so she should not be surprised he would target serving wenches to find out information.

Vernon stood up and crossed the room to the door, which he opened. 'Thank you for your assistance, Mr Parkes. I should be most grateful if you will ensure we are not disturbed. And…ah…' he reached into his pocket and withdrew a coin '…please take this in recompense for Alice here taking a short break from her duties.'

As soon as Parkes left the room, Vernon ushered Alice back to the table and bade her sit, which she did, a calculating light in her eye.

'Tell us about Daniel, Alice. When and where did you meet?'

'I don't know no Daniel.'

Thea leaned forward. 'You are lying. I saw your reaction when Ver…my uncle…asked Parkes about him.'

Scornful blue eyes turned on Thea. 'Well, that just shows what a know-nothing *you* are 'cause I don't know no Daniel and that's that.'

'Theo.'

The warning in that one word silenced Thea. She had been about to launch into a scathing put down, but Vernon's intervention reminded her she was meant to be a fourteen-year-old lad, not a mature woman confronted by a saucy servant. She clenched her jaw tight at the smug smile on Alice's face. Then Vernon jerked his head, indicating she should leave him to talk to Alice alone. She narrowed her eyes at him, folding her arms across her chest as she leaned back in her chair. A single twitch of his brow revealed Vernon's opinion.

He moved his chair closer to Alice, leaning towards her, capturing her gaze with his.

'But you *do* know Henry Mannington.' He smiled into her face. 'I was watching you. You reacted when I asked Parkes for his direction. Will you not tell me what you know of him?'

Alice blushed, lowering her lashes and peeping coquettishly at Vernon as she returned his smile.

'I don't know much about him, sir. Only the same as Mr Parkes told you. But I do…' She glanced towards Thea, then hunched a shoulder as she shifted around in her chair, turning her back to Thea and fully facing Vernon. She lowered her voice and Thea had to strain to hear her words. 'I do remember another man asking the same questions about Mr Mannington. *He* visited me several days in a row, looking for the gentleman, but he *weren't...*' she shot a look of disdain over her shoulder '...called Daniel. That I can say for certain.'

'I knew you were a smart girl, the minute I set eyes on you,' Vernon murmured.

He reached into his pocket and withdrew yet another coin.

What is it with him and money? He's forever throwing it at folk like it's worth nothing.

'What was his name? Can you remember?'

''Course I can remember.' The coin disappeared into Alice's apron pocket. 'It were Charles Leyton.'

Thea gasped, then clapped her hand across her mouth, worried she might put the girl off. Charles Leyton was the name of their manager at the glass works. She tried to signal to Vernon, miming he should ask Alice what this Leyton looked like.

'Very well done,' Vernon said. 'Can you describe him to me?'

'Why do you want to know?' she demanded, suddenly suspicious.

Vernon leaned closer to her and placed one hand on her arm as he said, 'It really is better you do not know. I should hate to put you in danger. Describe him to me and then forget we ever had this conversation.' He dropped his voice to a whisper. 'That is the only way to stay safe.'

'Oh! Well...he was tall...as tall as you, sir.' Her voice trembled slightly. 'And he was handsome as handsome can be, with lovely dark hair and big brown eyes and a *lovely* smile.' She sighed. 'And he were a proper gentleman, sir, that he was.'

'Did he visit you on horseback, or did he drive?'

'Horseback, sir. He rode a huge grey horse, sir. Oh, he were as dashing as any cavalryman.'

Thea's breath caught as her heart thumped against her ribs. She itched to fire questions at the girl, but knew she was wise to leave her to Vernon. She felt her brows twitch together as she mentally compared Vernon's way with women with her brother's and she barely contained her *hmph* of disgust.

Manipulative reprobates, the pair of them.

Chapter Ten

Vernon risked a quick glance at Thea's face. She was scowling, looking like she was ready to explode. He sensed the effort it cost her to sit still and stay quiet.

'Now, I need you think carefully, Alice. You told me this man, this Charles Leyton, asked questions about Henry Mannington. Did they ever meet, do you know?'

'Not here, sir.'

'Then where?'

She shrank back and he softened his tone. 'I did not mean to alarm you, Alice. Do you know where they met?'

'No. All I know is Charles… Mr Leyton, that is…was really angry. He got here last Thursday only to find Mr Mannington had been and gone. Mr M. were in a carriage and left heading for his home, so Charles…he just leapt on his horse and followed. He was about two hours behind.' She leaned closer to Vernon. 'I never seen him so angry, sir, and I never seen him since, neither, so it's no good you asking me where they met, because I don't know.'

Vernon sat back. 'Thank you, Alice. You have been a great help and I…we…are most grateful. You may return to your duties now. And please ask Mr Parkes to attend me here…we shall not, after all, be staying the night, but we shall need some luncheon before we leave.'

He barely noticed the tinge of disappointment in Alice's eyes. He only had eyes for the huge smile that lit Thea's face at the news they would soon be back on the road, following Daniel's trail. As soon as the door closed behind Alice, Thea bounded from her chair and began to pace the room.

'Do you think we should hire a post-chaise?'

She halted mid-stride and directed a serious look at Vernon, who had steeled himself to remain seated when she stood.

'We could use fresh horses along the way. It would get us there quicker.'

'Get us where?' Vernon followed her with his eyes as she began once more to pace, her agitation clear.

She stopped again. 'Why, to Worcester, of course.' She tipped her head to one side, staring at him, wide-eyed and eager. 'How many miles is it to Worcester? Do you know?'

Behind her, the door had opened to admit Parkes. 'It is twenty-eight miles, Master Boyton,' he said.

Thea whirled to face him. 'Twenty-eight? Why, that is not so far, if we—'

'Let us discuss this later, Theo,' Vernon interrupted. 'I am sure Parkes is busy. Our plans can hold no interest for him, other than the fact that we shall not, after all, require overnight accommodation.

'I shall, of course,' he added, smoothly, responding to the slightest firming of Parkes's lips, 'recompense you for the inconvenience.'

Parkes bowed. 'Very good, sir, I shall ensure your bags are brought back downstairs immediately. Alice said you would like to eat luncheon? I have come to inform you that food is being served in the dining room, if you care to follow me?'

It was gone two by the time they set out once again upon their journey, taking the Worcester road out of Birmingham. Thea sent Star ahead of Vernon on Warrior, her back stiff with her displeasure. Vernon sighed and nudged Warrior into a trot until they came alongside Thea.

'*Why* could we not hire a post-chaise?' She cast him a sidelong, accusatory look. 'You are happy enough to throw your money at every person you have dealings with, yet you baulk at spending on something so beneficial. Why?'

'You believe *that* is why I refused to hire a post-chaise? Because it would cost too much?'

Astounded, Vernon stared at her profile. Why was she so distrustful? Always ready to assume the worst of his motives? He'd had no opportunity to explain his reasoning to her...the busy dining room at the hotel had been too public for such a discussion.

'It is either that, or that you are reluctant, now it comes to it, to discover your cousin's part in some manner of villainy.'

Vernon reached across and halted Star. 'What is your plan, then, Dotty? What action do *you* say we should take?'

'If we hire a post-chaise we could reach Worcester before nightfall and then we can...'

She hesitated, her lips pursed and her brows bunched under the peak of her cap. Vernon saw the moment she began to doubt her plan.

'Hmph.'

She looked so disgruntled and so adorable he longed to reach out and gather her up and give her a big hug. He forbore to tease her, seeing how annoyed she was with herself.

'Why did I not think of that to start with?' The corners of her mouth drooped.

'Because you are always in such a hurry. You do not think through all the implications of what you want to do. I'll hazard a guess that you are not a good chess player.'

'*Chess*? I cannot abide the game. I always seem to...'

'Lose?'

She pouted, then laughed. 'Daniel always says I haven't the patience to play it well. I dare say I am a little...hasty... at times.'

She met his eyes with a silent apology. Then her frown flickered again.

'It is the same as when you rode from Stourbridge to Harborne,' she said, accusing again. 'You wish to stop and enquire at every inn we pass.'

'We *must* call at every inn if we are to establish what has happened,' Vernon said. 'Do you not see? All we know is that Henry Mannington lives somewhere to the south-west of Worcester, that he left here in his carriage on Thursday morning and that Daniel followed him, on horseback, two hours later. Yes, it will be slower, not only because of the need to stop at every inn, but also because we cannot ride too hard in this weather for the horses' sake, not to mention our own. But we are like to miss something if we bowl past in a fast-moving post-chaise. This way, we shall truly be following in Daniel's footsteps.'

'Or in Bullet's hoof-steps,' Thea said, with a flicker of a smile, 'if there is such a word.'

Vernon laughed, reached out and touched the tip of her nose. 'Are we friends again?'

'Friends,' she said, with a rueful smile.

The sun beat down on them from the afternoon sky as they continued on their way towards Worcester. Time passed quickly and with much laughter as Vernon taught Thea some of the slang words common in the rougher areas of London.

Thea had begun this journey determined to show no interest in the exclusive world to which Vernon belonged, but she couldn't curb her curiosity. She was fascinated by the contrast between the world in which he lived—rich, opulent, indulgent—and his descriptions of some of the poorer areas and the rookeries, where the poorest of the poor—and, from what she could gather, the criminals—scraped an existence.

In return, Thea told him tales of her world and the realities of life not only for manufacturers like her family, but also for the men who worked for them. She also told him of the hardships caused by trade embargoes, not only for manufactories like Stour Crystal, but also for the many ordinary hard-working men and women who lived in the area between Stourbridge and Birmingham and who made nails and chains at workshops in their own back yards. Something like a quarter of their output used to be sent to America, and the growing hostility between the two countries had forced many people to turn to poor relief to survive.

Vernon's fascination with her stories made Thea careless and she only just stopped herself confiding in him about her family's misfortune at the hands of Jasper Connor—she could not bear to be the object of his pity.

They rode on, stopping, as before, at every inn but no one knew—or would admit to knowing—Henry Mannington. No one had noticed a man of Daniel's description riding a light grey horse last Thursday. As the heat built, they discarded their jackets, taking full advantage of the filtered shade cast by roadside trees where possible but, when they had no choice but to ride in the open, Thea tilted her cap down until her eyes were almost covered.

At Vernon's questioning glance, she said, 'The sun brings out my freckles. I try to wear a bonnet with a large peak in the summer. This cap does little to protect my skin.'

'I had not thought you a woman to be concerned about such minor matters as freckles,' Vernon said. 'Besides…' he reached to her chin and turned her face to his '…your freckles are quite fetching.'

Her skin tingled at his touch, and she looked away. 'Freckles,' she replied, 'are most unfashionable.'

'Fashion? Bah! Fashion is merely a whim, based on a few persons' opinions.'

Thea laughed at him. '*You* say that? You with your coat from Weston and your boots from Hoby? What a plumper.' She frowned. 'Plumper? Is that the right word?'

It was one of the slang words Vernon had taught her. She was almost sure a plumper meant a lie.

'It is,' he said, with a grin. Then he sobered. 'But my usual attire, I shall have you know, is not a matter of fashion, but of dressing respectfully.'

'Respectfully? Respectful to whom?'

'To myself. To my peers. Fashion can be extreme—you should see some of the fops and the affectations of their dress. You would laugh, I promise you, to see them with their garish waistcoats adorned with fobs and seals, and their shirt points so high they cannot turn their heads. And many men—even moderately sensible men—wear padding at the shoulders and at the calves to exaggerate their shape and their muscle.'

Thea slid a sly sideways glance at Vernon's broad shoulders and then dropped her gaze to his calf, encased in his tight-fitting boot.

'Is *that* what it is?' she said. 'Padding?'

Vernon flicked her knee, laughing. 'Brat! I have no need for artificial help! No. Brummell has the right idea—simple and elegant. Unremarkable, even. A man should never aspire to be noticed for his clothing.'

'Do ladies indulge in such excesses as the fops?'

'Amongst the ladies of the *ton*, fashions are not so extreme, but they are fickle and they change every Season, necessitating the purchase of an entire new wardrobe if a lady does not wish to appear a pitiful creature in the eyes of her acquaintance.' He sounded almost mocking.

'Why do you continue to attend such events if you hold them in disdain?'

He shrugged. 'It is not disdain, precisely, it is what one does. To tell you the truth, I haven't thought about it much until now. You—' he flashed a smile in her direction '—have forced me to see my life through your eyes.'

'And your conclusion?'

He shrugged again. 'I have led a privileged life, there is no doubt of it. I will return to it willingly—I may jest about certain aspects of it but, overall, it is a good life and I am aware of my good fortune. But this journey...' He looked around, as though for inspiration. 'This journey and your stories have heightened my awareness of the injustices in society.'

'Do many in your position take on charitable work?'

'Many people take pride in donating to charity. They hold fund-raising events and so forth, but when you have wealth that is no hardship—you attend a ball and pay some money, you enjoy yourself and barely notice the loss of the money. That is not the same as actually *doing* something.'

He fell silent, staring at the road ahead.

'I have a role model within my own family,' he said eventually. 'Leo's eldest son, Dominic, Lord Avon—he is the patron of an orphan asylum and school. He is only two-and-twenty, and I confess he puts me to shame. My own nephew.' He shook himself out of his pensive mood, turned his head and winked at Thea. 'My *real* nephew, of course.'

They continued, riding at an alternating walk and trot, unfailingly enquiring after Daniel and Henry Mannington at each and every inn they passed, to no avail. Dusk began to fall and, as they crested a rise in the road, the welcome sight of a wayside inn appeared.

'We shall stop there for the night,' Vernon said.

He pretended not to hear Thea's soft sigh of relief. He was stiff and exhausted, so God knew how poor Thea must feel. He swung from Warrior's back, wincing at his aching muscles and, after a quick look round to make sure they were unobserved, he helped Thea from the saddle, his hands lingering on her slender waist, as he savoured the slide of her body down his and the tantalising brush of her peachy bottom against his groin. He stepped back, not wanting her to feel his arousal, but he found it a wrench to tear his hands from her waist.

The more time he spent with her, the more he…*liked* her. Not just wanted her, as a woman, but actually liked her and enjoyed her company. And he delighted in just watching her: she fascinated him.

He shook all such thoughts from his head as they led the horses into the stable yard, delivering them into the hands of the ostler, who pointed them to a side door, through which they gained access to the dim interior of the inn. The innkeeper—thin-faced and spindle-legged but with a pot belly—came to greet them, wiping his hands on a grimy towel.

'Welcome, sir, and to you too, young sir.' He bowed. 'Tom Jackson at your service. It is good to see you on this fine evening. What is your pleasure?'

'Good evening, Jackson. My name is Boyton, this is my nephew Theo. We should like two rooms for the night, if you please.'

'Ah.' Jackson's smile faded. 'Apologies, Mr Boyton, but we only have the three bedchambers here, and two are already taken…unless you do not object to sharing the room?'

Vernon's heart sank as the innkeeper regarded him hopefully. He dared not even glance at Thea. He could not think how they might contrive—any solution he came up with threatened to reveal their masquerade. A man such as Vernon Boyton would hardly allow his young nephew to sleep indoors in comfort whilst he bedded down in the stable and the opposite arrangement was unthinkable. He would not expose Thea to such a risk.

'In which direction are you travelling, sir?'

'Towards Worcester,' Vernon replied. 'How far is the next inn along this road?'

'A good five miles.'

A hand tugged at Vernon's sleeve. 'We can share the bed-chamber, Uncle,' Thea said in her husky voice. 'I promise I shall not complain when you snore.'

Chapter Eleven

Vernon glared down at Thea's innocent expression, gritting his teeth at the twinkle in her hazel eyes.

Little minx, baiting a man when there's no chance to reply.

His thoughts charged ahead with the possibilities of her suggestion, colouring in the details in lurid detail: him… and her…together all night long…in a room, with a bed.

Then, quietly, she added, 'I am weary, sir', and he could hear the truth of it in her voice, see it in the slump of her shoulders.

He recalled his own thoughts upon arrival—how tired he was and how much more Thea must be suffering for their long day, yet not a word of complaint had passed her lips. And here he was, a supposed gentleman, imagining her seduction. This would not do. Thea was under his protection, he could not take advantage of her. The innkeeper awaited his decision and Vernon was conscious of Thea watching him, now anxious.

'A single bedchamber will be acceptable, Jackson. Thank you.'

'And dinner, sir?'

Vernon glanced again at Thea. The less they saw of the other guests the better.

'Have you a private parlour we might use? We are both exhausted and we'd appreciate some peace and quiet.'

'Of course, sir. I shall show you to your bedchamber and send the girl up with hot water. Follow me.'

The room was not large, but there was a deep armchair by the fire as well as a large soft bed. Vernon dropped their bags at the foot of the bed.

'I shall be comfortable enough in the chair,' he said, without looking at Thea. He had never in his life felt quite as awkward with a female in a bedchamber. Not even his first time. Every movement felt contrived. 'You may take the bed.' Even his voice sounded strained.

'I thank you. I have to confess, it is all I can do not to flop down upon it now and go straight to sleep.' She crossed the room to him, peering up into his face. 'I can tell this arrangement makes you uncomfortable,' she said. 'But I trust you. If I did not, I should never have suggested it.'

Vernon had to smile at the earnestness in her voice and on her face but he wondered at her poise in this situation. Most of the females he knew would be either throwing themselves at him by now, or shrinking away with maidenly giggles. As far as Thea's reaction went, he might as well be Daniel.

Is that it? Does she view me as a brother?

There were times—a certain look, a particular reaction from her—when he had thought otherwise, but now…? He could not quite fathom her and he was unused to feeling so unsure of himself around a woman. However, he could do no more now than follow her lead, even though he still could not stop one dark corner of his mind from speculating quite how she hid her breasts so effectively. He would follow her lead and remain in the part of teasing uncle. He tweaked one of her curls.

'I beg you will not say as much to anyone else,' he said. 'I have a reputation to uphold.'

Her brows rose. 'A reputation for what, may I enquire? Is that your way of informing me you are considered something of a ladies' man in society?'

She grinned at him, then spun away to gaze out the window as a knock at the door heralded the arrival of their washing water. Vernon waited until the maid had placed the jug on the washstand and left them alone again. He badly needed some space to compose himself.

'I shall leave you in privacy for ten minutes whilst I check the horses. Then you can go downstairs and wait for me to join you in the parlour.'

He did not wait for her reply, but left the room and ran down the stairs. He quickly checked the horses—both comfortable in their stalls and munching hay—and then he returned to the inn, going into the bar. He had time for a quick beer before going back upstairs. A solitary customer sat in the bar and, upon finding out that Vernon was a fellow guest and traveller, he introduced himself as Wigbert Pooley, a salesman. Vernon did not linger, but soon excused himself and went upstairs to knock on the bedchamber door. It opened, and Thea—dressed as Theo, her red curls framing her face like a devilish halo—appeared.

'I shall leave you to freshen yourself,' she said and walked past him towards the stairs.

Vernon stripped off his shirt and unstrapped the bandage Thea had wrapped around his chest the previous evening. He twisted this way and that, examining it in the looking glass. It looked as though it was healing well, with no sign of swelling or redness, and there was no pain. He had got away lightly.

Ten minutes later, he opened the door into the private parlour and cursed beneath his breath. The room was empty. He pivoted on his heel and strode to the bar, stopping short on the threshold at the sight of Thea—colour high and her small fists clenched by her sides—confronting Wigbert Pooley, who was bent double clutching at his privates.

Rage pumped Vernon's blood as relief replaced fear on Thea's face at the sight of him. He didn't have to be a mind reader to guess Pooley—a beefy, middle-aged man with pendulous jowls—must have propositioned her in some way to provoke such a reaction. In two strides he crossed the room and hauled the man up by his lapels.

'What the hell are you doing with my nephew, Pooley?' he snarled, thrusting his face close to the other man's.

'Nay, sir.' The man's bulbous blue eyes were watering. ''Twas naught but…' he gasped for breath '…a bit of friendly banter. Ain't that so, m'boy?'

Vernon relaxed a little upon hearing him call Thea a boy. For a moment there, he had feared she had been recognised as a female.

'I bought him a beer 'n' all,' the man went on disjointedly. He groaned, feeling tenderly in the area of his wedding tackle. Vernon moved to shield Thea from the sight. 'Paid for out me own pocket. Man gets lonely on the road. Bit of friendly fun never harmed nobody.'

'Uncle.' Thea's hand was on his sleeve, her voice urgent. 'Leave him. There's no harm done. Our food will be served by now.'

Pooley attempted a chuckle. 'Typical lad, eh. Always thinking of his belly.' He straightened with a groan and then waved a hand at Vernon. 'Go on. No harm done, like the lad says.'

With a growl of disgust, Vernon shoved the man aside and ushered Thea from the bar and into their private parlour. He shut the door behind them.

'I thought I told you to wait in *here* for me? What the devil persuaded you to go into a public bar?'

'I am capable of making my own decisions,' she said,

elevating her nose. 'Jackson told me that man travels all around the Worcester area, taking orders and then returning with the goods. He calls at shops and houses alike. I thought he might know Henry Mannington.'

'You should have waited for me,' Vernon growled. 'Another time you might not be so fortunate.'

Thea grimaced. 'Do you *know*…he did not even realise I was female? And, even though he thought me a boy, still he said such things—'

Her mouth snapped shut as the door opened and two maids came in carrying salvers with roast meats and fish, pies and vegetables. Only after they had retreated, and the door had closed behind them, did Thea continue.

'*Disgusting* things.' Her cheeks were pink, but whether with embarrassment or indignation Vernon was unsure. Probably a combination of the two.

'So you kicked him?'

She nodded and his balls tightened in involuntary reflex. He could not be certain, but he thought he caught a smile flicker across her face and he shivered. Another involuntary reaction.

'Where did you learn such a move?'

'Daniel,' she said, shortly. 'He told me if ever I felt threatened, that was the quickest way to discourage a man.'

'Quick and extremely effective. Remind me to show you some further defensive moves as well. You never know when they might come in handy. Now, let us eat. I am ravenous.'

Vernon pulled out a chair for Thea, who hesitated and then sat, murmuring, 'Thank you.'

As soon as Vernon moved away to sit opposite her, Thea said, 'You must take care. If you show me such courtesies in private it will not be long before you forget yourself in public.'

Vernon sighed. 'You are right. I must pay more attention.'

They helped themselves to food and began to eat. Thea kept her attention firmly upon her plate, but Vernon could not prevent his gaze from straying in her direction, time after time. It was driving him wild, watching her slowly chew her food, the tip of her pink tongue darting out from time to time to lick a drop of gravy from her lips. What would he not give for a chance to kiss her...an opportunity to taste and explore her luscious mouth?

He tried to divert his thoughts to different subjects. He could do without feeding this craving—the night to come was already playing havoc with his senses. His brain kept insisting he was a gentleman, but his libido had other ideas. It was fortunate that Thea appeared to have put aside any awareness of him as a man or who knew what might happen? She chatted to him as easily and unaffectedly as though he were a brother. Or, even more lowering, a favourite uncle.

He came to a sense of his surroundings with a start. His mind had wandered and he had been eating mindlessly, ignoring his dining companion. She did not appear offended by his lack of manners, however—she had almost finished eating, her attention on her plate, her brow creased in a frown. Vernon reminded himself of their earlier conversation.

'Did you have an opportunity to question Pooley about Mannington?' he asked Thea.

'I did.' Her upper lip curled. 'He claimed to know the Worcester area well, but he has never heard of Henry Mannington. It was an utter waste of time. I should never have bothered with him.'

'Well, I hope you have learned your lesson.'

Thea glowered at Vernon. 'Learned my *lesson*? What lesson might that be?'

'The lesson, my dear Dotty, is that although you may

be *less* vulnerable as a youth than a woman, you are still not *in*vulnerable.'

'I dealt with him, did I not? I did not wait for you to rescue me. I am not some lily-livered society lady to swoon at the slightest provocation.'

And there it was again. A challenge, and a hint of scorn, as though every member of the aristocracy was capable of nothing more than a life of idle pleasure. He would not rise to it, suspecting she said such things to cover a deep-rooted feeling of inferiority, to convince him—and herself—that she and people like her had value. And yet he no longer needed convincing of that. The stories she had told him about her world and that of the people who lived around her…he could not help but contrast the toughness of their lives with the ease of his and for the first time in his life he felt an urge to get involved in politics and to try to make a difference in the world.

'Put your claws away, Thea, I am aware you have courage, but you still cannot face every challenge head on. And nor should you, when you have me by your side.' Her expression remained stormy. 'Come, you know it makes sense.' He covered her hand with his. It twitched, but she did not pull away. 'If I am constantly worried about what you are up to, I shall not be able to concentrate on finding Daniel. And that is our main concern, is it not?'

She bit her lower lip, her brows still bunched. 'Is that *your* main concern, Vernon? Or are you more interested in finding your cousin? What will you do after we have tracked him down?'

He sat back, removing his hand from hers. 'Is that what you believe? That I will abandon the search for Daniel if I find Henry?'

'No. Yes. I do not know. If I am honest…' she captured his gaze, searching '…I have wondered more than once about your motivations. You owe me nothing and you do not even know Daniel, so it is natural to question why you have put yourself out to help us.'

Vernon drummed his fingers on the table, thinking how to explain.

'In a strange way, I am enjoying it. And that is thanks to you.'

'Me?'

The intimacy of dining *à deux* made him speak more honestly than he might otherwise.

'Yes. You. You have not complained…not once…about your discomfort. You have borne the rigours of this journey with a smile and you have helped to ensure the time has passed more quickly.' He captured her gaze. 'I have enjoyed your company, Thea.'

She stilled, her eyes searching his. Then she dropped her gaze and stood up.

'I am weary. I wish to retire.'

Vernon rose to his feet. 'I shall allow you to get settled before I join you.'

An unfortunate choice of words and wholly inappropriate given their circumstances—words that stirred his imagination and fired his pulse. A flush of pink coloured Thea's cheeks, suggesting she, too, found his phrasing embarrassing.

'Goodnight.'

She avoided eye contact and slipped from the room, leaving Vernon to kick himself for such unaccustomed gaucheness.

Thea climbed the stairs, one hand clutching at the banister, the other pressed to her chest in an attempt to steady the erratic thump of her heart. Last night had been difficult enough, knowing Vernon—a stranger…a deliciously *attractive* stranger—had been sleeping in the adjoining bedchamber with only a door between them. Tonight, though…

Vernon might no longer be such a stranger, but that fact made her insides quake even more violently. They would be in the same room. All night.

She paused on the top stair, considering the past two days. How swiftly the time had appeared to pass, yet she felt as though she had known Vernon for much, much longer. And, as desperately as she fought it, she could not deny that the more time she spent in his company, the more she liked him…as a friend and, increasingly, as a man. A charming, intelligent, fascinating and kind man who—every time she felt his astute green gaze upon her—aroused the most wonderful and exhilarating swirl of anticipation deep in the pit of her belly.

Anticipation that was unwelcome. It was hard enough to trust Vernon with finding Daniel, but she must fight her growing feelings for him. She must protect her heart.

I can never trust another man. Not after Jasper.

She entered their bedchamber and made haste to undress, breathing a sigh of relief as she unwound the binding from her breasts, massaging them with her hands to ease them. She crossed to the washstand and used a washcloth to bathe the area, sighing with pleasure as the cool water soothed her itchy, sweaty skin, reaching around with difficulty to cleanse her back, too. The heat had increased her discomfort, but she dared not abandon the binding— her breasts might be small but, if someone was to catch sight of her at the wrong angle, her charade would be exposed and…

She shuddered as she pictured the ensuing scandal. Since they had left the Royal Hotel, during the lulls in conversation, she had found the time to look back upon her decision to follow Vernon. Her initial certainty that she need fear no repercussions if her escapade was uncovered had soon faded. The truth, she knew, was more complicated than that. It was not so much that she risked censure and being shunned—she did not have much time for pleasure and rarely attended their neighbours' parties, despite being invited. But that episode with Pooley had confirmed her worries about what conclusions would be drawn about her morals and her character if her conduct ever became known. Those conclusions, she was certain, would lead many men to think her little better than a whore and they would not hesitate to proposition her at every opportunity. She had seen it before with women who acquired a reputation. They became *'fair game'*.

Which led her to wonder about Vernon's true opinion of her. Over the past day or so she had detected a certain gleam in his eyes, a gleam she had recognised as the interest of a man in a woman. Did he, too, now view her as fair game? Had her impulsive action in following him, and her subsequent insistence upon accompanying him, led him to believe she would willingly share his bed? She hoped not. She hoped he would remain the gentleman, but she had nevertheless redoubled her efforts to conceal her growing fascination with him. She aimed to play the part of his nephew so well he would forget she was female.

She completed her ablutions and scrubbed her skin dry before delving into her saddlebag for the shift she wore at night. She donned it and then brushed her hair until it shone, tamping down her regret as she looked at her reflection in the mirror, mourning the loss of her ringlets even though she had cursed them most of her life. She tried to ignore the wash of heat at the memory of Vernon's fingers running through her curls as he tidied up Thea's choppy effort, consoling herself that her short hair was all the better to continue the illusion she was a boy, but her heart still ached at the sight.

As she cleaned her teeth there was a light tap at the door.

'Wait a minute,' she called.

She rushed to the bed and jumped in, pulling the covers up to her chin. 'You may come in.'

Vernon sauntered in—tall, assured and with a wicked gleam in his eye that stole her breath.

'I don't know, nevvy,' he said, with a wink and a grin. 'For a young lad you are surprisingly bashful…worse than a bride on her wedding night.'

Thea relaxed at his teasing. She had feared he might use his charm and attempt to seduce her, but his manner reassured. He was telling her, without words, that she had nothing to fear. Perversely, that provoked a nagging doubt about her desirability and that doubt was followed swiftly by irritation at her own inconsistency. One minute she was fretting he might think her a female of low morals and try to take advantage, the next she was upset that he did not find her attractive enough to seduce.

'Now, I have no wish to make you blush,' Vernon continued as he removed his jacket, 'but I have no intention of sleeping fully clothed tonight so I suggest you look away.' He turned to face Thea, reaching for the knot in his neckcloth. 'Unless, of course, you wish to ogle my chest again?'

Thea's cheeks burned. 'You flatter yourself, my lord,' she growled.

Vernon chuckled, aggravating her more.

'Your chest holds absolutely no interest for me. You forget I have a brother and have lived my life seeing the men working in the fields.'

'My apologies.' Vernon sketched a bow. 'I had not realised you were quite so *au fait* with the male form. I need not worry about offending your sensibilities then.'

He tossed his neckcloth on to a chair and reached for the fastening of his breeches.

Thea tore her gaze from the auburn curls visible in the V-shaped opening at the neck of his shirt. With a loud *hmph*, she threw herself on to her side to face the wall and gritted her teeth against the devilish chuckle from the other side of the room. She screwed her eyes tight shut, but her imagination supplied plenty of delicious images to accompany the sounds she heard—the swish of cloth, footsteps and then the splash of water. Unable to help herself, she opened her eyes and peeped over her shoulder.

Vernon stood at the washstand, shirtless, his back to her as he bent over the bowl. The candlelight danced across unblemished skin and she watched, fascinated by the play of muscles across his shoulders and back as he continued his ablutions. Her hands itched to touch, to stroke, to discover if his skin was as smooth as it looked. His breeches stretched tight, outlining taut buttocks—thrust temptingly in her direction—and long, lean thighs and her mouth dried as her skin heated. A thrilling sense of anticipation swirled in her belly, then slowed, arrowing in to the juncture of her thighs, provoking a strange restlessness.

An insistent need.

Thea resisted the urge to move, to turn on to her back, to push aside the covers, to extend her arms and invite him to hold her. How would it feel to throw aside morals and caution and pride, and follow that craving? She lay motionless, still watching as Vernon hummed a tune she did not recognise under his breath, seemingly perfectly relaxed.

Desire.

She recognised it instinctively although she had never before experienced it. Not even with Jasper. *Particularly* not with Jasper. The thought of her former betrothed, her vicious betrayer, had the same effect as though Vernon had snatched up that basin of water and dashed it into her face. She faced the wall again, bending her neck so her face was buried in the covers and only the top of her head would be visible should he glance her way.

She counted inside her head, willing him to hurry, to

snuff the candles and to settle down in the chair, upon which Thea had spread one of the blankets from the bed. There were several minutes of silence.

What is he doing? Is he looking at me?

The thought made her feel all...*fluttery* inside. She would not look. If she looked...if their eyes should meet...

The bed dipped and her pulse raced even as her body froze. Her hair stirred and then his hand was upon her head.

'Are you asleep, Thea?'

Thea! Not Dotty! Her heart quailed. She *needed* him to be teasing and provocative. Not kind.

'No.' She kept her face buried in the bedclothes. His hand moved to her shoulder and gently squeezed.

'You have nothing to fear. I shall not take advantage. You are perfectly safe.'

The bed moved again and she heard him move around the room and then the creak of the chair as he sat. A grunt. A bump. Another grunt and another bump. 'Sorry for the noise,' he said. 'Just removing my boots.'

'I made no objection,' she replied, her voice muffled under the bedcovers.

God, she was so hot, stifling, with her head under the covers, breathing in warm, stale air, almost gasping for the cool relief of fresh air.

She heard him shifting around in the chair, probably trying to get comfortable, and felt sympathy. They had both complained of aching muscles from spending so long in the saddle. A night in an armchair would provide little relief for poor Vernon.

'Goodnight. Sweet dreams.' His voice, deep and comforting, wrapped around her.

Thea straightened her neck, taking her face from under the covers, grateful to breathe the relatively cooler air of the bedchamber. The candles had been snuffed out; the room was dark. And intimate. Thea suppressed a shiver.

'Goodnight. I hope you sleep well.'

How strange it felt to say that to someone whilst she lay in bed.

It was a very long time before she slept.

Chapter Twelve

The following morning, Thea remained huddled under the bedclothes, feigning sleep, until Vernon left the room. Breathing a sigh of relief, she turned on her back and thrust the covers down. Vernon had stirred early and she wondered if he, too, had found sleep elusive.

Doubtless he did, but *his* discomfort would be as a result of sleeping in the chair. Unlike Thea, whose mind simply would not allow her to rest.

The maid had brought fresh water not long after Vernon had begun to move about. Looking at the chair, there was no way to tell that anyone had slept there—the blanket was folded neatly at the foot of the bed and, turning, Thea saw he had even dented the pillow next to hers, to make it look as though they had shared the bed. She arose, and crossed the floor to peer through the window, glazed with leaded, diamond-shaped panes. Vernon was just emerging from the stables—their room overlooked the yard at the rear of the inn—and he happened to glance up as Thea watched. His stride faltered and he smiled—a glorious smile that made her breath catch—as he waved. She returned his greeting even as her heart quailed at the effort she must henceforth make to conceal her growing desire to be held in his arms.

She spun away from the window, quashing her nerves. She must concentrate on Daniel, nothing else. She hurried across to the washstand.

Worcester.
At last!
It had been a day of frustrations. Vernon did not know why, but his every attempt at conversation had met with a short reply that effectively ended the exchange. There was none of easy repartee and banter of previous days. He had never known Thea to be so quiet for so long, but she had barely said a word the whole day. Neither would she look at him.

He longed to offer her comfort, but he could not. He could not risk any intimacy building between them, although it would have been so very easy to relax his principles and take her in his arms. But he would not whilst they were flung together in this unnatural charade. And, when they returned to real life, he was certain that his growing obsession with this little spitting kitten, who could also play and have fun and make him smile, would disappear and they would each return to their very different lives and, hopefully, be able look back upon this trip as an adventure.

Whether they would look back with joy or with sorrow depended, of course, on what they might discover about Daniel's fate. And maybe that was what was bothering Thea. They were that much closer to discovering the truth and she must dread the possibility of the worst news.

Vernon stifled a yawn and then circled his neck and rolled his shoulders in an attempt to work the cricks out of them. Never in his life had he spent a more uncomfortable night than last night. It was not only the chair, although that had grown harder and lumpier as the night progressed, but the knowledge that, not ten feet from him, lay a woman who had, almost without him noticing, crept into his heart.

They rode side by side, following the road down and through the city, until they arrived at a stone bridge, spanning a wide river, which was still running high and fast after the recent rains. Downstream, to their left, the huge mass of Worcester Cathedral squatted close to the riverbank, dwarfing the buildings around it. Upstream of the bridge, buildings lined the far bank of the river but downstream, opposite the cathedral, was green pasture land.

'That is the River Severn,' Thea said.

A sideways glance revealed a groove between her brows and tightly pursed lips. She looked like a woman deep in thought—a woman deeply worried, a woman exhausted. Vernon caught hold of Star's rein and steered both horses to the side of the bustling road, bringing them to a standstill.

'We could reserve rooms at that inn we passed in the centre. The Crown.'

'The Crown? Are you sure?'

She nudged her mare closer to Warrior...so close that Thea's leg pressed against Vernon's, sending the blood rushing to his groin. He gritted his teeth and tried to banish the image branded on his brain: Thea, curled on her side in bed, the thin blanket moulded to her frame, draping her narrow waist and accentuating the curve of her hip and the roundness of her bottom.

She leaned towards him. 'You said we should stay at an inn outside the town, where we shall be less likely to run into somebody either of us knows,' she whispered. 'If Mannington does live to the south-west, as Parkes told us, then would we not be better to find an inn over there?' She pointed across the bridge. 'We are more likely to find someone who knows him in that direction.' She heaved a sigh. 'Heaven knows, we haven't learned anything of any use up till now, despite all our enquiries.'

Her face was set, lines of fatigue bracketing her mouth. Vernon hauled in a breath, castigating himself for not standing firm and sending her home at the start. That thought was followed swiftly by the realisation she would not have gone. He had tried. She had been determined to come with him. But he had never known her to be so despondent. He missed his lively, bouncy firebrand.

'Cheer up, Dotty,' he said.

If anything was calculated to pull her free from the doldrums, it was him calling her Dotty. She barely glanced up, her eyes dull as she pulled her cap from her head and swiped her forearm across her glistening brow, in a gesture worthy of any young lad. Her cropped copper curls glinted momentarily in the bright sunshine before she replaced her cap, transforming her once again into Theo. Vernon had thought it would become progressively easier to think of her as the youth she portrayed, but it became harder by the day.

'What reason is there for cheerfulness? This is a foolish quest,' Thea muttered, completely ignoring his use of the nickname she detested.

Where was the fire in her eyes? The passion in her heart? This forlorn Thea was so very different to the woman he had come to know and to admire, with her drive and her verve and her ability to find fun in the everyday.

'Nobody remembered Daniel,' she said. 'And here…' she gestured to the town at their backs '…would anyone notice a stranger? It is so busy, how could anyone remember one man passing through, out of so many?' Then she straightened in her saddle. 'I am sorry. I do not mean to be such a misery. I convinced myself that *someone* would remember Daniel on the road between Birmingham and Worcester, that is all.' She met Vernon's gaze and he could see her fear. 'We cannot know if he ever arrived here—he might have ridden no more than a mile out of Birmingham before… before…' Her voice choked and she turned her head aside.

Vernon cursed himself for not realising how her worst fears must be haunting her. He might be committed to this quest, but he had not the same emotional stake in the outcome. He studied the land on the far side of the bridge.

'I have decided. We shall stay on this side of the bridge after all…who knows how far we would have to go before finding decent accommodation on the road out of town. You, my dear nephew, need some rest. You look exhausted.'

And his heart ached to see her instinctive female response to such a comment as she straightened her back, pinched at her cheeks and tidied her few stray strands of hair under her cap.

'I am fine.' She sounded more like the determined Thea he was used to, but he knew she was putting on a brave front for him. 'Once we've had something to eat and drink, we must begin our enquiries. Even if we find no trace of Daniel, surely *someone* will have knowledge of Mannington and he might hold the key to the mystery.'

She reined Star around and headed back into the town. 'Come along,' she said over her shoulder. 'There is no time to waste.'

Vernon followed, partly relieved to see her regain her former resolve but also worried at how adept she was at concealing her inner pain. He vowed to try again to persuade her to return home and leave him to continue the search alone.

Back outside the Crown, Vernon studied the façade. 'Let us go inside and see what the accommodation is like before we commit to staying. We can have a drink and something to eat, and see if it is suitable. At least we shall be rested.'

Twenty minutes later they were seated in their favoured position in the taproom, at a table in the corner, with Vernon facing out into the room and Thea with her back to it. There were only three other occupants: a man sitting alone, reading a newspaper and two men, their heads together over a table, deep in conversation. A glance reassured Vernon that all three were strangers and he felt he could relax. For now.

Platters of rolls and butter, cheese and cold roast beef, with a dish of pickles and two tankards of ale had been delivered to the table. Thea reached for her tankard and sipped cautiously. She still had not acquired a taste for it. If it was in his power, Vernon would buy her fine wine or champagne, but such a choice would excite too much interest in the youth Theo. The image of Thea, arrayed in a fine gown and jewels and sipping champagne, arose in his increasingly active imagination—an imagination he was helpless to quash, and an imagination that supplied ever more disturbing images of Thea, picturing her as part of his world—in his world and in his life.

Impossible images.

He raised his own tankard and drank long and deep. What the hell was wrong with him? He'd never been a man to indulge in obsessive fantasies, particularly of women.

You've never had to fantasise, that is why, a small voice whispered. *Women have always fallen at your feet. You're only interested in Thea because she is impervious to your charm.*

She is different. She is my friend. She feels a part of me. She is fun, good company and courageous. And sexy, beautiful and desirable.

And what you are starting to think...to hope for...is impossible. She has no interest in you as a man. She treats you as an older brother. Have you no pride? Will you prostrate yourself at her feet?

Vernon bit viciously into his bread roll and chewed, ignoring that infuriating inner voice. It was time for action, not for this idle conjecture. He was thinking like a lovesick youth, not a man of the world in his mid-thirties. He slammed the lid on his daydreams and vowed to focus his full attention on tracing Daniel and on finding out how Henry was involved. And the first step…

'I have been thinking,' he said.

Thea looked up, her brows arched.

'I think it is time you went home and left the rest of this to me.'

'No!'

Heads turned at Thea's loud exclamation and she shot Vernon a look of apology, then leaned across the table.

'I am sorry.' Her husky voice sparked such shivers of desire across his skin he was forced to clench his jaw to hide his reaction. 'I didn't mean to shout, but you *cannot* send me away. We are partners. We are in this together. You cannot expect me to go home when we are finally close to the truth.'

'It could be dangerous. I am a fool. I should never have brought you this far.'

'Dangerous? How so? You told me your Cousin Henry is a gentle soul.'

'He is. Was. It is many years since we have met. He went to live in Italy to feed his passion for the art and architecture, and he also longed to visit Greece and Egypt to view their antiquities. I cannot reconcile the Henry I knew with the man who made your brother so angry he shook with fury, as Janey told us. I have accepted I know nothing about this man and he could very well pose a danger. I should have sent you home on that very first day.'

'And if I point out it is not your place to dictate my movements? Vernon…' his name on her lips sent longing cascading through him '…look…you know I am sensible. If I promise to remain in the background, *please* allow me to stay.'

Vernon smiled at her and shook his head. 'You are inconsistent, my dear Dotty. You have just informed me I cannot dictate your movements and now you beg me to allow you to stay.'

Her lips firmed. 'I am not inconsistent. You can send me away, but I will not go. I am asking you to allow me to stay with *you*.' Her words ignited a fire in his belly. If only they were spoken in different circumstances. 'Otherwise...' she drew back, squaring her shoulders '...I shall simply stay at another establishment and conduct my own enquiries.'

She had taken the decision from him and he was, secretly, glad. He *wanted* her to stay, no matter how unwise.

'You leave me little choice,' he grumbled, determined not to reveal his relief. 'But, you must remain in the background. That idea you came up with, in Birmingham, about being my by-blow...we will keep that in mind. It will provide a good excuse for you not to accompany me when we find my cousin...it would be entirely reasonable for me to keep you away from any member of my family.'

Thea gave him a saucy smile. 'I am glad that is all settled. Might I suggest you go and reserve rooms for us?'

'Your wish is my command.'

Thea had finished eating and had pushed her plate aside when Vernon returned, but he resumed his seat and began to eat once more. All this fresh air and exercise was giving him an appetite.

'I have paid for two rooms,' he said. 'For three nights to start with.'

'I shall repay you, as soon as we go home.'

Again, the words she chose...*'as soon as we go home'*... sparked a need and a longing in Vernon that he did not care to examine too closely.

'There is no need to repay a single penny. I am happy to fund this little adventure of ours. I was going to say I have enjoyed it...but that is not entirely true, given the nature of our quest and the fact we have yet to find Daniel.'

Vernon resumed eating. The two customers who had

been in such deep conversation now stood up and walked towards the door, passing close behind Thea, who was absently crumbling a roll between her fingers. Vernon watched them idly. The first man, finely dressed, fair-haired and sharp-featured, appeared to be of a similar age to Vernon. The second man was older and heavy-set, with a ruddy face and bulging waistcoat. They paused at the door and he clapped the younger man on the shoulder.

'Now, Mannington…' Vernon's heart jolted in his chest as his eyes fixed on the fair-haired man. *Mannington!* The older man—an American, by his accent—continued to speak. 'Don't be a stranger. As soon as you get back, send me word and come dine with us—I know my Cordelia will be pleased to see you again. And we will hope you are not delayed like last time.'

Vernon looked more closely. This could not, surely, be Cousin Henry? Despite the man before him being similar in height, build and colouring, he could see no resemblance in his features and Henry had never been quite as fair… this man's hair was near white in colour.

'I should not be gone more than a couple of days,' Mannington said. No, definitely not Henry. Wrong voice altogether. 'And I shall be delighted to further my acquaintance with your charming daughter.'

Vernon glanced at Thea to see if she had caught Mannington's name and his heart jerked again, this time in alarm. Thea had frozen. Even her lips had drained of colour and each individual freckle stood stark against the pallor of her skin. Her fingers squeezed tight around the roll, her knuckles white, and her eyes were squeezed tight shut.

Vernon stretched his leg out under the cover of the table to nudge Thea, to try to provoke a reaction. Anything to interrupt that death-like stillness.

The two men left the room, but still Thea didn't move.

'What is it?' Vernon kept his voice to a whisper. He

longed to reach across the table, to take her hand, to offer her his strength, his presence. But he could not. Not whilst she was dressed as a boy. 'Thea! Talk to me. Please.'

She looked up at that. Shock and disbelief on her face. Eyes stricken. Her chest moving up and down too fast, too shallow. She licked her lips and her brows drew together in a distressed frown.

'That man.'

Her voice shook. Her hands trembled. Vernon stretched his leg forward again and pressed it against hers, offering his physical support in the only way he could.

'Hush. It is all right. I am here. Do you mean Mannington or the American?'

'M-Mannington. Did he see me?'

'No. Neither of them noticed either one of us. It is safe. You are safe. You know I will look after you. There is nothing to fear.'

'Fear?' Thea laughed. A harsh, low sound. 'Am I not to fear a ghost?'

Chapter Thirteen

A ghost?

A movement outside the window caught Vernon's eye. Mannington and the American stood on the pavement outside, still deep in conversation. Thea followed the direction of his gaze and a distressed mewl reached Vernon's ears. She had paled even further and appeared to shrink, her shoulders hunched and her head bowed.

Vernon shoved his chair back.

'I need to go after Mannington.'

'No!' Thea was on her feet, by his side, blocking his way, frantic fingers clawing his sleeve. 'No! You cannot, not until I…you *must* not.' She captured his gaze with glittering eyes. 'Let him go. He will be back. Mannington!' She all but spat the word. 'It is not his name,' she whispered fiercely. 'Oh, I cannot think…and Daniel…what did he do?'

'Hush,' Vernon whispered urgently as her voice rose in both volume and pitch.

He dropped his hand upon her shoulder. She was trembling violently.

'Come on, lad,' he said, in a loud voice for the benefit of the remaining customer who had abandoned his newspaper and was watching them with curiosity. 'Let us go and inspect our rooms.'

I ought to be following Mannington. Finding out what the devil is going on. But I can't leave Thea, not like this.

Thea nodded. Side by side they walked to the door and out into the lobby, from which an oak staircase rose to the first floor. Thea stumbled slightly as they crossed the lobby and Vernon slung his arm around her shoulders— to an onlooker it would be a friendly gesture but, in reality, his fingers gripped her upper arm and he remained ready to support her if she stumbled. Once they had left the bar, Thea seemed to regain some of her strength and they climbed the stairs to the first of the rooms Vernon had reserved for their use.

He realised precisely how much effort it had taken for Thea to walk from the bar and climb the staircase as soon as they entered the bedchamber. He released his hold upon her to turn and close the door and, when he turned back, she had sunk to the floor. She had not swooned, however. She sat, huddled in a heap, with her face sunk into her hands as she rocked to and fro in absolute silence.

He fell to his knees beside her and gently rubbed her back. He ducked his head to try to see her face, but it was completely covered by hands that visibly shook.

'Thea. Please. Talk to me. You recognised Mannington?'

She nodded, her face still hidden.

'Who is he? What has he done?'

A high-pitched whimper escaped her, quickly stifled. Vernon bit back a curse and gathered her into his arms, then regained his feet and carried her to the bed. He set her down near the head, pulling the pillows behind her to cushion her, and then he clasped her wrists and tugged her hands from her face.

She shook her head violently. 'No! No!'

Vernon settled beside her and held her close. 'There is nothing to fear. I am here. He cannot hurt you.'

His mind whirled with conjecture. What was that man to

Thea? What had he done? A black, murderous rage swelled deep in his chest and he swore he would make the bastard suffer. Gradually her quivering stilled and her breathing steadied. She relaxed into Vernon's embrace. He pulled back, to look into her face, putting his hand under her chin to force her to meet his gaze.

'I am going downstairs for a few minutes—'

'No!' Terror lit her eyes and she grabbed frantically at his hand. 'I beg of you. He cannot find out I am here. For Daniel's sake! You must not!'

'Calm yourself. I promise I shall not confront him—I am going to fetch some brandy. You have had a shock; it will help steady your nerves. I shall return before you know it and then we shall talk. No matter how difficult it is for you to confide in me, you must.'

Had the bastard attacked Thea? Possibly even raped her? That rage—hot as molten lava only moments before—had solidified into a cold hard mass that demanded revenge— a revenge that required a cool, logical approach, not the hot-headed, fists-flying solution he had initially craved.

He stroked her cheek, smoothing her curls away, re-lieved to see a touch of colour in her face again. 'Do you understand?'

Her eyes searched his and his heart stuttered at the trust that shone from them. She nodded—tiny, rapid movements.

'And you must promise me you will not leave this room until I return.'

She nodded again.

'Let me hear you say it.'

'I promise. And…' She paused for so long he wondered if she had forgotten what she had been going to say. 'Thank you,' she concluded eventually.

He smiled at her and pulled her close into a brief hug. Unable to resist, he dropped a kiss on to her curls, pausing for one second to breathe in her evocative scent before leaving to go downstairs.

Before going to the bar to request a bottle of brandy and two glasses, he stepped outside the front door, fully prepared to exchange at least a few words with the man who had evoked such an extreme reaction from Thea—not to challenge him…merely to establish a preliminary connection—but both Mannington and the American were gone.

At least we know he is here and he will be returning.

As he crossed the lobby, after ordering brandy to be sent to his room, the innkeeper, Mr Horwell—a spare, dark-haired man of indeterminate age—was descending the staircase. Vernon waited for him to reach the lobby.

'Mr Boyton,' Horwell said, with a nod of his head. 'I trust your rooms are to your satisfaction?'

'Indeed they are.'

'You have a further requirement?'

'I do.' Vernon glanced around the lobby. It was quiet now, but when he had reserved their rooms it had been busy with people coming and going. He did not want to be overheard. 'I should like a word with you, if you will? Do you have somewhere private we may talk?'

Horwell bowed. 'But of course, sir. This way.'

He showed Vernon into a back room clearly used as an office.

'Would you care to sit, Mr Boyton?'

Vernon thought of Thea and declined. He must get back to her as soon as possible, but he could not pass up this chance to question the innkeeper.

'I shall not take up much of your time,' he said. 'I shall come straight to the point. Do you know the name Daniel Markham?'

'No, sir, I do not.'

'What about Charles Leyton?'

Horwell shook his head decisively. 'No, sir.'

'And—' Vernon watched him closely '—what can you tell me about Mr Henry Mannington?'

A subtle change came over Horwell. He straightened— almost imperceptibly—and ran one finger around his neck, easing his neckcloth.

'Not a great deal, sir. He visits the Crown from time to time, but he has never been a paying guest.'

Caution radiated from the man.

'Has he lived in the area a long time?'

Horwell's gaze flicked to Vernon's face and then away. He cleared his throat.

'If it will make this easier, Horwell, you should know that I have never met Mr Mannington, but that I do seek information about him. I saw him here earlier in the company of an American gentleman, which is why I thought to ask you about him.'

A muscle leapt in Horwell's jaw.

'Your discretion does you credit, Horwell. I give you my word as a gentleman that anything you tell me will go no further.'

Other than to Thea.

'There will be no repercussions. And I, in return, will be honest with you. Are you willing to help me?'

Horwell stared at Vernon, then nodded, releasing a pent-up breath.

'I shall aid you to the best of my ability, sir, although I do not know a great deal about the gentleman other than he claims kinship to a duke and he is lying to one of my guests.'

Vernon had been gone an age. Still shivery with shock, Thea clambered under the eiderdown and curled in a ball, tugging the folds around her, trying to warm herself. Her brain appeared to be mired in quicksand—the more she tried to free a thought to follow it through and try to make sense of what she had heard and seen, the more she felt as though she was sinking. Her chest squeezed tight, making breathing a chore, and her limbs felt heavy, anchoring her to the bed. She had not managed to follow even one thought to a conclusion when she heard the door open.

'Put the tray on the nightstand, if you please,' Vernon was saying, in a loud voice. 'As you see, my nephew is unwell.'

Thea kept her head buried as light footsteps neared the bed and then retreated. Finally, the door clicked shut and she fought her way out from the cocooning eiderdown, blinking her eyes against the brightness of the room. Strong hands clasped her upper arms and helped her to sit, propping her once more against the pillows leaning against the headboard. Her hand was taken and her fingers wrapped around a glass.

'Sip at this,' Vernon ordered. Then, 'Steady. Do not gulp', as she tilted the glass to her mouth.

She coughed and spluttered as the liquid scorched its way down her throat. She raised watering eyes to Vernon's.

'What is that?'

'Brandy. I did say I would bring some. Have you never drunk it before?'

She shook her head. This was it. He would expect an explanation…and how could she admit the truth and own up to her culpability in the chain of events that had culminated in the loss of their fortune and had caused Papa's stroke? But she must. If they were to find Daniel…she could not hamper the search because of her own guilt and shame.

She sipped again at the amber spirit and this time it warmed and it soothed as she swallowed. She sucked in a determined breath.

'I scarce know where to start.'

Vernon eyed her approvingly and she realised he had expected more reluctance on her part to reveal her story.

'Try the beginning,' he said, sitting on the bed, then swivelling to face her. 'You recognised the man calling himself Henry Mannington.'

'That man…he is not your cousin?'

'No.'

'I am glad. He is…he is *not* a good man. And, yes, I know…*knew* him.'

She chewed at her lip. There was no dodging this. She must face the truth, incredible as it seemed. Perhaps talking of it would finally allow her to make sense of what she had heard and seen this afternoon. Her stomach still roiled with nerves and disbelief.

'I told you I had been betrothed once, several years ago?'

'You did and that you decided by mutual consent that you would not suit.'

'That was not entirely true,' Thea said. She rubbed her eyes, then her mouth. She bent her legs and clasped her arms around her knees, hugging them close to her chest, and sighed. 'His name was Jasper Connor. We met at the assembly room in Bewdley and he asked me to dance. Over the following few weeks we met several times and he asked permission to call upon me at home. We began courting. I was flattered. He was charming, attentive, handsome…he was possessed of all the attributes to turn a young woman's head.'

'How old were you?'

'Twenty, when we met.' She raised her gaze to his. 'He was most plausible. I have thought about it since then…oh, so many times I have gone over what happened. Should I have known? Were there clues I missed? But I can think of none. It was a leisurely courtship. There was no rush… no chivvying me into accepting a proposal…and when he did offer for me, it felt…oh, I do not know how to explain… it felt *natural*. As though it were the next logical step. Do you understand? How could any of us have known what would happen?'

She dipped her head, resting her forehead on her knees.

'How long after you first met did he offer for you?'

'Five months. To the day.' She laughed mirthlessly. 'He even spoke of it as the anniversary of the day we met and he said he hoped it would not be another five months before we could be wed.'

Vernon stroked her hair. 'Tell me the rest, Thea. None of this reflects badly upon you.'

She raised her head and stared at him, reading nothing but concern on his handsome face. 'Does it not? It was I who introduced him into the lives of my family. I who caused…who caused…'

Vernon took her hand, caressing her palm with his thumb. 'Do not distress yourself. Do not talk of culpability. Tell me the facts. What happened after he proposed? You accepted him…and then…?'

She swallowed past the aching lump that had formed in her throat. 'We set the date for our wedding. Papa…' Her voice hitched and she coughed to clear the rasp. 'Papa and Jasper agreed the marriage settlements…and then, and then…three days before the wedding Jasper came to Stourwell Court in such excitement…he had been given *such* an investment opportunity…it could not fail, he said…he would make a fortune. And he said he had thought of Papa and why should he not also benefit from such a wonderful opportunity? But it had to be quick. If Papa did not commit immediately, he would miss this *chance of a lifetime…* and Papa said, afterwards, that he should have known better…he *did* know better…but he trusted Jasper. We all did. Why should we not? And so they went into Stourbridge together, to Papa's bank, and he withdrew his savings and handed them to Jasper and then he raised more by way of a loan secured against the manufactory and then…then…

they went to Jasper's solicitor in Birmingham. He handled all the paperwork…'

Vernon stirred and Thea paused.

'Why did your father not use his own solicitor to validate the paperwork?'

'There was no time, according to Jasper. Papa's solicitor is in Kidderminster, but the deal had to be done in Birmingham and Papa *trusted* Jasper. He was like a son to him. He was part of our family.'

'This Jasper…he absconded with the money?'

Her stomach clenched and then churned again as the events of the past unfolded in her memory. She shook her head. 'That was the *cruellest* part, when I look back. No, he did not. Not immediately. He dined with us, as expected, the following day. He…he acted so *normal*. None of us suspected a thing when he said he would not see me again before the wedding, that there were various business matters he must attend to and that he would see us at the church in two days' time. That was the last we saw of him.'

'So you…you went to the church?'

Thea nodded, tears stinging, throat thick. Every moment of that dreadful day was etched into her soul. Her initial anxiety…had there been an unavoidable delay? An accident? Was Jasper ill? Her hurt and humiliation as the minutes passed and no word arrived from the groom. Her heartache and despair when a messenger sent to Jasper's lodgings returned with the news that he had packed his bags and left the minute he had returned after that final dinner at Stourwell Court.

'He did not come.'

That was all Vernon needed to know. She had no words to describe the aftermath…the utter disbelief and the sheer panic of her father in particular as the implications slowly sank in… Jasper had gone. And the money…as hard as they tried to convince themselves there had been some dreadful

mistake…a misunderstanding… Papa had the share cer-
tificates. Surely the investment was sound… Deep down
inside Thea suspected they had all known the truth.

'The next day…' The day that should have been Thea's
first day as a married woman. 'Papa and Daniel went to
Birmingham to speak to Jasper's solicitor. His office was
locked and bare. They discovered the shares were not worth
a single penny. The mining venture Papa had invested in
did not exist.'

'I am sorry, but what has Henry Mannington to do—?'

'They returned home,' Thea spoke over Vernon, gab-
bling slightly in her haste. She must tell him the whole now
she had come thus far. 'And, as Papa was telling Mama and
me…*confessing* to us…telling us we were ruined…that is
when he…he…'

A huge sob gathered in her chest and, try as she might,
she could not suppress it. Vernon's arms came around her
and she leaned into him, grateful for his strength and his
calm presence.

'That is when he had the stroke?'

Thea nodded, sniffing. 'It is all my fault! If I had not
allowed myself to be flattered by Jasper, none of it would
have happened. It is my fault Papa is bedridden and cannot speak properly—'

'You are not to blame. Jasper Connor bears the blame.
Nobody else. What happened next? Did you try to trace
him?'

'Daniel did. He spent weeks following leads but then,
when he finally tracked him down, it was too late.'

Thea felt her pulse kick and gallop as she recalled the
reason why she was telling all this to Vernon. The impossible…the unbelievable…

'Go on.'

A gentle hand smoothed her hair. Comforting. Reassuring. Giving her the courage to say the words out loud.

'Daniel finally caught up with Jasper at his funeral.'

She felt Vernon tense. She pulled away, staring up into his face. 'He had been travelling ever since…*that* day. He had stopped overnight at an inn and there was a fire. Jasper died in that fire. Daniel watched as his coffin was placed in the ground.'

'So…' Vernon's brows had drawn together in puzzlement. 'What has this to do with Henry Mannington?'

'Do you not see? Henry Mannington is Jasper Connor.'

Chapter Fourteen

Vernon had not seen it coming. He had been caught up in Thea's tale, heart sore at the pain she had endured, furious at the dirty trick paid on her and her family. He stood up and paced the room as he sorted through the facts, then he returned to sit on the bed again. No wonder Thea had spoken of ghosts. No wonder she had been in such shock.

'We must ensure he does not see you,' he said.

Thea stiffened. 'Is that all you have to say? Your only concern? That Jasper… Mannington, I mean, might recognise me?'

Vernon swept his hand through his hair. 'No. Of course not. I was thinking aloud. It is one of my concerns…the others…'

He could barely order his thoughts. Every instinct he possessed screamed at him to chase after Mannington. Find him…and put his hands around his neck and squeeze the life from him. He had never known his own self-control so precarious. He rarely lost his temper. He was not a violent man. But something about this woman stirred some primeval force deep within him, a snarling beast that urged him to take action. To protect. To avenge.

He poured himself a glass of brandy and tossed it down

his throat, then proffered the decanter to Thea. Wordlessly she held out her glass.

'We need to discuss this in a calm manner,' Vernon said. 'We must try to work out how and why Jasper is still alive and how that ties in with my cousin and your brother.'

Thea sipped her brandy. He was pleased to see she had more colour in her cheeks now. She shuffled around on the bed until she was sitting facing him, cross-legged. If only she knew what she did to him…her shapely legs outlined by the breeches she wore… Vernon averted his eyes, concentrating on her face. The fact that she was completely unselfconscious about her appearance, and about being here, alone, with him in a bedchamber…never had he felt so overlooked as a man.

He cleared his throat and marshalled his thoughts.

'I gleaned some information from Horwell when I went downstairs to order the brandy,' he said. 'It sounds as though Connor… Mannington, that is…is up to his old tricks. He lives at a place called Crackthorpe Manor, which is about four miles out of town on the road to Great Malvern and he has befriended an American businessman, Mr Samuel Temple—'

'Was that the man we saw him with? I thought he had a strange accent.'

'Yes. He is in Worcester on business and is staying here at the Crown. He is very wealthy and is accompanied by his daughter, Cordelia, who stands to inherit his entire fortune.'

Thea sucked in an audible breath. 'An heiress?' She swivelled around, lowering her feet to the floor. 'We must warn her!'

Vernon grasped her arm, restraining her. 'Steady. According to Horwell, Mannington's plans are not going as smoothly as he would like. Mr Temple is set on snaring a nobleman for his daughter.'

'That, at least, is some protection for her. Mannington

cannot conjure a title from nowhere no matter what other lies he tells,' Thea muttered. 'And with no title to turn her head, *she* will not be so foolish as to arrive at a church in the expectation of finding her betrothed waiting at the altar.'

'Hey.' Vernon pinched her chin. 'You were not foolish. He is clearly an accomplished fraudster. Now, we must plan how to approach him when he returns—'

'Returns? Why? Where—?'

'You must have heard what they said…'

Vernon fell silent as Thea turned huge, bruised eyes on him.

'I cannot recall. I did not…could not…'

He brushed the back of his fingers along her cheekbone, aching to take her in his arms again. But he resisted, not certain how she might react now those hurtful memories were in the open.

'I'm a fool,' he said. 'Of course you did not take in what was being said. The gist of their exchange was that Mannington has gone away for a couple of days and Temple was inviting him to dine here with him and his daughter upon his return. So, we have that time to plan how we tackle him. And Thea, trust me…at this moment, there is nothing we can do other than try to make sense of all this.'

Thea was still looking up at him. 'Tell me what else Horwell said.'

'Well, he does not trust Mannington, that is for certain. He overheard him tell Temple that Crackthorpe Manor is his ancestral family home, but Horwell knows for a fact that he has only been living there a matter of weeks because he took on Horwell's niece as a housemaid when he moved in. So he knows Mannington is lying to the Temples, but he hasn't said anything to them because he does not want his niece to lose her job.'

'But someone must warn this Mr Temple and his poor daughter.'

'And we will.' Vernon bit back a curse. 'God knows how many people he has swindled, blackening the Beauchamp name into the bargain. Horwell told me he is still claiming to be a cousin to the Duke of Cheriton and not even a distant cousin at that.'

'But he is not your cousin, is he? It is not that Henry Mannington is his real name and Jasper Connor was false?'

'No. At least…we cannot say for sure that Jasper Connor was not a false name, but I do know without the slightest doubt that he is not my cousin.' Vernon scratched his jaw, frowning. 'The fact that he is openly living as Henry… I hate to even think this, but it suggests, does it not, that he has no fear of being exposed as an imposter by the *real* Henry.'

Thea stirred and took his hand between hers. 'I thought the same,' she said. 'I am sorry.'

She was offering him comfort even though her heart must be breaking. And they had not even touched on what this new revelation might mean about Daniel's disappearance.

Vernon surged to his feet and paced to the window. For all his words to Thea, he did not want to sit idly, talking over problems and formulating plans. He longed to be *out there*…doing…taking action. He was a man…it's what men did.

'So will he be sorry when I get my hands on him,' he growled, clenching his fists and leaning on the sill, gazing unseeingly through the glass. 'Two days! It cannot pass quickly enough for me. I shall take great pleasure in exposing him for the charlatan he is.'

He heard the creak of the bed and the pad of her feet as she crossed the room to stand behind him. A small hand settled against his shoulder blade.

'Let us plan. There are questions that need answering, and we must consider them in a logical fashion. We must not allow our emotions to sway our thinking.' Her hand circled, soothing. Then patted. 'I *told* you we made a good partnership. When one of us veers away on a tangent, the other is there to haul them back on the right road.'

He turned. She was so close, gazing up at him. Trusting. Open. How much courage did it take for her to set aside her emotions in order to comfort him? And *his* anger had been directed at Mannington for besmirching his family name; his distress was for a distant cousin he had not even thought of in years, whereas Thea had been jilted by that bastard and now her brother was missing. He forced a smile, and pushed an errant curl back from her forehead, resisting the urge to cup her cheeks. To lower his head. And to kiss those full, tempting lips.

'You are right. We do make a good partnership.'

He sidestepped around her, but she grabbed at his hand, pulling him round.

'Look!'

Her nose was all but pressed against the window. Vernon leaned forward to peer down at the street below.

'That is him, is it not? Mr Temple?' Thea said. Then she straightened, drawing back. 'And *that*, I presume, is *Miss* Temple.'

Vernon gave her a sidelong look—distracted by the change in her tone—before studying again the two figures in the street below. Temple it was, with a lady upon his arm. She was certainly young enough to be his daughter, but there was little resemblance between the portly American and this dark, willowy, exotic-looking creature. Vernon just managed to contain his low whistle of appreciation. Miss Cordelia Temple was stunning. Conscious of Thea quietly bristling by his side—and why was it women always seemed to take an instant dislike to beautiful females?—he moved away from the window.

'Yes, that is him,' he said. 'Come, let us sit over here...'

he steered her to a small round table and pair of chairs that were set back in the corner '…and we shall plot Mannington's downfall. But first, our priority must be to work out what has happened to Henry and to Daniel. What are those questions you spoke of?'

They sat across the table from one another. Thea held up a finger.

'First: where is the real Henry Mannington?'

Vernon recognised in Thea's expression the same resignation that weighed on his mind.

'I fear that, if it was not Jasper who was buried that day, it must have been my cousin,' he said.

Thea reached for his hand and squeezed. 'I am sorry but I agree. That is the most rational explanation.'

'Which poses an additional question,' Vernon said. 'Did Jasper simply seize upon an opportunity that presented itself to him, or was he involved in Henry's death? Did he set the fire, perhaps?'

'And that is a question only he can answer,' Thea said. 'Now…next…how did Daniel learn that Jasper was still alive?' Her amber eyes searched his. 'Do we agree that Daniel somehow discovered Jasper was alive and set off to track him down?'

'Agreed.' He thought back to what they had learned in Harborne and Birmingham. 'He must have seen Jasper at the Royal Hotel and learned he was using a false identity. Maybe Jasper… Mannington, I mean…left before Daniel could confront him and so, when he learned Mannington was due to stay there on his return journey, Daniel decided to go to the hotel every day until he saw him again.'

'And, in the meantime, he wrote to your brother.'

'And we know that, when Mannington did stay again overnight, he left very early in the morning…'

'Keen to get back to his heiress,' Thea muttered, her brows lowering.

'And Daniel therefore missed him.'

'And decided to follow him, knowing now that he lived near to Worcester and would be travelling on the Worcester road.'

'I wonder why, once he knew Mannington would return, your brother did not simply stay at the hotel until Mannington returned?'

'I think I can answer that,' Thea said. 'He would not stay away overnight unless he had no choice. He has taken on the mantle of head of the family. He feels responsible for us: Papa and Mama and me. He would rather ride all that way every day than not come home. And, of course, the cost would be a consideration. Our finances might be improved, but they are still not fully secure.'

Which makes his failure to return now even more troubling.

Vernon saw the effort it cost Thea to contain her worry and her grief and his heart swelled.

'Try not to think the worst,' he said, taking her hands across the table and caressing her knuckles with his thumbs. 'There still could be a good explanation for Daniel's silence.'

Although I cannot think of a single one.

He hated to think how desolate Thea must be feeling at this very moment. He felt it, too: grief for Henry, even though he had not seen him for years, and apprehension about what had happened to Daniel. But he must remain positive for Thea's sake.

'What we need to decide is how we move forward from here,' he said. 'Can you recall the name of the inn that burned down?'

'No, but I do know it was in the village of Yarncott, near Oxford.'

'Oxford? That is too far for us to go to make enquiries, with only two days at our disposal. I need to establish a relationship with the Temples before Mannington returns and, through them, with him.'

'*You* need to? Do you not mean we?' She stared challengingly, then her shoulders slumped and she shook her head, her curls bouncing. 'No. Sorry. Of course I cannot be involved. Mannington will know me in an instant.' Her mouth drooped.

'I promise you, Thea,' Vernon said. 'Mannington *will* pay for the suffering he has caused you and your family.'

She drew back. 'Pay? In what way? Money?' She laughed bitterly. 'Money will not buy Papa his health.'

'But it might give him peace of mind, to know the culprit is brought to justice.'

'How do you intend to lure the Temples into trusting you? You cannot use your real name and you do not look much like a wealthy gentleman, dressed as you are.'

'That is true.' Vernon jumped to his feet. 'First, I need to ensure Mannington has really gone away...we already know he is a consummate liar, do we not? Plus, you have given me an idea, Thea. Now, do not leave your bedchamber, or you might ruin my plans. I shall see you at dinner.'

'What is your idea? Tell—'

But Vernon had gone, closing the door on the remainder of her sentence.

Thea did not see Vernon again until it was time to dine, when she answered a knock upon her door, her heart bumping in her throat even though it was illogical to think it might be Mannington who knocked. Vernon had raised such doubts in her mind...what if Mannington *had* lied to Mr Temple and he was still skulking around the area?

But it was not Mannington. Vernon, looking very pleased with himself, stood on the landing outside and her pulse leapt with fierce joy.

'Oh. It is you,' she said, struggling to conquer her involuntary reaction to the sight of him.

'Were you expecting somebody else?'

'Of course I was not.'

'Come, then,' he said. 'Enough of your dawdling. I am ravenous. I have reserved a private parlour for us to dine.'

Thea stomped on to the landing and banged the door shut behind her. She cloaked herself in anger. She could not bear it if he guessed the strength of her feelings for him.

Infuriating wretch! Leaving me all alone for hours, *to worry myself silly. And then he reappears when it suits him, all smug and self-satisfied. No doubt he has been 'establishing a relationship' with that woman. Well, I wish him luck with her.*

She would not give him the satisfaction of questioning him about his whereabouts—he obviously could not care less that she'd had been going quietly mad, left alone with her thoughts.

'I hope you have not left your bedchamber since last I saw you, Dotty,' Vernon said, tweaking one of her curls as they walked downstairs together.

She had been oh-so-tempted to defy him. But common sense—and fear that Mannington might indeed still be lurking around—had stopped her. They still needed to find Daniel and blundering about when Vernon was establishing…well, whatever he was establishing…would not help.

'I am not foolish enough to ruin our chances of finding the truth,' Thea said, sticking her nose in the air as she stalked past him into the parlour, 'even if *you* are unfeeling enough to leave me in ignorance all this time. But you need not think that means I shall remain confined to my room day after day whilst you gallivant about *establishing relationships* and searching for clues, because I shall not.'

Vernon regarded her with an arched brow and a smile playing on his mouth. 'Are you miffed with me, Dotty?'

She rounded on him. 'Miffed? Why, pray, should I be miffed?'

He shrugged carelessly. 'Oh, I don't know,' he said. 'Just an impression. I am pleased I am wrong.'

She could see by his expression he knew he was right. And that he thought it amusing. He thought *her* amusing.

'Now, this parlour will do nicely for our meals, do you not agree?' Vernon said. 'The less other guests, or the staff, see of you, my dearest Dotty, the better. Then Mannington's return will not coincide with the sudden elusiveness of my young nephew. I shall invent a disorder for you, I believe.' His green eyes twinkled. 'What say you to a disorder of the brain? Shall that suffice to keep you confined to your chamber, do you think?'

'There is no need for me to remain out of sight when Mannington returns, as long as we are not introduced,' she said. 'I am dressed as a boy and, as long as I wear my cap, there is no reason for him to even notice me. And *that*, my dear Lord Vernon, is to our advantage. You need my help. A lad may loiter without exciting comment and a man such as Mannington is less likely to censor his conversation in front of a youth than in front of a full-grown man. It will be an excellent opportunity to find out some of his secrets.'

'Oh, no. Absolutely not.' They were seated at the table by now, opposite one another, and Vernon pierced Thea with a narrowed gaze. 'Do not imagine for one minute, Dotty, that I shall permit you to risk your safety by sneaking around and eavesdropping on that scoundrel. Besides, it is not safe for you to wander about on your own in a town this size. You are entirely too innocent. Do you forget that incident with Pooley? There are any number of things that might happen to an unsophisticated lad…things that would make your hair curl. Or—' his eyes glinted '—perhaps I should say, make your toes curl. Your hair needs no assistance in that department.'

Thea glared at him, raising a hand involuntarily to smooth her hair, a hopeless task as she very well knew. Why could she not have smooth, sleek, shining hair? In the mental images she had formed of the ladies with whom Vernon no doubt consorted in his normal, privileged life not one of them had wild curls that spiralled and bounced. And unsophisticated…well, she could not argue with that description of her, not compared to the females he was accustomed to.

She thrust aside her inadequacies, telling herself there were far more important issues at stake.

'Where have you *been* all afternoon?' *So much for my resolve not to question him.* 'I kept thinking about what you said—that Mannington might not have gone away after all. I kept wondering if you might bump into him unawares.'

And if he did, she just knew Vernon would confront him. The fear had plagued her the entire afternoon, worry eating at her in case Vernon was in danger. How would she know? What would she do if something happened and he failed to return, like Daniel? She could not bear it if he simply vanished too.

Vernon's brows shot skywards. 'Is *that* why you are so scratchy? Were you worried about me?'

He grinned at her and she scowled back, desperate to hide the truth. Yes. She had been worried. Frantic, even. And now he sat there, seemingly without a care in the world, looking suave and gorgeous despite his travel-stained clothes, whilst she looked like a scruffy schoolboy with badly cut hair. Oh, how she wished they were sitting there in different circumstances, with her clad in a pretty gown, with her hair nicely dressed…

She tamped down those wishes; they were nonsense.

A man such as he would never look at a woman like her.

Besides. Men were not to be trusted. She had seen the living proof of that not five hours ago in this very inn.

'Why should I worry about a great oaf like you? I have no doubt you can take care of yourself.'

But she had thought the same about Daniel and now she could only pray he was out there somewhere, safe.

Two maids came in carrying trays and served their food and wine, precluding further conversation. Thea drummed her fingers on the table, waiting for the women to leave the room, her stomach churning. It took her several minutes to work out the cause…it was dread. Pure and simple. Now they seemed close to discovering the truth she realised there was a growing part of her that was simply terrified of what they might learn. At least at the moment she had hope. What if her worst fears were realised? What, then, would she have left?

At last the women left, closing the door behind them.

'Well?' She almost spat the word out, fear making her sharp. 'Will you tell me what you have been doing or am I to be kept in total ignorance?'

Chapter Fifteen

Vernon gave Thea a rueful smile. 'I am sorry. I should not tease. This is a difficult time for you, I know. And I am at times guilty of forgetting quite how much is at stake.'

She stared. 'You almost sound as though you are enjoying yourself.'

Vernon winced. 'Put like that, I sound heartless indeed. But I am not. I care about you and I pray we shall find Daniel safe and well but, to be brutally honest, I *am* enjoying the change. Or, more accurately, the challenge. You have accused me of being an idle aristocrat with too much money and too much time on my hands and, despite my business interests, you are right. My brother and I, we employ people to do the hard work. We only need be involved when and if we wish to be. This is…*different*. I am needed. Indispensable. And it is that feeling I relish, not the actual circumstances.'

Somewhat mollified, Thea sipped at her wine.

'So, I shall enlighten you as to how I have spent this afternoon. I spoke to Horwell, following which I wrote two letters, and then Horwell drove me out to Crackthorpe Manor, ostensibly to visit Annie, his niece, but actually to ascertain that Mannington has indeed gone away for a couple of days as he said. Which Annie confirmed.'

That, at least, is a relief. 'But why did Horwell drive you out to Crackthorpe Manor?'

Vernon frowned. 'I asked to hire a post-chaise, and he offered to take me himself. I did think it a bit odd, but…' He shrugged. 'I told him Mannington had fleeced a friend of mine and that I hope to bring him to book, so perhaps he is just relieved to have an ally against the man.'

'Did you meet the Temples?'

Another thought that had plagued her throughout that long afternoon. Vernon, with that…that… *beauty.*

'No. I have a plan and that does not include making their acquaintance just yet. When Bickling arrives—'

'Bickling?'

'My groom.'

'I know he is your groom, but he is at Stourwell Court.'

'And that is why I sent my letter to Stourwell Court,' he said in an exaggeratedly patient tone. 'I have summoned him to come to Worcester and to bring my curricle and also my own clothing. I—'

'You wrote to Stourwell Court and you did not think to tell me?'

'I am telling you now.'

'But… I could have sent for some of *my* clothes.'

'But that makes no sense, Dotty my dear. You cannot parade around here as Dorothea Markham. Quite apart from the risk of Mannington seeing you, I need to gain the trust of Mr and Miss Temple, not drive them away with outrage and scandal. No, you have no choice but to remain as my nephew, Theo, for the time being. But take heart…at least you may remain as my nephew and not my by-blow,' he added with a chuckle.

Thea gazed gloomily at her plate. 'I suppose you are right.' She tried to shake free of the feeling that events were sweeping past her, leaving her mired in a backwater. 'You were telling me of your plan.'

'I was indeed. The reason I have sent for my curricle and my own clothes is that I, my dear Dotty, am about to become *Viscount* Boyton—no more plain Mister for me. I told Horwell this afternoon—in the strictest of confidence, of course—that my trunk has been delayed and that I've been forced to dress in borrowed clothing until it arrives. He is thrilled that a member of the aristocracy is patronising his inn and I have little doubt that particular tale will spread in no time and will reach the ears of Mr Samuel Temple and his lovely daughter, Cordelia, to whom I shall be *particularly* attentive.'

A sharp pain arrowed through Thea and she battled to keep her expression blank, appalled at the jealousy that erupted in her chest. She knew, logically, there was no reason to be jealous. But emotions were not logical.

'This plan of yours,' she said. 'Would it not be better to target Mannington direct? Why bother with the Temples at all?'

Vernon, chewing a mouthful of food, did not immediately answer, but his eyes were on her and, uncomfortable with his scrutiny, she began to eat her own meal. What if he could read her mind? There were times when she was certain he knew exactly the thoughts that chased around inside her head. She focused on her plate.

'That would take too long. A man such as Mannington learns to be cautious of any new acquaintance. If I successfully charm my way into the lives of Mr Temple and his daughter—and I can be *most* charming when I try, Dotty, even though I say so myself—Henry Mannington will have no choice but to acknowledge my acquaintance. He will—quite wrongly, I do assure you—view me as a rival to the hand of Miss Temple.'

Thea pushed her plate aside, any appetite flown. 'I am in no need of your assurances, sir. I am sure it is none of my concern if you *do* aspire to the hand of Miss Temple.'

She stole a look through her lashes to gauge his reaction, then stiffened. 'You laugh at me, but it is scarce five hours since I told you I was jilted at the altar. I envy *no* woman the attentions of *any* man. Of that, *I* assure *you*.'

Vernon shook his head at her. 'Not every man is deceitful in matters of the heart, Thea.'

'Are they not?'

She found her hand captured, engulfed by his much larger one, and her stomach performed a slow somersault.

'They are not,' he said firmly. 'Thea…you are weighed down by the guilt over what happened to your papa and you tell yourself it is your duty to stay at home and help your mother. But what happened…it was not your fault. You must know that. All you did was trust the word of a scoundrel. Your father—older than you and, presumably, a shrewd man—was also taken in. Fraudsters such as Mannington are clever with words. They often have charm in abundance. *No one* would blame you for believing his lies and you should not blame yourself or allow your experience to sour you against all men.'

He lifted her hand and pressed his lips to the back, sending jolts of energy sparking through her veins and setting her pulse racing.

'What is more,' he added in an even softer, infinitely more intimate tone, 'you should not continue to punish yourself.'

Thea snatched her hand from his, heart hammering, cheeks burning. 'I don't know what you mean. I do not punish myself.'

He raised his wine glass and drank, his eyes never leaving her face.

'I do *not*.'

'You have buried yourself at Stourwell Court. You never go anywhere. You have given up on life and you should not. You have too much to offer.'

A lump swelled in her throat. She must change this conversation. She could not bear sympathy. Or kindness. She did not deserve it.

'You said you wrote two letters?'

His eyes narrowed, as though he knew exactly why she had changed the subject.

'Indeed. I also wrote to Leo. My brother.'

Thea still could not become accustomed to hearing Vernon talk about his brother—a *duke*—in such a casual manner and the reminder of the inequality in their positions in society added to the ache in her heart. She had battled so hard not to succumb to him. To protect her heart. She had failed. And that terrified her because, on top of what had happened to Daniel, she must face the agony of losing a man she feared she was falling in love with.

'May I ask why?' Her voice, remarkably, did not quiver.

'I updated him on what has happened and asked him to send his man to Yarncott to make enquiries about that fire and then to come here to help us search for Daniel.'

And where was the role for her in Vernon's plans? He would be busy building his rapport with the Temples—there would be little place for a young lad in their adult world, even if she could risk coming face to face with Mannington. Still less, she thought ruefully as she looked down at her nondescript clothing, a boy dressed as she happened to be. Thea's involvement from henceforth would be strictly limited. The thought of Vernon leaving her behind whilst he nurtured his acquaintance with Miss Cordelia Temple and her father stirred a cauldron of fervent imaginings in her brain. She already disliked that woman with a quite unreasonable intensity.

She hadn't heard Vernon move and yet, there he was, right beside her, his finger beneath her chin.

'Chin up, Dotty. At least we are making some progress.'

She gazed up at him, their eyes locking, and his hand

moved to cradle her cheek, setting her pulse skittering and anticipation swirling deep in her core. Before she could react—either to rebuff or to encourage—he snatched his hand away with a muttered oath and returned to his chair.

'Finish your meal,' he said. 'It is growing late and I suggest we should retire early tonight…the less we are seen until my clothing arrives, the better.'

The following afternoon Thea pressed her nose against the window of her bedchamber, which overlooked the street outside the Crown. Vernon was below, on the street, his chestnut waves gleaming in the sunlight as he spoke to Bickling, who stood at the heads of Vernon's blacks.

Thea propped her elbow on the windowsill and her chin on her hand and brooded. For all her talk about eavesdropping on Mannington upon his return, she knew very well she had not the courage. The thought of being unmasked… she shivered with fear. There was much at stake from Mannington's point of view and who knew what lengths he would be driven to in order to protect himself? For that matter, who knew what lengths he had already gone to? No. Vernon's plan did have the best chance of success but, with the duke's man also coming to assist, where did that leave Thea? What was there left for her to do?

Sit here and brood, that is what.

At least they were safe within the inn. Mr Horwell had acted precisely as Vernon predicted, unable to keep the true identity of his illustrious guest to himself, and now the entire inn knew he was really a lord. Thea—as the Viscount's nephew—had been assumed his heir and was accordingly treated with much respect by the staff.

And now, here was Bickling, and Vernon had not even bothered to tell Thea he had arrived. She felt the gap between the two of them widening already. She flung away from the window and went to the door. She needed fresh air and exercise. Perhaps she could persuade Vernon to accompany her on a ride.

Vernon and Bickling were still deep in conversation when Thea reached the street. Both men looked up on her approach and she hesitated, but Vernon smiled and beckoned her over.

Not by a flicker of an eye did Bickling reveal his surprise.

'Master Theo,' he said, touching his cap.

She smiled and nodded at the groom, then said to Vernon, 'I thought I might go for a ride. It is like being in prison, being cooped up indoors all day and, strangely, I have missed the activity.'

'Have you indeed? Well, there is no accounting for it, I suppose. I thought you might enjoy the rest. Wait there, I shall instruct the groom to saddle the horses and we can leave Bickling to see to these two.'

Vernon strode through the arch to the stable yard. Before Bickling could follow him, Thea said, 'I trust all was well at the Court when you left?'

The groom nodded. 'Well enough,' he said. He lowered his voice. 'Though that man of yours… Malky…he took a might of persuading not to come along with me, 'e's that worried about you.'

'There is no need for him to worry. He knows I am with Lord Vernon.'

'That,' said Bickling, flicking a glance towards the archway through which Vernon had disappeared, 'appears to be what troubles him. Only I told him, I did, 'e's no need to fret on that account 'cause…beggin' your pardon, miss…you'm not to his lordship's usual taste and I told him so, I did.'

His words were no surprise, but she nevertheless felt the blow to her heart. It was quite one thing to tell yourself that you weren't *up to snuff*—another slang term taught to her by Vernon—but quite another to be told the same by someone else.

She raised her chin. 'What you fail to realise, Bickling, is that—even were I to his lordship's *usual taste*, as you so charmingly put it—his lordship would be destined for quite a disappointment for he is most definitely not to *mine*.'

She ground her teeth as she caught Bickling's smirk before he leaned into the curricle and extracted a bag from beneath the seat.

'Malky got one of the maids to pack you some clothes, miss. Dresses, they are. Just in case, he said, though it doesn't look like you'll have need of them. I'll have the bag sent up to your room, shall I?'

Slightly mollified, Thea thanked Bickling and watched as he began to lead the horses through to the rear of the hotel. It was not long before Vernon returned, leading Warrior and Star.

'Do you not wish to change your clothes before we go?' she asked him.

'There is little point, with you still resembling a barrow boy,' Vernon said with a wink. 'Unfortunately, there is little we can do about that. And, besides, there is no time to waste. Are you able to mount without help?' he added, as he checked Star's girth.

'You know that I am,' she responded sharply and pushed her left foot into the stirrup iron, springing up to the saddle. 'You have seen me do so often enough during our journey.'

'True.' Vernon mounted Warrior and then reined him around to ride in the direction of the river. 'But I should like to be able to treat you as I would normally treat a lady. I cannot help but feel guilty about everything you have been forced to endure over the past few days.'

'There is no need,' Thea said as Star ranged alongside Warrior. 'It was my choice to accompany you. And, before you suggest it again, I have no intention of going home.'

'I am glad.'

'You are? I thought you were eager to be rid of me.'

She glanced at his profile, glimpsing his rueful expression even as he kept his attention squarely on the road before them.

'I should not admit to this, but I would miss you if you went.' A muscle twitched in his jaw. 'I have become accustomed to having you around.' He turned to look at her, his green eyes boring into her. 'I have enjoyed being with you.'

Thea's stomach swooped. What did he mean? Did he have feelings for her? Should she speak words of encouragement? But fear kept her silent. She could not bear the humiliation of misunderstanding him...of him trying to explain what he really meant...

Bickling's words came back to haunt her.

You'm not to his lordship's usual taste.

And who should know his master's predilections better than his groom, who would accompany him almost everywhere he went?

'You will soon forget me, when you go back to London,' she said dismissively.

Vernon reached for her hand. 'I shall not fo—'

Thea knocked his hand aside. 'Stop that,' she hissed. 'What if someone were to see? They would think you no better than that Wigbert Pooley.'

For once it was not Thea's cheeks that reddened, but Vernon's. 'My apologies,' he said, stiffly. 'I was forgetting myself.'

'I am sorry if you think I overreacted,' Thea said, following a pause, needing to soothe, hating that she'd made him uncomfortable. 'I did not mean to snap at you.'

'No. You were right, I was wrong. Look, Thea...' Vernon reined Warrior to a halt and twisted in the saddle to face her '...this...' he gestured between the two of them '...I feel a little as though...' He stared down at his hands,

then heaved in a breath. 'I don't know. This is not real...
We are in such a strange...'

His voice trailed into silence. They had stopped by the
bridge and Vernon now looked over the river. Thea followed his gaze. On the opposite bank she could see a portly
gentleman, clad in a black tailcoat and a tall-crowned hat,
walking by the river. On his arm was a tall figure Thea had
no trouble recognising: Miss Cordelia Temple.

'*There* they are,' Vernon said and sent Warrior forward
across the bridge.

Thea followed. 'You sound as though you expected to
see them.'

'They are the reason we have come this way. Horwell
told me it is their custom to take an afternoon promenade
along the river in fine weather. I hoped we might encounter them.'

'But...you said I must stay hidden from them.'

'Another thing I was wrong about. Well, not wrong precisely. Unfair? Yes. Unfair. You were right, you cannot
remain hidden away for however many days it takes to un-
cover the truth about Daniel. You can develop—oh, I don't
know, a fever of some description once Mannington returns. Until then, you may consider yourself out of prison.'

He threw her a crooked grin that sent her heart racing.
Then she looked again at Miss Cordelia Temple and that
surge of excitement drained away as she took in the American girl's elegant figure, draped in a silk gown that matched
the blue of the sky. White lace and ribbons adorned both
her gown and her matching bonnet, and she twirled a white
lace parasol over one shoulder.

'But—'

'Shhh, now. Take care.'

Chapter Sixteen

As they passed by the Temples, Vernon reined Warrior around and raised his hat. 'Good afternoon,' he said with a bow of his head. 'Do I have the pleasure of addressing Mr Temple?'

His voice, unlike the softer, gentler tone he used when conversing with Thea, was clipped and haughty. Aristocratic. His transformation into an entitled nobleman despite his slightly disreputable-looking clothing made Thea stare. This man was far removed from the Vernon she had come to know. Was this how he normally looked and behaved and spoke? Self-confidence appeared to ooze from every pore—as it had, she realised with a start of memory, the day they first met.

Mr Temple and his daughter halted, and Temple frowned as he studied Vernon with something approaching disdain.

'You do,' he said, his accent strange to Thea's ears.

'Forgive my informality in addressing you without an introduction,' Vernon said, 'but we are fellow guests at the Crown and I could not ride past without acknowledgement. Boyton is the name.'

Temple's eyes widened. '*Lord* Boyton?'

'Indeed. I beg you will excuse my appearance. I am

afraid our luggage has been waylaid and my nephew and I have been forced to resort to borrowed clothing.'

'I did hear a story of the sort,' Temple said. 'So it is true.'

Vernon inclined his head, whilst Thea lurked in the background, her eyes fixed on Cordelia Temple, taking in her poise, her glowing, golden skin and, glimpsed under that *exquisite* bonnet, her smooth black hair.

I'll bet Miss Cordelia Temple is 'to his lordship's usual taste'.

Jealousy, hot and sour, burned in her throat.

'Might I present my daughter, Cordelia?' Temple said.

Vernon slid from Warrior's back with fluid grace and tossed the reins to Thea. She watched, her heart twisting as Vernon took the heiress's proffered hand and raised it to his lips.

'*Enchanté*, Miss Temple.'

The girl inclined her head gracefully and then raised her gaze to Vernon's, meeting it with self-assurance. Dismay weaved its tentacles through Thea. How could she bear this? She could not even comfort herself that Cordelia was ugly, or coarse. She soon found herself the object of scrutiny from those dark eyes. Cordelia's lips curved as she raised her beautifully arched brows.

'And your companion, my lord?'

'My nephew, Theo,' Vernon said. 'He is somewhat shy, I fear. That is why we are travelling around England together, in an effort to accustom him to strangers.'

'Then we must help you to help him,' Miss Temple said. 'Pops, we should invite Lord Boyton and Master Theo to join us for dinner. That—' she switched her smile from Thea to Vernon '—is the best way for Theo to engage in conversation.'

Thea smiled a secret smile at Vernon's horrified expression. 'But he is too young to dine with adults.'

'Oh, we do things differently back home and that's a

fact,' Mr Temple said. 'Of course the boy is welcome. Not tonight, mind you. I'm dining with a couple of businessmen, making contacts and building relationships for the future.' He winked and tapped his nose with one finger. 'There's trouble ahead for our two nations and Samuel Temple will be one step ahead of the competition, you better believe me. That's the way to make money and that's a fact. Now, how long did you say you are in the area, my lord?'

'A week or so, I should imagine,' Vernon said.

A week? Thea almost gasped out loud in her horror until she realised how much time Vernon would need to get close to Mannington once he returned. A whole week, watching Vernon toadying up to that…that… She realised Miss Temple's gaze was upon her and she blanked her expression.

'How old are you, Theo? Fourteen? Fifteen?'

'Fifteen, miss.'

These past days had been the only time since her childhood that Thea had blessed her naturally deep voice. Before she had always cursed it, hating how unfeminine she sounded and the fact that she could not sing to save her life. Daniel had teased her about it mercilessly. The thought of her brother steadied her. They had to find out what had happened to Daniel. Nobody had seen him since he left Birmingham. It was as though he had vanished into thin air. It did not matter how much she might dislike Miss Temple, Thea must play her part.

'Will you do me the honour of taking my arm, Miss Temple?'

Vernon sketched a bow and crooked his elbow. Cordelia smiled graciously as she tucked her hand in his elbow and they began to stroll along the riverbank. Mr Temple, a wide beam lighting his face, walked on her other side, leaving Thea, riding Star and leading Warrior, to bring up the rear.

'My lord, this will not do.' Cordelia slipped her arm

from Vernon's after a few minutes and stepped aside, waiting for Thea and the two horses to draw level. 'You say it is your aim to accustom your nephew to strangers and yet you abandon him to ride alone in our wake.'

The full force of her smile—smooth cherry-red lips and sparkling white, even teeth—was directed at Thea. She felt her cheeks heat and, at that, Cordelia laughed—a low, musical sound—then reached up and patted Thea's hand.

'No need to be embarrassed. Come walk with me…may I call you Theo? And you must call me Cordelia.' She tossed her head in Vernon's direction, then turned her attention back to Thea. 'What do you say? Let the gentlemen walk ahead and talk of business and other tedious matters, and you may tell me about your life and I shall confide in you about mine.' She winked. 'Although you must promise not to reveal my secrets to your uncle,' she added in a whisper.

Thea's spirits plunged. Cordelia was *nice*. She was being kind to a youth who she thought was feeling awkward and unsure of himself. That knowledge made Thea feel worse for her dislike, which was not based upon the woman herself but upon Thea's own irrational jealousy. Given other circumstances, Cordelia Temple might be a friend.

'Miss Temple!' Vernon had halted and turned. He glanced at Thea, an impish gleam in his green eyes, before striking a dramatic pose, one hand pressed to his chest, the other extended to Cordelia. 'You strike a callous blow to my pride and my heart,' he pronounced. 'Will you indeed desert me for so green a youth? Come. Take my arm once more. Do not, I beg you, abandon me.'

Thea stared. This man, again, was nothing like the man she had come to know, but neither was he the haughty aristocrat of earlier. Was this how Vernon flirted with the females of the *ton*? Or was he mimicking those men he had told her of…the ones who made *cakes* of themselves, spouting poetry and prostrating themselves at the feet of a pretty girl, all for the sake of a pair of fine eyes? Those tales had kept Thea entertained during their long days in the saddle.

Miss Temple appeared impressed, however, for she started towards him, hands stretched out, crying, 'My lord! Never! I shall not forsake you so cruelly.'

She caught his hand between hers and somehow their entwined hands were pressed to Vernon's chest. Anger licked deep in Thea's belly.

Mr Temple let forth a guffaw. 'Delia, you are a naughty minx. Let go of his lordship this instant. And as for you, sir,' he added as both Vernon and Cordelia broke apart, laughing, 'I'll thank you not to encourage my daughter in such nonsense.'

'I cannot believe you saw through me so quickly,' Vernon said, grinning. Then he sobered. 'Not that I did not mean every word, of course.'

Cordelia laughed again and slapped his arm. 'Of course.'

'My lord! Tell her that ladies in London must not laugh uncontrollably nor make fun of gentlemen,' Mr Temple said, his thick grey brows beetling. 'We are going there in the fall, but you will be shunned if you make such a spectacle of yourself, Delia, and that's a fact.'

Vernon raised his brows as he smiled ruefully. 'I am afraid your father is correct, Miss Temple. I cannot conceive why, for it has never made sense to me that ladies are expected to control their emotions at all times, but it is so. You may smile, but it is frowned upon to laugh. Or to voice your opinion too forcefully. Or, indeed, to show enthusiasm. It is the height of fashion to be *ennui*.'

'Well, that does not sound much fun to me,' Cordelia announced. 'I am not sure I wish to go to London after all, Pops. I can't think of anything worse than spending my time a-fretting and a-flustering in case I've broken some unwritten rule.'

Thea, following behind once more, found herself in full agreement.

'Well, well, we shall see,' Mr Temple said. 'There is time yet to change our plans. I must say...' he tipped his head towards Vernon '...I have wondered if it is wise to take my Cordelia to London. I didn't expect that news about Perceval. Shocking! I expect such lawlessness in America—it is very primitive in parts, with savages and such—but I never thought to hear of a British Prime Minister being assassinated and that's a fact. Is London safe?'

'It is as safe as anywhere, sir. No one can pre-empt a madman, such as the fellow who shot Perceval. It is quite unprecedented. Your daughter will be perfectly safe from gunmen, although I cannot promise the same safety against fortune hunters. I fear London society has its fair share of such men—as does Worcester, no doubt—and you will do well to be on your guard. You can never be too careful.'

Mr Temple slapped Vernon on the back. 'You can be sure I've got my wits about me, my lord. It'll take a real sly critter to put one over on Samuel Temple and that's a fact.'

They reached a point on the bank opposite the cathedral and Temple turned to Vernon and thrust out a large hand.

'Good to meet you, my lord. You too, Theo, m'lad. We get the ferry here, back across to the cathedral.' A white and green boat, the name *Betty* painted on her bow, was moored by a small wooden jetty. 'Shall we say dinner at six tomorrow? It'll only be us and our friend Mr Mannington if he is back in time, so no need for young Theo to get himself in a fuss about it.'

'Mannington?' Vernon flicked a warning glance at Thea and she realised she had gasped out loud. 'Is he from America, too?'

'No. We met in Liverpool the night our ship docked. It was a lucky coincidence...we both have interests in the cotton manufactories in the Manchester area, so we travelled there together and then, blow me down, when we came here it was only to find he lives not four miles away. He persuaded us to stay here for the summer rather than go to Brighton as I intended.' He nudged Vernon with his elbow. 'He's the cousin of a dook, y'know. One up on a viscount—eh, m'lord?'

Thea bit back a grin as astonishment flitted across Vernon's expression. No doubt he was unused to such familiarity.

'Oh, indubitably so,' he murmured. 'Although…much as I hate to correct you…a duke is, in fact, *three* up on a viscount.'

'Three up!' Mr Temple emitted a low whistle. 'Well, I'll be.' He nudged Vernon once again. 'I bet you wish you were related to a dook, eh, my lord?'

'I am perfectly content with my birthright, sir,' Vernon said.

A smile was by now tugging at the corner of his mouth. He bowed.

'It was a pleasure to meet you both,' he said, 'and I thank you for the invitation to dine tomorrow, which we gladly accept. I, for one, cannot wait to make the acquaintance of a real-life cousin of a duke.'

'Aw, shucks, now you're pulling my leg, my lord. You'll have to forgive me and my rough-and-ready ways. So long, young Theo, m'lad.' He waved to the ferryman, leaning on his oars. 'Come along, Delia, time we moved along.'

He raised his land in farewell and Cordelia smiled, first at Vernon and then at Thea.

'Goodbye,' she said. 'I shall look forward to seeing you both tomorrow.'

Vernon remounted Warrior and they enjoyed a canter, still following the course of the Severn. As it curved, beyond the city, an encampment came into view and Vernon brought Warrior to a halt.

'A gipsy camp, by the look of it,' he said. 'We shall turn back. It is better not to intrude.'

'I have always found the gipsies to be friendly enough,' Thea said, taking in the colourful wagons, the tents and the cooking fires. 'I had not thought you to be prejudiced against them, not after what you said to the constable in Harborne.'

'I am not prejudiced. They often camp on my land in Devon and work during the harvest or mend bits and pieces. They are friendly to a point, but they do not welcome outsiders and they are protective of their own.'

A tall man with dark, curly hair emerged from the nearest tent. He watched them expressionlessly, his hands relaxed by his sides.

'That camp is their home, albeit temporary,' Vernon continued, turning Warrior. 'I have no wish to stir resentment.'

She smiled at him. 'You are right.' She reined Star around, pointing her head back upstream. 'Come on. I'll race you.'

Vernon followed with a whoop. He seemed to hold Warrior back at first, but Thea—familiar with both animals— knew Star needed no preferential treatment. Vernon clearly reached the same conclusion and he gave the bay his head. They finished nose to nose, both riders slightly breathless, the horses blowing.

'We must walk them now and let the horses cool,' Thea said, stroking Star's damp neck.

The road back to the Crown was busy with carts and coaches and they were forced to ride in single file, precluding conversation, for which Thea was grateful. When they arrived back, Bickling came out to take charge of the horses.

'You go on up,' Vernon said to Thea. 'I must speak to Bickling. I will see you at dinner.'

* * *

That evening, Vernon raised a forkful of pigeon pie to his mouth and chewed, eyeing the woman sitting opposite him at the dining table in their private parlour. He still cringed at the memory of his ridiculous posturing after Cordelia had asked Thea to walk with her. It had been the only way he could think to divert her—he didn't believe Thea's disguise would pass such close scrutiny—and so he had put on an act. Thank goodness neither of the Temples had been fooled into thinking he was serious; he did have some pride.

'Miss Temple seems nice,' Thea remarked after a period of silence.

He had wondered how long it would take her to bring the conversation around to the American visitors. He still could not fathom her feelings. Was she angry with him? Or—and his heart twitched in hope at the thought—was she perhaps a little jealous at the attention he had paid to Cordelia Temple?

She was so easy to read in so many ways and yet when it came to her feelings for him she was a closed book. He felt…he groped for the right word. Off balance. That was it. An uncomfortable and unaccustomed feeling for him, especially where women were concerned. But then, his uncertainty about what she thought and felt was no greater than his uncertainty about what *he* truly thought and felt.

About her.

He did not deny he liked Thea. He liked her very much indeed. And the more time he spent in her company, the more he liked her. He looked forward to seeing her every day. But did his feelings run deeper than that? Yes, he wanted her physically, but was that desire partly driven by these extraordinary circumstances, and because he was honour bound to safeguard her virtue, even from himself… *especially* from himself? All he did know was it was getting harder to stick to his principles.

He had never before, he realised with a start, been such close friends with a woman he was not related to. And that thought led to another…what if she *were* a member of his family? The thought rattled him. He had no need to wed. His life was fulfilled as it was. Why look for complications?

He swallowed his food, conscious she was waiting for him to respond.

'You did not give the impression that you much cared for her company,' he said.

She pierced him with her hazel eyes, green specks glinting in the candlelight.

'It did not take two of us to act like lovelorn fools,' she snapped.

Vernon pondered that as he continued to eat. *Was* there a hint of jealousy there, or was this simply more of her scathing dismissal of the idle aristocracy? She did not appear to be waiting for his reply, attacking her food with more enthusiasm than he had yet seen.

'*Acting* being the pertinent word here,' he commented finally.

She raised her gaze to his.

'My dear Dotty…'

Her eyes flashed her anger. It did help, somewhat, if she was irritated with him and teasing came naturally…it was easier to tease her than to find himself resorting to charm. God knew where that might lead.

'You forget that I am not a viscount in need of a wife and family to continue my family name and to inherit entailed estates. I am still a bachelor for a reason… I have no need to wed.'

She swallowed her food. 'Very sensible. I should imagine rakish aristocrats do not make comfortable husbands.'

'You look for comfort in a husband?'

'I look for nothing. I look for no husband, as you well know.'

'But if you did look for one?' He couldn't help himself, even though this conversation could become treacherous. '*Comfort* would be your first consideration?'

Their gazes fused, the food forgotten.

'I think an *uncomfortable* husband would result in an unhappy life.'

'But what of passion? Desire? Did you not feel those emotions with…?' His voice trailed into silence.

Her jaw set. 'With Jasper? Mannington, I mean.' She sighed, her shoulders dropping, and used her knife to push her remaining food into a neat heap at the side of her plate. 'I felt… I don't know…happy, flattered, eager to set up home together. I suppose I must have thought myself in love with him, but—looking back—I wonder if I was more in love with the notion of being married and having a family than with the man himself.' A tight, bitter smile stretched her lips. 'I was very soon cured of that nonsense.' She put down her knife with a clatter. 'Quite what my marital intentions have to do with your flirtation with Miss Temple I fail to understand, but I warn you…do not raise false expectations as to your intentions merely because it suits your purpose.'

'She is no fool. I'll wager she knows enough of the world to understand that not every man who pays her some attention wishes to marry her and she has her father to protect her from rakes and fortune hunters.'

'And yet they are friends with J—Henry Mannington and I notice she hung on every word that left your mouth.'

Vernon shrugged. 'Can I help it if I have that effect on women?'

Thea flushed a deep red. 'Not every woman,' she said in her endearing, gruff little voice. 'You believe yourself to be irresistible, but you are not.'

'Am I not, Thea?'

Vernon stretched across the table and captured her hand,

holding just firmly enough to stop her tugging it free. It was tiny and warm and soft, the bones fragile, and his heart swelled with the urge to take her in his arms and kiss her senseless, to show her what real desire and passion was, to demonstrate what she was missing, what she had shut out of her life.

'Vernon…'

She pulled again at her hand, but he tightened his grip. A light blush crept from her neck to wash her cheeks. Without any conscious thought as to his actual intention, he stood up and rounded the table, tugging her to her feet. He reached for her other hand and stroked her knuckles with his thumbs. Her lids lowered to shield her gaze, but he saw the tremble of her lip. Surely he could not be mistaken? She was not unaffected. She no longer tried to pull free, but her posture was stiff. Tense.

What would I give to know exactly what she is thinking? A king's ransom, that's what.

He released one hand and nudged her chin up so her face tilted to meet his gaze. Her eyes were wide—questioning and, yes, uncertain. Then they darkened as her pupils dilated, her shoulders slumped and he felt the warmth of her breath as it feathered across his cheek and heard her whispered gasp as it escaped her lips. A wave of desire sent the blood powering to his groin and he felt the heavy weight of arousal. He pulled her close to his chest, folding his arms around her. She was so tiny. Fragile. And yet she was strong, too, in her spirit and her resolve. The desire to protect, and to avenge, flowed through him and he breathed a deep sigh before letting her go, dropping his arms to his sides.

He had proved to himself she was not immune to him, but he felt an utter bastard, particularly because he still wasn't sure these feelings she aroused in him were not just as a result of them being thrown together in this unnatural way.

But Thea did not step away when he released her. Instead, she reached up and slipped one hand behind his neck, pressing the length of her body to his. Her eyes asked a different question now, no longer uncertain but assured as she went on tiptoes and her mouth sought his.

Chapter Seventeen

Her lips were warm and sweet and open to his questing tongue. With a deep groan, Vernon gathered Thea to him, his exploring hands registering the strangeness of the rough cloth of her jacket and the peculiar rigidity of her back and sides due to the bindings under her shirt. His hands moved lower and he cupped her softly rounded cheeks, lifting to pull her hard against him. He thrust aside the warnings that screamed through his mind as he kissed her and allowed his hands to roam. Her fingers combed through his hair, caressing his skull. He should stop, but...

He did not want to. He wanted more. He wanted her.

He cradled her face in his hands, her cheeks silky to his touch as he devoured her sweetness. He speared his fingers through her soft curls, scattering butterfly kisses over her cheeks, her brows, her eyelids. He feathered kisses along the angle of her jaw and slid his lips to her ear, sweeping his tongue around the delicate shell, then caught her lobe between his teeth and tugged gently, nibbling. She moaned, pushing her hands beneath his jacket and around his back, caressing as she pressed closer.

Time stood still. Nothing else existed. Only Thea, in his arms, her soft lips open to him and her body nestling into his. His heart felt as though it cracked open, welcoming her in to fill a gap he had not known existed until now, but a gap that had always been there. And it was Thea-shaped. She fitted perfectly. She made him whole.

It was Thea who ended that kiss, who stepped back, bringing her hands between them, resting them on his chest. Reluctantly, he released her, shoving his fingers through his hair.

'Someone might come in.' She pressed her fingers to her mouth, her eyes huge and luminous, her cheeks rosy. She uttered a strangled-sounding laugh. 'That would take a bit of explaining.'

Vernon returned to his chair and stood behind it, watching her closely and, once again, uncertain of which path to take. He was cautious of forging ahead, as he'd like to. After her experience with Mannington, her trust would be slowly gained. It could not be demanded.

'Should I apologise?' he asked.

'No!' Startled. Vehement. 'Why should you apologise? *I* kissed *you*.' She sighed and dropped down on her chair, propping her elbows on the table and dropping her head into her hands. 'Shameful as that must seem to you.'

Vernon gripped the back rail of the chair. 'Shameful? Why should I think it shameful?'

She huffed a bitter laugh. 'I might not be part of your world, Vernon, but I do know that my behaviour would be viewed as scandalous. And in my world, too, come to that.'

She avoided his gaze. 'Whereas your behaviour…you would no doubt receive a pat on the back from your peers and an indulgent shrug of the shoulders from your womenfolk. Men are permitted indulgences such as stealing a kiss when the opportunity presents. A woman behaving in such a way is to be scorned.'

'Then it is fortunate that no one other than you and I were witness to it.' Vernon sat down again, feeling curiously deflated. Did it mean nothing more to her than a stolen kiss? 'After all, what is a kiss between friends?'

Her eyes shuttered. 'Indeed.' Her tone was careless. 'It was merely a…a *trifling experiment* between friends.'

Vernon cursed himself for his clumsiness, knowing he had hurt her feelings. Never had he felt more out of his depth with a woman as he floundered for the right words.

'Thea. I—'

Thea interrupted. 'We need to discuss tomorrow before we go upstairs.'

Did his failure to find the right words matter? Maybe this was for the best—for now. If they spoke now of other matters, it might help dispel the awkward aftermath of that kiss and they might return to their former friendship until they found out what had happened to Daniel. And when they did…after they did…then, perhaps, they might think about what the future might hold.

'I cannot dine with the Temples tomorrow,' Thea said. 'Not if Mannington might be present.'

'I agree. Meeting Mannington in passing on the street is quite different to sitting with him at a dining table. He could not fail to recognise you, especially as you would not be wearing a cap. I shall go alone and tell the Temples you are unwell.' He half-smiled at her, attempting to tease. 'I shall tell them I caught you at the brandy.'

'That,' said Thea, stiffly, as she shoved back her chair and stood up, 'is unnecessary. There is no need to pile lie upon lie. Simply informing them that I am unwell is sufficient.'

Vernon rounded the table. He skimmed her curls back from her face. 'I was teasing, Thea.'

She stared up at him, her eyes searching his. 'I know. And I know you are trying to make this better, to make it easier for me. But…'

'But it is hard for you. Take courage, though. Mannington will be back tomorrow.'

Thea clutched Vernon's sleeve. 'You must promise to tell me *every*thing. Good or bad.' She shook his arm. '*Please.* I need to know you will not try to protect my feelings.'

Vernon cupped her cheek. 'I promise.' It was not enough. He needed to give her the reassurance she craved, to shield her as far as possible from the fear that must gnaw at her day and night. 'I promise I will not conceal *anything* I discover.' He raised his brows slightly and smiled into her eyes. 'We are partners, are we not, you and I? Who else can I discuss strategy with?'

She tipped her head, pressing her cheek into his palm, like a kitten seeking a caress.

'Thank you,' she whispered, and for a moment he was gliding, effortlessly, across the waters that so often in the past few days appeared likely to swamp him.

'I must go,' she whispered. 'Goodnight, Vernon. I hope you sleep well.'

Vernon reached the door before her, preparing to open it. Thea halted, her brows raised pointedly, and he released the handle again and stepped aside.

'I forgot,' he said. 'Again. I keep forgetting, but how I wish…'

He shook his head, knowing that to speak his wishes—that he could treat her as a lady—was not wise. Not now. He gestured for her to open the door.

'Goodnight, Thea,' he whispered as she passed him by. 'Sweet dreams.'

The following day was an utter waste of time from Thea's perspective. In keeping with the tale that she was ill, she remained in her bedchamber all day, with just her thoughts for company. And if she wasn't fretting about Daniel, she was fretting about that kiss…about how *she* had kissed *him*. She had never before behaved so shamefully.

But he started it.

He'd hauled her from her chair and studied her face with such intent, his green eyes glinting in the candlelight and his lips…his kiss…

He kissed me as though he meant *it.*

She hugged that knowledge close. And—from time to time—she allowed herself to glory in the memory of the most wonderful moment in her life so far. That kiss had lit a slow-burning fuse deep down inside her that, no matter how she tried to douse it, simply refused to be extinguished.

Apart from a couple of brief visits from Vernon—when she strove to act as though that kiss had never happened— she had not seen him. He was, he assured her, pursuing his acquaintance with the Temples and had sent Bickling to tour the numerous public houses in Worcester to enquire after Daniel. He promised to call in on her before he went down to dine and Thea found herself pacing the floor from five o'clock, waiting for his visit.

Finally, there was a tap at the door. She flew across the floor, hauled the door open and grabbed Vernon's arm, dragging him into the room.

'My dear Dotty,' he drawled, removing her hand from his sleeve and tugging at the cuff to smooth out the wrinkles. 'I beg you will refrain from manhandling my second-best coat in such a very uncouth manner.'

Thea blinked and stepped back, taking in his appearance. He looked…magnificent. Utterly gorgeous. Handsome, sexy and every inch the wealthy aristocrat he was. And all for the benefit of Cordelia Temple…

Bickling had delivered these clothes yesterday, but Vernon had not thought Thea worth dressing up for last night. Her heart sank, remembering his dismissal of that kiss.

'And I have to say,' he went on as he strolled over to the

window and peered into the street outside, 'in all my years I cannot recall ever being hauled into a lady's bedchamber in quite such a…shall we say…*enthusiastic* manner.'

She was too dazzled by his appearance to take much notice of his teasing. She had thought him resplendent when he first arrived at Stourwell Court, but *this*…

He wore an olive-green tailcoat over a cream waistcoat glittering with gold embroidery and cream pantaloons and at his throat a stunning emerald pin nestled in his beautifully tied neckcloth. She gulped and turned to fiddle with the comb on her dressing table. This was not the Vernon she knew. This was Lord Vernon Beauchamp and she felt… shy. How should she behave? Should she have curtsied? She certainly should not have dragged him into her room as she did.

Vernon appeared not to notice her turmoil as he continued to watch the street outside.

'I say enthusiastic,' he continued, musingly, 'but it could, I think, even be described as *desperate*.'

He turned to look at her, a mischievous grin on his face, which vanished the instant he caught sight of her. 'Thea?' He was by her side in two strides, lightly cupping her shoulders. 'What is it?'

Thea gulped. Reminded herself this was still Vernon. 'You look…splendid.'

Vernon tipped his head to one side, frowning. 'You sound different. Where is my spiky little kitten?'

Kitten? Is that how he thinks of me? As a ball of fluff to amuse and entertain him? A joke? I bet he wouldn't refer to Cordelia Temple as a kitten.

But then what did that kiss mean?

He is a man, a lord who no doubt has enjoyed mistresses galore. What does a kiss mean to him? Nothing!

'You took me by surprise. Your clothes make you look so different. Almost a stranger.'

Vernon tweaked a curl above her ear. 'I am no stranger, Dotty. I am still me.'

His eyes crinkled...an almost-smile that had Thea grinding her teeth. Why did she always feel so...so...*fluttery* around him? And how was he *always* so self-assured? She had never been a woman to simper and flirt and yet, with him, she had to constantly control her urge to do exactly that. And, worse, she worried that the search for Daniel was almost being overshadowed by her growing fascination with Vernon.

She must keep her focus on Daniel, even though it was increasingly hard to keep her hopes alive.

She perched on the edge of the bed, thrusting down that tangle of guilt and desire, hope and dread. Emotions could not help; they could only confuse and lead her astray. Weak, female emotions must be controlled...particularly this ridiculous infatuation for Vernon. She could not bear to put her trust in another man only to be let down again. Once more, she heard Bickling's amused declaration that she was not to his lordship's usual taste.

'Tell me about your day,' she said.

Vernon, she noticed, did not sit on the bed, but chose the wooden chair by the dressing table. He swung it around to face her and sat, stretching his long legs out, crossing them at the ankle, and folding his arms across his wide chest—supremely confident, relaxed, in charge. And very...*deliciously*...masculine.

Thea contained her inner *hmph* and averted her gaze.

'Actually, I have little to report. I have made myself indispensable to Miss Temple by escorting her to the shops this morning, whilst her father attended business meetings, so she and I are fast becoming friends.'

The pain that pierced Thea's heart could be borne. She had no choice.

'This afternoon Bickling and I visited more of the public houses in the city,' Vernon continued, 'but we found no one who recalled either Daniel Markham or Charles Leyton.' He sat up, leaning forward, his elbows on his knees. 'I worry you were right the other day.' All trace of teasing had vanished and Thea could not doubt the genuine concern on his face. 'It is as you said: Birmingham is the last place where Daniel was definitely seen. Even though we stopped and asked at every inn we passed, we have found no one who remembers him.' He leapt to his feet and paced the room. 'He must have gone *somewhere* when he left there. Where did he go? Who did he see? Did he ever meet Mannington face to face?'

Thea rubbed her upper arms as she listened to his questions. Her heart swelled as she watched him pace, not with awe this time but with gratitude. How much she owed this man. Without him, she would never have dared to set out on this mission. Although they had found no trace of Daniel, they were close to uncovering the truth. She could feel it. Mannington—shivers of loathing chased up and down her spine at the mere thought of the man—was the key to finding Daniel, of that she was convinced. And without Vernon she would never know the truth because she would never have the courage to confront the man who had jilted her and defrauded her family.

'I must go.'

Vernon stood and Thea followed suit. Vernon came to her and touched her shoulder, fleetingly. Their gazes fused, and Thea felt a lurching tug deep inside.

'I must not be late.' Again he touched her, this time one finger beneath her chin. Again, it was fleeting. 'I have asked Horwell to send up some food on a tray for you.'

Thea forced a smile, dreading the solitary evening ahead of her.

'Please do not be tempted to leave this room,' he said

softly, taking her hand. 'I know you are bored, but it will only be for a few more days.'

He pressed warm lips to the back of her hand, sending delightful tingles chasing across her skin.

'Goodnight, sweet Dotty. I shall tell you all in the morning.'

And he was gone, leaving the scent of his cologne lingering in the air and a dull ache in her heart.

Chapter Eighteen

Vernon straightened his sleeves and smoothed his lapels as he waited in the private parlour rented by the Temples for the duration of their stay in Worcester. It was twice the size of the parlour Vernon and Thea had at their disposal, but Vernon preferred the cosiness and the intimacy of their smaller room. The table, at one end of the room, was set for five—one place at the head and two on either side—and a sofa and two upholstered chairs were arranged around the unlit fireplace at the opposite end of the room.

Vernon thought of Thea, all alone in her bedchamber. He would far rather eat his meal in her company than with the Temples and Mannington, even though the point of this was to gain an introduction to the man. Poor Thea, stuck in her bedchamber all day and still uncomplaining, although she was clearly bored. And still as enigmatic as ever. From their very first meeting that morning she had exhibited not one hint of awkwardness after that kiss last night. It was as though nothing had happened…as though that kiss was truly, as she had claimed, a trifling experiment. His own inconsistency irritated him. Her behaviour was precisely what he had hoped for—for them to return to their former easy camaraderie.

Why, then, did he feel so…*rejected*?

The sound of the door opening jolted him from his thoughts. Cordelia Temple wafted into the room on a cloud of expensive perfume and a swish of silk skirts.

She crossed the room, holding out her hand with a smile.

'Good evening, Lord Boyton. How nice to see you again. I am delighted you could join us.'

Vernon took her hand and bowed over it. As he did so the door opened and Horwell entered.

'Mr Henry Mannington has arrived, Miss Temple.'

He stood aside and Henry Mannington strolled in, then stopped short as he caught sight of Vernon with Cordelia. Vernon deliberately lingered over Cordelia's hand, pressing his lips to it as he gauged Mannington's reaction from under his brows.

He is good.

Other than his abrupt halt, not a hint of anger marred Mannington's expression. Vernon straightened, releasing Cordelia's hand. There was no need for Mannington to suspect he was purposely needling him. Subtle and sly, those were to be Vernon's watchwords. He slammed the lid on his desire to throttle the man for what he had done to Thea and her family. If ever there was a time for cool and calculated detachment, this was it.

'Mr Mannington.' Cordelia turned to the newcomer with a radiant smile. 'Such a delight to see you again. Was your business trip a success?'

'Good evening, Miss Temple, and indeed it was. I have every hope this particular deal will prove a huge success. Better, indeed, than I had originally hoped.'

He took her hand, as Vernon had done, and he too bowed over it and pressed his lips firmly to the back, flicking a sideways glance at Vernon as he did so.

Vernon recognised the possessiveness of the gesture and the glance. The man was marking his territory.

We shall see about that.

A light blush had coloured Cordelia's cheeks, confirming she was not immune to Mannington. Vernon would have to work hard to gain her trust before she might believe any warning he might give her about him, particularly as her father clearly trusted him. This task might prove more delicate than Vernon had anticipated. He must bide his time, watch the three of them together, and exploit any chink he could find in their relationship.

'Mr Mannington, may I introduce Lord Boyton?'

Vernon, standing in what he knew was an arrogant pose, thrust out his hand. 'Mannington,' he said.

If he hadn't been watching Mannington very closely, he might not have seen the caution that flashed across his expression, could easily have missed the minute hunch of his shoulders that, in an animal, would be the slink of a lesser male before the leader of the pack. Vernon knew he must be on his guard—such a man, feeling the threat, would think nothing of attacking from behind.

'My lord,' Mannington said. He bowed his head, briefly, and shook Vernon's proffered hand. 'It is always a pleasure to meet newcomers to the area.'

If Vernon had not caught Mannington's first, instinctive reaction, he would have been completely fooled by the man's current open expression, pleasant smile and firm handshake. No wonder Thea's family had been taken in by this scoundrel... He trapped that thought before it could develop further. He must take care not to dwell on such thoughts lest Mannington was watching him as closely as Vernon was studying Mannington. Let him believe that Vernon's only interest in him was as a rival for Cordelia. That was a simple conflict compared to the truth.

'His lordship is a guest here at the Crown, together with his nephew,' Cordelia continued. 'Papa and I made their acquaintance yesterday. Speaking of Theo...' Cordelia tilted her head to one side, smiling at Vernon '...where is he, my lord? I do hope you did not forbid him to attend? Do you know, Mr Mannington, Lord Boyton was quite horrified at the idea of a fifteen-year-old youth joining us to dine?'

'Miss Temple, I protest. You do me a gross disservice. Alas, Theo is unable to join us because he is unwell. He asked me to convey his apologies.'

'What?' Mr Temple had joined them. 'Young Theo not well? Does he need a doctor? Henry, my boy, you must know of a decent man hereabouts. Give me his name and I'll send for him immediately to attend the lad.' A heavy hand landed on Vernon's shoulder. 'Can't be too careful with matters of health, m'lord, and that's a fact.'

Mannington's gaze darted between Temple and Vernon, but the only indicator of his feelings was the slightest twitch of his left eye. 'I am certain his lordship will not hesitate to ask for a recommendation should his nephew require medical attention.'

The weight of Temple's hand was uncomfortable—made him feel trapped...controlled, somehow—and Vernon sidestepped, causing it to slip from his shoulder. Not wishing to offend the man, he then placed his left hand between the American's shoulder blades.

'I am grateful for your concern, sir,' he said, 'but Theo has no need of a physician. Rather...and I trust you will think none the worse of him after this confession, Miss Temple...he is in sore need of a darkened room and bed rest. His ills are entirely self-inflicted.'

Temple guffawed. 'The downfall of many a youth. I trust you will curb any excessive tendency in that direction, m'lord...the demon alcohol can all too easily become a master instead of a servant and that's a fact.'

'It can indeed,' Vernon murmured, biting back a smile

as he imagined Thea's reaction were she privy to this conversation.

The door opened to admit a maid carrying a soup tureen.

'The food's here; time we sat,' Temple said, heading for the chair at the head of the table. 'My belly feels like my throat's been cut.'

Vernon pulled out a chair for Cordelia, leaving a vacant seat between her and her father. 'Miss Temple?'

'Thank you, kind sir.'

She sat in the proffered seat and, from the corner of his eye, Vernon saw Mannington stalk behind his back to commandeer that vacant chair. Vernon allowed himself a quiet smirk of satisfaction. The seating arrangements suited him perfectly: sitting opposite the pair of them, on Temple's right-hand side, would mean he could watch all three with ease.

'That's it, sit where you will, gents,' Temple boomed. 'No formality at my table and that's a fact. None of that *only talk to your neighbour* here, no matter how highfalutin' our guests might be.'

Vernon could not hold back his grin at that. He leaned down to murmur into Cordelia's ear.

'Highfaluting?'

On the far side of Cordelia, he could see Mannington straining to hear what he said. Taking the opportunity to stir the other man's temper, he lowered his voice to a whisper.

'I cannot say I have *ever* had the pleasure of being described as highfaluting before. What, precisely, does it mean? Is it *exceedingly* unflattering?'

Cordelia gurgled with laughter. 'It means…well, I guess it is a little unflattering. Pops! You must not insult his lordship with unfamiliar American slang.'

'Rubbish! His lordship won't take offence at some good-natured joshing, will you, m'lord?'

Cordelia smiled over her shoulder at Vernon. 'It kind

of means high-flown, grandiose. I do hope you are not offended.'

'Of course I am not.'

He rounded the table and took his own seat.

Dishes were set in the centre of the table and wine poured, and the servants left the room. Mannington's plan became clear—by sitting next to Cordelia he could serve food to her plate and speak quietly in her ear as he did so without risk of censure, for who would call him on his manners were he merely asking her what morsels she might prefer?

The meal progressed. Temple held forth on matters of business and Vernon took little part in the conversation, but was surprised at the extent to which Cordelia joined in. She appeared knowledgeable about all her father's many interests, from their cotton plantation in Georgia to their coal mines in Pennsylvania. It appeared, however, that father and daughter lived much of the time in Washington.

'For that is where the power is, m'lord,' Temple said. 'And that is where I can lobby on matters that will benefit me. It is not like here, where all the power is in the hands of the landowners and very little in the hands of manufacturers who employ the people and make goods to export to bring money into the country. You mark my words...' he waved a fork '...change will come here, too.'

'Wealth will always count,' Vernon said.

'That is true,' Mannington said, his long fingers playing with his wine glass. 'But the balance of wealth—and therefore influence—will gradually shift away from the landed gentry and towards those who, as our host has said, actually produce goods.'

Vernon might suspect he was right, but could not resist challenging him.

'What about food? People will always need to eat.'

'I do not deny it...' Mannington tore his bread roll in

half and buttered it '…but the war with France will not go on indefinitely and grain will be imported once more. Where there is competition the price will drop. That is a basic tenet of business.'

Vernon quashed his irritation at the implication that he knew nothing of business. It fitted the part he played to be thought an idle aristocrat by these people, even though he hated Thea to think of him as such. And how did she always creep into his thoughts even when she was not present?

He forced a shrug of nonchalance, peering down his nose at Mannington. 'The ruling classes will always be just that,' he said in his most condescending voice. 'I do not expect such as you to understand quite how society and government work together for the common good.'

The other man's jaw tightened. Both Vernon and Mannington had ceased eating, and Temple's gaze darted from one to the other, consternation writ large upon his face.

'*Henry,*' he said, 'is the cousin of a *dook*, my lord. I'm sure we told you that when we met yesterday.'

'A duke, you say?' Vernon held Mannington's gaze as he sipped his wine.

How Leo would relish slapping down the presumption of this scoundrel. And how I would love to see the two come face to face.

He permitted himself an arrogant smile. 'It must have slipped my mind. And which duke might that be?'

'The Duke of Cheriton.'

Not by a flicker did Mannington reveal the tension he must be feeling. After all, for all he knew, Vernon and the Duke of Cheriton might be the closest of friends.

'Ah, yes.' Vernon sipped again at his wine, his eyes never leaving Mannington's face. 'Cheriton. A cousin, you say? Close, are you?'

The muscles around Mannington's eyes tightened imperceptibly. 'Close enough, although we do not, of course, move in the same circles. I have a living to earn. Leo…his Grace…does not.'

'You do not consider running huge estates and being responsible for vast numbers of employees and tenants to be work?'

'No. Managers, agents and bailiffs take care of most of that,' Mannington said carelessly. 'As is no doubt the same in your case, Boyton.'

Vernon shrugged again. 'As you say. I do not concern myself with the day-to-day running of my estates. However, neither do I pretend to move in such exalted circles as Cheriton. I have little interest in politics, for instance.'

'But you are able to sit in the Lords?' Temple interjected. 'You do hold some influence there?'

Vernon turned his gaze on the American. This remark, together with his earlier comment on living in Washington, in order to be close to the men who ran the country, provided him with the perfect lever to unsettle Mannington and keep Temple—and hence his daughter—on his side. Viscount Boyton, as a peer, would indeed be eligible to sit in the Lords even though Lord Vernon Beauchamp, with merely a courtesy title, could not.

He shrugged. 'Oh, I can wield influence if I choose. I have yet, however, to discover a cause about which I am passionate.' He smiled across the table at Cordelia. 'Becoming too embroiled in worthy causes does tend to distract one from the more…shall we say, *pleasurable* aspects of London life.' He raised a brow. 'And Worcestershire life, come to that.'

Cordelia laughed. 'Would you care to expound on that statement, sir?'

He allowed one corner of his mouth to quirk up. 'Expound in what way, Miss Temple?'

Out of the corner of his eye he was aware of Mannington's displeasure. He had straightened in his seat and his chin jutted, although his expression remained one of polite interest. Temple, on the contrary, looked smug.

'I should be interested to hear what aspects of life in London you find the most enjoyable, sir. As Papa said yesterday, we have the intention of visiting London in September to sample its delights.'

'In that case, you have come to the right man,' Vernon said. He switched his gaze to Mannington. 'I take it *you* are not familiar with London society, Mannington?'

'I choose not to waste my time on such frivolity,' he replied. 'But I might make an exception in the autumn…the attractions of the capital become more obvious by the day.'

'It will be pleasant to have at least one acquaintance in London this fall,' Cordelia said, 'and, if you should choose to go, too, Mr Mannington, that will be even better. Two acquaintances in the whole of the city, Pops. We shall be spoilt for choice.'

'You may rest assured I shall do all in my power to ensure you enjoy your stay,' Vernon said. 'You may only claim two acquaintances. *I* can lay claim to many more and I shall be honoured to introduce you to anyone you choose.'

'Splendid, splendid.' Temple rubbed his palms together with an unpleasant rasping noise. 'Now, are we all finished? I hope you'll not object to drinking your brandy with Delia present, my lord? I know it isn't customary, but we don't stand on ceremony here.'

Vernon did object, as it happened, but didn't say so. He had been hoping to engage Mannington in a more frank conversation than was possible with Cordelia in the room. But his time would come. He could be patient.

Thea's face floated into his mind, her troubled eyes and her repressed fears pricking his conscience. But not too patient, he promised himself. They needed to find out what had happened to her brother as soon as possible.

As Temple busied himself at a sideboard with a decanter

and glasses, Mannington assisted Cordelia from her chair and proffered his arm, which she accepted with a smile. Mannington led her from the table towards the sofa, leaning in to whisper in her ear as he did so. Vernon could not hear what Mannington said, but the flush at the nape of Cordelia's neck suggested his comment was not one that would have been uttered within her father's hearing.

He watched closely, but Cordelia gave no hint that she did not welcome Mannington's attention, neither drawing away nor slapping him down with words. Vernon prayed she had not already developed a *tendre* for the man. Her behaviour at dinner did not suggest her feelings were engaged, but she clearly enjoyed Mannington's company and her behaviour around him was both relaxed and familiar, although that could be due to her upbringing. Vernon was accustomed to society events where strict formality was observed. Woe betide any lady who behaved familiarly with a man who was not a relative. From what he had observed of Samuel Temple and his daughter, American society seemed very different. Perhaps it stemmed from being in business.

And that thought led inexorably and inevitably back to Thea. What was she doing? No doubt she would be fretting about tonight, wondering what he might discover. He briefly entertained the notion of knocking on her door upon his return…of going into her room…sitting on her bed and telling her about the evening's conversation. Then, savagely, he rejected that image. Even the thought of being in her bedchamber with her again rattled him. If he did go in, could he resist trying to seduce her? She was an innocent, for God's sake, and she had been badly hurt in the past. He could not risk hurting her again, not until he knew for certain what he wanted from her. If it was merely carnal… a false craving due to their unnatural proximity over the past few days…then he must resist his urges.

'My lord?'

He came back to the present with a start. 'I do apologise,' he said, smoothly. 'I was wondering how my nephew fares and whether his head will still be sore in the morning.'

Temple chortled. 'Never you mind about young Theo. He'll learn, same as the rest of us had to as youngsters. Now, m'lord, try this.' He thrust a glass of amber liquid into Vernon's hand. 'That is a top brandy and that's a fact. I'll wager you've not tasted such a fine one in a long, long time.'

Sceptical of the other man's ability to detect a fine brandy, Vernon sipped. His brows rose.

'That, sir, is a wager I shall not accept. It is a very fine brandy indeed. What is its provenance?'

Temple winked. 'Ask me no questions, I shall tell you no lie, m'lord. Suffice it to say Henry here had a hand in supplying it.'

Vernon knew what that meant—his estate was in the county of Devonshire and many people, at all levels of society, turned a blind eye to smuggling.

'Now, Samuel, don't you go revealing all of my secrets,' Mannington said, from his place on the sofa, next to Cordelia.

His tone was jovial, but there was an edge of steel to it. Vernon took his place on a nearby chair and Temple stood by the fireplace, hands clasped behind his back as he rocked to and fro on the balls of his feet, spouting forth once again about his business.

Again, the seating arrangement suited Vernon even though the triumphal glint in Mannington's eye set his teeth on edge. The man was laying claim to Cordelia and, although Vernon had no interest in her in a romantic sense, he knew himself well enough to recognise his metaphorical hackles rising at the other man's challenge—his mind stilling and crouching even as his body remained outwardly relaxed. He would bide his time, however, and work on gaining Cordelia's trust and, in the meantime, he would circle and he would watch.

His time would come.

Later, after saying goodnight, he trod up the stairs, waging an inner battle with himself. He should not disturb Thea…he should not put himself in the way of more temptation…but…what if she was lying awake…unable to sleep…worrying about Daniel…wondering if Mannington had showed up, and if Vernon had discovered anything.

He hesitated outside her door. Ridiculously, his heart beat a little faster in his chest merely at the thought of seeing her. How had he come to this? A man of such experience, reduced to the behaviour of a lovesick youth by a little curly-headed kitten of a woman who could change into a tiger before his eyes.

His thoughts strayed to Leo and his recent marriage to a woman he had met, quite by chance, on a country lane. A woman not of their world—the daughter of mésalliance between a duke's granddaughter and a silversmith's son— but a woman who had changed Leo's life beyond recognition and for the better, who had brought joy and laughter into his world of duty and distrust. Leo had sworn never to marry again: he had his heir and his spare and a beautiful daughter. But his vow could not withstand love. His heart—once he had allowed himself to listen to it—had overruled all his rational objections.

Vernon bowed his head, resting his forehead against the wooden door. Is that what was happening? *Was* it love he felt for Thea? It was different to anything he had ever felt for any other woman. More than lust. But love?

He lifted his head. Stared at the knots in the door, traced the grain with his eyes.

How can I know? How can I be sure?

Chapter Nineteen

At last!

Thea would know Vernon's footsteps anywhere. She listened to him walk along the landing and heard him pause outside her door. Her pulse quickened. He had said he would see her in the morning, but she had prayed he would change his mind. Then her heart sank at the unmistakable sound of him walking away. She gave herself no time for second thoughts. She darted to her bedchamber door and wrenched it open.

'Vernon!'

He pivoted on his heel to face her.

'Come in. Tell me what happened.'

His jaw set…he looked anything but pleased to see her and pain speared her heart. She had wrapped a sheet around her shoulders as she had no shawl with her and now she pulled it tight around her, defensively. And why would he be pleased to see her, when he had spent the past few hours in the company of Cordelia Temple, dressed in fancy dresses and wearing fine jewels? Had he fallen under Cordelia's spell? Thea clenched her jaw. Not for the world would she reveal even the tiniest hint of her jealousy, but how she wished she was wearing her gown—the bag Bickling had brought from Stourwell Court had contained her two favourite gowns and her pearl necklace and matching ear drops. She could not take such a risk however. She had stowed the bag beneath her bed, to put temptation out of her sight.

Vernon prowled slowly back along the passage, his gazed travelling from her head—and she knew her hair must be dishevelled after she had speared her fingers through it countless times that evening—to her toes, bare on the wooden floor.

'Get back inside,' he growled as he neared her, his frown thunderous. 'What if anyone was to see you dressed like that? Or should I say, undressed?'

Thea backed inside her bedchamber, tugging the sheet closer still to cover her shift, which barely reached her knees, feeling suddenly vulnerable, the intent in his hooded gaze sending shivers over her skin.

He banged the door behind him, then remained still, glowering at her, the muscles either side of his jaw bunched.

'Are you *trying* to get discovered?'

Thea hunched her shoulder as she turned away. 'Of course I am not. There was no one there to see me.'

She went to sit on the bed and then changed her mind. She did not want him looming above her, not when he was in this sort of mood.

'What did you discover?'

'If you mean about Daniel, nothing.'

'Nothing? But—'

'And what did you expect? Did you imagine I would question Mannington over the soup? *And when was it you last saw Daniel Markham?*'

'No.' Thea shook her head, disappointment flooding her. How foolish. Of course he could not baldly ask Mannington about Daniel. 'I did not think. I am sorry, I was just... I built my hopes up.'

Vernon paced across the room and twitched the curtain aside to peer out into the night.

'I need to gain Cordelia's trust,' he said, his back still to Thea. 'Mannington was unhappy to see me there and he made his prior claim to her very clear.'

'What did he say?'

Vernon faced her, a puzzled smile on his face. 'He did not have to *say* anything, Thea. His behaviour was enough. He is wary of me and that is good. I hope Cordelia—and she is an intelligent woman—will see him with different eyes now I am on the scene. If she does not, however, then I shall have to tell her some of what I know about him.'

'But—'

'Do not worry. I shall not expose you. I shall tell her in more general terms. Mannington is already talking of a lucrative business deal and casting his lure to entice Temple to invest. And I fear my presence might force his hand over Cordelia. If we do not find some clue about Daniel very soon, I think I shall have to send Bickling to retrace our journey from Birmingham to see if he can discover something we missed.'

He paced into the centre of the room, pausing at the foot of the bed.

'I have arranged to take Cordelia for a drive tomorrow afternoon, whilst her father is out on business. I suspect Mannington will also show up—on horseback, probably. He will be on his way home from somewhere and will insist on accompanying us, out of concern for Cordelia's reputation.' Vernon laughed, but there was little mirth in the sound. 'Although her father appears to suffer no qualms about allowing me to drive her around the countryside unchaperoned.'

Mr Temple might have no qualms, but Thea found herself hoping Mannington *would* show up, as Vernon predicted. Her jealousy battled to break free. Hearing the familiar way in which Vernon called the heiress Cordelia burned in Thea's chest and, before she knew what she was doing, she was standing in front of Vernon, gazing up at him. Would he kiss her again? Give her some sign that she meant more to him than just a funny little kitten to amuse himself with?

His eyes darkened and he swayed towards her. Her lids drifted shut and she tilted her face to his. She heard a groan and peeped through her lashes. His gaze was still fixed upon her face but then, as she watched, every plane of his face hardened and, taking her by the shoulders, he set her aside and strode past her to the door.

'Go to bed,' he said in a harsh voice. 'I shall see you in the morning.'

The following afternoon Cordelia Temple, charmingly dressed, with a white lace parasol over her shoulder, joined Vernon as he waited patiently by his curricle for her to appear.

'Good afternoon, Lord Boyton.'

'Miss Temple.' Vernon bowed. 'How very charming you look today. However...' He glanced at the sky. It was still blue, with fluffy white clouds, but from his bedchamber window he had glimpsed black clouds massing in the west. 'I fear you might have more need of an umbrella than a parasol. We shall be wise not to venture too far today.'

'I am thankful for any opportunity to pass the time whilst my father is occupied, Lord Boyton,' Cordelia said. She lowered her voice. 'Even if I do suspect your main purpose was to rile our mutual friend, Mr Mannington. Who, I must tell you, is now *especially* displeased at being thwarted by Pops.'

The laughter in her eyes belied the censure in her words. Vernon handed her up into his curricle and—aware that Henry Mannington stood nearby talking to Samuel Temple—he brushed the back of her gloved hand with his lips before releasing it, conscious of Mannington's glare boring into him. He had ridden into Worcester, as Vernon had predicted, in time to accompany them on their drive. Samuel Temple, though, had forestalled him—begging to discuss the 'unmissable' business deal Mannington had spoken of last night.

A slight movement from above caught Vernon's eye. A curtain twitched at an upstairs window and his heart sank as he caught a glimpse of Thea's red curls as she turned away, her hand to her mouth. She had made no secret of her contempt for the game of flirtation he played with Cordelia and, despite his reassurance it *was* merely a game, relations between the two of them had been strained when they met over the breakfast table that morning.

He tried to push Thea from his thoughts. He must concentrate on Cordelia.

'And what about *your* feelings, Miss Temple? Are you sad that your faithful swain will not accompany us?'

'Oh, I shall see plenty of Mr Mannington in the next two days, my lord. He is throwing a house party at Crackthorpe Manor from tomorrow and, not only are Pops and I invited, we are to be guests of honour and are to be introduced to more of his business associates. Pops is thrilled at the opportunity to cultivate more useful contacts over here.'

A bad feeling was forming in Vernon's stomach. He liked the Temples and he did not want to see either of them hurt, but he was not yet in a position to confront Mannington or to confide his distrust of the man in the Temples. He could furnish no proof and he still had no clue what had happened to Daniel. For now all he could do was gain Cordelia's trust in the hope she would believe him when he warned her against Mannington.

He was aware that both Samuel Temple and Mannington were now behind him and within earshot.

'Miss Temple, I am distraught,' he protested, pressing

his left hand to his chest. 'How shall I survive without your presence for even one day?'

'No need for you to be left out, m'lord.' Temple slapped Vernon on the back as he spoke. 'I'm sure you can squeeze one more guest in, eh, Mannington?'

Vernon turned and looked directly at Mannington, raising his brow. Again, only the minutest twitch in one eye betrayed the man's ire.

'But of course.' He inclined his head. 'You are most welcome to join us.'

'That is most gracious, Mannington, but I am loath to leave my nephew alone in a public inn overnight.'

Satisfaction gleamed momentarily in Mannington's eyes.

'However,' Vernon continued, 'I shall be delighted to join you for your daytime activities and for dinner, of course.' He smiled. 'I look forward to it with great anticipation.'

It'll be an ideal opportunity to snoop around.

He smiled at Cordelia and bowed again.

'It seems I am not to be deprived of your company after all, Miss Temple. You see before you a happy man.'

'Well, well, that's all sorted. We'll see you later, Delia, m'lord. Come along, Mannington...' Temple slung his arm across Mannington's shoulders and urged him back to the inn '...and tell me again how this investment works.'

Cordelia chuckled, bringing Vernon's attention back to her. 'It is fortunate for you, my lord, that I am not so easily duped by compliments and sweet smiles,' she whispered, 'particularly when the minute we are on our own your manner is more that of an uncle to a favourite niece than a beau.'

They had strolled down to the river and back that morning, and Vernon had deliberately refrained from any behaviour that could be construed as courtship. Instead, their conversation had centred on London society to help Cordelia prepare for her sojourn in the capital in the autumn.

Quite apart from anything else, she was far too young for his taste. Why, she could only be a year or two older than his niece, Olivia. *Far* too young. And besides, he only wanted Thea.

He swallowed. He had lain awake half the night trying to unpick his feelings and then one simple question had given him his answer. How would he feel when the time came to say goodbye? He did not have to puzzle over the answer to that. He *never* wanted to say goodbye.

Vernon rounded the curricle and climbed on board, nodding at Bickling, who was at the horses' heads, to release them. The blacks, eager to get going, pranced on the spot until Bickling hopped on behind and Vernon eased his hold on the reins. They set off, heading towards the bridge over the Severn.

'Well, I *am* old enough to be your uncle and my behaviour is called being a gentleman,' Vernon said. 'You deserve to be treated as a lady and you must remember that when you go to London. I know you are aware you will be a target for fortune hunters, so my advice is: do not be fooled into going *anywhere* alone with a man. There are scoundrels in all walks of life, including the *ton*. If you have doubts, never be afraid to say *No*. A decent man will respect you for it and you need not concern yourself with what the other sorts might think.'

'Yes, Uncle Vernon.' Cordelia nudged him with her elbow, laughing, and he smiled down at her.

'Seriously, though,' she continued, 'I am grateful for your advice about how to behave in London. I am sure without it I should end up breaking all kinds of unwritten rules, there are so many to abide by. You men do not know how lucky you are.'

'That is true,' Vernon said. 'But you are a sensible—'

A fork of lightning lit the sky and, after a tense pause, they heard a grumble of thunder ahead of them. Bruised purple clouds roiled over the horizon, building higher by the minute.

'The storm is a few miles away yet,' Vernon said, 'but we will not go too much further. I understand the river here floods quite readily and it is still high from the heavy rain last week.'

He felt Cordelia shudder and he glanced at her.

'Are you scared of thunder? Do you wish to return now?'

'No, it is not that. I was remembering that poor young man who fell into the river last week. They never did find his body.'

Vernon's heart seized in his chest.

'What young man?'

'Nobody knows who he was.' She bit her lip. 'Pops and I...we saw it happen.'

Another flash of lightning forked from the sky, followed by another crash of thunder. Closer now.

'Tell me.'

'I do not know much more. It had been raining for days and, when it finally stopped, we walked down to the river. It was quite a sight, several people were on the bridge, watching the torrent. Papa said he noticed the man ride across the bridge from the city end. His horse was light grey and it caught his eye because it looked like it had been ridden hard. Then, not long after, people started shouting and screaming and pointing. The sky was still dark with clouds. We could not see clearly...it was all a blur...there was a scuffle on the bank and, next thing, a man was in the water. He was swept away *so* fast. Someone on the other end of the bridge said the other man had stabbed him, before galloping off on a dark-coloured horse. They formed a party to search along the river, but found nothing. It was horrible. Pops reckons they were drunk.'

Sorrow gathered—a solid lump in Vernon's chest—as Thea's face surfaced in his mind's eye.

Cordelia frowned. 'You look troubled.'

'Yes.' He sent the blacks up the road at a brisk trot, looking for a place wide enough to turn. 'I apologise, but I must cut our drive short. I need to return.'

'Of course,' Cordelia replied. 'I am sorry. Did you...do you think you know that man?'

'It is possible.'

Vernon cursed himself. He had deliberately not said Daniel was missing when he had enquired after him around Worcester, worried that word of his search would reach Mannington. If only he had said, someone before now might have mentioned the drowning of a mysterious stranger.

'What happened to his horse?' That had been Thea's hope from the start, that Daniel's horse had not found its way home.

'No one knows. It ran off in all the confusion.'

A crossroads loomed ahead and, although there was not much room, there was enough to effect a turn.

'May I ask a favour of you?' Vernon manoeuvred the curricle and pair into a tight circle.

'Of course.'

'Please do not mention my interest in that man—not to your father, not to *anyone*. I cannot explain more now, but I need to keep my connection to him a secret, just for a short while.'

'It is your business, my lord. I shall say nothing.'

Vernon threw her a grateful smile. She really was a remarkable young lady...so young and yet such a level head on her shoulders. Did that come from growing up in America? Or from the travelling? Or both?

'Bickling,' Vernon spoke over his shoulder, 'that goes for you, too. Not a word. We shall say we turned around because of the storm.'

'Very good, milord.'

They completed the remainder of the journey in silence, Vernon in a fever of impatience. He would seek out the constable and find out more about this drowning and then… reluctance crept through him. Once he had more details, it would fall to him to deliver the bad news to Thea and shatter her world. That lump of sorrow threaded through with dread rose up to fill his throat.

Thea felt better once she'd indulged in a little weep after seeing Vernon kiss Cordelia's hand when he handed her into his curricle. The incident had brought all her insecurities to the fore. She lay on her back, staring at a dark patch on the ceiling above her head, and tried to put her thoughts in order. Vernon had spent most of today with that woman…that *girl*…walking with her that morning and driving her around even though thunder threatened. He *said* he must gain her trust and Thea did believe that…but she also knew he must be bored with only her—a scrap of a woman dressed as a boy—for company. Why wouldn't he prefer the society of an American heiress who made him laugh?

She was younger than Thea: prettier, taller, curvier. And more fun. And much, much more suitable for Vernon than the daughter of a glassware manufacturer who even Bickling could see was not his type.

A flash of light illuminated her room, followed a minute later by an ominous rumble.

I hope they get soaked.

Thea swiped at her tears. It was easy to be fun when your father was rich and indulged your every whim, and when your only brother was not missing. She scrubbed her hands over her face. What did it matter? There was no point in worrying about her complexion, or her red eyes, or the mouth that—these days—had a permanent droop. She could do nothing to improve her appearance even if she wanted to. And Vernon wouldn't notice if she did. He had not kissed her again last night, even when she had blatantly offered her lips, and today he had spent as little time alone with her as possible.

And you do not help by scolding him and nit-picking whenever you are together.

Can I help it if he irritates me? With his teasing ways and his flirting with Cordelia and his, 'Stay out of sight as much as possible, Dotty. We don't want Mannington seeing you.' Hmph! What he really means is: Stay out of sight so I can romance dear, sweet, clever Cordelia.

Another flash, this time followed more quickly by a clap of thunder. The storm was nearing, the air thick and oppressive.

She should be happy for him. They would no doubt suit very well, with each of them in possession of a vast fortune, and Vernon in possession of that all-important title—

She sat up at the rap on the door, that bitter inner conversation stumbling into a silence that echoed frighteningly in her head. No one apart from Vernon ever came to her door at this time of day. Vernon was out. Horwell? She found herself praying it *was* the innkeeper, because the other face that hovered in her imagination was that of Henry Mannington, who she knew was here, somewhere, in this inn.

Rap! Rap!

Lightning flared again.

Thea scrambled from the bed and ran lightly to the door. She waited for the thunder to die away before putting her ear to the wood.

'Who is it?'

'Me. Are you decent? We need to talk.'

Vernon. Why is he back?

Thea fumbled with the latch and pulled the door open, walking backwards so she remained hidden from anyone else outside. If he had brought that Cordelia… She caught sight of his expression and, again, her circling thoughts slammed to a halt. Her temples throbbed. Her heart climbed into her throat, her stomach clenching in fierce dread.

'You have news.'

She stumbled to the bed and, clinging to the corner post at the foot, she pivoted and slumped on to the mattress. Their charade would be over soon, but first she must bear what Vernon had to tell her. She wanted to run away, to ram her fingers into her ears—she already knew the worst without listening to the detail. But she would not. She owed Daniel that much.

'Tell me.' How steady her voice sounded when all she wanted to do was scream and scream and scream and then curl into a ball and never wake up. Never have to deal with the truth.

He came and sat next to her, on the edge of the mattress, his legs wide, elbows on knees, forearms dangling between. His head was bowed.

She found the strength to say, 'The news is not good.' A small part of her marvelled that, even now, she cared about easing his task. 'Tell me the end, then tell me the details. I need to know.'

His back expanded as he sucked in a breath, then he looked her in the eyes. Put his hand to her cheek.

'I am so sorry. It seems Daniel fell into the Severn during an altercation. He drowned.'

She willed herself not to cry. There would be time, soon, for tears. Now, she needed to know. She shuddered and Vernon's arm slipped around her, pulling her close, supporting her with his strength and his vitality. She leaned into him, relishing his warmth.

'Tell me. Please.'

He told her what Cordelia and her father had seen, and that he had spoken to the constable who told him that descriptions of the assailant varied wildly and the only detail all the witnesses agreed upon was that he was dressed as a gentleman and that he'd had a knife. The constable doubted they would ever discover his identity.

'When?'

'The day Daniel went missing.'

'But we cannot know for certain it was Daniel.'

'Mr Temple noticed a young man of Daniel's age ride across the bridge on a light grey horse. He said it was sweat-stained. It had been ridden hard. It was that man who fell in the river.'

'You said during an altercation? Who with? Was it Mannington?'

'Nobody knows. The light was failing and no one was certain exactly what happened.'

'But…' There was a straw of hope and Thea grabbed it. 'Daniel can swim. He—'

'Hush, sweetheart. There had been heavy rain—do you remember? In the early part of last week? The river was brimming full and turbulent. The constable told me that if a man fell into the river in full spate, he would almost certainly drown.'

The sobs began deep down, deeper inside her than she believed possible. Deep, racking sobs that wrenched her stomach, robbed her of air, left her gasping and juddering as they scraped her throat raw. Dimly, she felt herself gathered into a strong, familiar embrace and she pressed her face into Vernon's chest and allowed all her pent-up misery and fear and despair to escape the shackles that had kept them buried ever since Daniel had failed to return home.

Chapter Twenty

Finally, Thea slept. Carefully, inch by inch, Vernon moved to sit with his back propped against the headboard and his legs stretched along the bed, Thea cradled on his lap. At some point, as the day outside grew dim and the noise from the bar downstairs grew louder, there was a tap on the door and Bickling popped his head around. He held a lighted candle that illuminated his expression and Vernon answered the questioning lift of his brow with a nod.

Bickling came in, treading quietly, and drew the curtains across the window before lighting the candles. He mimed eating and Vernon nodded again, blessing the man's forethought and understanding, and his lack of questions or, indeed, of censure. Vernon's behaviour had gone way past censure. Whether she liked it or not, Thea would be his wife. He would not leave her to support her parents on her own, nor to try to keep their manufactory running without her brother's support.

Bickling soon returned with a platter laden with slices of cold game pie, cheese, bread and cold beef and a tankard of ale. Vernon eased Thea from his lap. She frowned and grumbled under her breath as he moved her, but she soon settled again.

'Thank you, Bickling.'

'Shall I bring some wine, m'lord, in case Miss Markham awakens? And maybe fruit?'

'Yes, please.'

When he returned, Vernon said, 'I cannot leave her alone tonight. Tell Horwell Master Theo is ill and that you and you alone are to enter this bedchamber in case of infection.'

'Yes, milord.' Bickling slipped from the room as quietly as he had arrived.

It was a little before three in the morning before Thea stirred. Vernon, dozing next to her on the bed—his senses alert for any sound from the woman by his side—came fully awake immediately. She moaned as she surfaced from the depths of her sleep and tossed from side to side, her arms flailing. Vernon caught her in his arms and held her tenderly, cradling her skull as he gathered her to him. He knew the instant she remembered, her muscles rigid with shock as she sucked in a sharp breath.

'Shh. I am here.'

'Tell me it was a dream. A nightmare.' Her voice sounded harsh in the hush of the night. A tremor shuddered through her. 'No. It was real,' she muttered almost immediately. 'He is gone. Daniel is gone.' She pushed free of Vernon's arms, sitting bolt upright. 'I need to go home. I have to tell Mama. And P-Papa. Oh! Wh-what will this d-do to them? H-how can I t-tell them?'

'You can do nothing right now, Thea.'

Vernon stroked, tracing the delicate bones of her shoulders through the coarse linen shirt she wore as Theo. So fragile. She would not bear this burden alone. He vowed to stay with her. Protect her. Help her. Avenge her and her brother.

He levered himself off the bed and crossed the room to pour a glass of wine. There was food still on the platter,

but it looked unappetising after several hours. He selected
a dish of berries to offer her, but she shook her head.

'I couldn't eat a thing,' she said. Her voice quavered.
He could see the effort she made to keep her emotions in
check. She took the glass from his hand and drank, drain-
ing the glass.

*She is stronger than I think. It is not all about physical
strength, or how could any female bear the sorrows that
assailed them?*

She had such resilience, a mental strength that he could
not but admire—an admiration that had grown throughout their journey together. He would give anything to protect her against this devastating blow but, no matter how
he raged against God, it was not in his power to make
such a gift.

Thea held out her glass and, wordlessly, Vernon poured
more wine. Again, she tipped the glass back.

'Steady on,' he said. 'Getting foxed will not help.'

She stared up at him, her eyes glittering. 'Then what
will?'

Vernon turned away, suddenly uneasy at her mood, at
the intent in her gaze. 'Time.'

'Hah! Time. I do not want time. I want to forget. Time
means nothing—it can be gone in the blink of an eye. Or
the flash of a knife...that *bastard* Jasper... I'll...'

She banged her glass on the nightstand and scrambled
from the bed.

'Hi! Where—?' Vernon ran after her and stretched his
arm above her head, propping his fist against the door to
hold it shut.

'Let me out!' She tugged at the door.

'No.'

She leant back, putting all her weight into her effort to
open the door but it did not budge. She released the handle
and turned to Vernon, stamping her foot.

'I want some fresh air.'

'You do not.'

She stepped very close to him, her body brushing his. 'Do you call me a liar, Lord Vernon Beauchamp?'

Her voice was silky, challenging. Her upturned face was close—temptingly so. Vernon hauled on the reins of his control, reminding himself why they were there…what this conversation was really about.

'You know I do not, but I shall not let you out. Besides, you have bare feet.'

She looked down, studying first her feet, then his. She lifted one foot and stroked it over his.

'So do you,' she whispered.

Heat spiralled through his body, sending shocks of desire and tingles of need radiating to every cell. Every organ.

She captured his gaze again, placed both hands, very deliberately, on his chest and stroked, then slid her hands to his shoulders. His belly clenched and he grew harder still.

'Thea—'

She lifted her hand to his mouth, pressing her fingers to his lips, silencing him.

He closed his eyes, tilted his face to the ceiling. He knew where this was going. Knew what she wanted. What she needed. Could he withstand her? That was a question to which he feared there was only one answer.

As if she sensed his weakening resolve, she slid her hand around the back of his neck and went up on tiptoes, fitting her body into his. Her fingers speared through his hair, drawing his head down.

Their lips met in a storm of urgent need. Tongues tangled and quiet moans punctuated the night's silence. Without volition, his arms wrapped around her and she leapt, her legs encircling his hips, her heat driving him wild. He stumbled to the bed, lips locked to hers, and lowered her to the mattress, following her down. She tugged at his shirt and he broke away just long enough to pull it over his head, then gathered her to him again, reclaiming those soft, sweet lips and surrendering to the demands of her tongue.

His hands swept lower and encountered the coarse weave of her shirt, the stiff bindings beneath. A woman such as Thea should be dressed in satins and silks. He lifted his torso from hers and tugged at her shirt, pulling it over her head before taking her lips again. Blindly, he fumbled with the knot that held her bindings in place.

She tore her mouth from his. 'Let me,' she breathed, and in seconds the knot was loose and he unwrapped her, his eyes riveted to the prize as small, perfect, pink-tipped breasts bounced free. Her skin was hot and damp and he blew gently across the slopes of her breasts, watching her nipples tighten as his breath cooled them. He massaged and plumped, as he had done in his fantasies, and then he lowered his head, his tongue sweeping across her tender flesh.

His heart pounded with a primal need as he forced himself to go slowly…to give her the pleasure she deserved.

His hands skimmed lower, following her curves to the fall of her breeches. In seconds, they were off and he played his thumb around the rim of her navel and then circled her flat belly with his palm, pressing lightly. Her hips lifted helplessly, pushing against his hand, as he licked at her taut nipple then grazed it lightly with his teeth. She moaned, clutching at his hair.

'Hush, my sweet,' he whispered. 'Lie still. Let me pleasure you.'

Her hands came between them then, to his chest, and pushed. He pulled away, disappointment flooding him as he looked down at her.

'Do you want me to stop? You only have to say the word.'

Dazed hazel eyes searched his face. Then she levered herself up on her elbows and looked down, her eyes locking on the erection that strained his breeches.

'No. I want to see you.'

He hadn't thought he could get any more aroused, but he was wrong. He had thought to give her pleasure and to sacrifice his own but…once his breeches were gone…

'Thea—'

'I want *you*.'

'You do not know—'

'I do. Mama told me. The night before my wedding. I know, Vernon. And I know that I want you.'

She sat up fully now. Her hands splayed against the muscles of his chest, then moved lower. Not hesitantly, but sure…determined… She unbuttoned his breeches and then slipped her hand inside and grasped him. He could not contain his groan of pleasure as he seemed to swell even more at her touch. She stroked and he grabbed her wrist and pulled her hand away.

'Not yet, sweetheart, or this will be finished before we start.'

And Thea—and how was he still surprised when she took control like this?—scrambled on to her knees and pressed her mouth to his in a hard, demanding kiss.

'Then let us start,' she said, and lowered her head to nip at his nipple, sending shock waves rippling through him.

He stood and took off his breeches—her wide-eyed stare sending his pulse soaring even higher—and then lay her back on the bed, kissing her lips as his hands again traced the curves and hollows of her body. He followed the trail of his hands with lips and tongue, lower and ever lower, lingering at the sensitive spots where she arched and moaned, seeking her scent—not the floral, summer garden scent she had worn as Thea, but the scent…the essence…of *her*.

The scent that was driving him wild.

Her thighs parted as he stroked the soft cleft hidden between and he slipped a finger inside. He groaned out loud.

So hot. So wet. So ready.

He hauled on the reins of his control and stroked and played, finding the little nub that would help her find her release. Soft, feminine gasps and moans accompanied the arching of her body as she pressed into his touch. He trailed his lips down the silken skin of her stomach and then traced a path with his tongue through crisp auburn curls to her swollen lips. He pushed into the wet folds and licked, teasing her tender flesh and sucking lightly.

Dear God!

Her evocative scent triggered an eruption of hot molten desire within him. He moved, covering her, his leg between hers, and he cradled her face, kissing her open-mouthed, his tongue pushing inside. She moaned, clutching at him, and he shifted, settling between her widespread thighs. He flexed his hips and nudged into her, then pushed steadily into the welcoming heat, stretching her. His jaw clenched with the need to go slow. To take care.

He was taking too long. She wanted…she needed…she tilted her hips as she clutched at his hips.

Come on!

'Please! Vernon?'

She rocked her hips against him once more and, with a loud groan of surrender, he pushed fully into her, stretching her more than she ever thought possible. He lay still then and she could feel her throbbing flesh tighten around him.

Is that it?

There had been no pain, as Mama had warned, just a little discomfort. But…instinctively she knew there was more…just out of her reach. She lifted her knees and wrapped her legs around his hips, rocking her pelvis again. And then, he began to move and those feelings…those wonderful, elusive, exhilarating feelings…surged again. They grew and they swelled, and she reached and she yearned, higher and higher until, with a helpless scream, her entire body went rigid before exploding into a thousand brilliant, white-hot stars—scattering and soaring, up and up and up into a vast nothingness. Pulses of pleasure radiated through her entire body as Vernon drove into her harder and faster than ever. Then he, too, tensed, as he roared his climax. She felt his seed pump into her as she drifted, dreamily, back down to earth.

Vaguely, she was aware of Vernon kissing her and then settling down beside her. She snuggled into his warmth and slept.

Chapter Twenty-One

Thea woke with pain stabbing at her temples and a mouth that tasted like…well, she did not want to think *what* it tasted like. Something nasty. That was as far as her sluggish brain would allow her thoughts to stray. She rolled on to her back and her left shoulder wedged up against something solid. Something *warm* and solid. Her breath seized. She cranked one eyelid open. She knew what she would see before she turned her head. Who else could it be? The huff of quiet breathing reached her straining ears. He still slept. She swallowed and moved her right hand over her own body. She swallowed again, her heart pitter-pattering, as she encountered her naked belly.

Memories—hazy and disjointed—floated, disembodied and surreal, through her thoughts: memories of kisses, caresses, murmured endearments. Her fingers sought the triangle of soft curls at the apex of her thighs and heat flooded her as she remembered the touch of his hand, his…her brain stumbled over the memory…his *mouth*. The memory of him inside her, covering her. The weight of his body on hers. And the memory of pleasure. Intense, glorious pleasure.

Nerves now invaded her stomach. *She* had enticed him. Just as with that kiss. That memory was the sharpest yet.

She had needed him so badly: needed his comfort, his re-assurance, needed something…*anything*…to ease the pain of losing Daniel. This was no seduction of an innocent, even though she *had* been an innocent. She had known what she was doing.

Thea's fingers again strayed to where her thighs joined and to the soft, secret folds hidden within. She felt a little sore, but she remembered no physical pain from last night, only pleasure. There had been a momentary discomfort as he entered her…stretching her…but that was all. She shuddered in remembered delight.

The bed rocked.

'Good morning.'

She snapped her head to her left, feeling the flush of embarrassment flood her face as she met a pair of smiling green eyes. Vernon had turned to face her, propping himself up on his elbow. She managed a faltering smile in response, battling the urge to allow her gaze to roam that wonderful chest, bared to her eyes as the sheet slipped to his waist.

His hand cradled her cheek. 'How are you? Head sore?' He sobered. 'Heart sore?'

She nodded. He eyed her thoughtfully, then put his arms around her and pulled her into his chest.

'I wish I could protect you from the pain of the next few days, weeks and months, sweetheart, but I cannot.' He stroked her hair back and tilted her face to his. 'Thea…last night… I should not have given in—'

Thea, beginning to relax against him, stiffened and pulled away. 'You do not have to explain. It was my fault. I do not blame—'

A large hand covered her mouth and he laughed, shaking his head at her. 'Thea. *Please* will you allow me to finish? I was about to say I shouldn't have given in to my base desires.'

'Oh,' she said in a small voice.

'You were vulnerable. I took advantage.'

'No. No, you did not. I—I *wanted* you. I do not blame you.'

He smiled, a devastatingly smile full of charm that set her heart racing. 'And I wanted you, my sweet. In fact, I want you again, right now—' he moved his hips and she felt the proof of his desire '—but I shall resist.' He lay back and lifted her across his chest, and he kissed her, slowly and dreamily, his eyes closed as his hands gently caressed her back and bottom. All too soon, he ended the kiss, settling her back on the mattress by his side.

'I must return to my room before the maids are up and about or we shall start the scandal of the century.'

He brushed a kiss to her cheek, then rolled away, pushed the blanket aside and left the bed. Thea's gaze roamed his body—the broad shoulders, slim waist, firm buttocks— and her mouth dried as she realised she wanted him, too. But he was right. It was too risky.

He pulled his shirt over his head and picked up his boots and the rest of his clothing. 'It's still early. Try to sleep. We will talk later.'

And he slipped out of the door, closing it softly behind him.

Sleep was impossible. Thea lay on her back, staring up at the now familiar stain on the ceiling, as she moved the tips of her fingers in circles over her temples. Her spinning thoughts steadied, seeming to mirror the movement of her fingers. She slowed the speed at which she rubbed her temples and the words, images and fragmented thoughts whirling around her brain began to coalesce into comprehensible sentences.

Daniel was dead. Nothing could change that. And it must fall to her to tell her parents. But, first, she would confront Mannington. Jasper Connor. And he would pay for what he had done.

* * *

Later, over the breakfast table, Thea buried her awkwardness at facing Vernon again and she told him her intentions as he tucked into a plate of ham and eggs. A single slice of toast, barely nibbled at, lay disregarded on the plate in front of her.

'Will you come with me to face Mannington? Now?'

Vernon frowned. 'We need to discuss this. It will do no good rushing in at half-cock.'

'But he must pay for what he has done.'

'The only way he will pay is for the law to convict him.' He reached to take her hand. 'Thea. Sweetheart. Think! If we *were* to confront him this morning…where is our proof? All we will do is warn him that we are on to him. A man such as he might produce any number of men prepared to attest to his character or to give him an alibi on the night Daniel was attacked.'

'But you can expose him as a fraud. He is not Henry Mannington.'

'He is not Henry Mannington, cousin to the Duke of Cheriton. But I cannot prove he is not called Henry Mannington. We can only expose him as a liar…a man who has claimed an important connection that is not true. That will destroy his credibility, but it will not convict him. He will be free to move elsewhere and to continue with his fraudulent ways.'

'But he cannot deny he stole from Papa…' She stopped. He could. Of course he could. 'We need proof he is really Jasper Connor.'

A brief smile curved Vernon's mouth. His eyes were sympathetic. Thea sipped at her coffee, quelling her irritation. She did not want sympathy. She wanted justice.

She sucked in a deep breath. 'What do *you* suggest then?'

He raised a brow. 'Do not be cross with me, Thea. I *am* trying to help.'

'I know. I am sorry. I am just…'

Frustrated. Angry. Impatient.

'I am listening.' She mollified her tone. 'Do you have a plan?'

He gave her a twisted smile. 'I am not sure plan is quite the right word. It is four days since I wrote to Leo. I would expect that whomever he sent to Yarncott to enquire into the fire at the inn will get here today. If we can prove my cousin was a guest at that inn the night it burned down, then we will have some proof that Jasper survived and the man buried was Henry Mannington.'

He sighed, thrusting a hand through his hair. 'It will not be easy to make any accusation stick.'

'Then why not let me confront him? If you are with me, he cannot harm me. He might be so shocked he will let something slip.'

'No! Absolutely not. I am letting you nowhere near that villain.' He frowned and she thought she detected a hint of guilt in his eyes. 'Thea…with everything that happened yesterday… I didn't have a chance to tell you this. Mannington is throwing a house party at Crackthorpe Manor, starting this afternoon, with the Temples as guests of honour.'

She swallowed. 'How long for?'

'Two days. Thea… Mannington has some business scheme that he has been dangling under Temple's nose, as a carrot to a donkey. This party…this gathering…is more about business than pleasure. Temple is already keen to invest and I fear it is the same sort of scheme with which he swindled your father.

'I am honour bound to warn Temple—although I worry he will see only the usefulness of Mannington and not realise the danger—but before I warn him I want to use this house party to snoop around Crackthorpe Manor and see if I can find any proof of Mannington's real identity.'

'So…' her voice quivered despite her effort to prevent it '…you will be gone until tomorrow?'

Vernon shoved back his chair and rounded the table to crouch by Thea's side. He put his hand on her thigh and, in spite of her misery, she felt the echo of pleasure throb in her core.

'I shall be back here tonight. The moon is nearly full and it is only four miles away. But…' He leapt to his feet and paced the small parlour, back and forth. 'You know the man, Thea. Would he compromise Cordelia to force a marriage, do you think? I worry my presence will drive him to take desperate measures if he thinks he might lose such a wealthy prize.'

Their eyes met and any disappointment that he would be spending so much time away from her vanished beneath the sick fear she felt on Cordelia's behalf.

'Is he capable of such a thing?'

'I think him capable of almost anything,' Thea said. 'You have to warn her…and her father, too, before you leave the Manor to come back here. They must be on their guard.'

'I shall,' Vernon said grimly.

'What about the other guests? What if you are recognised?'

'I doubt I shall be. I understand most of the guests will be businessmen and their wives. They do not move in the same circles as me.'

Those words reminded Thea of the gulf that still yawned between the two of them, that Vernon, no matter how kind and no matter how much he appeared to desire her…

And does he? Or is it merely that I am the only available female and I threw myself at him last night?

He was an aristocrat. Brother to a duke. And Thea… she belonged in the same circles as those businessmen of whom he spoke.

Her pain at that thought was submerged by the agony

of Daniel's death and her concern for the Temples, and it was utterly dwarfed by the thirst for revenge.

'You must warn them but, before you do, *please* do what you can to find out the truth about Mannington.'

She dropped her gaze to her plate, to hide the tears that had gathered without warning. How could she sit here, calmly discussing Daniel's killer? She was aware that Vernon had regained his feet. He took her hands and urged her, too, to stand.

'I know just what you need. Come.' He grabbed her cap from where she had hooked it on the back of her chair and plonked it on her head, before urging her towards the door. 'Let us go for a ride. I don't know about you, but I find myself in need of a dose of fresh air and the rush of wind in my face. What do you say to a gallop?'

She forced a smile. Staying indoors, sinking into the mire of her grief, would help no one. And the thought of getting away from the inn and spending time with Vernon, whilst she still could, was appealing. 'I say let's go.'

Then she frowned. 'Wait!'

Vernon, halfway to the door, stopped and spun on his heel to face her, his brows raised.

'Tell me again what Cordelia told you about Bullet,' she said.

'He ran off. Many of the people on the bridge who saw what happened raced down to the riverbank. They would have been shouting and screaming—enough to terrify the most placid animal.'

'So why did he not come home?' She clutched Vernon's hand. 'Do you not see? Daniel…he could have survived. He could have got Bullet and—'

'And what? Thea.' The pity in his green eyes made her heart sink. 'If Daniel did survive, where is he? Why has he not been in contact? Bullet will turn up sooner or later. Come, enough of this. Let us go for that gallop.'

* * *

No sooner had Vernon left for Crackthorpe Manor that afternoon than Thea began to pace. She could not settle. She tried to read, but she could not concentrate. Instead, she picked over all that had happened since the day Daniel had left home. Their refreshing morning ride along the river—this time straight past the gipsy encampment—had temporarily assuaged Thea's desperation to take action. Some action. *Any* action. But now she was once again cooped up in this inn whilst Vernon investigated Mannington.

And the knowledge that he would also be with Cordelia Temple—the Temples had set off in Mannington's carriage at noon—did nothing to help. Frustration and insecurity scoured her insides despite the night before. How could Vernon possibly prefer a woman like Thea over one like Cordelia?

I wish I could go there and see for myself what is happening.

Around and around the parlour she paced, like a caged animal. If only she could do something to help.

Then she stopped. Stared at the window, her thoughts whirling.

Bullet! What if...?

Why did I not think of that before? What if Mannington *has him?*

She would recognise him in an instant. To Vernon, he would just be another grey horse. She went to the window. The weather was fine but breezy, the heat not so oppressive since yesterday's thunderstorm had cleared the air. Vernon had pointed out Crackthorpe Manor—its stone walls glowing a warm buttery yellow in the June sunshine—as they had turned away from the bank of the Severn and returned to the road that led from Worcester to Great Malvern.

I am sure I can find it again.

There was no one to stop her as long as she could evade

Bickling and his inevitable awkward questions. She rummaged through her saddlebag and extracted the pistol she had packed when she left home to follow after Vernon. It occurred to her that she was doing the same thing—following him once again, against his express orders.

Orders. Pfft. He cannot tell me what to do.

A commotion arose in the street outside and she crossed to peer again from the window. A mud-spattered carriage had drawn up outside the Crown and, as she watched, one of the two men on the box jumped down and ran to let down the steps and open the door. An elegant gentleman with black hair emerged. He settled his hat upon his head then turned, reaching to help someone else from the vehicle.

She leaned forward, wondering if these newcomers might recognise Vernon. A fashionably-dressed lady came into sight, pausing on the top step, and then Horwell appeared on the pavement below, bowing, and Thea spied Bickling hurrying out from the passage that led to the stables. Here was the perfect opportunity for her to leave without awkward questions and opposition. Determined to grab it with both hands, Thea did not stay to watch, but rushed down the stairs and out the rear door. She sped across the yard and into the stables, where she was brought up short by a figure standing in the shadows inside the door.

'Oh! You startled me.'

The man moved into the light. 'Sorry.'

Thea blinked. It was the Gipsy they had seen at the camp, the day they first met the Temples.

What is he doing here?

A groom coming out of the tack room at the rear distracted her, and when she looked again, the Gipsy had vanished.

'Yes, master?'

She shook the puzzle of the Gipsy from her mind. 'Saddle the black, will you?'

It was done in no time. She was up in the saddle and riding away from the Crown within ten minutes of first thinking of the idea and without being noticed by either Bickling or Horwell, both still occupied with the smart couple and their companion, an elderly, stooped man with white hair.

Thea kicked Star into a trot. She would ride to Crackthorpe Manor. Tether Star somewhere out of sight and then…somehow…she would search Mannington's stables. Without being seen. Her heart faltered.

What if Mannington sees me? Recognises me?

Stop this! He'll be busy with his guests, as will his servants, too busy to notice one extra strange face around the place. She fingered the hard shape of the pistol in her pocket, gaining comfort from it.

She found Crackthorpe Manor with little difficulty. The house and stables were sheltered on three sides by a narrow belt of woodland and Thea approached the buildings through the trees, not bold enough—or foolish enough—to ride up the main carriageway. She tethered Star to a sturdy sycamore in the middle of the belt and continued on foot to where the trees gave way to smooth, verdant lawns. Here, she could see the stable yard set to the side and behind the house, at a distance of a hundred yards or so. All appeared quiet there but, from the far side of the house and over the sounds of leaves rustling in the breeze and the birdsong, she could make out the faint drone of conversation and the occasional guffaw of laughter. The guests had arrived, then, and the party had begun.

She examined the stables again, noticing a track leading behind them and through the trees. Did she dare? She could look around openly and search for Bullet, and where better to hide Star than in plain sight? She ran back to her mare and leapt into the saddle and soon found that track.

She pulled the peak of her cap to shade her eyes, and headed Star towards the stables.

As she rode through the stone pillars of the gateway a groom emerged from the barn.

'Afternoon,' she said, deepening still further her already deep voice. 'I've brought a message for my uncle, Lord Boyton. He is a guest here.'

'Boyton? Oh, him. He's the one with that pair of blacks.' A note of envy crept into his voice. ''andsome pair, they are, and no mistake.' The groom took Star as Thea slid to the ground. 'D'you know the way?'

'Yes. Are there many guests? Their horses must keep you busy.'

'There aren't too many: them from Birmingham shared carriages and the guvnor sent our carriage to Worcester to bring some others, so it's not too bad.'

The groom led Star into the barn and into a vacant stall where he tethered her before loosening her girth. Thea followed, trying to penetrate the dim interior with eyes accustomed to bright sunlight, searching for Bullet.

'I'm trying to persuade my uncle to buy me a grey hunter,' she said. 'Do you have any greys here?'

'Greys? Only the dappled mare down there and she's a pig. Don't like 'em myself…too much hard work to keep 'em clean.'

Disappointment dragged at Thea. This had been a waste of time. She had been foolish to think…the phrase clutching at straws came to mind. She should return to Worcester. But she had told the groom she had brought a message for Vernon. He suspected nothing now, but he would think it odd if she left without seeing Vernon first.

'I had better go and find my uncle,' she said. 'Thank you for taking care of my mare.'

Chapter Twenty-Two

Vernon's bad feeling about this house party—and about Henry Mannington's intentions towards the Temples and, in particular, Cordelia—intensified as he was introduced to his fellow guests. It seemed that Henry Mannington harboured greater ambition than Jasper Connor ever had. Not content with attempting to reel in Samuel Temple, it appeared—from the snippets of conversation Vernon overheard—that all the guests here were eager to invest in this 'opportunity of a lifetime'. Mannington was clever. He had clearly prepared his ground in advance...he had no need to use further powers of persuasion. His guests seemed quite capable of selling his scheme to each other and, simultaneously, themselves. It was depressing there were so many fools in this world. Mayhap they deserved to be fleeced.

Vernon sipped his wine and wandered along the terrace to the corner. Mannington had sent his carriage to convey the Temples to Crackthorpe and they had been here since noon, sharing luncheon with their host before the remaining guests arrived. Cordelia—looking, it had to be said, a little uncomfortable—had been persuaded to step into the role of hostess, as there was no lady of the house. Vernon had not had a chance to speak privately to her; Mannington had kept her occupied and mostly by his side.

He propped his shoulders against the wall and planned how and where to begin his search. On this side of the house four French windows faced on to the terrace, the two furthest from him standing open. They led into a salon, through which Vernon had been shown upon arrival.

Most of the guests were outside, although a couple of the ladies remained in the salon, complaining of the bright sun and the brisk breeze. Altogether there were twenty people in attendance, including himself and Mannington, but only five of them were women. Temple was holding court in the middle of the largest group gathered on the terrace, but... Vernon straightened, every muscle tensing ready for action...there was no sign of either Mannington or Cordelia.

They were here five minutes ago.

He sauntered along the terrace, heading for the open windows, peering again through the other windows he passed to see if they were inside that room—a corner room, furnished as a sitting room, with two further windows that overlooked the rear of the house. There was no sign of either Mannington or Cordelia and Vernon's concern mounted. Then, as he neared the first of the open windows, he released his pent-up breath as Cordelia stepped through, Mannington on her heels.

'Miss Temple.' Vernon bowed. 'I thought you had deserted me.'

He caught her flash of relief before her face relaxed into a smile. 'Lord Boyton, how pleasant to see a familiar face.'

Behind her, Mannington's smile widened but it did not reach his eyes. Vernon proffered his arm.

'Would you care for a stroll in the garden?'

Mannington stepped forward, between Vernon and Cordelia. 'Miss Temple is eager to rejoin her father, Boyton.' He turned to Cordelia. 'If you care to see the garden later, Cordelia, I shall be delighted to escort you. I can tell you anything you wish to know about the flowers growing there.'

'You must be a keen plantsman, to be able to put a name to so many flowers, Mannington,' Vernon drawled. He had caught a glimpse of the abundantly stocked borders on his approach to the house. 'Most impressive in such a short period of time.'

'A short period of time, Lord Boyton?' Cordelia's smile was perplexed. 'How so, when this is Mr Mannington's family home?'

'It is?' Vernon held Mannington's glare. 'I must have misunderstood. My mistake.'

A muscle leapt in the side of Mannington's jaw.

'I suggest you pay more attention to the facts in future, Boyton,' he said silkily, 'or you *might* discover that misinformation can result in all kinds of unfortunate consequences.'

Vernon was conscious that Cordelia had paled as she looked from one man to the other. He laughed and leaned close to put his lips to her ear, drawing a scowl from Mannington.

'It would appear our Mr Mannington does not take kindly to being teased, Miss Temple,' he said, loud enough for Mannington to hear. 'It is, I fear, a serious shortcoming for a man to have no sense of humour.'

'Come, Cordelia.' Mannington cupped her elbow in a proprietary manner and indicated the group that included her father. 'I shall escort you to your father.'

Vernon maintained his polite smile as Cordelia shook her head and pulled her arm from Mannington's grasp. She smiled at him, patted his hand, and said, 'No, you go ahead, sir. I know how eager you are to discuss business, but I shall be of more use entertaining your female guests. Go on, now.' She made a shooing motion with hand.

Reluctance in every line of his body, Mannington stalked

off to join his other guests. Vernon recalled Cordelia's look of relief when she had first seen him.

'Has he been bothering you, Miss Temple?'

'Only in as much as he appears to believe there is an understanding between us, which I have assured him is not the case. It is nothing I cannot handle, however.'

'I trust you are correct. Remember my warnings about fortune hunters and, please, take care.' On the drive over to Crackthorpe, a question had begun to plague Vernon. 'I apologise for resurrecting an unpleasant memory, but I must ask…on the day that man drowned in the Severn, did Mannington call upon you during the day? Or later that evening?'

She stared up at him. 'Why, no. He was due to dine with us, but he did not keep his appointment and then, later, he sent word that he had left Birmingham later than intended and hence arrived home too late to join us.'

Vernon's pulse kicked. At last! Their first proof… The maid at the Royal Hotel had told them Daniel was angry at missing Mannington, who had left Birmingham *early* that day. Not late. And the information settled a discrepancy that had nagged at Vernon: Mannington had been in his carriage; Daniel's assailant had left on horseback. Vernon hadn't been able to reconcile the two. But…what if Mannington had driven straight home, then ridden back to Worcester to dine with the Temples? And what if he had then come face to face with Daniel at the far side of that bridge? Witnesses had spoken of an altercation…the two men running…shouting…raised fists and the slash of a knife. He cast a swift glance at where Mannington stood talking to his guests.

'Cordelia.' He injected a wealth of serious intent in that one word.

She frowned. 'What is it?'

'There is something you need to know about our host.

We need to talk in private. Meet me in that room at the far end of the terrace.' He pointed to it. 'You go first. I shall follow in a few minutes.'

'Lord Boyton…you are not intent on compromising me, are you?'

'No. Please trust me on that. But I *am* intent on saving you and your father from a huge mistake.'

Five minutes later, Vernon slipped into the sitting room and closed the door behind him. Cordelia waited by the fireplace, her hands clasped before her. Vernon crossed the room to her and began to talk. He did not mince his words, but told her everything he knew, including how Mannington had jilted Thea. The only secret he kept was that Theo was Dorothea Markham. The colour slowly leached from Cordelia's face as he spoke and, when he finally told her that the man who had drowned was Daniel Markham and that his murderer was Henry Mannington, she swayed, one hand to her mouth, eyes stricken.

'Oh, my goodness,' she whispered. 'I cannot believe…'

Vernon clasped her upper arms, supporting her, and she leaned into him. He folded his arms around her.

'I am sorry,' he said. 'It is a harsh tale to tell, but I can no longer stand by and see you and your father taken in by such a villain.'

Despite the risk of being seen, Thea could not resist the urge to see for herself what was happening at the house party. She hugged close to the house wall, following the murmur of conversation until she reached the corner. She could see several knots of people gathered on a terrace, glasses in hand as they chatted and laughed. She scanned the people, but could not see Vernon's tall figure and chestnut hair amongst them. Neither, she realised with a jolt of annoyance, could she see Miss Cordelia Temple. The few women present were middle-aged matrons. She risked poking her head around the corner of the house and there he was, with Cordelia as Henry Mannington—and this was the first time she had seen him so clearly since discovering he was still alive—strode from them to join a group of men, including Samuel Temple. Although Henry's—*Jasper's*—expression was agreeable, his stiff gait signalled his displeasure. Either Vernon or Cordelia had angered him and Thea would bet on the former being responsible.

Vernon stood close to Cordelia, their faces serious as they spoke. Then Cordelia disappeared inside the house and Vernon stood, idly contemplating the view from the terrace as he sipped his wine. Thea ducked back behind the corner, seeking Mannington amongst the groups on the terrace. Good, he hadn't noticed her and was still deep in discussion with Samuel Temple and a couple of others. She watched him, noticing as he grew increasingly uneasy, glancing several times back towards the house, to where Vernon stood. Eventually, Thea took a chance and peeped around the corner again. Vernon had disappeared.

Where is he?

He had not crossed the terrace to mingle with the other guests, which meant…

He has followed Cordelia!

She tried to persuade herself that Vernon—as he had said he would—was searching for evidence against Mannington. But then where was Cordelia? And all her old insecurities and distrust reared up to mock her for daring to wonder if Vernon might truly care for her.

She withdrew once more around the corner, her insides in turmoil, and she made her way back along the house wall. At the first window some sixth sense made her hesitate, even though the room had been empty when she passed it earlier. Cautiously, she peered around the edge of the window frame—and bit back a gasp, her heart plummeting, bruised and sore.

Cordelia was in Vernon's arms, her head on his shoulder. Tenderness shone in his expression as he held her. Thea's throat tightened with misery. Only last night, he had made love to her. He had given her pleasure—such intimate pleasure that she blushed to even think of it. And now he was making love to Cordelia.

Had he imagined Cordelia in his arms last night and wished it was her?

Once a fool, always a fool!

Not content with allowing herself to be deceived by Jasper Connor, she had gone and fallen in love with the most unsuitable man she could ever imagine. A rake. An aristocrat who—if he ever chose to wed—would choose either a high-born lady so as not to dilute his blue blood, or a woman with a fortune to add to his wealth and his consequence.

Neither of which I am. How could I be so stupid?

Tears smarted in her eyes and stung her nose.

I will not stay here. I cannot face him, ever again. I will go home, devote myself to Mama and Papa and we will mourn Daniel together. I will spend my life atoning for the misery I've brought to my family.

But she remained, despite her avowals, her gaze riveted to the couple in the room, misery coursing through her. Then a movement caught her eye. The door was easing open and Henry Mannington slipped into the room, behind Vernon's back and, before Thea realised his intention, he had crossed the room and grabbed Vernon's shoulder, hauling him away from Cordelia and around to bring them face to face.

His voice was a muffled roar as he drew back his fist. Thea gasped, but then sighed with relief as Vernon blocked his punch with almost leisurely ease.

She could see him reply to Mannington, his hands raised, palms facing his furious host. But if he intended to placate the other man, he failed, for Mannington once again let loose with a wild punch. Vernon, in an almost contemptuous gesture, shoved Mannington aside, then turned to Cordelia, whose eyes were round with shock above her hand-covered mouth. Mannington, however, reached into his sleeve and withdrew a wicked-looking, thin-bladed knife. Cordelia screamed and Vernon spun on his heel to face the threat.

Thea waited no longer. She delved into her pocket as she sped around the corner of the house and on to the terrace, where the first French window also led into that sitting room.

Let it be unlocked.

The gods were on her side and she wrenched it open and charged inside, holding her pistol aloft. She skidded to a halt, six feet away from where Vernon faced Mannington, who was crouched slightly, knife in hand.

Vernon glanced at Thea and sighed. 'Dotty… I do *not* need rescuing.'

'But—'

'Dotty?' Cordelia looked from Thea to Vernon and back again. 'Who…? Are you…? Do you mean…?'

'Thea?'

Holding Mannington's horrified gaze, Thea reached up and pulled her cap from her head. In that same instant Vernon pivoted on the ball of one foot and let loose a well-aimed kick at the knife, which flew from Mannington's grasp. Vernon then grabbed the other man's lapels, pulled him around to face him, drew back his fist and let fly at Mannington's jaw. Mannington spun around with the force of the punch and collapsed on to a side table that held a collection of porcelain figurines, knocking the entire display over as he fell to the floor. There was an almighty crash and Thea allowed herself a moment to savour the sweet taste of revenge before bleak reality shrouded her again.

Daniel was still dead and Cordelia had been in Vernon's arms.

She was vaguely aware of the sound of running footsteps and raised voices from the hall. Then the door crashed wide, wrenching her gaze from the prostrate form of Daniel's killer.

'Thea!'

The roar rocked the room.

The world seemed to tilt on its axis.

Then she realised—dimly and from a distance—that it was she who was tilting as her legs gave way and she crumpled to the floor.

The man who filled the doorway occupied Vernon's attention for less than a second. He recognised him, vaguely, but his focus was on Thea. Was she all right? He fell to his knees beside her and snatched the pistol from her senseless fingers. He held it out in Cordelia's direction.

'Take it,' he bit out, without looking at her. 'Use it if he—' he indicated the newcomer with a flick of his head '—causes trouble.'

As soon as she took the gun, he turned back to Thea, leaning over her as he checked her over, making sure...

She's breathing. She's only passed out. She—

'Why, you—! Get your filthy hands off my sister!'

Sister?

Slowly, Vernon straightened and turned his head to look properly at the newcomer. From the corner of his eye he could see Cordelia, pistol gripped in both hands, pointing it unwaveringly in the direction of the man. He pictured the portrait Thea had shown him. The portrait of Daniel Markham.

So that is why he's familiar.

Vernon stood up, then bent and scooped Thea into his arms.

'I'm warning you, mister...'

He settled her gently on a sofa before turning to face Daniel and thrusting out his hand.

'Beauchamp,' he said.

Daniel ignored it. '*Beauchamp*? Another one claiming kinship to the Duke?' A sneer twisted his mouth.

'As it happens,' a smooth, familiar voice interposed, 'that particular claim is not without foundation.'

A tall figure—this time *very* familiar—had appeared in the open doorway.

A laugh gathered, deep down, swelling Vernon's chest and filling his throat. Trust Leo. Always there at the opportune moment. His brother, suave and assured as ever, sauntered into the room. He took in the prostrate form of Mannington and then the gently stirring form of Thea. His brows rose and he met Vernon's gaze, a quizzical gleam lighting his silvery-grey eyes, and as swiftly as that bubble of laughter had risen, it subsided.

Vernon held Leo's stare, daring him to take control. Leo's eyes narrowed slightly, then his lips quirked and he wandered over to the window, hitching one hip on to the sill. The slightest of hand gestures confirmed the stage belonged to Vernon.

'Lord Vernon Beauchamp,' Vernon said to Daniel. '*Brother* to the Duke. And you are Daniel Markham.' He gestured at Thea. 'We thought you dead. Your sister has been distraught. How the hell could you be so insensitive, and put her through such needless agony?'

Daniel stepped closer, almost toe to toe with Vernon, and thrust his chin forward belligerently. 'I was protecting her,' he growled. 'Unlike you. How the hell could *you* be so irresponsible as to allow her to jaunt around the country dressed like...like *that*?'

Vernon stood his ground, ready to deal with him if the other man became physical, but otherwise careful to make no move that might set that particular fuse alight. Fighting with his future brother-in-law was not wise.

'Have you *ever*,' he said, 'attempted to stop your sister doing anything she set her mind to?'

Their gazes held. Then Daniel blinked and his glare softened. He stepped back and lifted his arms sideways in a hopeless gesture.

'Why do you think I didn't tell her what I'd seen?' he said, through gritted teeth. 'When I knew I would be away from home for a while I wrote to Mama, but I swore her to secrecy. She was *supposed* to tell Thea I was visiting friends so she wouldn't worry. What do you imagine Thea's reaction would be if she found out that bas—*he*—' he gestured at Mannington, still prone on the floor '—was still alive? Do you think she would sit quietly at home and leave me to bring him to justice? Hah!

'And *you*…' this directed at Cordelia '…whoever you are, will you please put that da—*blasted* gun down?'

Cordelia glanced at Vernon, who nodded. Daniel scowled, then paced across the room and back again.

'You will have to marry her,' he said. 'I shall accept no less.'

Behind Daniel, Vernon saw Leo suppress a grin, stoking his irritation.

'I know my obligations,' he said. 'Of course I will marry her. I would not see your sister suffer.'

'And do I get a say in all of this?'

Vernon turned. Thea was on her feet, fists on her hips, her curls in a wild halo around her head: a hissing, spitting, fluffed-up kitten.

Chapter Twenty-Three

'First of all—' Thea strode to Daniel and poked him in the chest '—no letter from you arrived. I thought you dead. And second—' she whirled to face Vernon '—*I*, and only I, will make the decision about if, when and who I will marry. And…and…' All her fight appeared to drain away. She sucked in a long, juddering breath, her eyes huge, haunted. 'What *happened*?'

A sob exploded from her, followed by another. Vernon wrapped his arms around her and gathered her to him. 'Shh…' He half-carried her back to the sofa and sat with her tucked close to his side, his arm around her. Mannington, at his feet, was beginning to stir.

'Markham,' he said. 'Cover him with the pistol, will you? This scoundrel—whatever his real name is—has a lot of questions to answer before he goes off to jail.'

Cordelia handed the gun to Daniel, then looked around.

'I suggest you come over here and sit with me in the audience,' Leo said, patting the sill next to him. 'This promises to be most entertaining.' He raised an innocent brow in response to Vernon's glare.

'Who is *that*?' Thea whispered to Vernon as Cordelia did as she was bid. 'I saw him at the Crown.'

'My brother.'

'The *Duke*?'

She wriggled away from him, leaving at least six inches of empty sofa between them. Vernon frowned. He wanted her close to him. Touching him. So he *knew* she was safe, beyond all doubt. But maybe this was not the time and place to explain how things would be in the future. Once this charade was played out, however, he would tell her in no uncertain terms. She was his. And they *would* be married.

'One fact I have established,' Daniel said, 'is that his name is definitely Jasper Connor.' He nudged the man with his toe.

Jasper groaned, his hand going to his jaw. 'It's broken. You've broken it!'

'Good,' Daniel said. 'You deserve worse. Far worse. And I have no doubt you'll get it.'

Jasper rolled on to his side and pushed himself into a sitting position.

'You can't prove a thing,' he spat, speaking remarkably well for a man with a broken jaw.

'We can prove enough. We have witnesses.'

'What witnesses?'

'You'll see. Watch him, will you?'

Daniel went to pass the gun to Vernon, who rose to his feet and waved the gun away.

'I don't need that.' He formed a fist with his right hand and smacked it into his left palm. Jasper winced.

Daniel left the room and soon returned with four people—two men and two women—two of whom were strangers and two of whom Vernon recognised: Horwell's niece, Annie, and the Gipsy he had seen at the camp. A gasp burst from Jasper and then the second woman was flying across the room, fingers crooked into claws as she launched herself at Jasper Connor.

'You devil, you! How could you do it? Abandon me and

our children?' She raked his face with her nails, drawing blood, as he tried, unsuccessfully, to fend her off.

The older of the two men rushed to her and pulled her away. 'Now, now, Gladys. This will get us nowhere. Allow the law to deal with him. I'm sure they'll not see you and the children penniless.' She turned into his chest, sobbing.

Vernon stared at Daniel. '*Children?* Are they...? Is she...?'

'His wife. Yes. And this is her father, Mr Morgan. He is a merchant in the town of Aberystwyth, on the Welsh coast.'

A whimper sounded from the sofa behind him. Vernon sat down again and put his arm around Thea. She shrugged him off and stood up.

'How did you find them, Daniel?' Thea planted herself in front of her brother, hands again on her hips. 'How did you know he was married?'

'I didn't know it. Look, let us sit down and I will tell you what happened.'

Thea ignored the space next to Vernon and marched over to an armchair and flung herself into it, crossing her arms. 'Go on.'

'First, allow me to introduce Annie Horwell, who works here as a maid, and Absalom Gray, the Romani who saved my life by hauling me from the river after I fell in.'

'So you did fall,' Vernon said. 'You were not pushed?'

'Not pushed, but I had little choice. It was either the river, or his knife,' Daniel said bitterly. 'I had crossed over the bridge from the city when I saw him riding towards me. I hauled him off his horse and we fought. I had the upper hand, too. I intended to take him back home and press charges against him. But he broke away and ran to the riverbank. I chased after him and grabbed him and then he pulled the knife. I released him, thinking he would run again, but he did not. He came at me. I had the river at my back and no time to get my pistol from my pocket. I went in deliberately.'

'We were told the current was ferocious that day.'

'It was. More powerful than I could ever believe. And so fast. It tossed me about as it pleased and I could do nothing but try to keep catching my breath every chance I got.' He shuddered. 'Then I surfaced and I found myself in a sort of whirlpool, close to the bank. And, thank God, Absalom had seen me and stretched out a branch. I caught hold just when I thought I could fight it no longer and would be sucked under for good. He managed to pull me on to the bank.'

Daniel smiled at Absalom who stood to one side, watching. He acknowledged Daniel's smile with the slightest of nods. Thea leapt from her chair and went to Daniel, hugging him.

'Thank you,' she said to the Gipsy. 'What happened then?' she asked Daniel.

'Absalom's people were camped by the river, not far from where he rescued me, and he took me to them to recover. I racked my brains about how I could bring Connor to justice… I needed proof the man calling himself Henry Mannington was actually Jasper Connor and that he had swindled our father. I also wondered who had been killed in the fire in which Connor had supposedly perished. I had written to the Duke about his cousin, but I did not have much hope he would respond.

'And then I remembered Connor talking about the beauty of the Welsh coast, and about Aberystwyth, and I wondered if someone there might know him, or have information that might help. Sheer desperation drove me there, little believing what I would find.

'Absalom agreed to watch Connor. He enlisted Annie's help and then found out, through her uncle, that Connor was targeting the Americans and, later on, that a viscount was asking questions about Connor.'

'But why didn't Horwell tell me this when I asked if he knew you?' Vernon asked.

'Only I and my people knew that the man who had been swept away had not drowned, or that his name was Daniel Markham.' It was the Gipsy who spoke. 'Horwell never knew Daniel's name, or that he was alive, or that Connor had anything to do with it.'

'I swore them to secrecy,' Daniel said. 'My biggest fear was that Connor would find out I was still alive and disappear again.'

He turned to Thea. 'I *did* write to Mama. I would never have left you thinking the worst, even though I did not dare to tell you the truth.' He paced the room again, stopping in front of her. 'And I have been proved right, haven't I? The minute my back was turned, you... *Look at you!*'

He reached to grasp a handful of curls and Vernon tensed, ready to intervene but, with a groan, Daniel wrapped his arms around Thea and pulled her close.

'What have you done to your beautiful hair? Foolish, impetuous woman.'

Thea wriggled free. 'Never mind that now, Daniel. It will grow again. What happened to your letter?'

Daniel looked at Absalom, who shrugged.

'I gave it to a passing group of Rom,' he said. 'They were heading north. They'll have delivered it by now, I expect.'

'Bickling made no mention it,' Vernon said. 'My groom,' he added in response to Daniel's querying look. 'He came to Worcester from Stourwell Court three days ago.'

Daniel grimaced. 'Why would my mother mention a letter to a servant, particularly someone else's servant? Anyway, when I arrived back in Worcester, with Mr Morgan and Gladys Connor, Absalom told me that you...' he directed a hard stare at Vernon '...were staying at the Crown and had been asking about me, that you and the Temples were guests at this house party and that the Duke had arrived at the Crown. What I did *not* know was that you were the Duke's brother and that your *"nephew"* was my sister, whom I thought safe at home with our parents.'

'You must take the blame for your sister's panic and her subsequent actions,' Vernon retorted. 'If you had been less secretive—'

'And allowed this villain to get away with it? As soon as he had a sniff anyone knew the truth of his identity he would have vanished just as effectively as he did at Yarncott.'

'Speaking of which… Leo, I cannot believe you decided to make those enquiries yourself.'

'I confess to a certain amount of curiosity as to what convinced you to remain up here to search for a stranger.' His gaze settled on Thea for a moment and his mouth twitched. 'And, as Rosalind and I were escorting her grandfather to Birmingham, it was not too great a detour to travel via Oxford and Worcester.'

'What news from Yarncott?'

'I spoke with the former innkeeper and he confirmed that there were two guests at the inn the night it burned down: Jasper Connor and Henry Mannington. They evidently spent much of the evening playing cards and, from what he remembers, one man lost heavily to the other. He is unsure which, however…' He stood up and walked across to where Jasper sat sullenly on the floor, still cradling his jaw. 'Because after the fire—which began, incidentally, in Connor's bedchamber—he at first thought it was Connor who had somehow survived. But then the man who escaped the fire told him he had muddled the two men and that he was, in fact, Henry Mannington.' Leo leant down and took hold of Jasper's chin, tilting his face and moving it from side to side. 'There is a certain superficial likeness; it is not hard to understand why the innkeeper fell for your lies.'

'Stop! You're hurting!'

Leo jerked his jaw again. 'Dear me, how clumsy of me,' he murmured before releasing it. 'You may console yourself, Connor, that however painful your bruised jaw might be, it is as nothing compared to the agony of being burnt to death.'

'He didn't burn to death…he was already de—'

Vernon crouched down in front of Jasper and grasped his neckcloth, twisting. 'How did he die?'

Jasper shrank from him. 'I don't know.' He coughed and spluttered as Vernon tightened his grip. 'He just did.'

'In *your* bedchamber?'

'No. Yes.'

Holding the man's terrified gaze, Vernon said, 'Markham? Get the women out of here will you? We need a *private* chat with Jasper here.'

Daniel began to usher the women, plus Mr Morgan, to the door. Thea broke ranks and rushed to crouch next to Vernon, glaring at Connor.

'Tell them! You owe me that much. You are not going to wriggle out of this one…why make it harder for yourself?'

Jasper, sheer terror in his eyes, nodded. Vernon released his neckcloth and regained his feet, pulling Thea up with him. He nodded at Leo, then towed Thea out of earshot.

'You did not really believe I would use physical force on him, Thea?'

She stuck her nose in the air. 'I am sure *I* do not care what you do, Lord Vernon, but you cannot want Cordelia to think you capable of such barbaric behaviour.'

'Cordelia?'

She hunched her shoulder and pulled free of his grip. 'Do not try to pretend. I *saw* you embracing her. Now, I want to hear what that villain has to say for himself.' She took one pace towards where Leo continued to interrogate Jasper before spinning back to stare up at Vernon. 'Don't you?'

'No.'

Her mouth opened in silent surprise.

'Leo will fill in the details later.' He reached out and fingered a curl that dangled provocatively over her ear. '*You* are my priority now.'

Vernon's voice deepened as he spoke, raising a delicious shiver that danced across the surface of Thea's skin. His green eyes darkened as they bored into hers, as though he could see deep, deep inside her and knew her every thought.

Her every desire.

Her pulse quickened and she tore her eyes from his, disconcerted by the immediate response of her treacherous body.

Can I trust him? Is he playing a part?

Would he uncomplainingly sacrifice his freedom and his future because he was a gentleman and she was hopelessly compromised? He had been embracing Cordelia—she could not mistake the evidence of her eyes. Her restless gaze swept the occupants of the room.

Daniel: he had made his expectations of Vernon clear.

Jasper: she had trusted him and he had jilted her, humiliated her and almost destroyed her family.

The Duke: he, surely, would object to his brother marrying a woman so far beneath him?

She caught the eye of Absalom Gray, standing apart, once more watching the proceedings without taking part. *He* knew his place. *He* knew where he belonged. The only surprise was that he had involved himself in Daniel's affairs in the first place. Most of the gipsies Thea had met liked to keep themselves to themselves.

Absalom's eyes narrowed and Thea realised, with a start, that she had been staring at him. She felt the heat build in her cheeks and swung her gaze back to Vernon. His hand rested lightly on her shoulder. Not detaining her if she wished to go, but keeping that connection between them.

'How can *I* be your priority?' she said. 'I have my duty to my family; you have your duty to yours.'

His fingers tightened. 'You cannot mean that. What about…?' He put his lips to her ear. 'What about the way I feel about you?'

'What about Cordelia?'

She watched him closely. His astonishment appeared genuine, then his brows drew together.

'That is the second time you have mentioned her. Whatever you think you saw, you are wrong. I told you before, I have no interest in her: she is too young, too tall, and her hair…' he spread his fingers and pushed them through her curls '…is *far* too boring. And besides…' he curved his fingers around the back of her skull and pulled her closer even as he tilted her face to his '…she is not you.'

Her lids lowered and her lips parted as desire coiled in the pit of her stomach.

A loud cough interrupted them. Embarrassed, Thea pulled away. However many doubts her brain raised, it seemed her body held no qualms. Her feelings for Vernon were too complicated…she could not think straight, not with everyone here, and so she focused on the practicalities.

She spoke to her grim-faced brother. 'What about all the guests?'

'That girl, the American, she's gone to tell them their host has been taken ill. They will soon be gone. And then you and I, Sis, will be having a chat.'

She went to him, lay her hand on his arm.

'Not here,' she whispered. 'Not in front of the Duke.' She glanced over her shoulder to where he still interrogated Jasper Connor, having hauled him up to sit on a chair. He scared her. She had never met anyone quite so high-born before.

Except Vernon. He is of the same parentage, only younger. You are not scared of him.

She brushed away that errant thought. Whatever happened, she did not want it to be here, in this house.

'How did you get here?' Daniel said.

'On Star. She is in the stables.'

She caught Daniel's scowl as he eyed her legs. 'You will return in the post-chaise with Mrs Connor and Mr Morgan.'

'She will not.' Vernon had joined them. 'Thea will be with me, in my curricle. The Temples will need transport back to town, so they can go in the post-chaise. Leo?'

Vernon's brother looked around, raised a dark brow and sauntered across the room to join them, his silvery-grey gaze on Thea, making her feel like squirming. She firmed her lips and elevated her chin, and he smiled. She narrowed her eyes at him. He was as bad as Vernon.

'You called?' The Duke executed a mock bow.

'How did you get here? Carriage?'

'As it happens, no. I rode out from the Crown, in company with the charming but somewhat uncommunicative Mr Gray. And you will be pleased to hear that the ever-obliging Horwell is sending the constable out to take charge of Connor.'

'Good. I wondered how we were to transport him back. Markham?'

Daniel looked his query. 'You may ride alongside my curricle if you so wish, but your sister is coming with me.' He grasped Thea's arm and started for the door. 'We will see you all back at the Crown.'

Thea hung back. 'Do I not get a say?'

Vernon looked at her. 'No.'

Chapter Twenty-Four

Thea huddled at one end of the curricle seat, her arms folded tightly across her chest, brooding. She was happy… she really was…that Daniel was safe but, at this moment in time, she wished she could consign all men—and, in particular, these two bristling, belligerent specimens—to Hades.

Vernon handled the reins and his whip with relaxed skill, but his profile appeared to have been carved from rock and he had spoken not a word since handing her into the curricle at Crackthorpe Manor. Daniel, astride Bullet—who, she had learned, had been tracked and caught by the gipsies after Daniel's rescue—and leading Star, rode beside the curricle, casting black looks at Vernon and Thea alike.

So much for gratitude. You'd think he'd appreciate us coming to search for him.

Back at the Crown, Vernon handed his blacks over to Bickling and, holding Thea's arm, he marched her into the inn. And stopped dead, cursing under his breath, as an attractive, finely dressed lady standing at the foot of the staircase turned and smiled.

'Good afternoon, Vernon,' she said. Her shining golden-brown hair was swept into a smooth chignon. 'Did Leo find you?'

Her words confirmed she was the Duchess. Thea swallowed nervously, tugging the peak of her cap lower over her eyes.

Vernon's fingers tightened around Thea's upper arm. 'He did and good afternoon to you, too, Rosalind. I understand you are escorting Mr Allen home to Birmingham?'

The Duchess's hand went to a silver locket that hung on a simple chain around her neck.

'We are, although he is only going back to collect his belongings. I don't know if Leo told you, but Grandpa has agreed to come and live with us at Cheriton Abbey. It is time he retired.' Her gaze settled on Thea and her brows twitched. 'Are you going to introduce us?'

The front door of the inn opened behind them and a quick glance over her shoulder confirmed that Daniel had entered the Crown. Vernon, too, had seen Daniel and he tugged Thea closer to his side.

'Not just at this moment, Rosalind,' he said, as he manoeuvred Thea in the direction of their private parlour. 'Please forgive me, but there is a matter that demands my urgent attention.'

Thea did not dare look at the Duchess as Vernon towed her past. He threw open the door to the parlour but, before he could shut it, Daniel barged in behind them.

'You are not needed, Markham,' Vernon bit out. 'Your sister and I have matters to discuss.'

Daniel crossed his arms. 'I go nowhere without Thea.'

Vernon thrust Thea behind him as he faced Daniel, who cocked his head to one side. 'Do *you* have a sister, Beauchamp?'

Thea marvelled at Daniel's bravery in confronting a member of the aristocracy even as she resented them both for taking control and talking about her as though she weren't even there.

'I do,' Vernon growled. 'What does—?'

'Would you allow *your* sister to remain even one minute, unchaperoned, in the company of a man who had already thoroughly compromised her?'

Vernon's rigid back relaxed somewhat but, far from relieving her, that made Thea more nervous. Matters were tricky enough without Vernon and Daniel forming an alliance against her. She pushed past Vernon.

'Neither of you has the right to *allow* me to do anything.'

'Now, Thea—'

'Do *not* "Now, Thea" me,' she hissed at Daniel. 'I—'

He put his arm around her. 'We only want what is best for you.'

'You...both of you...seem to think me incapable of deciding what is best for myself,' she said, wriggling to free herself. Daniel tightened his hold. 'You are wrong,' she hissed. 'I have a brain. I can decide my own future.'

'Markham?'

She felt Daniel stiffen. 'Beauchamp?'

'Might we leave this discussion until later?' Vernon moved forward and, somehow, Thea was free of Daniel's grip and Vernon was ushering her towards the door. 'Your sister is tired and she has suffered a huge shock. Allow her to rest. We can discuss this later.'

Thea glanced back at Daniel, who looked as dumbfounded as she felt. How had Vernon managed to manipulate them so smoothly? He opened the door for Thea. She walked out of the room, but Vernon remained inside.

'Go and sleep. I will see you at dinner.'

'Promise me you will not fight with Daniel.'

'I promise. Now, go.' He shut the door.

At half past five that evening Vernon knocked on Thea's bedchamber door. He heard a muffled 'Come in' and he opened the door. It had taken some doing, but he had persuaded Daniel Markham to allow him time to prove to Thea he was not marrying her because he ought to, but because he wanted to. It was the one thing the two men had agreed upon: Dorothea Markham could not be forced to do anything. She needed to make up her own mind.

As he stepped through the door he blinked in surprise. Sitting at the dressing table, dressed in a pale primrose silk gown, was Thea, frowning ferociously above a mouthful of hairpins. Vernon closed the door behind him as she pulled another curl straight and jabbed a pin through it. The end sprang up again. Thea sighed and scooped the pins from her lips, scattering them across the top of the dressing table.

'It is hopeless,' she declared. Her eyes sheened. 'It's even harder than before to make them lie flat.'

'But why do you want to flatten your curls?' Vernon wandered over to stand behind her and skimmed his fingertips across her nape and along her shoulder to the edge of her neckline, watching the skin pucker in response to his touch. 'They are beautiful. I love your curls.'

Their eyes met in the mirror. 'You do?'

He fingered one curl and tugged it gently before releasing it to spring and bounce back into shape. 'I do.'

She sighed. 'I will look an utter fright next to Cordelia and the Duchess.'

He dipped his knees and brushed a kiss to the sensitive spot below her ear. 'You will outshine the pair of them.'

She stretched her head to one side, exposing more of her neck for him to nibble and kiss. She sighed, her lids fluttering closed, but before long her eyes sprang open again.

'What will the Duchess say about me? Will she be *very* disapproving?'

Vernon paused in his ministrations. '*Rosalind?* Disapproving? Thea, sweetheart, if that is what you are worrying about, let me tell you that Rosalind is the least judgemental person I know.'

'Oh. And what about the Duke?'

Vernon grinned at her reflection and saw an answering smile quiver at the corner of her luscious lips. Lips he longed to kiss.

'Rosalind has worked wonders on him since their marriage. He is learning to have more fun and to take himself less seriously. Being a duke can be lonely, but he finally has someone to share the burden.'

'But…how long have they been married? I thought they have adult children.'

'A month. And Leo *does* have adult children. Three of them. Their mother died when they were young. Thea… I have not come here to discuss Leo and Rosalind, I have come to talk about us. But, first, where did that gown come from?'

'Malky got one of the maids to pack a bag for me. Bickling brought it with him.'

He had not known. He was pleased, for Thea's sake, she had a gown to wear this evening. He could not care less what she wore, but she had already proved to him that she *did* care.

'I like you in that colour. It suits you.'

She blushed. 'I'm sure anything is preferable to what you are used to seeing me wear.'

'*My* preference,' Vernon said, 'is to see you naked. Although maybe not until later this evening.'

Thea, her cheeks fiery red, grabbed at a velvet drawstring pouch and withdrew a pearl necklace and a pair of pearl ear drops. Vernon reached over her shoulder.

'Allow me.' He opened the clasp and draped the single strand of pearls around her slender neck, admiring how the lustre of the pearls complemented her flawless skin. 'Perfect,' he breathed.

She held his gaze in the mirror, then her lashes swept low to veil her thoughts as she fitted her ear drops to her lobes.

'I want to talk to you about Cordelia,' she said.

Vernon frowned. He thought he'd dealt with that misunderstanding.

'What about her?'

'Do you care for her? Because, if you do, you owe me nothing.'

'No! I—'

She rushed on: 'You must not feel obli—'

He hauled her from her chair and into his arms. 'Foolish Dotty. Will you just let me speak? Is that not just like you…rushing full tilt ahead without listening first?'

Thea stood rigidly in his embrace. 'I saw you embracing her.'

'It wasn't an embrace. Not as you mean it.' He slid his hands down her arms to take her hands, drawing them into his chest. 'I was comforting her after I told her the truth about Mannington's identity and that he was responsible for that man drowning in the river.'

'Oh.'

'She was upset.'

Thea stared at the floor between their feet. 'Oh.'

'Thea.' She looked up. He traced the line of her brow with a gentle finger. 'You saw us and yet still you rushed in to help us, even though you were hurting—'

'Angry! I was angry.'

'Angry. Of course.'

'But I was angrier with Jasper.'

'And now you know the truth of what you saw, are you still angry with me?'

She searched his face. 'No. Not angry.'

'But…?'

'Scared.'

'Thea, you are the most courageous woman I've ever met. What are you scared of? Me?'

'I am scared of the future. Daniel said you must marry me and I know you will, because it is your duty and because you are an honourable man. But you will regret it, because your family will not approve and society will not approve. I am not of your world. I could not bear to be an… an *embarrassment*.' Her voice choked on that final word.

'Thea…you could never be an embarrassment.'

She snatched her hands from his and spread her arms wide. 'Look at me! Of course I will be an embarrassment. You need a real lady. You need someone tall and elegant and smooth and sophisticated and—'

Vernon held his hand aloft and, miraculously, Thea halted her tirade of self-deprecation.

'When you have *quite* finished telling me what you think I *need*, Dorothea Markham,' he said, 'please allow me to tell you what I *want*. Or, to be accurate, what I do *not* want.

'I do *not* want a real lady, if by that you mean a female born into the aristocracy. I have met any number of them since my youth and not one of them has wriggled her way into my heart the way you have.

'I do not want someone tall.' He reached for her shoulders and pulled her into a gentle hug, propping his chin on top of her head, her curls tickling his jaw. '*You* are the perfect fit for me.'

He set her back again, and looked her up and down. 'You look beautifully elegant to me, so I *will* accept I need—and want—an elegant wife.'

She was watching him closely, a slight crease between her brows, but the light of hope beginning to dawn in her eyes.

'Smooth? I do not even know what you mean by smooth. If you mean your hair… I *adore* your hair and I'll have you know that many society ladies spend hours trying to get their hair to curl or to fall in ringlets. You will be the envy of all.'

'But it is *red*!'

'It is the colour of a fine sunset and of an autumn leaf. It is warm and happy and perfect, and I would not have it any other colour.

'Now. What else? Oh, yes: sophisticated. You, Thea, are an intelligent and knowledgeable woman. You are stylish— maybe not when you are dressed in breeches, but…look at yourself, sweetheart.' He turned her to face herself in the mirror. 'You are the exact degree of sophistication I want and the exact degree of sophistication I need.'

He turned her to face him again. '*You* are the one I want and the one I need, Thea. You and only you. I love you.'

He lowered his mouth to hers. He had no more words to describe what he felt, so he poured his heart and his soul into that kiss, desperate to show her the deepest yearnings of his heart. She responded, melting into him, her fingers clutching at his shoulders and her tongue stroking his.

Conscious of the passing time, Vernon ended the kiss. 'Thea, I love you. Please do me the honour of being my wife.'

Her face was serious as her eyes searched his. 'I love you, too, Vernon. But I…'

His heart cracked. Surely she would not refuse him? What could he say to convince her? He searched desperately for the words, but they would not come.

'I need time to think,' she continued. She caressed his cheek, then averted her face. 'After Jasper, I swore never to trust another man.'

'You do not trust me?'

She captured his gaze again. 'It is my own judgement I do not trust. Give me time. Please.'

'How much time?'

'Does it matter?'

Yes, he wanted to roar. *It matters. I want you with me always, starting now.* He swallowed his pain.

'You may take as much time as you need,' he said. 'Although your brother might not prove so amenable. It seems impatience is a family trait.'

Chapter Twenty-Five

Dealing with her brother would be easy compared to summoning the courage to accept Vernon's proposal. She wanted to. She really wanted to. She had become so attuned to Vernon's feelings she could feel his suppressed pain and she hated that she was the cause. But something held her back from saying 'yes' there and then.

'You have often said I am impulsive,' she said, trying to lighten the suddenly sombre mood. 'You should be happy I am considering my answer seriously.'

'Happy is not how I would describe it,' he said, 'but I accept your right to answer in your own time.' He proffered his arm. 'Come. It is time to go downstairs. We have all been invited to dine with the Temples in their private parlour tonight, as it has a bigger table.'

'All?'

Thea took Vernon's arm and they left the bedchamber, heading for the staircase.

'You and your brother, and me and my family.'

'What has happened to Mrs Connor and her father?'

'There was no room for them to stay here and they declined to join us this evening. They are weary after their journey and also, I believe, in a state of shock at what Jasper has done.'

'What will happen to him?'

'He's been arrested and will be kept in jail until he stands trial at the next assizes. There's little doubt he killed Henry Mannington and set the fire to cover up his crime and it was only by the greatest of good luck Daniel survived. I'm afraid he will almost certainly be sentenced to hang.'

Thea swallowed. He deserved to be punished, but it was hard to think of him dying in such a way. They had reached the door of the small parlour they had used during their time at the Crown.

'We have arranged to meet the others in here before we join the Temples,' Vernon said. 'I shall introduce you formally to my brother and his wife—who will have conveniently forgotten they have ever set eyes upon my supposed nephew, Theo—and to Rosalind's grandfather, Mr Allen.'

He opened the door for Thea. Three pairs of eyes turned to look at her and her stomach roiled violently and her mouth dried as she took in the figures of the Duke and Duchess and Mr Allen.

What will they say? What will they think of me?

With a flash of insight she realised that here was the 'something' that was holding her back. *They* were the reason she had not accepted Vernon straight away. It was not that she didn't trust him. She did. And she loved him, but part of loving him meant she would also protect him. During the past week she had learned that the Beauchamps were a close and loving family and she could not bear to be the cause of conflict between them. Their acceptance of her was crucial.

Yes, it is crucial. But I can still fight for him.

Vernon's hand was at the small of her back, large and reassuring, urging her forward. Thea swallowed, rolled her shoulders back, raised her chin a notch and walked forward.

Vernon made the introductions and Thea dropped a curtsy.

'Oh, there's no need to bother with curtsies,' the Duchess said, with a smile. 'To tell you the truth, I still haven't become accustomed to all that formal nonsense and I doubt I ever shall. Have you ever been to London, Miss Markham?'

'Why, no,' Thea said.

'Do not worry about it. If I can adapt to it, I am sure you will have no difficulty.'

'But I am not—'

Vernon was by her side in an instant. 'Thea has yet to agree to marry me, Rosalind,' he said, with a warning note in his voice.

'Oh!' The Duchess's cheeks washed pink. 'I am so sorry… I assumed…that is…'

'Hush, my sweet.' The Duke was quick to protect the Duchess's embarrassment and Thea warmed to him, although she still felt rather overawed in his presence. 'I am sure Miss Markham will agree to overlook your…er…eagerness to enrol her into the family.'

Thea studied both of their expressions, but could detect no hint of insincerity. The Duke smiled at her—not the amused, slightly cynical smile she recalled from Crackthorpe Manor, but a genuine, friendly smile.

'You do quite right to keep him guessing, Miss Markham,' the Duchess said. 'These Beauchamp men are far too accustomed to having females fall at their feet.' She dipped her head closer and whispered, 'But do not delay too long, will you? I can see you are besotted with one another and it will be pleasant to have a fellow newcomer in the family.'

They seemed welcoming enough. But what of her birth? What had Vernon told them? She wanted answers, but she knew no one in that room would be impolite enough to address such a vulgar question. She decided to tackle it head on.

'My father is a manufacturer, your Grace,' she said to the Duke.

He raised a dark brow, looking so like Vernon for a moment that she gaped at him.

'I am aware of your parentage, if that is what is bothering you, Miss Markham. Stour Crystal, is it not? Very fine lead-crystal glassware…you should be proud.'

'I *am* proud,' Thea said.

'There's nothing amiss with working for a living, bab.'

It was the first time Mr Allen had spoken and he did so with the flat Midlands accent Thea had been familiar with her whole life.

'I've been a silversmith all my life,' he went on, his chin jutting belligerently. 'Nothing to be ashamed of.'

The Duke grinned. 'Quite right, Grandpa. Not a thing to be ashamed of.' He then said to Thea, 'Mr Allen is my wife's paternal grandfather.'

'And my son, her father, was a common soldier,' the old man said. 'Leo here, he came and found me before he married my Rosalind and took me to London for the wedding. I hadn't seen her since she was six years old, but I never forgot her and she never forgot me. And now, I'm going to retire and spend the rest of my days with my grandchildren and, God willing, my great-grandchildren.'

The door opened and Horwell came in to announce dinner was about to be served. Daniel was already in the larger parlour, chatting to Cordelia, who seemed smitten with him. Thea noticed she barely glanced at Vernon when he entered the room. There was little chance for Thea to join in the conversation at dinner. Samuel Temple was so enthused about having a real-life 'dook and duchess' as his guests that he dominated the conversation, questioning Vernon's brother about almost every topic under the sun and not holding back with his own opinions. The Duke did not appear to object, but answered him patiently, exchanging loving smiles from time to time with the Duchess.

Thea watched. And thought. And reached the conclusion she had been fretting about nothing. She appreciated Vernon giving her time to consider what she wanted and was grateful neither he nor Daniel were harrying her to accept him. It was important to her, if she married, that her husband would respect her opinion. Any residual doubts about Vernon and Cordelia had vanished. Cordelia only had eyes for Daniel, and Vernon... Thea shivered in pleasure as his hot gaze lingered on her neckline.

She waited until there was a lull in the conversation.

'Vernon.'

A sudden hush fell over the table and Thea's courage nearly deserted her. Then she braced herself. Everyone here knew Vernon was waiting for her answer. She owed him this.

'Do you recall that question you asked me?'

He pursed his lips, his eyes dancing with merriment, the absolute devil.

He knows what I am going to say.

'I do,' he said.

'May I give you my answer now?'

He nodded.

'My answer is yes.'

A huge grin split Vernon's face. He shot to his feet and thrust his arms high in the air, as a cheer arose around the table. Before she realised he had moved, he was by her side and pulling her to her feet.

'Ladies and gentlemen,' he said. 'Oh...' with an ironic bow in his brother's direction '...and your Grace. Allow me to introduce the future Lady Vernon Beauchamp. The woman I adore. The love of my life.'

He kissed her soundly on the lips to a chorus of congratulations and a loud, 'I'm pleased *someone* has managed to talk some sense into her' from Daniel, which brought forth much laughter.

Horwell popped his head around the door to investigate the noise and added his best wishes to the happy couple.

'Horwell…two bottles of your finest champagne,' the Duke said. 'This calls for a toast.'

Later that evening—her head pleasantly swimming from the effects of the champagne and her heart full and happy and content and excited—Thea undressed to prepare for bed. She washed at the basin and slipped on her shift, then sat at the dressing table to brush her hair. She could not wait for it to grow properly.

She froze as a movement in the mirror caught her eye, her heart leaping into her throat as she realised the door behind her was opening. But her terror lasted only a second. Vernon—in open-necked shirt and trousers—slid through the opening. Their gazes fused in the looking glass and she saw the heat in his, and that recognition stoked such a fire in her blood she could barely sit still. But she forced herself to remain seated as Vernon padded across the carpet. He took the brush from her hand and drew it through her curls, a look of total absorption on his face.

'I adore your hair,' he murmured, his deep voice melting through her.

He knelt behind her, pushed her hair aside and kissed her nape, then feathered kisses along her shoulder, pushing the neck of her shift aside to allow him access.

'I adore your skin.' She looked up at him, over her shoulder and he gently flicked the tip of her nose. 'I adore your freckles.' He reached around and cupped her. 'I adore your breasts.'

She shuddered, pushing into his touch, wanting more.

He rose behind her and urged her to stand, kicking the chair out of the way. His hands were on the hem of her shift, lifting, and she raised her arms, and then she was naked, her torso from thigh to neck reflected in the mirror. His hands were on her arms, holding them aloft, and he groaned—a deep, heartfelt sound that vibrated through her.

She could wait no longer. She wriggled and turned, tugging his shirt from his trousers and over his head. She stroked eager hands over the heavy muscles of his chest and shoulders, then fumbled at the fall of his trousers. He eased away from her and then he was as naked as she.

He cupped her chin and kissed her, hard.

'And I adore your impatience. And your impulsiveness. And...*you*!'

This time the kiss lingered, explored, feasted, as did their hands.

Vernon swung her into his arms and carried her to the bed, following her down.

Later, as she floated in the aftermath of their lovemaking, Vernon raised his head, suddenly serious.

'I love you, Dorothea Markham. I love you with all my heart and soul, and I swear to you now that I will make you happy.'

She stroked his lean cheek and along his jaw, relishing the scratch of his whiskers against her fingertips. She kissed him then, her heart bursting with all the love she felt.

'And I love you, Vernon Beauchamp, and I cannot wait to walk down the aisle and see you standing at the altar, waiting for me.'

'No doubts? You trust me?'

'I do.' She leaned up and kissed him again, pouring her heart into it. 'I do.'

* * * * *